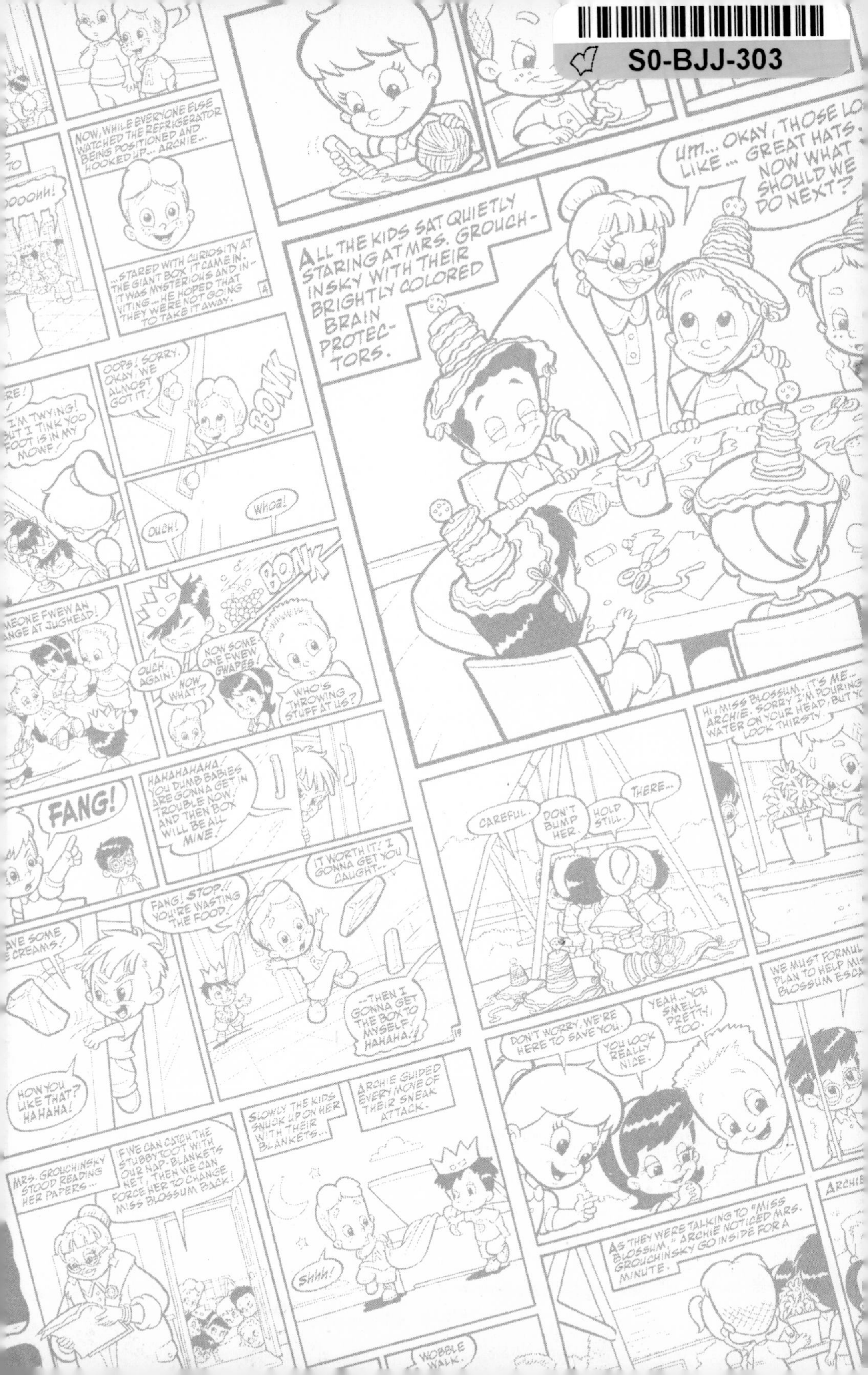
NOW, WHILE EVERYONE ELSE WATCHED THE REFRIGERATOR BEING POSITIONED AND HOOKED UP... ARCHIE...
...STARED WITH CURIOSITY AT THE GIANT BOX IT CAME IN. IT WAS MYSTERIOUS AND INVITING... HE HOPED THAT THEY WERE NOT GOING TO TAKE IT AWAY.
ALL THE KIDS SAT QUIETLY STARING AT MRS. GROUCHINSKY WITH THEIR BRIGHTLY COLORED BRAIN PROTECTORS.
OOPS! SORRY. OKAY, WE ALMOST GOT IT!
BONK
I'M TWYING! BUT I TINK YOO FOOT IS IN MY MOWF!
OUCH!
WHOA!
BONK
OUCH, AGAIN!
NOW WHAT?
NOW SOMEONE FWEW GWAPES!
WHO'S THROWING STUFF AT US?
HI, MISS BLOSSUM. IT'S ME... ARCHIE. SORRY I'M POURING WATER ON YOUR HEAD, BUT YOU LOOK THIRSTY.
HAHAHAHAHA! YOU DUMB BABIES ARE GONNA GET IN TROUBLE NOW. AND THEN BOX WILL BE ALL MINE.
FANG!
CAREFUL.
DON'T BUMP HER.
HOLD STILL.
THERE...
IT WORTH IT! I GONNA GET YOU CAUGHT--
FANG! STOP!! YOU'RE WASTING THE FOOD!
--THEN I GONNA GET THE BOX TO MYSELF! HAHAHA!
HOW YOU LIKE THAT? HAHAHA!
DON'T WORRY, WE'RE HERE TO SAVE YOU.
YOU LOOK REALLY NICE.
YEAH... YOU SMELL PRETTY, TOO.
MRS. GROUCHINSKY STOOD READING HER PAPERS...
IF WE CAN CATCH THE STUBBY TOOT WITH OUR NAP-BLANKETS NET, THEN WE CAN FORCE HER TO CHANGE MISS BLOSSUM BACK!
SLOWLY THE KIDS SNUCK UP ON HER WITH THEIR BLANKETS...
ARCHIE GUIDED EVERY MOVE OF THEIR SNEAK ATTACK.
Shhh!
AS THEY WERE TALKING TO "MISS BLOSSUM," ARCHIE NOTICED MRS. GROUCHINSKY GO INSIDE FOR A MINUTE.
WOBBLE WALK.

THE Archie® BABIES™

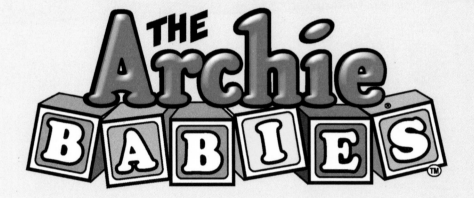

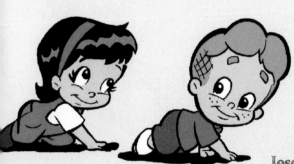

THE Archie BABIES™

CREDITS

SCRIPT BY
MIKE KUNKEL (CHAPTERS 1-4)
IAN FLYNN (CHAPTER 5)

PENCILS BY
ART MAWHINNEY

INKS BY
RICH KOSLOWSKI

COLORS BY
MATT HERMS

LETTERS BY
JACK MORELLI

COVER & FRONTIS COLORS BY
ROSARIO "TITO" PEÑA

ARCHIE COMIC PUBLICATIONS, INC.

JONATHAN GOLDWATER, co-ceo
NANCY SILBERKLEIT, co-ceo
MIKE PELLERITO, president
VICTOR GORELICK, co-president/e-i-c
BILL HORAN, director of circulation
HAROLD BUCHHOLZ, exec. director of publishing/operations
PAUL KAMINSKI with MIKE PELLERITO, editors
JOE MORCIGLIO, project coordinator
STEPHEN OSWALD, production manager
VIN LOVALLO, DUNCAN MCLACHLAN
& JON GRAY, production

Archie Babies Book One
Published by Archie Comic Publications, Inc.
325 Fayette Avenue, Mamaroneck, New York 10543-2318.

ISBN: 978-1-879794-72-6   10 9 8 7 6 5 4 3 2 1   Printed in U.S.A.

TABLE OF CONTENTS

USA
A

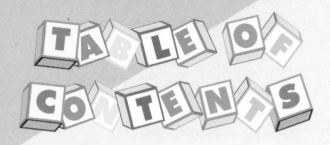

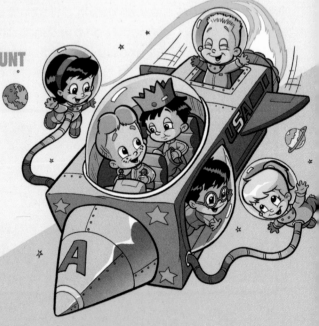

INTRODUCTION
by MIKE PELLERITO

About seven years ago, my first baby was getting ready to come into the world.

My wife and I were getting all sorts of shower gifts with baby versions of every character under the sun, and suddenly it seemed a shame that there were none of the Archie Gang. We needed Archie Babies!

So I went to work, idea in hand. The project first got the green light, then was put on hold, then back and forth until recently when new Co-CEO (and son of the Archie's creator) Jon Goldwater gave the final go-ahead. Now we were no longer crawling, but going full-steam to get the Archie Babies out to the world!

Now would come the hard part: who would help bring these Babies to life? Always, always, there was one artist that was just right—Art Mawhinney. Art is a well-known children's book illustrator, and we had worked together previously on the "Sonic the Hedgehog" comic. The way Archie Babies existed in my imagination was exactly what Art's look captured on these pages. He was perfect!

The next choice was who would write these Archie Babies adventures, and two names were always at the top of the list. The first was Mike Kunkel, who has worked in comics and animation for years and knows how to capture the wonder of childhood and imagination. The other writer is one of the best in comics, and seems to be able to write everything perfectly: Ian Flynn. Luckily we got both writers!

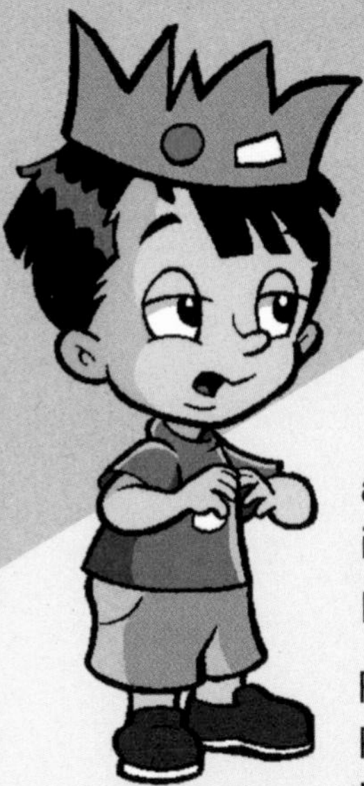

Finishing out the team were inker-extraordinaire Rich Koslowski, the amazing letterer Jack Morelli, Matt Herms and his perfect coloring, and Paul Kaminski, who helped skillfully, took on the lion's share of editing the book, and got the Archie Babies to be just perfect.

It has been a crazy journey with ups and downs—a lot like childhood, actually—but finally, you have in hand one of the most enjoyable and exciting projects Archie Comics has produced. And that's saying a lot, considering that all Archie Comics does is create excitement and fun!

The stories are a wonderful world of adventure, bright color and wild fun where babies rule and the universe is as limitless as a child's imagination. I couldn't be happier or prouder of this project or the wonderful people who helped bring Archie Babies into the world.

So, I dedicate this book to the people who made this happen, to Archie Comics for letting us have so much fun with comics and show the world-famous Archie teenagers in diapers, and to all the babies out there who grow up and fall in love with the Archie Gang. And of course, more than anything, to my own wonderfully perfect babies!

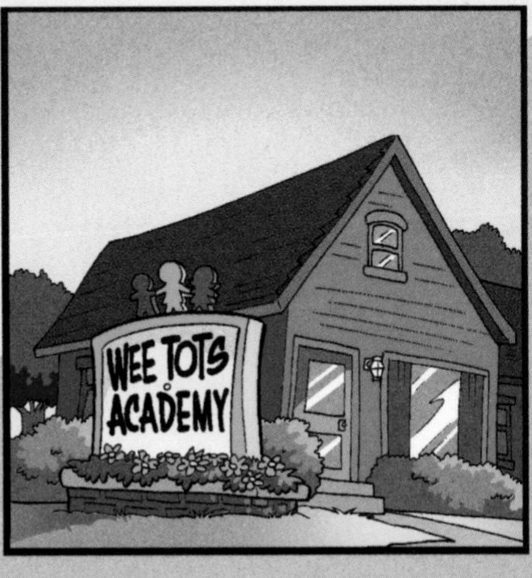
WEE TOTS ACADEMY

- MIKE

THE Archie BABIES

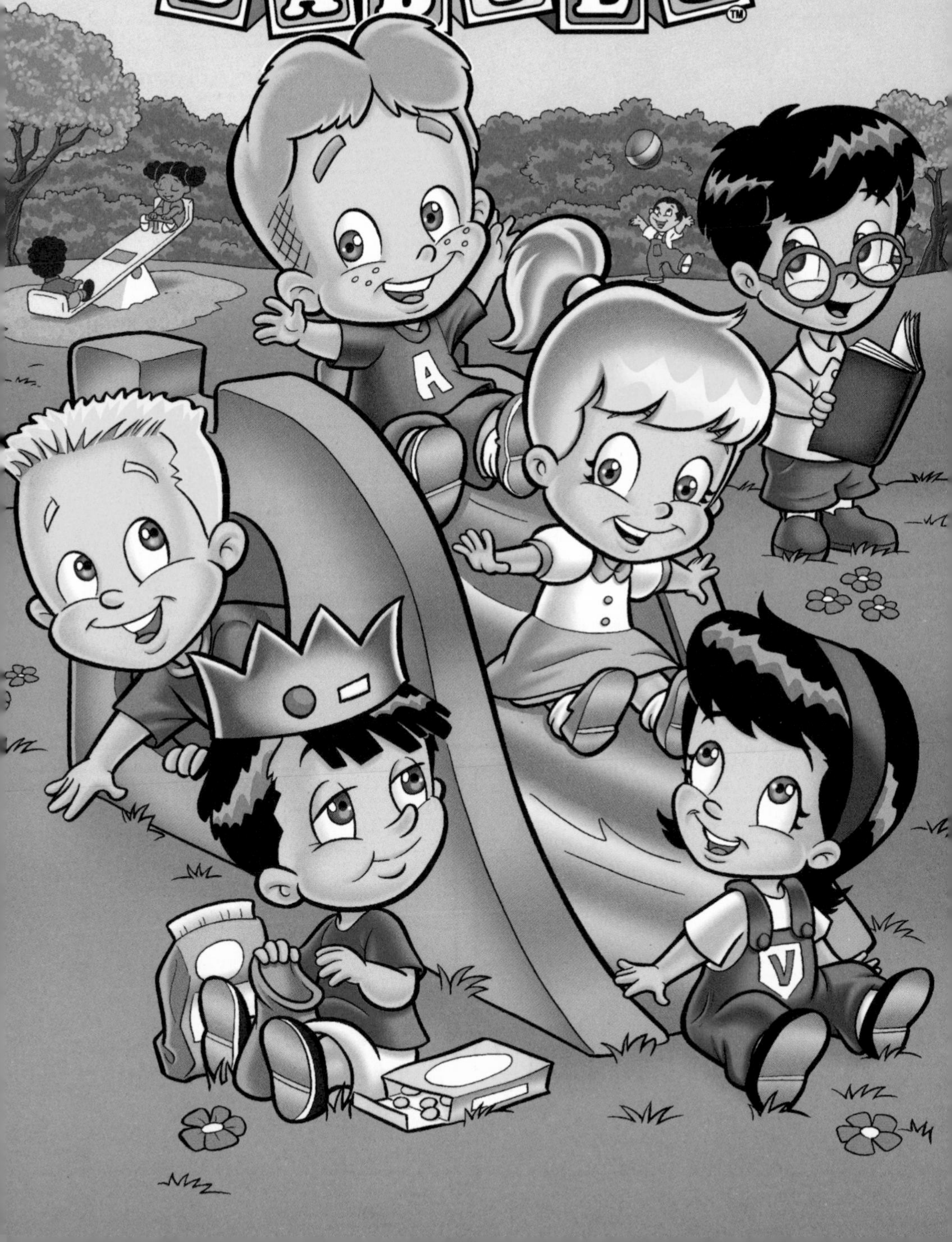

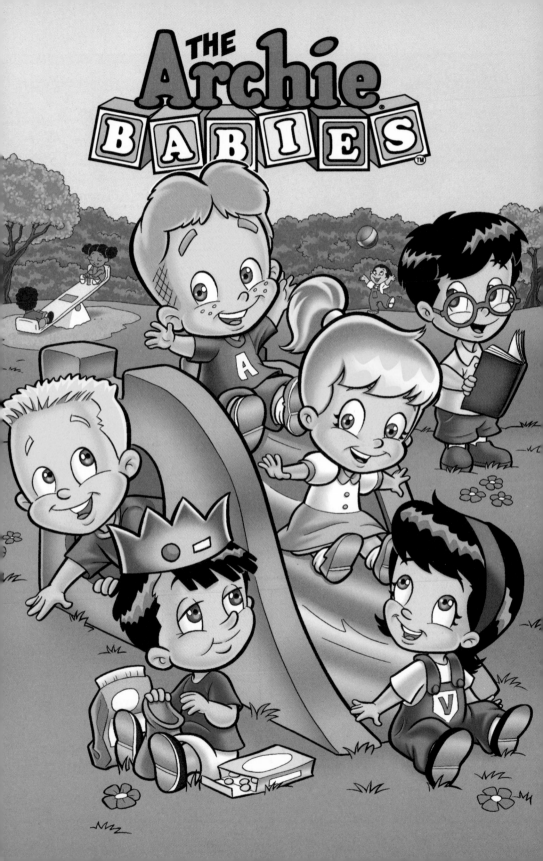

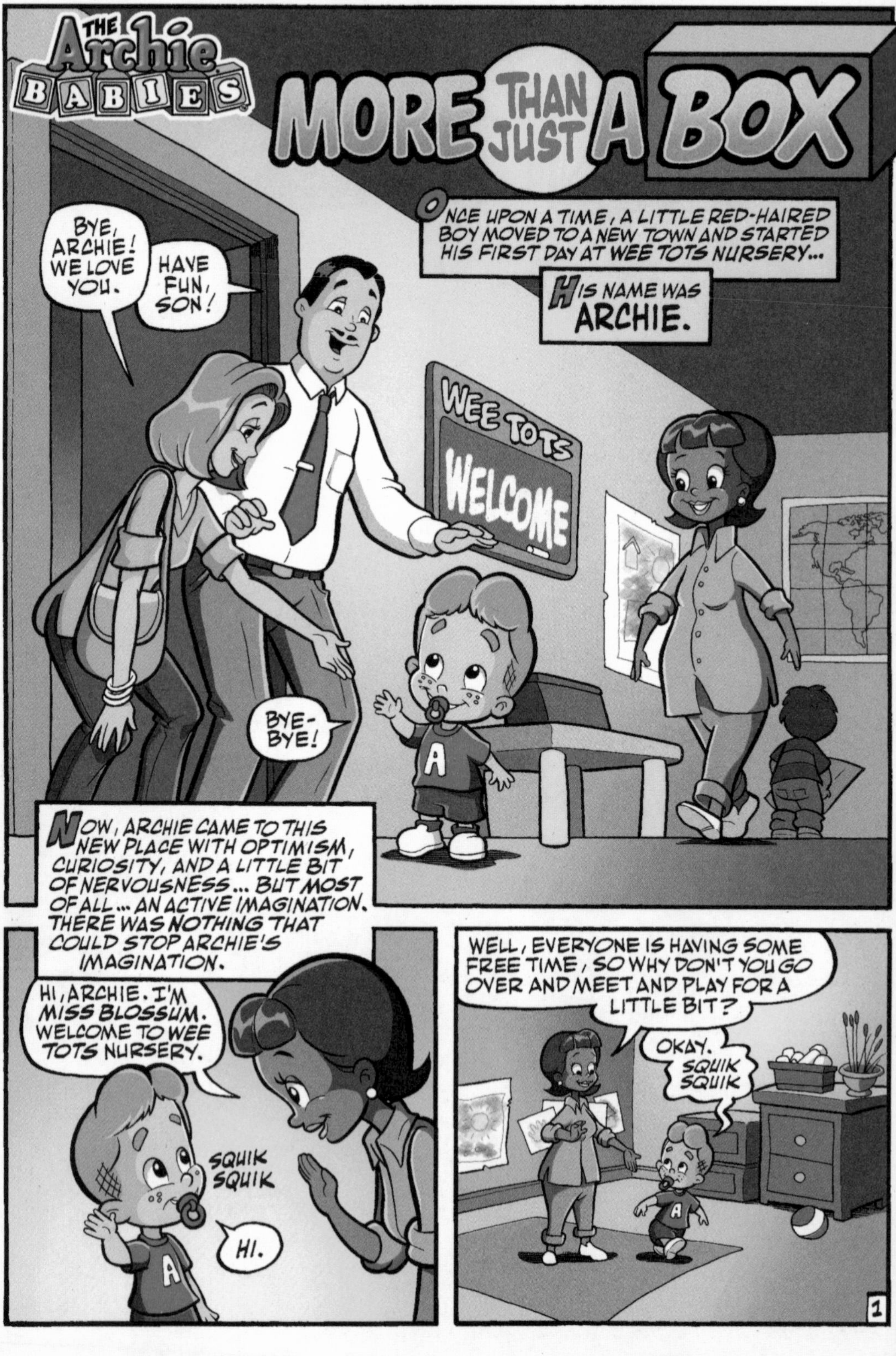
THE Archie BABIES
MORE THAN JUST A BOX
ONCE UPON A TIME, A LITTLE RED-HAIRED BOY MOVED TO A NEW TOWN AND STARTED HIS FIRST DAY AT WEE TOTS NURSERY...
HIS NAME WAS ARCHIE.
BYE, ARCHIE! WE LOVE YOU.
HAVE FUN, SON!
WEE TOTS
WELCOME
BYE-BYE!
NOW, ARCHIE CAME TO THIS NEW PLACE WITH OPTIMISM, CURIOSITY, AND A LITTLE BIT OF NERVOUSNESS... BUT MOST OF ALL... AN ACTIVE IMAGINATION. THERE WAS NOTHING THAT COULD STOP ARCHIE'S IMAGINATION.
HI, ARCHIE. I'M MISS BLOSSUM. WELCOME TO WEE TOTS NURSERY.
SQUIK SQUIK
HI.
WELL, EVERYONE IS HAVING SOME FREE TIME, SO WHY DON'T YOU GO OVER AND MEET AND PLAY FOR A LITTLE BIT?
OKAY.
SQUIK SQUIK

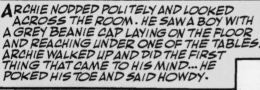

ARCHIE NODDED POLITELY AND LOOKED ACROSS THE ROOM. HE SAW A BOY WITH A GREY BEANIE CAP LAYING ON THE FLOOR AND REACHING UNDER ONE OF THE TABLES. ARCHIE WALKED UP AND DID THE FIRST THING THAT CAME TO HIS MIND... HE POKED HIS TOE AND SAID HOWDY.

HOWDY.

SQUIK SQUIK

HEY, THERE! WHATCHA DOIN'?

Oh, I'M TRYING TO SEE IF THERE ARE ANY LEFTOVER FRUITY HOOPS OR CHEERFUL O'S UNDER HERE. I'M STARVING.

DIDN'T YOU EAT BREAK- FAST?

Uh-HUH. BUT I'M ALWAYS STARVING. YOU DON'T HAPPEN TO HAVE ANY BREAD ON YOU, DO YOU?

um...NO.

hmm...TOO BAD. I FOUND SOME PEANUT BUTTER AND DIDN'T WANT IT TO GO TO WASTE. I'LL SAVE IT FOR LATER. SO, MY NAME IS JUGHEAD. WHAT'S YOURS?

I'M ARCHIE.

COOOL.

ARCHIE THOUGHT JUGHEAD WAS VERY COOL, TOO. HE WASN'T SURE, BUT HE THOUGHT THAT HE WAS WHAT HIS PARENTS WOULD CALL... MELLOW. HE KNEW RIGHT AWAY THAT THEY'D BE FRIENDS FOR A LONG TIME...

SO, HAVE YOU MET EVERYONE ELSE, YET?

NOPE.

EVERY- ONE, SAY HI TO ARCHIE.

HI, MY NAME'S BETTY.

HI, MY NAME'S VERONICA.

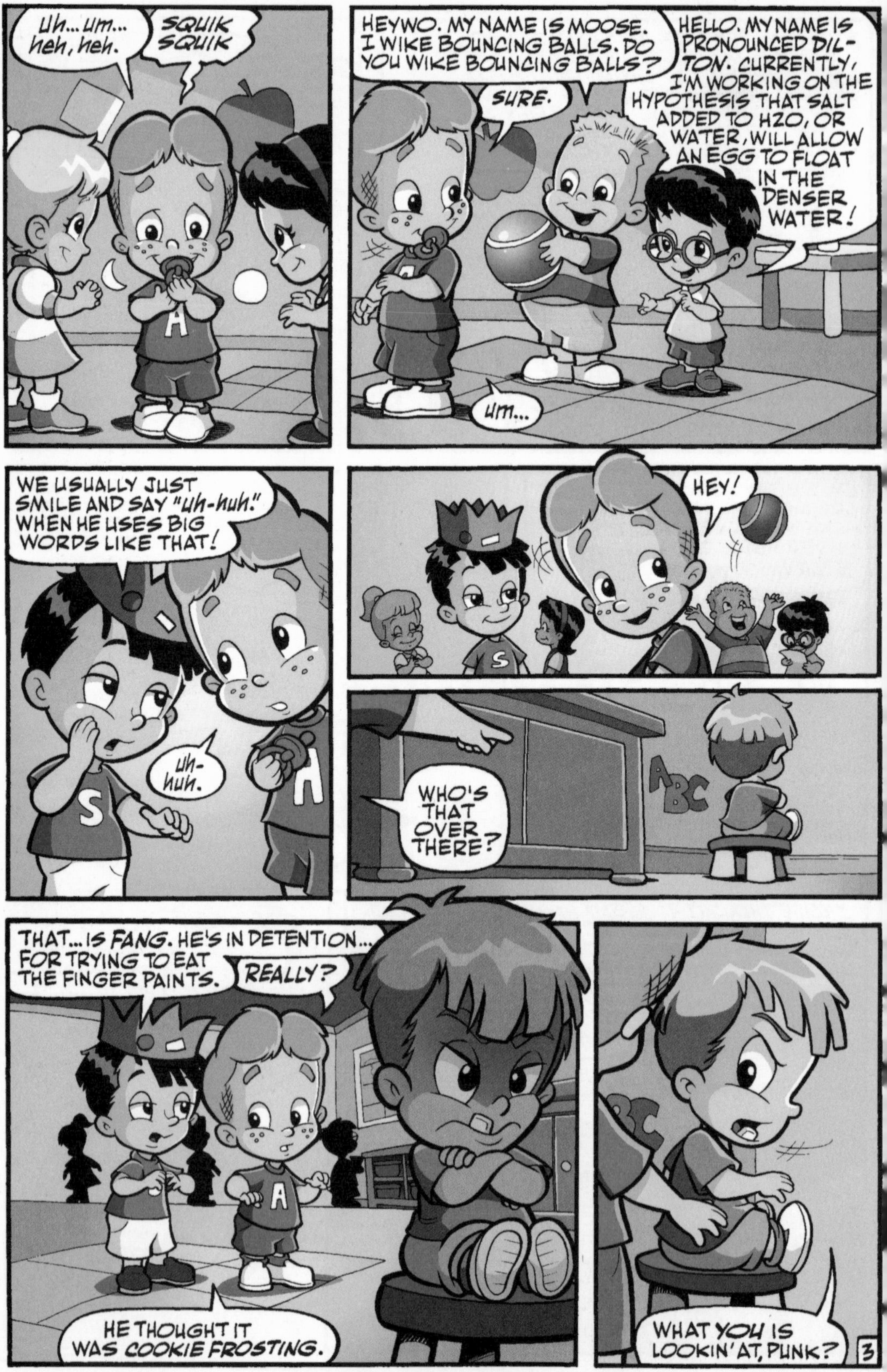
uh... um... heh, heh.
SQUIK SQUIK
HEYWO. MY NAME IS MOOSE. I WIKE BOUNCING BALLS. DO YOU WIKE BOUNCING BALLS?
SURE.
HELLO. MY NAME IS PRONOUNCED DIL-TON. CURRENTLY, I'M WORKING ON THE HYPOTHESIS THAT SALT ADDED TO H2O, OR WATER, WILL ALLOW AN EGG TO FLOAT IN THE DENSER WATER!
um...
WE USUALLY JUST SMILE AND SAY "uh-huh." WHEN HE USES BIG WORDS LIKE THAT!
uh-huh.
HEY!
WHO'S THAT OVER THERE?
ABC
THAT... IS FANG. HE'S IN DETENTION... FOR TRYING TO EAT THE FINGER PAINTS.
REALLY?
HE THOUGHT IT WAS COOKIE FROSTING.
WHAT YOU IS LOOKIN' AT, PUNK?

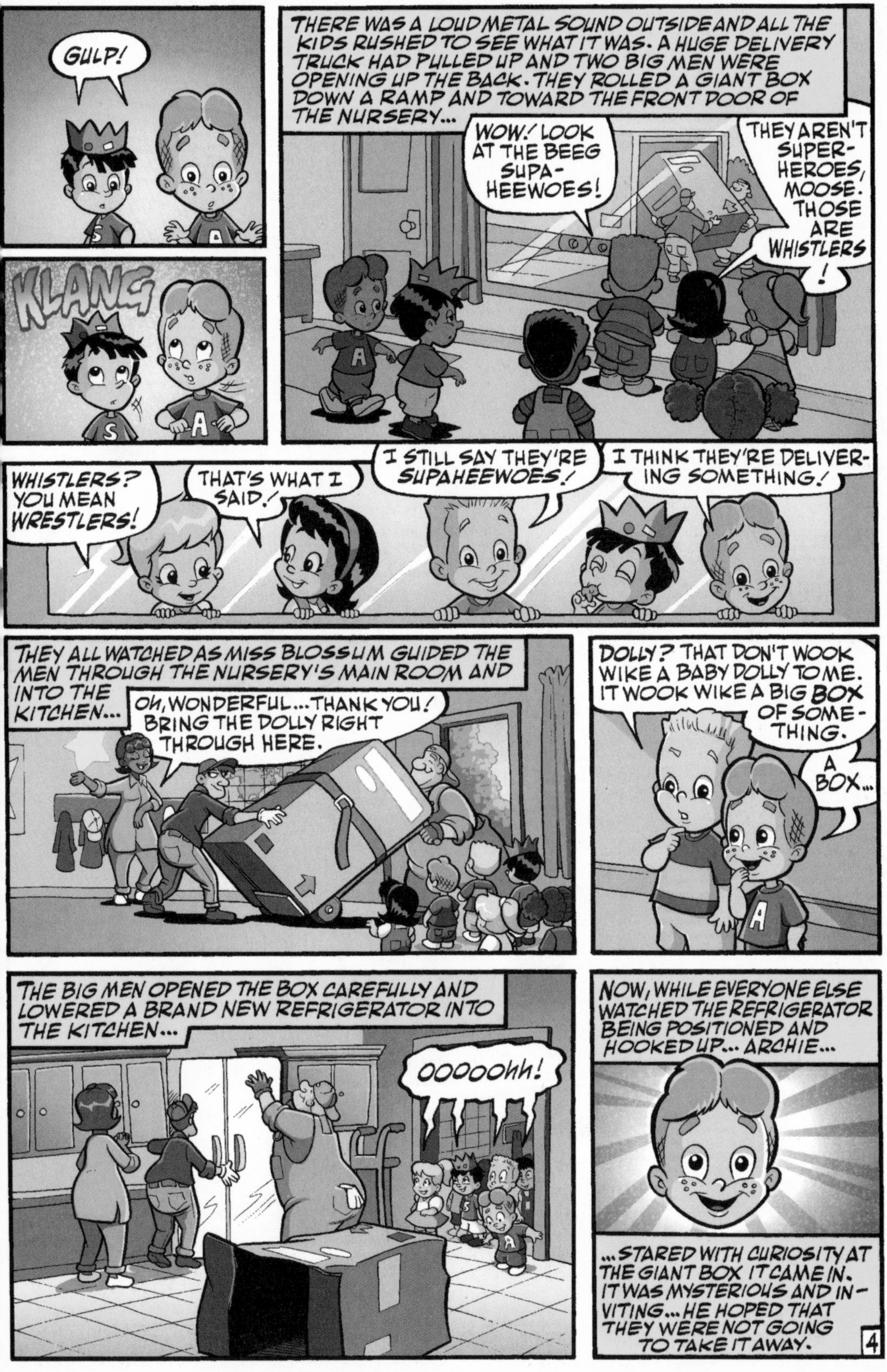
GULP!
KLANG
THERE WAS A LOUD METAL SOUND OUTSIDE AND ALL THE KIDS RUSHED TO SEE WHAT IT WAS. A HUGE DELIVERY TRUCK HAD PULLED UP AND TWO BIG MEN WERE OPENING UP THE BACK. THEY ROLLED A GIANT BOX DOWN A RAMP AND TOWARD THE FRONT DOOR OF THE NURSERY...
WOW! LOOK AT THE BEEG SUPA-HEEWOES!
THEY AREN'T SUPER-HEROES, MOOSE. THOSE ARE WHISTLERS!
WHISTLERS? YOU MEAN WRESTLERS!
THAT'S WHAT I SAID!
I STILL SAY THEY'RE SUPAHEEWOES!
I THINK THEY'RE DELIVER-ING SOMETHING!
THEY ALL WATCHED AS MISS BLOSSUM GUIDED THE MEN THROUGH THE NURSERY'S MAIN ROOM AND INTO THE KITCHEN...
Oh, WONDERFUL... THANK YOU! BRING THE DOLLY RIGHT THROUGH HERE.
DOLLY? THAT DON'T WOOK WIKE A BABY DOLLY TO ME. IT WOOK WIKE A BIG BOX OF SOME-THING.
A BOX...
THE BIG MEN OPENED THE BOX CAREFULLY AND LOWERED A BRAND NEW REFRIGERATOR INTO THE KITCHEN...
OOOOOhh!
NOW, WHILE EVERYONE ELSE WATCHED THE REFRIGERATOR BEING POSITIONED AND HOOKED UP... ARCHIE...
...STARED WITH CURIOSITY AT THE GIANT BOX IT CAME IN. IT WAS MYSTERIOUS AND IN-VITING... HE HOPED THAT THEY WERE NOT GOING TO TAKE IT AWAY.

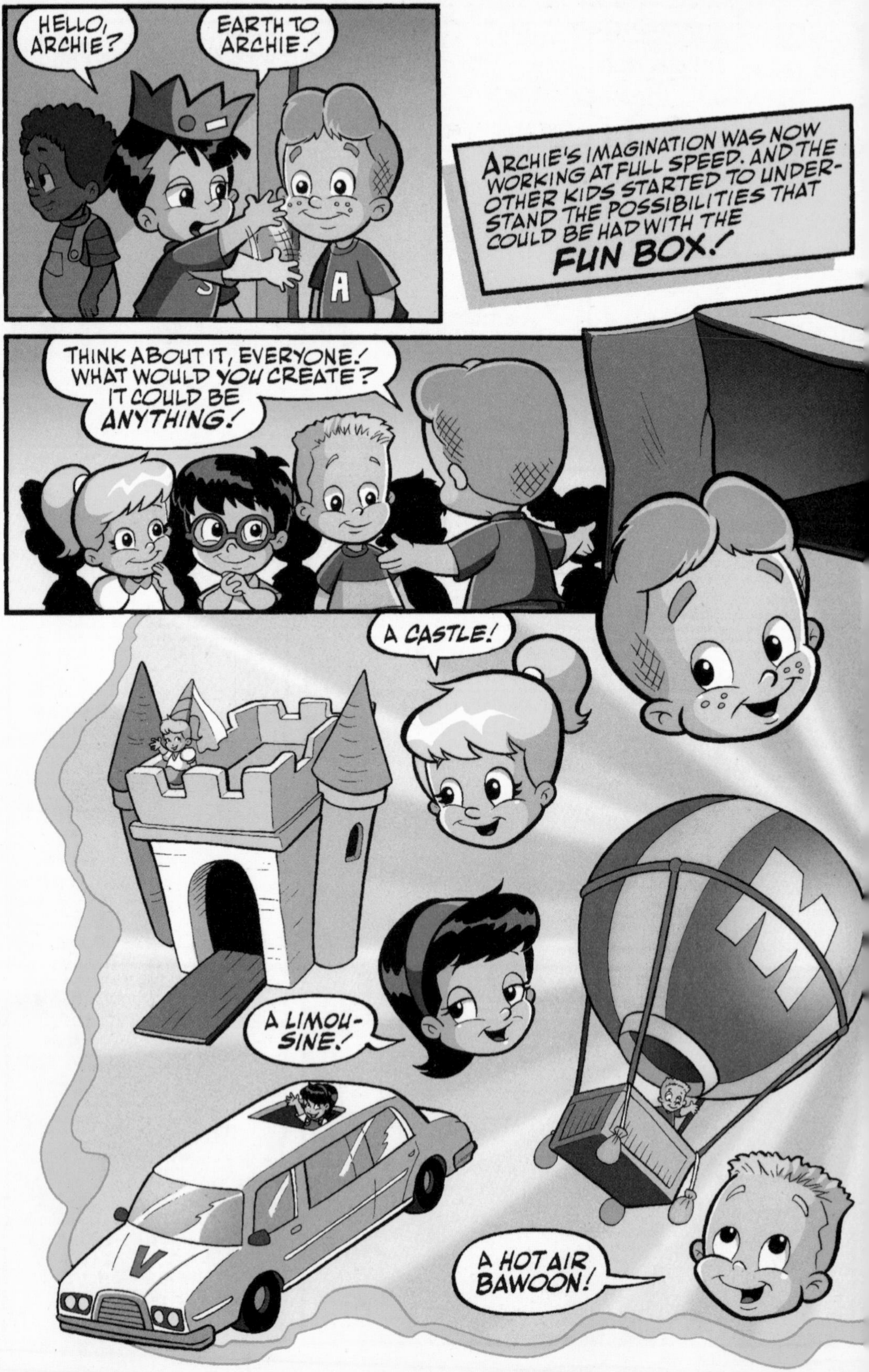
HELLO, ARCHIE?
EARTH TO ARCHIE!
ARCHIE'S IMAGINATION WAS NOW WORKING AT FULL SPEED. AND THE OTHER KIDS STARTED TO UNDERSTAND THE POSSIBILITIES THAT COULD BE HAD WITH THE FUN BOX!
THINK ABOUT IT, EVERYONE! WHAT WOULD YOU CREATE? IT COULD BE ANYTHING!
A CASTLE!
A LIMOUSINE!
A HOT AIR BAWOON!

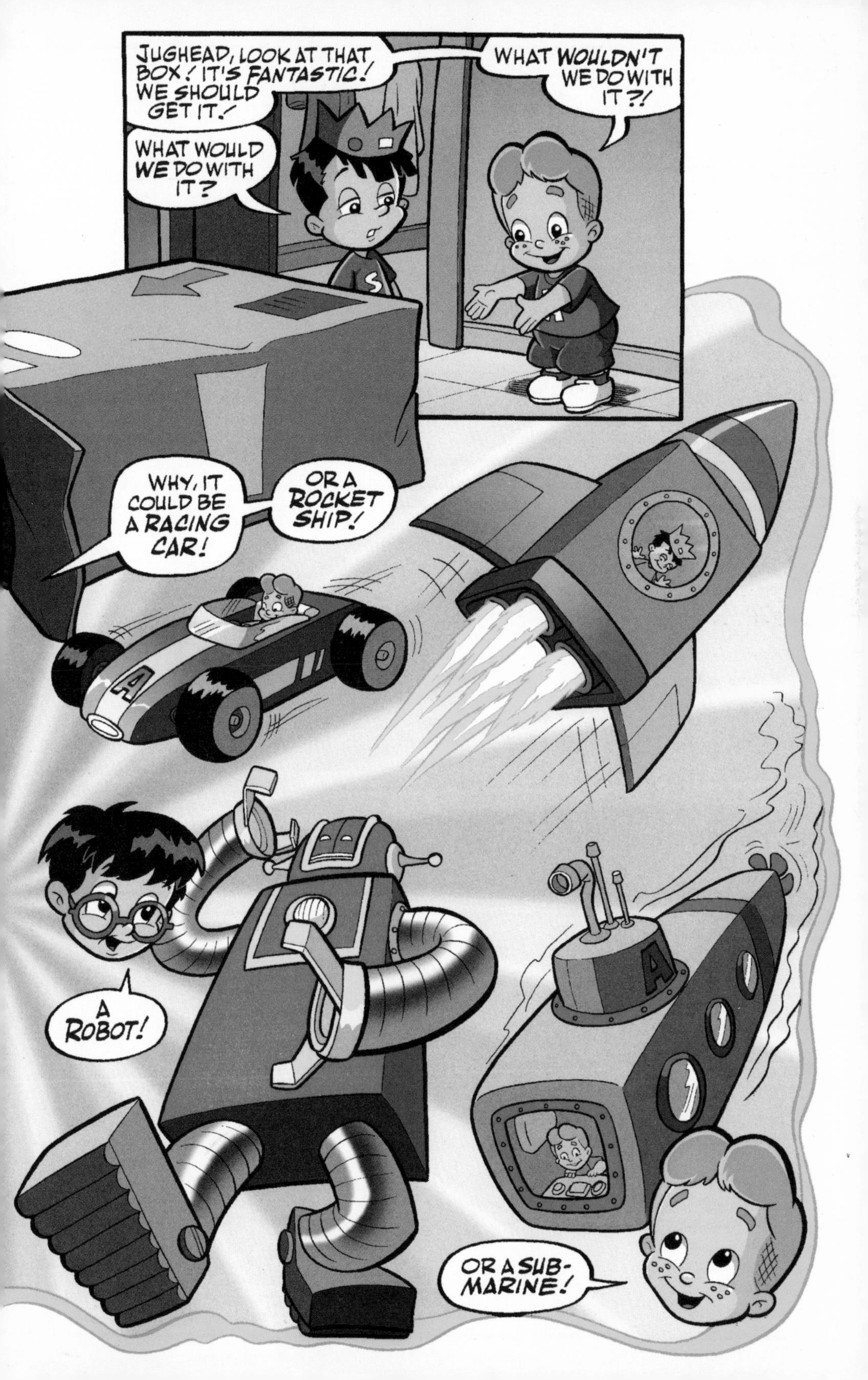
JUGHEAD, LOOK AT THAT BOX! IT'S FANTASTIC! WE SHOULD GET IT!
WHAT WOULD WE DO WITH IT?
WHAT WOULDN'T WE DO WITH IT?!
WHY, IT COULD BE A RACING CAR!
OR A ROCKET SHIP!
A ROBOT!
OR A SUB-MARINE!

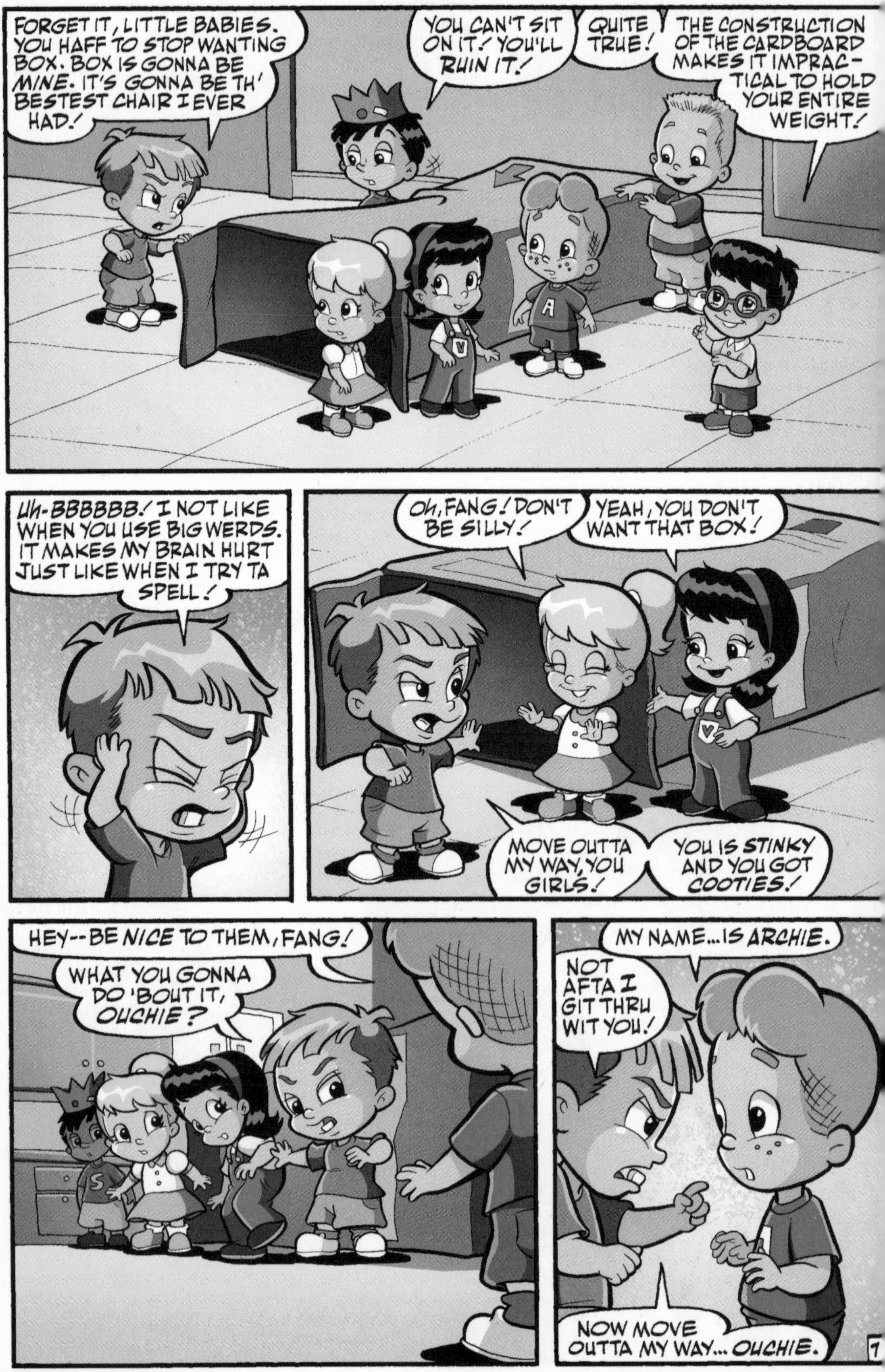
FORGET IT, LITTLE BABIES. YOU HAFF TO STOP WANTING BOX. BOX IS GONNA BE MINE. IT'S GONNA BE TH' BESTEST CHAIR I EVER HAD!
YOU CAN'T SIT ON IT! YOU'LL RUIN IT!
QUITE TRUE!
THE CONSTRUCTION OF THE CARDBOARD MAKES IT IMPRACTICAL TO HOLD YOUR ENTIRE WEIGHT!
Uh-BBBBBB! I NOT LIKE WHEN YOU USE BIG WERDS. IT MAKES MY BRAIN HURT JUST LIKE WHEN I TRY TA SPELL!
Oh, FANG! DON'T BE SILLY!
YEAH, YOU DON'T WANT THAT BOX!
MOVE OUTTA MY WAY, YOU GIRLS!
YOU IS STINKY AND YOU GOT COOTIES!
HEY--BE NICE TO THEM, FANG!
WHAT YOU GONNA DO 'BOUT IT, OUCHIE?
MY NAME...IS ARCHIE.
NOT AFTA I GIT THRU WIT YOU!
NOW MOVE OUTTA MY WAY... OUCHIE.

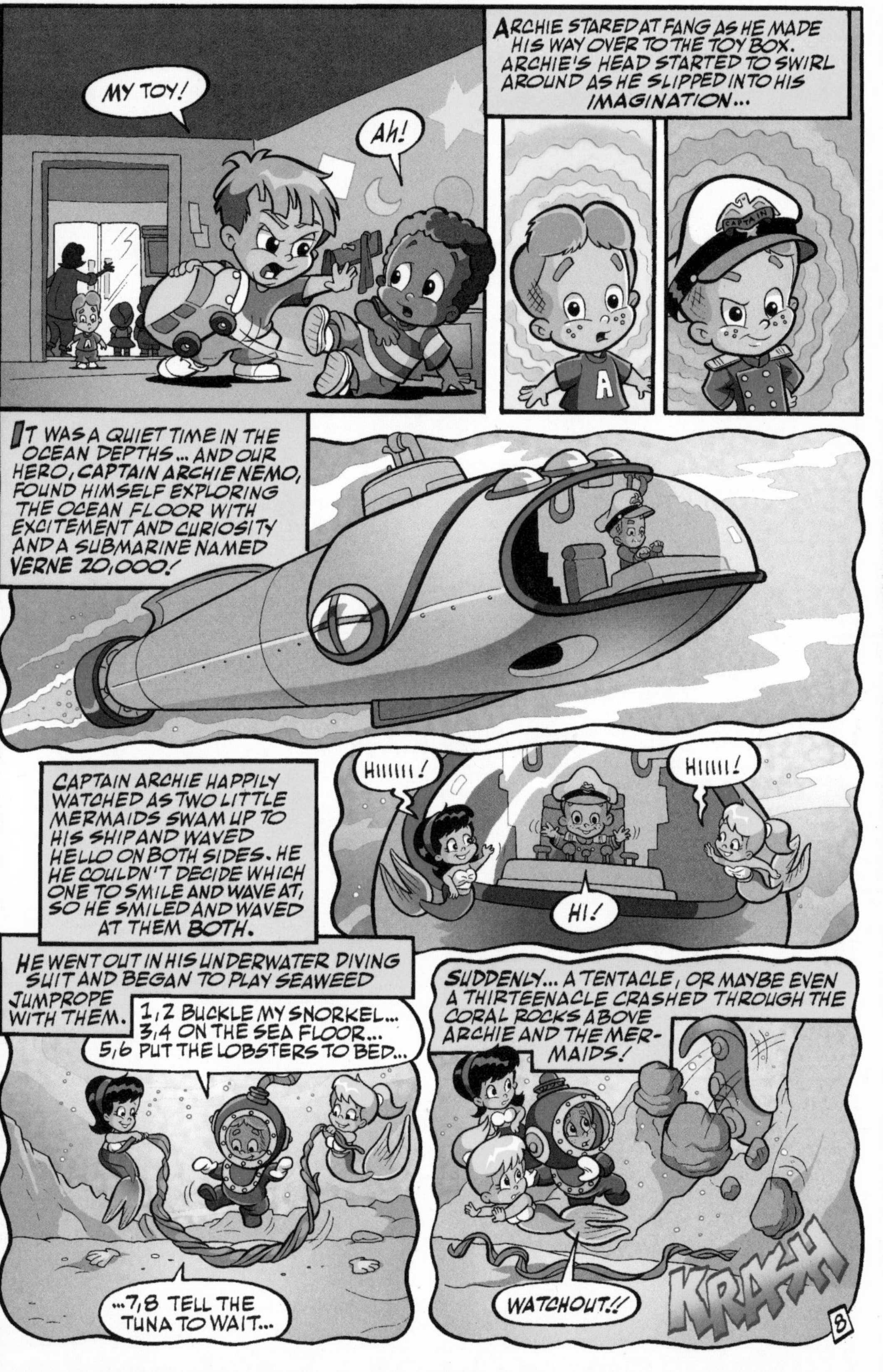

MY TOY!
Ah!
ARCHIE STARED AT FANG AS HE MADE HIS WAY OVER TO THE TOY BOX. ARCHIE'S HEAD STARTED TO SWIRL AROUND AS HE SLIPPED INTO HIS IMAGINATION...
CAPTAIN
IT WAS A QUIET TIME IN THE OCEAN DEPTHS... AND OUR HERO, CAPTAIN ARCHIE NEMO, FOUND HIMSELF EXPLORING THE OCEAN FLOOR WITH EXCITEMENT AND CURIOSITY AND A SUBMARINE NAMED VERNE 20,000!
CAPTAIN ARCHIE HAPPILY WATCHED AS TWO LITTLE MERMAIDS SWAM UP TO HIS SHIP AND WAVED HELLO ON BOTH SIDES. HE HE COULDN'T DECIDE WHICH ONE TO SMILE AND WAVE AT, SO HE SMILED AND WAVED AT THEM BOTH.
HIIIIII!
HIIIII!
HI!
HE WENT OUT IN HIS UNDERWATER DIVING SUIT AND BEGAN TO PLAY SEAWEED JUMPROPE WITH THEM.
1,2 BUCKLE MY SNORKEL... 3,4 ON THE SEA FLOOR... 5,6 PUT THE LOBSTERS TO BED...
...7,8 TELL THE TUNA TO WAIT...
SUDDENLY... A TENTACLE, OR MAYBE EVEN A THIRTEENACLE CRASHED THROUGH THE CORAL ROCKS ABOVE ARCHIE AND THE MER-MAIDS!
WATCHOUT!!
KRASH

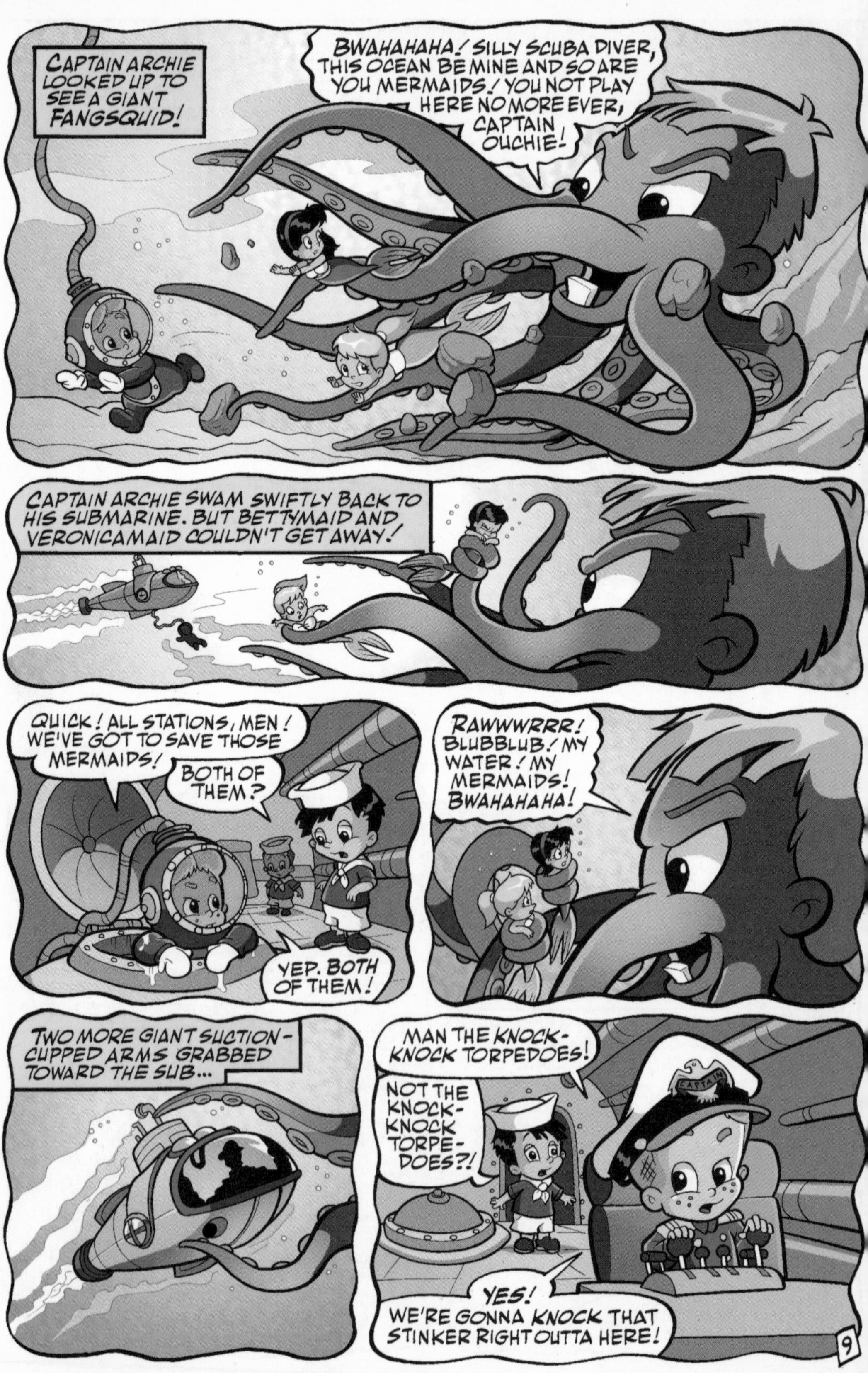
CAPTAIN ARCHIE LOOKED UP TO SEE A GIANT FANGSQUID!
BWAHAHAHA! SILLY SCUBA DIVER, THIS OCEAN BE MINE AND SO ARE YOU MERMAIDS! YOU NOT PLAY HERE NO MORE EVER, CAPTAIN OUCHIE!
CAPTAIN ARCHIE SWAM SWIFTLY BACK TO HIS SUBMARINE. BUT BETTYMAID AND VERONICAMAID COULDN'T GET AWAY!
QUICK! ALL STATIONS, MEN! WE'VE GOT TO SAVE THOSE MERMAIDS!
BOTH OF THEM?
YEP. BOTH OF THEM!
RAWWWRRR! BLUBBLUB! MY WATER! MY MERMAIDS! BWAHAHAHA!
TWO MORE GIANT SUCTION-CUPPED ARMS GRABBED TOWARD THE SUB...
MAN THE KNOCK-KNOCK TORPEDOES!
NOT THE KNOCK-KNOCK TORPE-DOES?!
YES! WE'RE GONNA KNOCK THAT STINKER RIGHT OUTTA HERE!
9

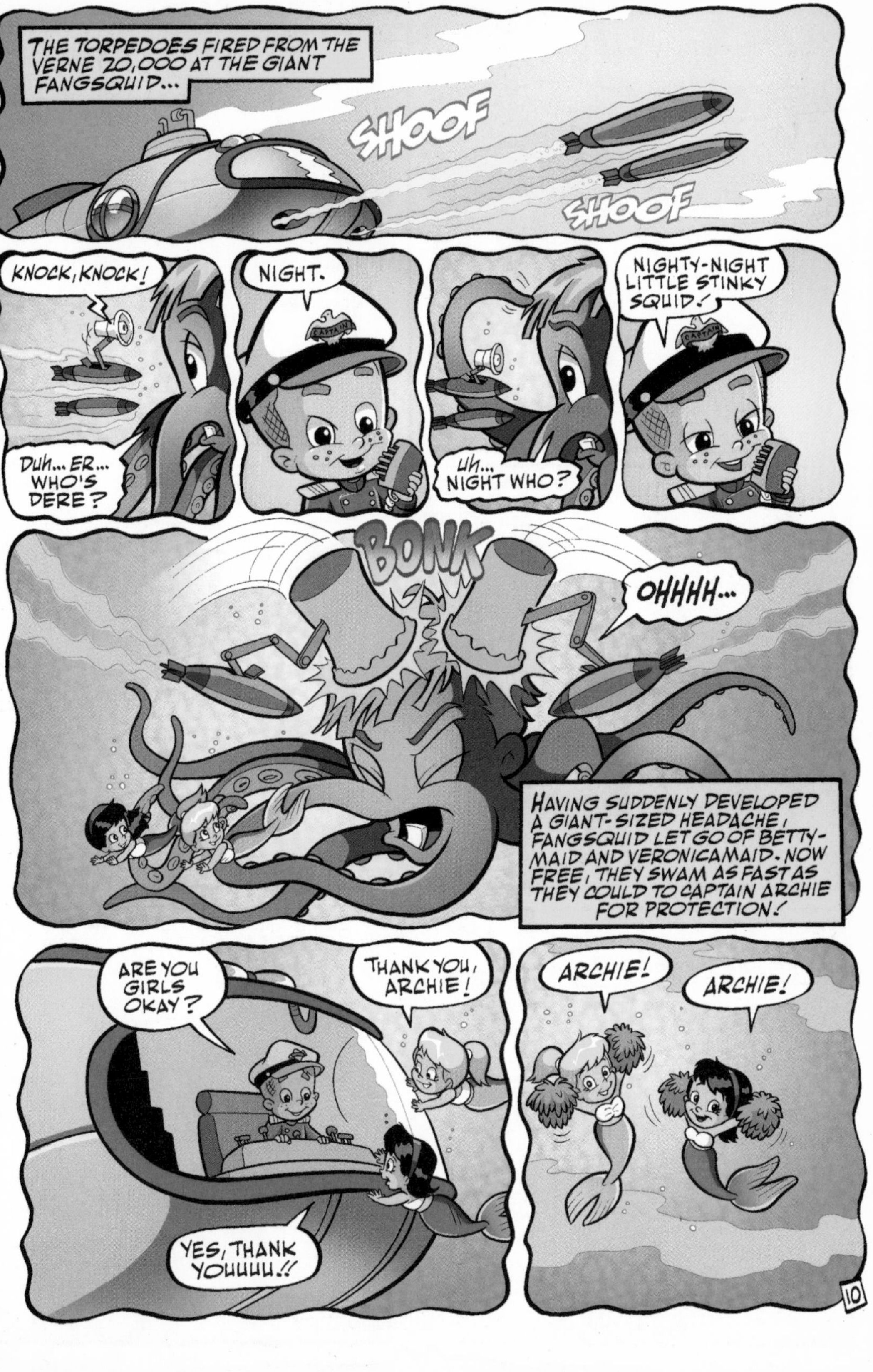
THE TORPEDOES FIRED FROM THE VERNE 20,000 AT THE GIANT FANGSQUID...
SHOOF
SHOOF
KNOCK, KNOCK!
DUH... ER... WHO'S DERE?
NIGHT.
UH... NIGHT WHO?
NIGHTY-NIGHT LITTLE STINKY SQUID!
BONK
OHHHH...
HAVING SUDDENLY DEVELOPED A GIANT-SIZED HEADACHE, FANGSQUID LET GO OF BETTY-MAID AND VERONICAMAID. NOW FREE, THEY SWAM AS FAST AS THEY COULD TO CAPTAIN ARCHIE FOR PROTECTION!
ARE YOU GIRLS OKAY?
THANK YOU, ARCHIE!
YES, THANK YOUUUU!!
ARCHIE!
ARCHIE!

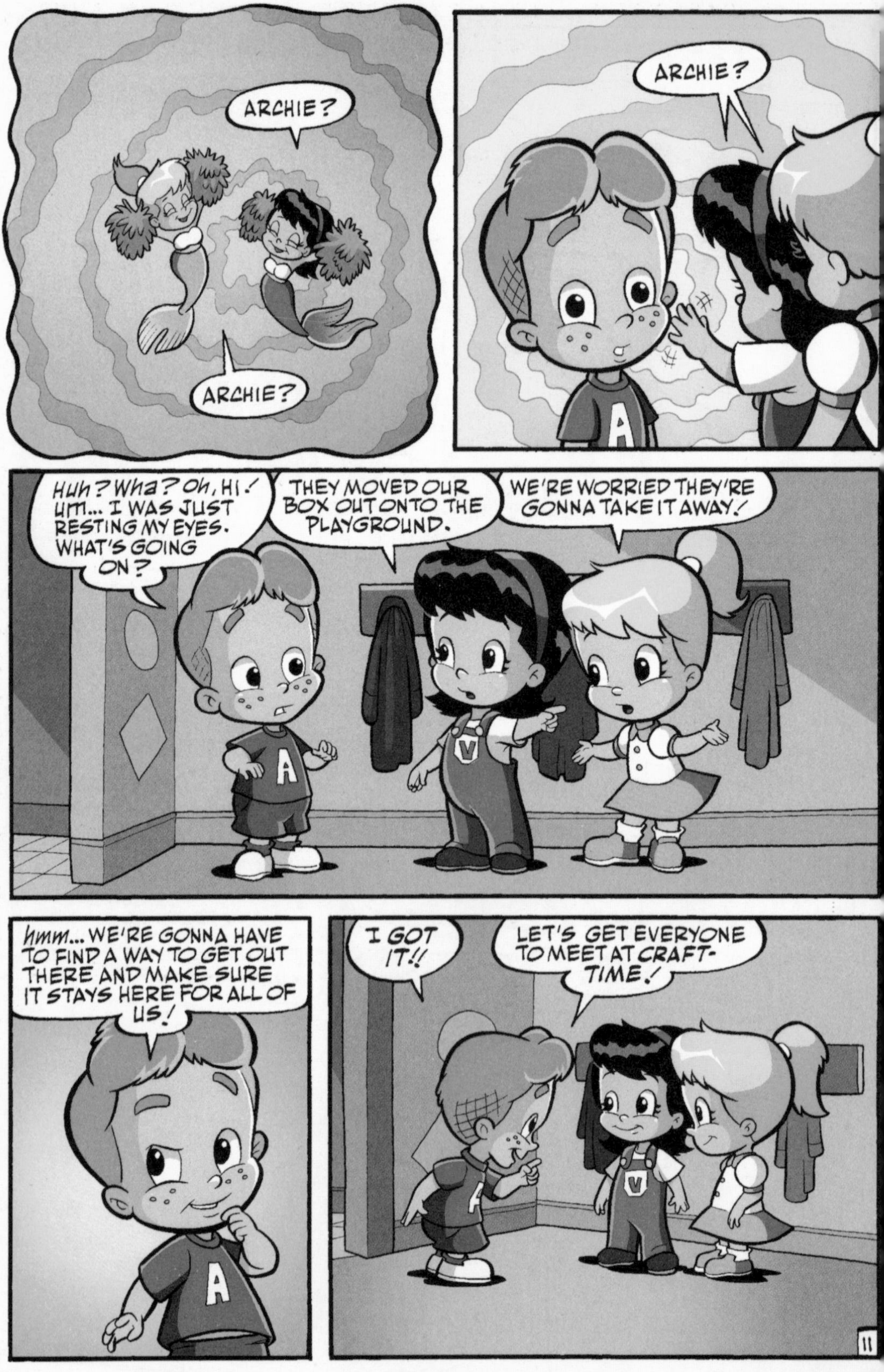

ARCHIE?
ARCHIE?
ARCHIE?
Huh? Wha? Oh, Hi! Um... I WAS JUST RESTING MY EYES. WHAT'S GOING ON?
THEY MOVED OUR BOX OUT ONTO THE PLAYGROUND.
WE'RE WORRIED THEY'RE GONNA TAKE IT AWAY!
hmm... WE'RE GONNA HAVE TO FIND A WAY TO GET OUT THERE AND MAKE SURE IT STAYS HERE FOR ALL OF US!
I GOT IT!!
LET'S GET EVERYONE TO MEET AT CRAFT-TIME!

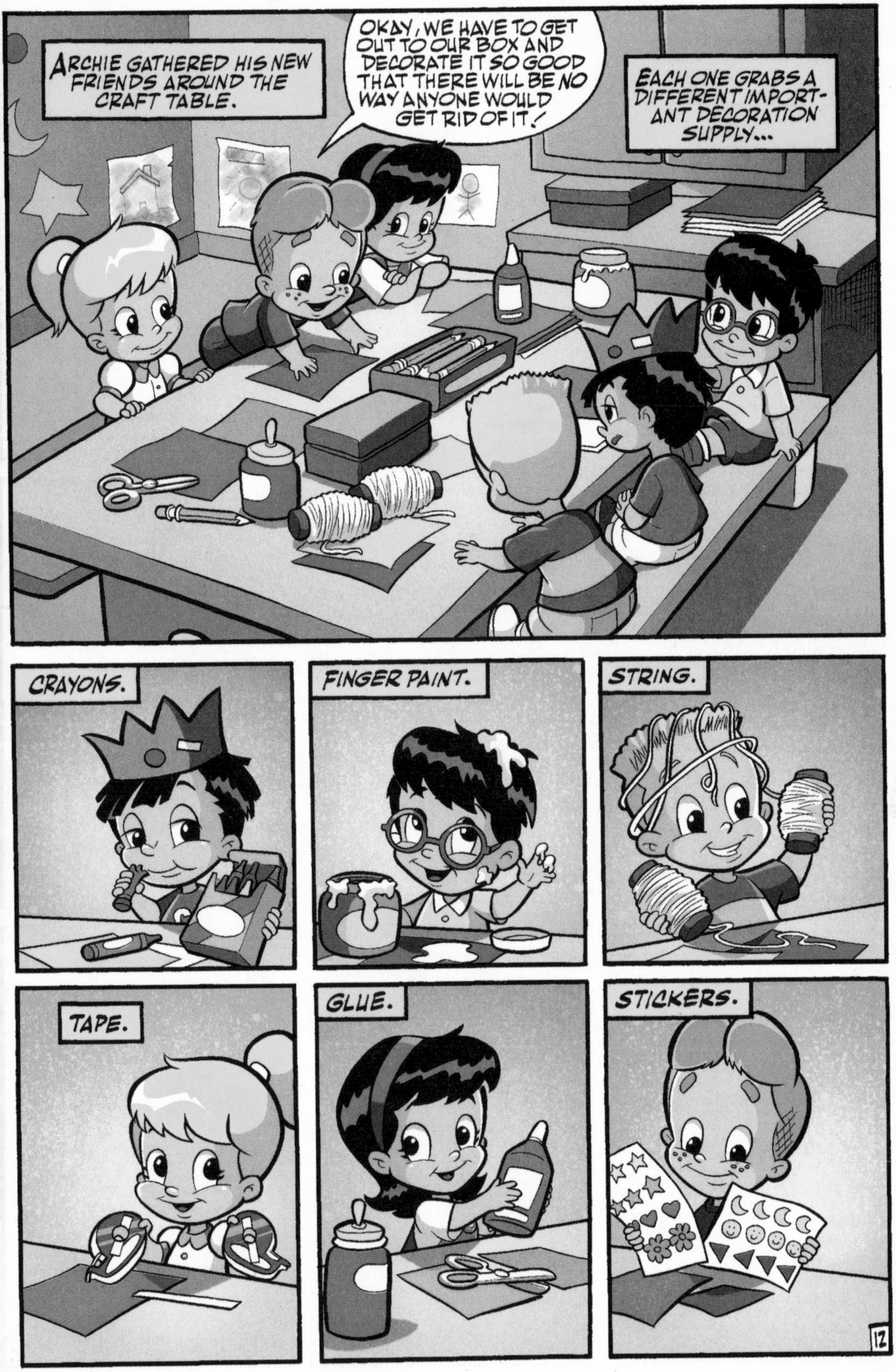
ARCHIE GATHERED HIS NEW FRIENDS AROUND THE CRAFT TABLE.
OKAY, WE HAVE TO GET OUT TO OUR BOX AND DECORATE IT SO GOOD THAT THERE WILL BE NO WAY ANYONE WOULD GET RID OF IT!
EACH ONE GRABS A DIFFERENT IMPORTANT DECORATION SUPPLY...
CRAYONS.
FINGER PAINT.
STRING.
TAPE.
GLUE.
STICKERS.

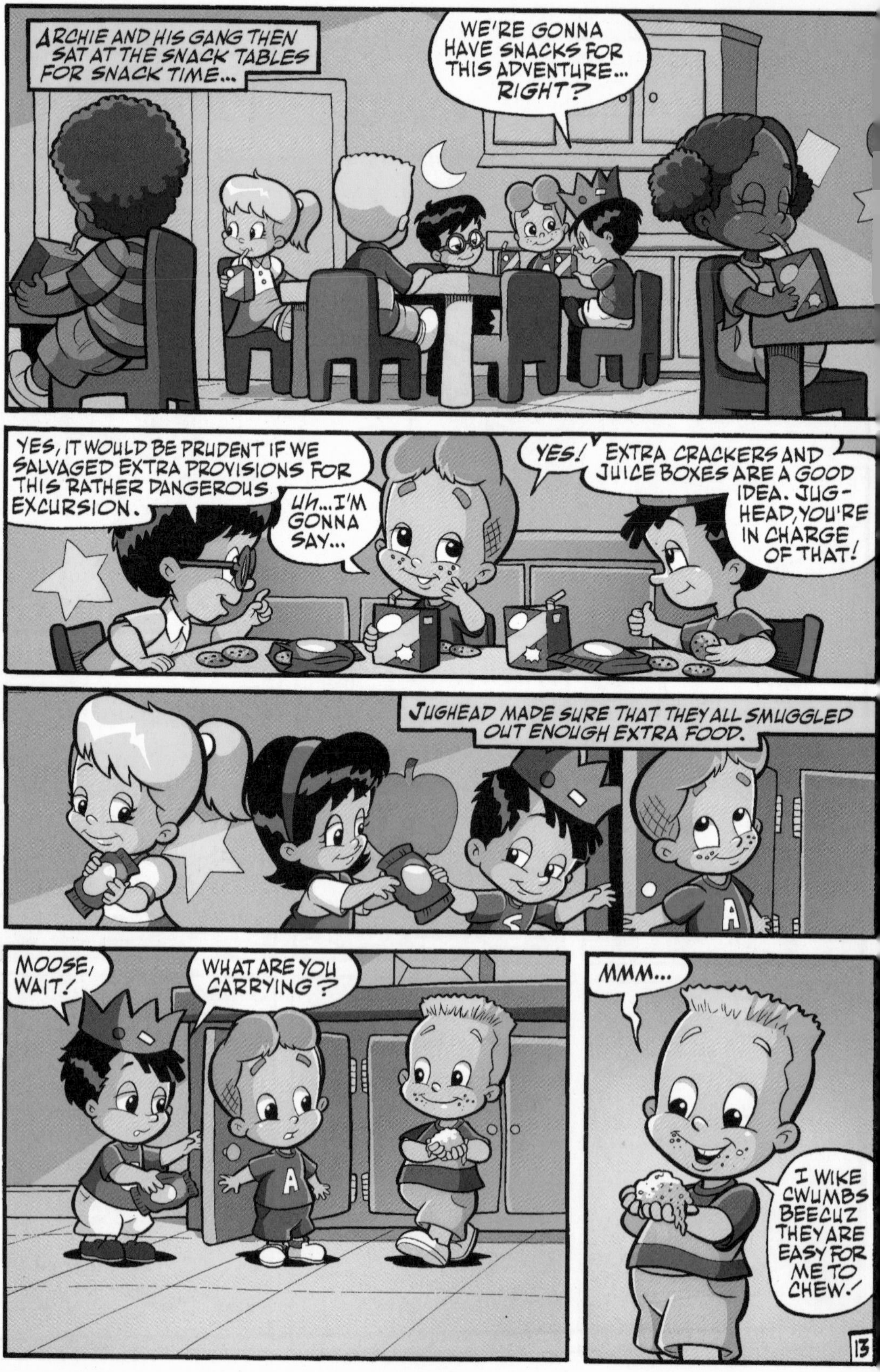
ARCHIE AND HIS GANG THEN SAT AT THE SNACK TABLES FOR SNACK TIME...
WE'RE GONNA HAVE SNACKS FOR THIS ADVENTURE... RIGHT?
YES, IT WOULD BE PRUDENT IF WE SALVAGED EXTRA PROVISIONS FOR THIS RATHER DANGEROUS EXCURSION.
uh...I'M GONNA SAY...
YES!
EXTRA CRACKERS AND JUICE BOXES ARE A GOOD IDEA. JUG-HEAD, YOU'RE IN CHARGE OF THAT!
JUGHEAD MADE SURE THAT THEY ALL SMUGGLED OUT ENOUGH EXTRA FOOD.
MOOSE, WAIT!
WHAT ARE YOU CARRYING?
MMM...
I WIKE CWUMBS BEECUZ THEY ARE EASY FOR ME TO CHEW.!

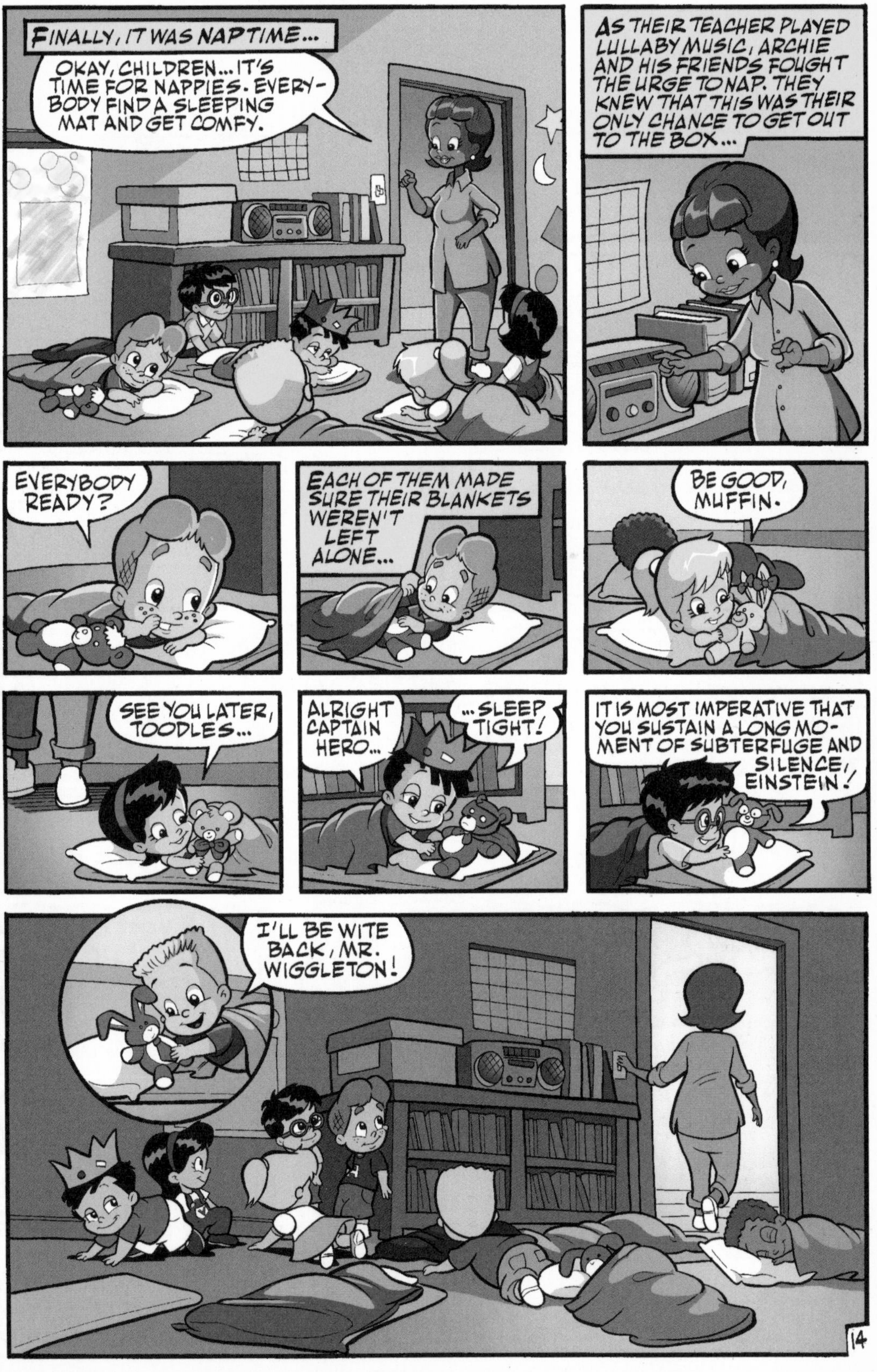
FINALLY, IT WAS NAPTIME...
OKAY, CHILDREN... IT'S TIME FOR NAPPIES. EVERY-BODY FIND A SLEEPING MAT AND GET COMFY.
AS THEIR TEACHER PLAYED LULLABY MUSIC, ARCHIE AND HIS FRIENDS FOUGHT THE URGE TO NAP. THEY KNEW THAT THIS WAS THEIR ONLY CHANCE TO GET OUT TO THE BOX...
EVERYBODY READY?
EACH OF THEM MADE SURE THEIR BLANKETS WEREN'T LEFT ALONE...
BE GOOD, MUFFIN.
SEE YOU LATER, TOODLES...
ALRIGHT CAPTAIN HERO...
...SLEEP TIGHT!
IT IS MOST IMPERATIVE THAT YOU SUSTAIN A LONG MO-MENT OF SUBTERFUGE AND SILENCE, EINSTEIN!
I'LL BE WITE BACK, MR. WIGGLETON!

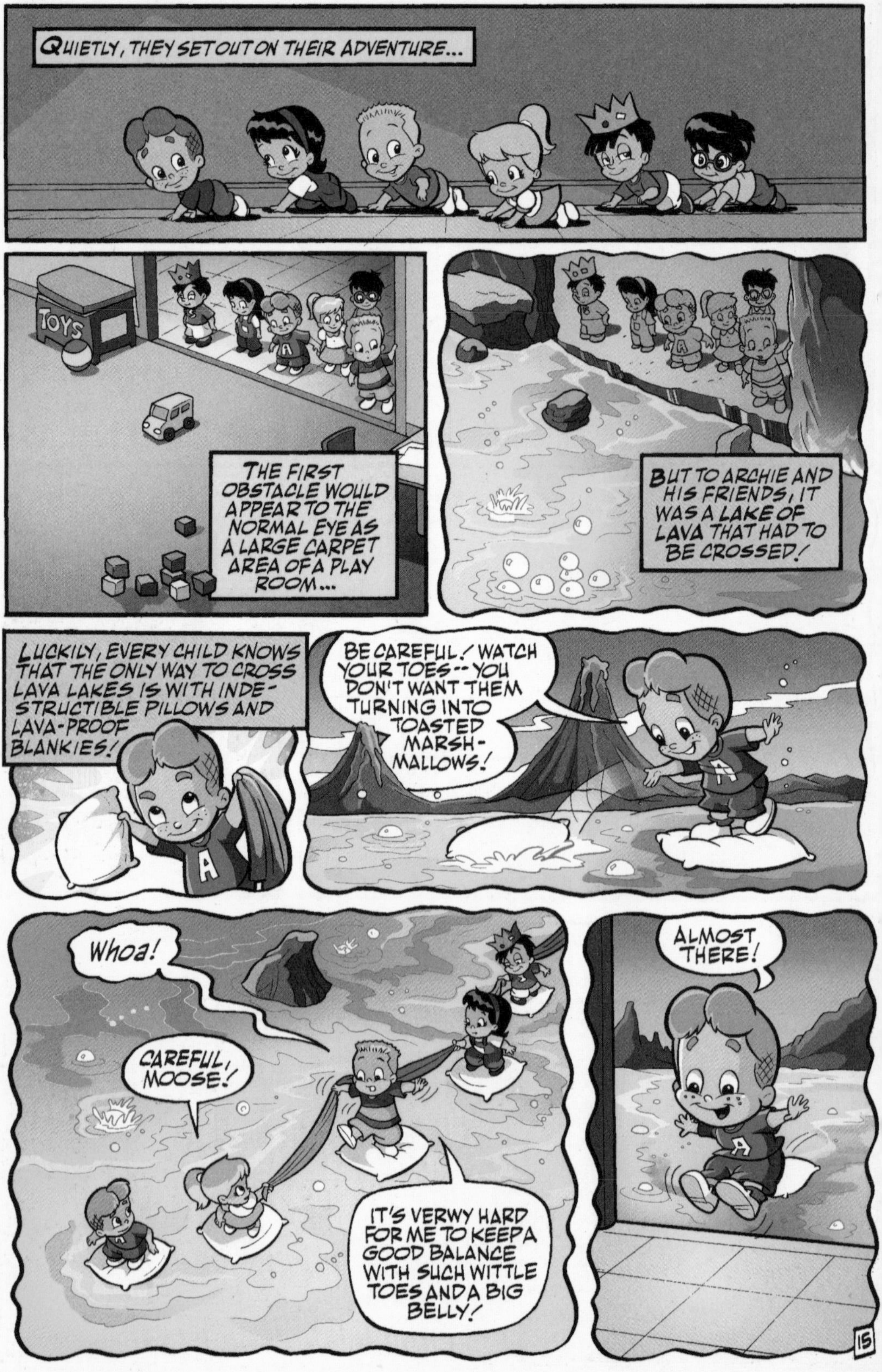
QUIETLY, THEY SET OUT ON THEIR ADVENTURE...
TOYS
THE FIRST OBSTACLE WOULD APPEAR TO THE NORMAL EYE AS A LARGE CARPET AREA OF A PLAY ROOM...
BUT TO ARCHIE AND HIS FRIENDS, IT WAS A LAKE OF LAVA THAT HAD TO BE CROSSED!
LUCKILY, EVERY CHILD KNOWS THAT THE ONLY WAY TO CROSS LAVA LAKES IS WITH INDE-STRUCTIBLE PILLOWS AND LAVA-PROOF BLANKIES!
BE CAREFUL! WATCH YOUR TOES-- YOU DON'T WANT THEM TURNING INTO TOASTED MARSH-MALLOWS!
Whoa!
CAREFUL, MOOSE!
IT'S VERWY HARD FOR ME TO KEEP A GOOD BALANCE WITH SUCH WITTLE TOES AND A BIG BELLY!
ALMOST THERE!

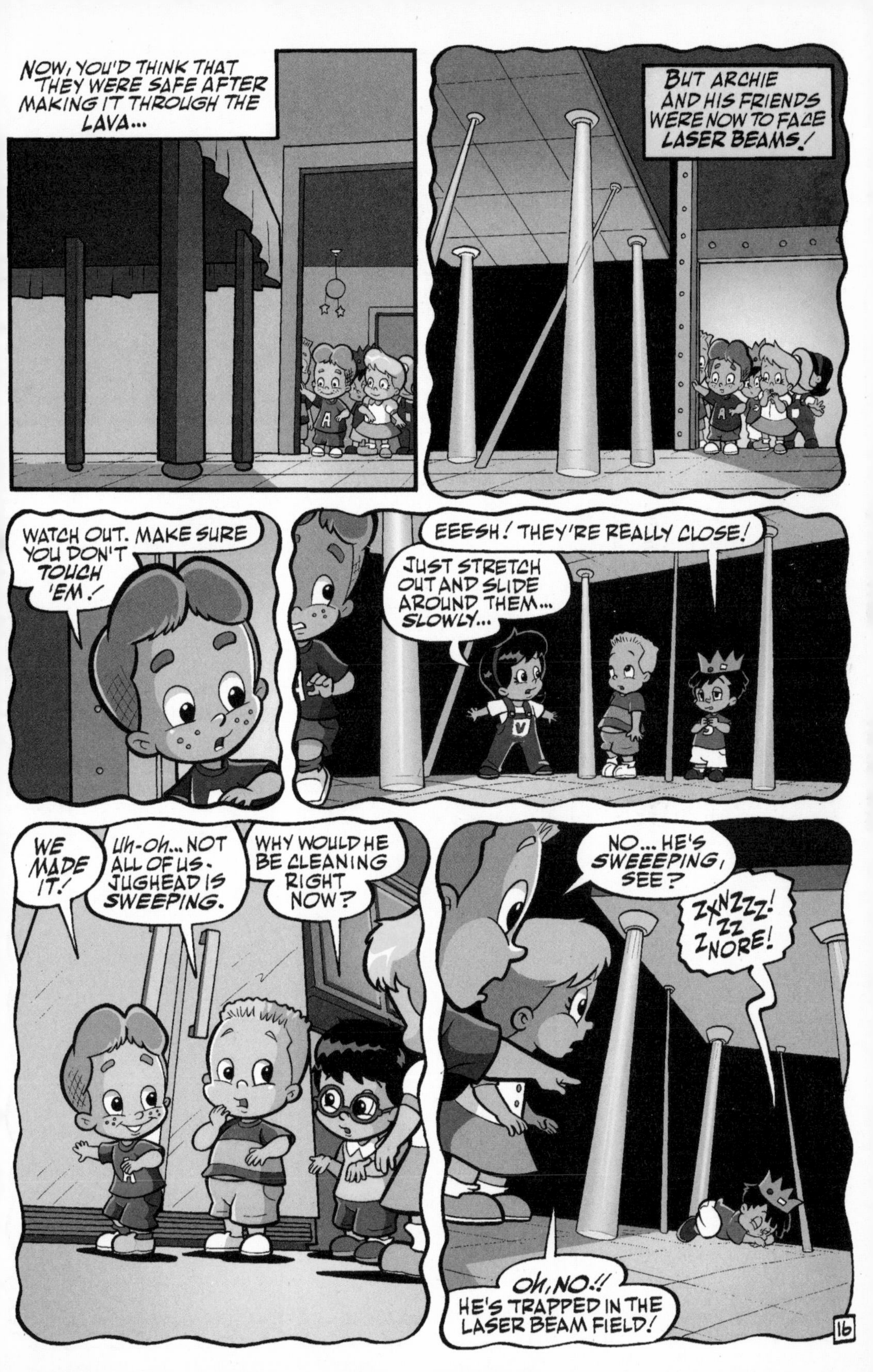

NOW, YOU'D THINK THAT THEY WERE SAFE AFTER MAKING IT THROUGH THE LAVA...
BUT ARCHIE AND HIS FRIENDS WERE NOW TO FACE LASER BEAMS!
WATCH OUT. MAKE SURE YOU DON'T TOUCH 'EM!
EEESH! THEY'RE REALLY CLOSE!
JUST STRETCH OUT AND SLIDE AROUND THEM... SLOWLY...
WE MADE IT!
Uh-Oh... NOT ALL OF US. JUGHEAD IS SWEEPING.
WHY WOULD HE BE CLEANING RIGHT NOW?
NO... HE'S SWEEEPING, SEE?
ZXNZZZ! ZZ ZNORE!
Oh, NO!! HE'S TRAPPED IN THE LASER BEAM FIELD!

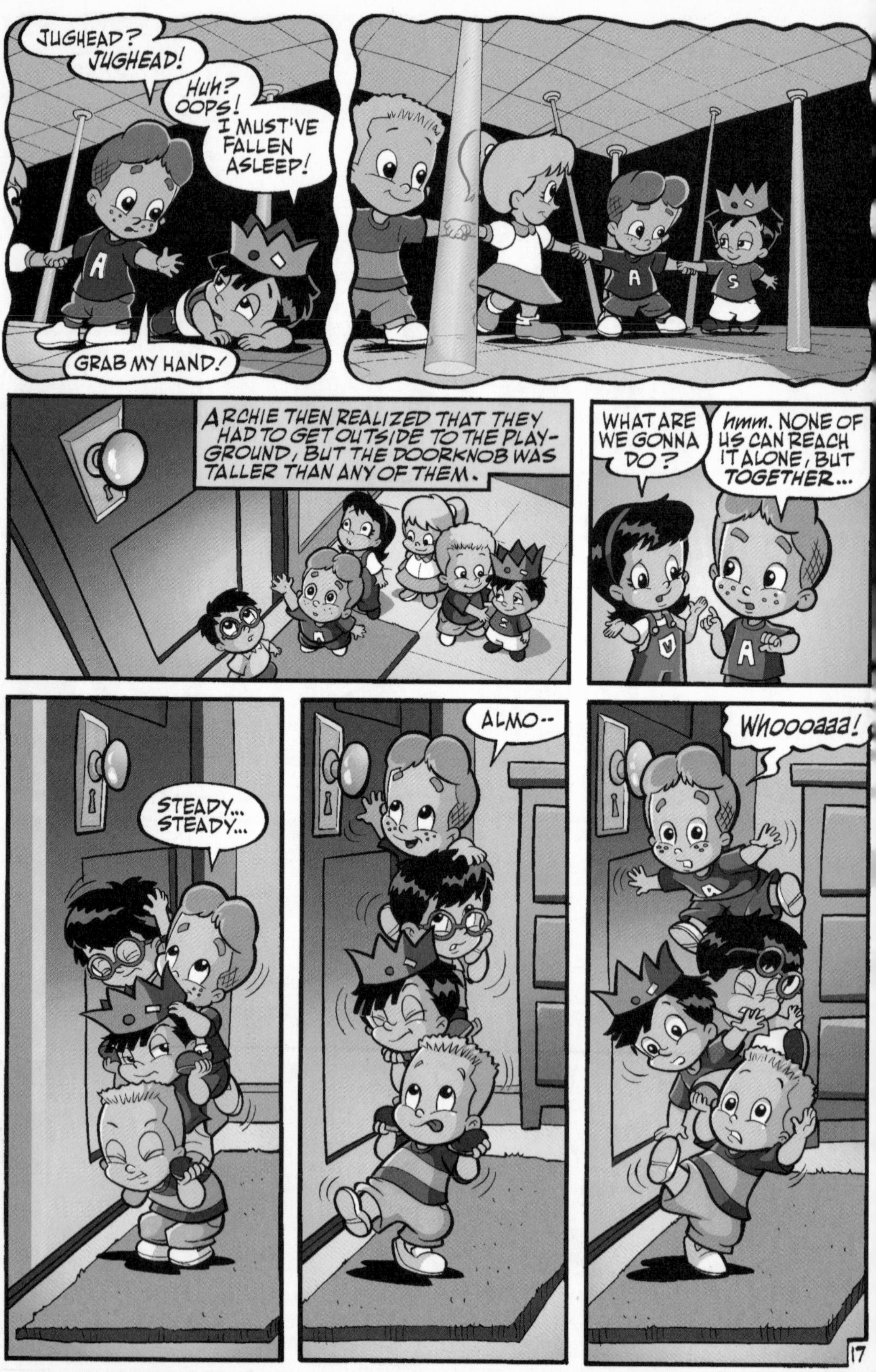
JUGHEAD? JUGHEAD!
Huh? OOPS! I MUST'VE FALLEN ASLEEP!
GRAB MY HAND!
ARCHIE THEN REALIZED THAT THEY HAD TO GET OUTSIDE TO THE PLAY-GROUND, BUT THE DOORKNOB WAS TALLER THAN ANY OF THEM.
WHAT ARE WE GONNA DO?
hmm. NONE OF US CAN REACH IT ALONE, BUT TOGETHER...
STEADY... STEADY...
ALMO--
WHooooaaa!

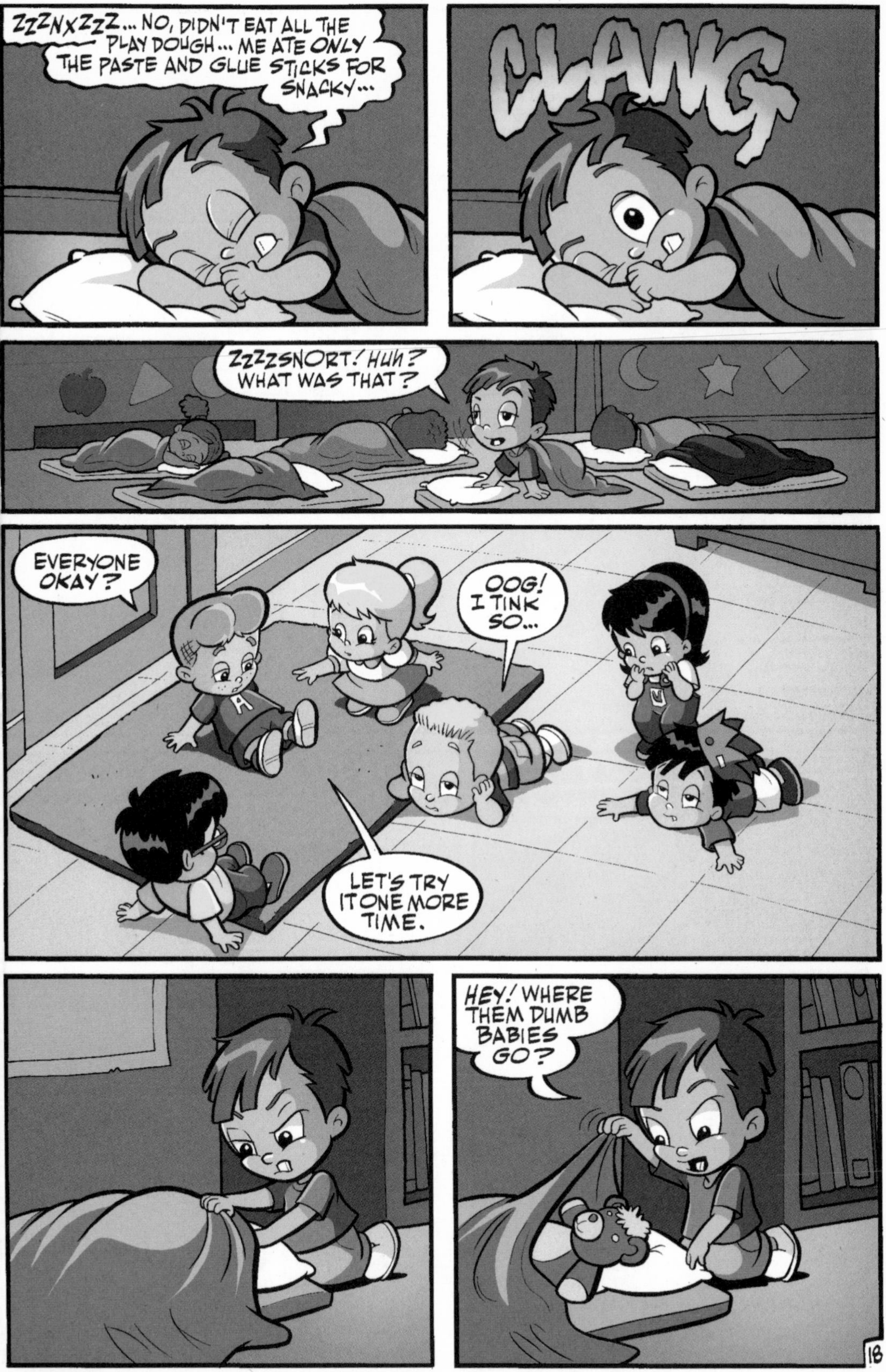
ZZZNXZZZ... NO, DIDN'T EAT ALL THE PLAY DOUGH... ME ATE ONLY THE PASTE AND GLUE STICKS FOR SNACKY...
CLANG
ZZZZSNORT! HUH? WHAT WAS THAT?
EVERYONE OKAY?
OOG! I TINK SO...
LET'S TRY IT ONE MORE TIME.
HEY! WHERE THEM DUMB BABIES GO?

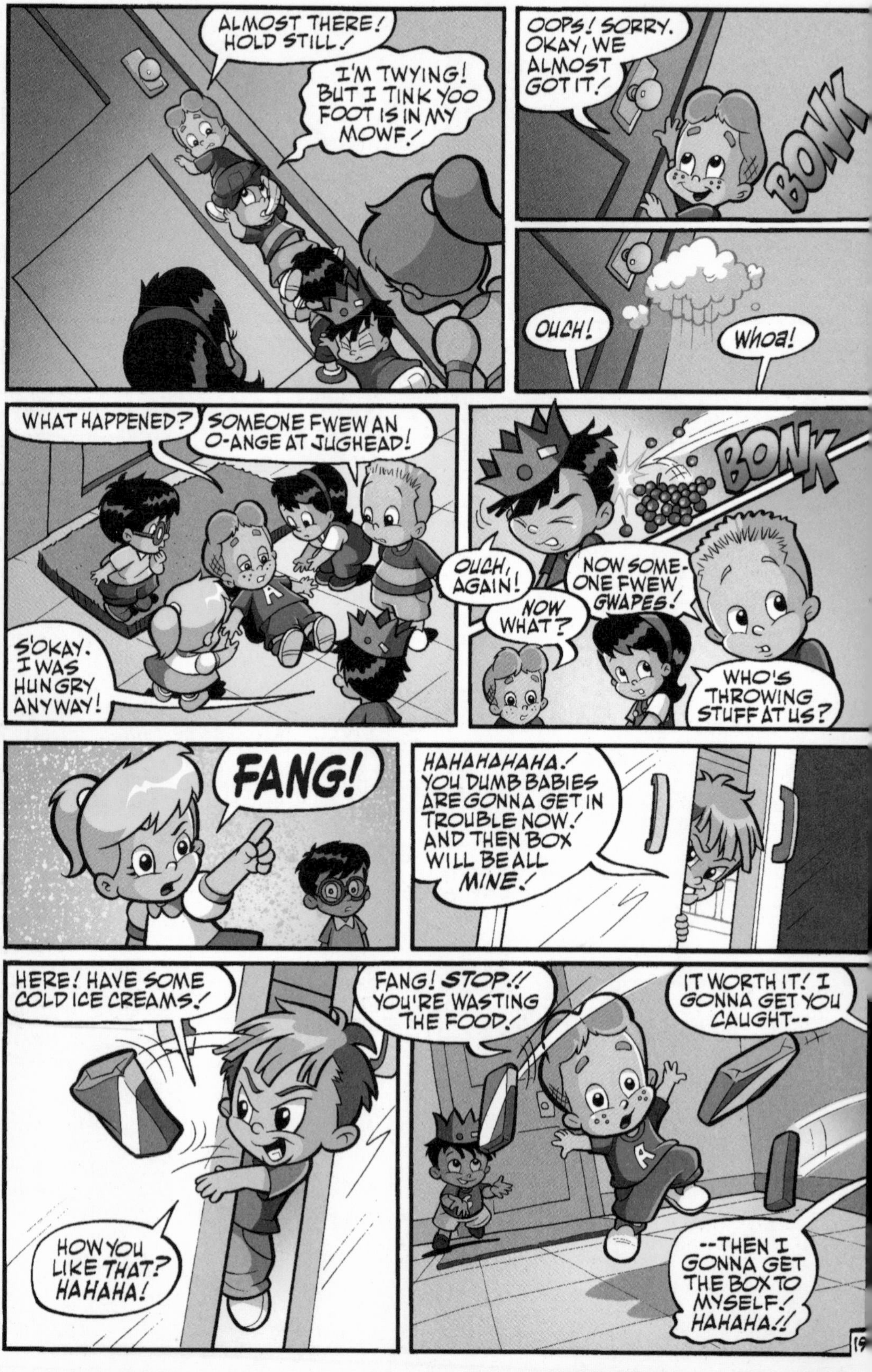
ALMOST THERE! HOLD STILL!
I'M TWYING! BUT I TINK YOO FOOT IS IN MY MOWF!
OOPS! SORRY. OKAY, WE ALMOST GOT IT!
BONK
OUCH!
Whoa!
WHAT HAPPENED?
SOMEONE FWEW AN O-ANGE AT JUGHEAD!
S'OKAY. I WAS HUNGRY ANYWAY!
BONK
OUCH, AGAIN!
NOW SOME-ONE FWEW GWAPES!
NOW WHAT?
WHO'S THROWING STUFF AT US?
FANG!
HAHAHAHAHA! YOU DUMB BABIES ARE GONNA GET IN TROUBLE NOW! AND THEN BOX WILL BE ALL MINE!
HERE! HAVE SOME COLD ICE CREAMS!
HOW YOU LIKE THAT? HAHAHA!
FANG! STOP!! YOU'RE WASTING THE FOOD!
IT WORTH IT! I GONNA GET YOU CAUGHT--
--THEN I GONNA GET THE BOX TO MYSELF! HAHAHA!!

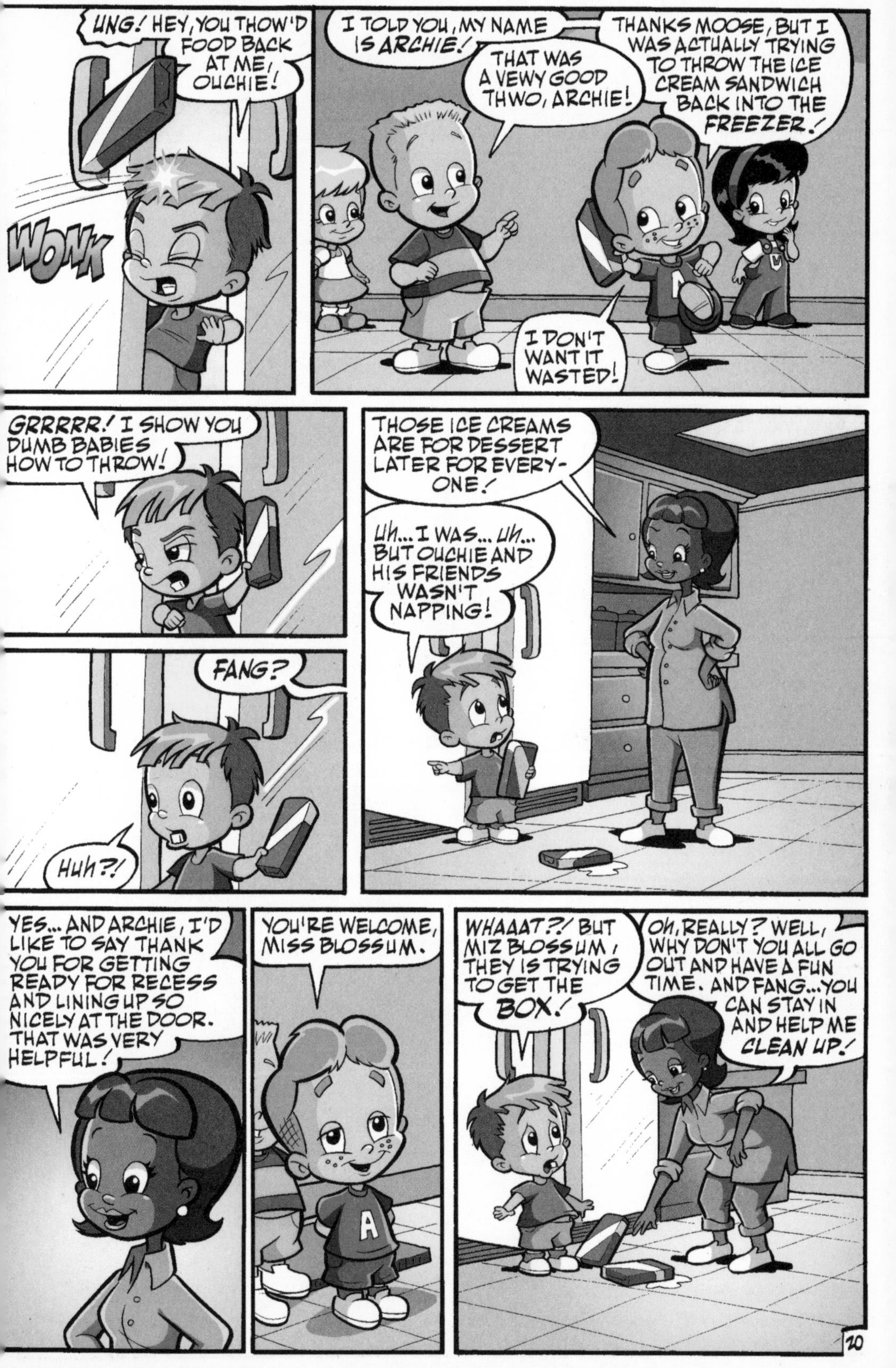
UNG! HEY, YOU THOW'D FOOD BACK AT ME, OUCHIE!
WONK
I TOLD YOU, MY NAME IS ARCHIE!
THAT WAS A VEWY GOOD THWO, ARCHIE!
THANKS MOOSE, BUT I WAS ACTUALLY TRYING TO THROW THE ICE CREAM SANDWICH BACK INTO THE FREEZER!
I DON'T WANT IT WASTED!
GRRRRR! I SHOW YOU DUMB BABIES HOW TO THROW!
FANG?
HUH?!
THOSE ICE CREAMS ARE FOR DESSERT LATER FOR EVERY-ONE!
UH... I WAS... UH... BUT OUCHIE AND HIS FRIENDS WASN'T NAPPING!
YES... AND ARCHIE, I'D LIKE TO SAY THANK YOU FOR GETTING READY FOR RECESS AND LINING UP SO NICELY AT THE DOOR. THAT WAS VERY HELPFUL!
YOU'RE WELCOME, MISS BLOSSUM.
WHAAAT?! BUT MIZ BLOSSUM, THEY IS TRYING TO GET THE BOX!
OH, REALLY? WELL, WHY DON'T YOU ALL GO OUT AND HAVE A FUN TIME. AND FANG... YOU CAN STAY IN AND HELP ME CLEAN UP!

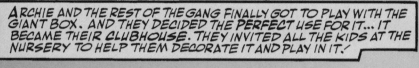

ARCHIE AND THE REST OF THE GANG FINALLY GOT TO PLAY WITH THE GIANT BOX. AND THEY DECIDED THE *PERFECT USE* FOR IT... IT BECAME THEIR *CLUBHOUSE*. THEY INVITED ALL THE KIDS AT THE NURSERY TO HELP THEM DECORATE IT AND PLAY IN IT.

WELL, THAT EXCURSION TURNED OUT TO BE MOST *EXHILARATING!*

YOU SURE DO!

YEAH, ARCHIE! YOU SURE KNOW HOW TO MAKE A FIRST DAY *FUN!*

MMMM... THIS IS THE BESTEST CWUBHOUSE EVER!

YOU CAN SAY *THAT* AGAIN, MOOSE!

MMMM... THIS IS THE BESTEST CWUBHOUSE EVER!

HAHAHA HAHA HA H A HAHA!

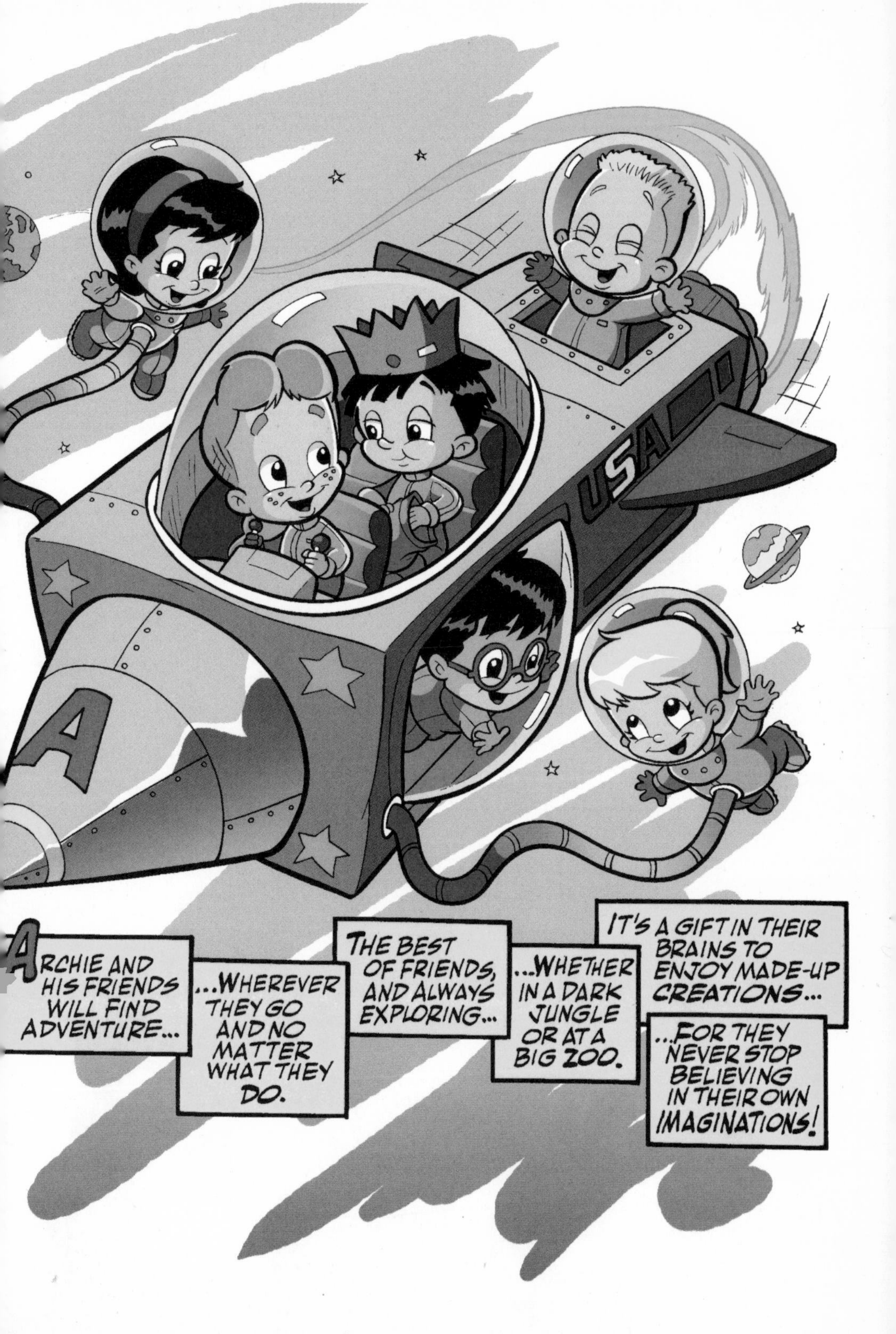
ARCHIE AND HIS FRIENDS WILL FIND ADVENTURE...
...WHEREVER THEY GO AND NO MATTER WHAT THEY DO.
THE BEST OF FRIENDS, AND ALWAYS EXPLORING...
...WHETHER IN A DARK JUNGLE OR AT A BIG ZOO.
IT'S A GIFT IN THEIR BRAINS TO ENJOY MADE-UP CREATIONS...
...FOR THEY NEVER STOP BELIEVING IN THEIR OWN IMAGINATIONS!
USA
A

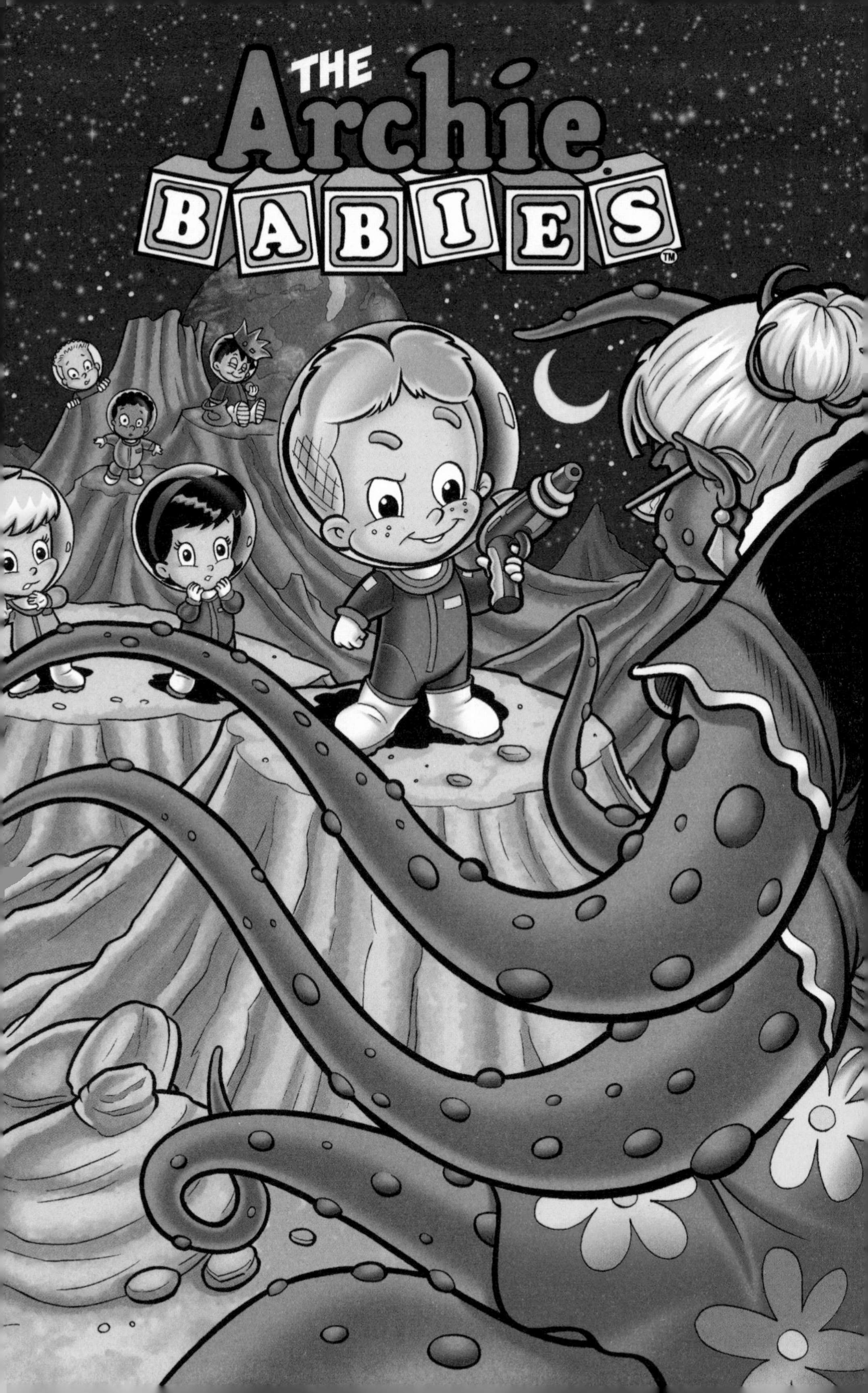
THE
Archie
BABIES
TM

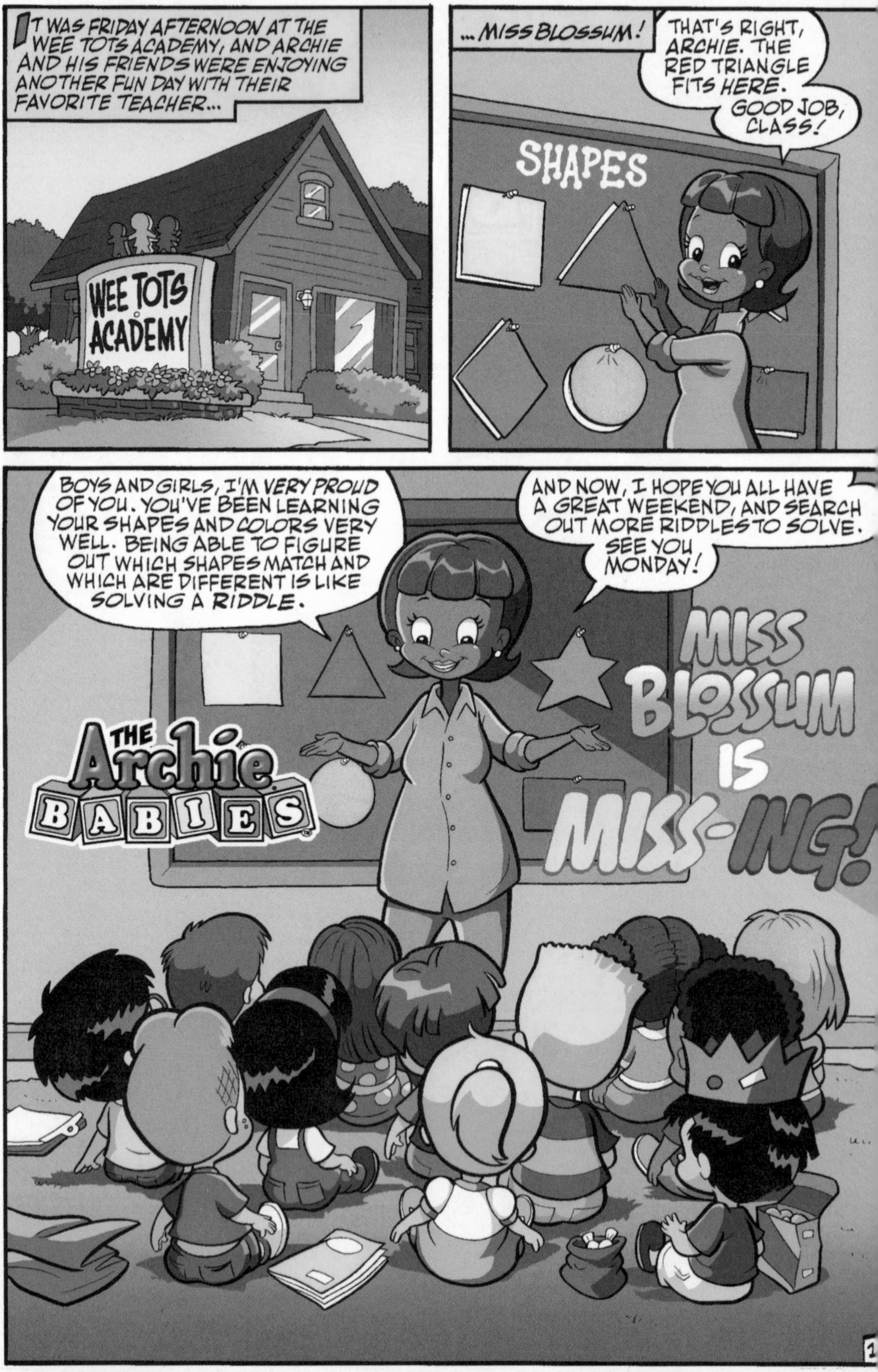
IT WAS FRIDAY AFTERNOON AT THE WEE TOTS ACADEMY, AND ARCHIE AND HIS FRIENDS WERE ENJOYING ANOTHER FUN DAY WITH THEIR FAVORITE TEACHER...
WEE TOTS ACADEMY
...MISS BLOSSUM!
THAT'S RIGHT, ARCHIE. THE RED TRIANGLE FITS HERE.
GOOD JOB, CLASS!
SHAPES
BOYS AND GIRLS, I'M VERY PROUD OF YOU. YOU'VE BEEN LEARNING YOUR SHAPES AND COLORS VERY WELL. BEING ABLE TO FIGURE OUT WHICH SHAPES MATCH AND WHICH ARE DIFFERENT IS LIKE SOLVING A RIDDLE.
AND NOW, I HOPE YOU ALL HAVE A GREAT WEEKEND, AND SEARCH OUT MORE RIDDLES TO SOLVE. SEE YOU MONDAY!
THE Archie BABIES
MISS BLOSSUM IS MISS-ING!

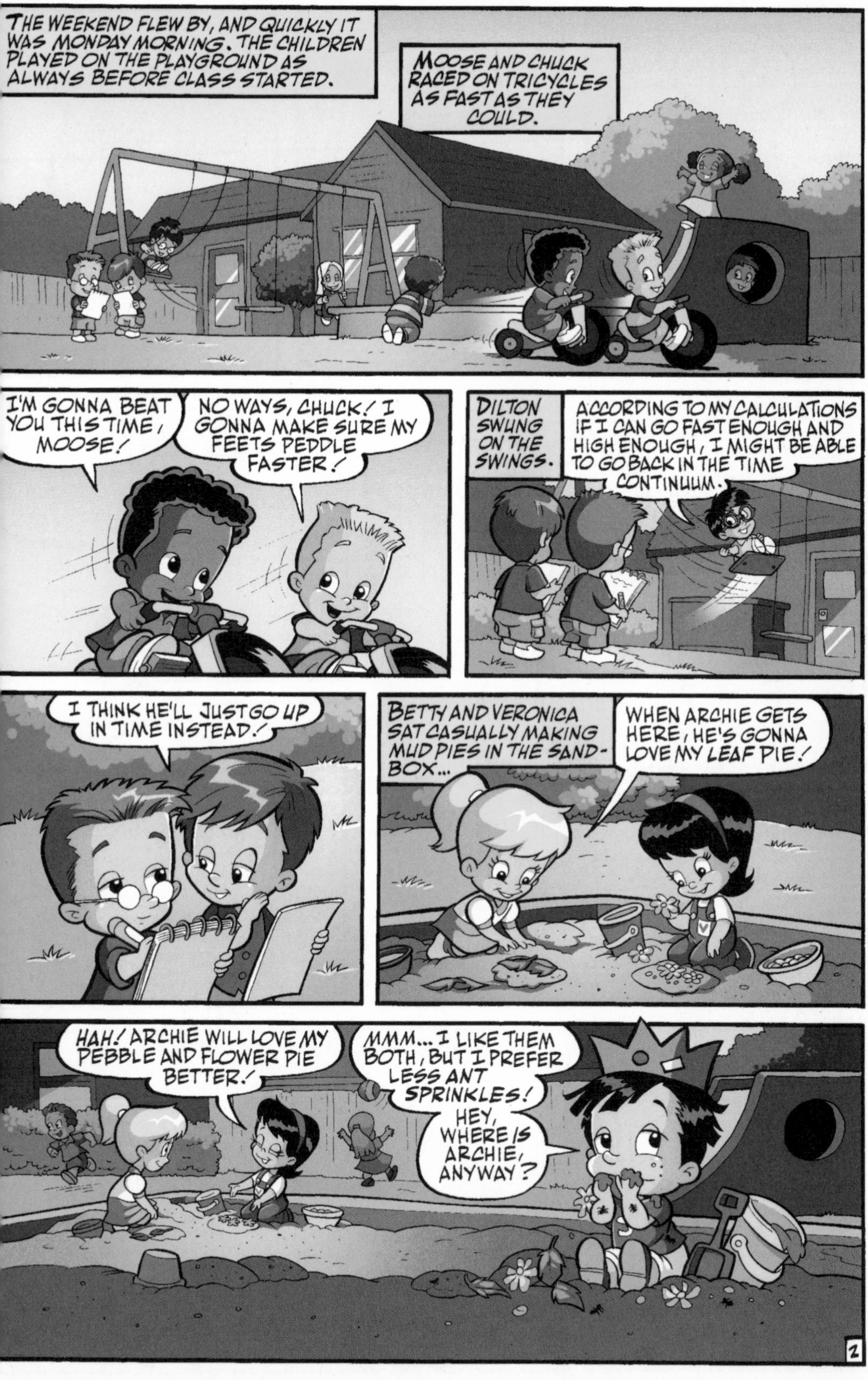
THE WEEKEND FLEW BY, AND QUICKLY IT WAS MONDAY MORNING. THE CHILDREN PLAYED ON THE PLAYGROUND AS ALWAYS BEFORE CLASS STARTED.
MOOSE AND CHUCK RACED ON TRICYCLES AS FAST AS THEY COULD.
I'M GONNA BEAT YOU THIS TIME, MOOSE!
NO WAYS, CHUCK! I GONNA MAKE SURE MY FEETS PEDDLE FASTER!
DILTON SWUNG ON THE SWINGS.
ACCORDING TO MY CALCULATIONS IF I CAN GO FAST ENOUGH AND HIGH ENOUGH, I MIGHT BE ABLE TO GO BACK IN THE TIME CONTINUUM.
I THINK HE'LL JUST GO UP IN TIME INSTEAD!
BETTY AND VERONICA SAT CASUALLY MAKING MUD PIES IN THE SAND-BOX...
WHEN ARCHIE GETS HERE, HE'S GONNA LOVE MY LEAF PIE!
HAH! ARCHIE WILL LOVE MY PEBBLE AND FLOWER PIE BETTER!
MMM... I LIKE THEM BOTH, BUT I PREFER LESS ANT SPRINKLES!
HEY, WHERE IS ARCHIE, ANYWAY?

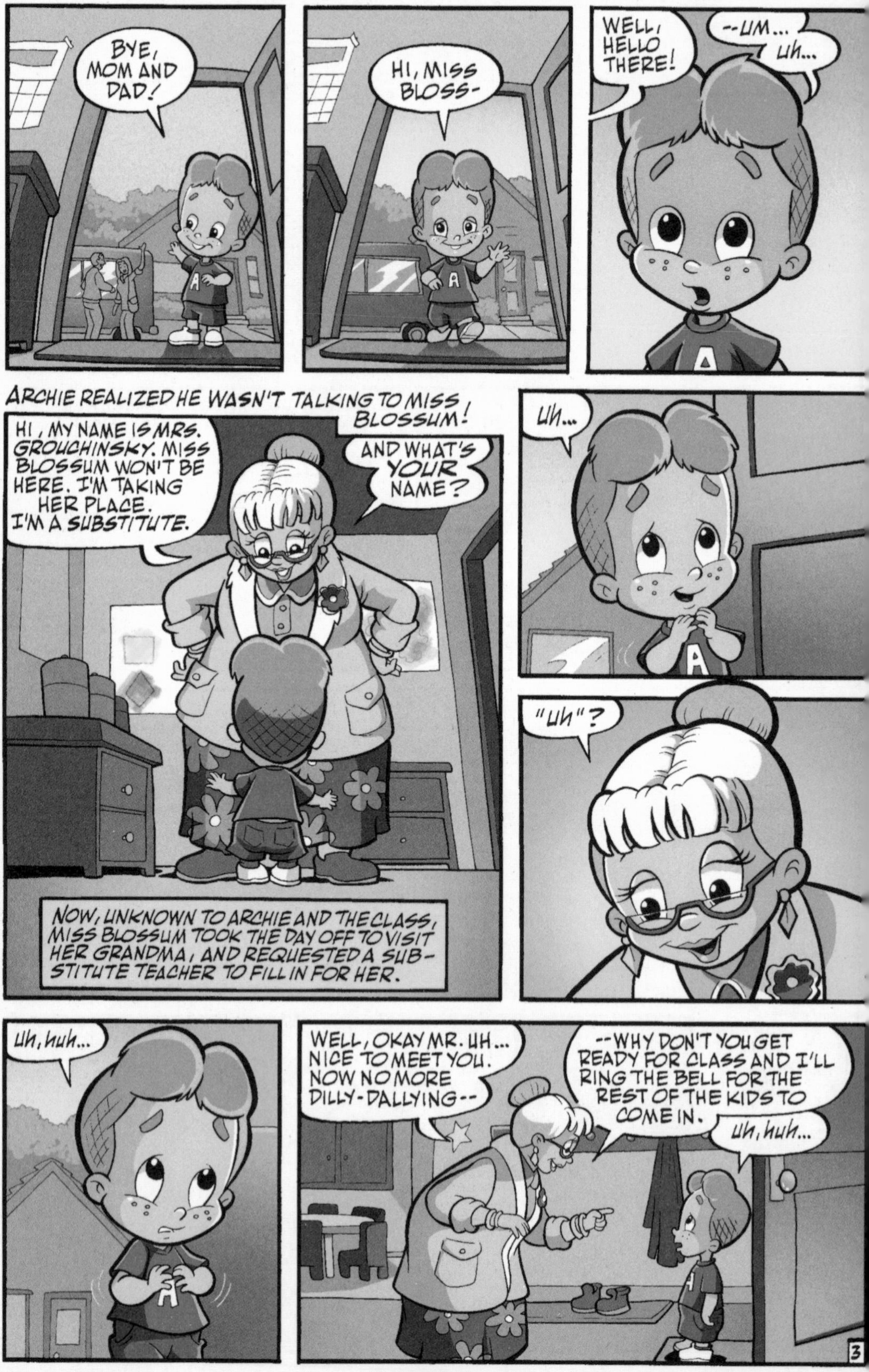
BYE, MOM AND DAD!
HI, MISS BLOSS-
WELL, HELLO THERE!
--UM... UH...
ARCHIE REALIZED HE WASN'T TALKING TO MISS BLOSSUM!
HI, MY NAME IS MRS. GROUCHINSKY. MISS BLOSSUM WON'T BE HERE. I'M TAKING HER PLACE. I'M A SUBSTITUTE.
AND WHAT'S YOUR NAME?
UH...
"UH"?
NOW, UNKNOWN TO ARCHIE AND THE CLASS, MISS BLOSSUM TOOK THE DAY OFF TO VISIT HER GRANDMA, AND REQUESTED A SUB-STITUTE TEACHER TO FILL IN FOR HER.
UH, HUH...
WELL, OKAY MR. UH... NICE TO MEET YOU. NOW NO MORE DILLY-DALLYING--
--WHY DON'T YOU GET READY FOR CLASS AND I'LL RING THE BELL FOR THE REST OF THE KIDS TO COME IN.
UH, HUH...
3

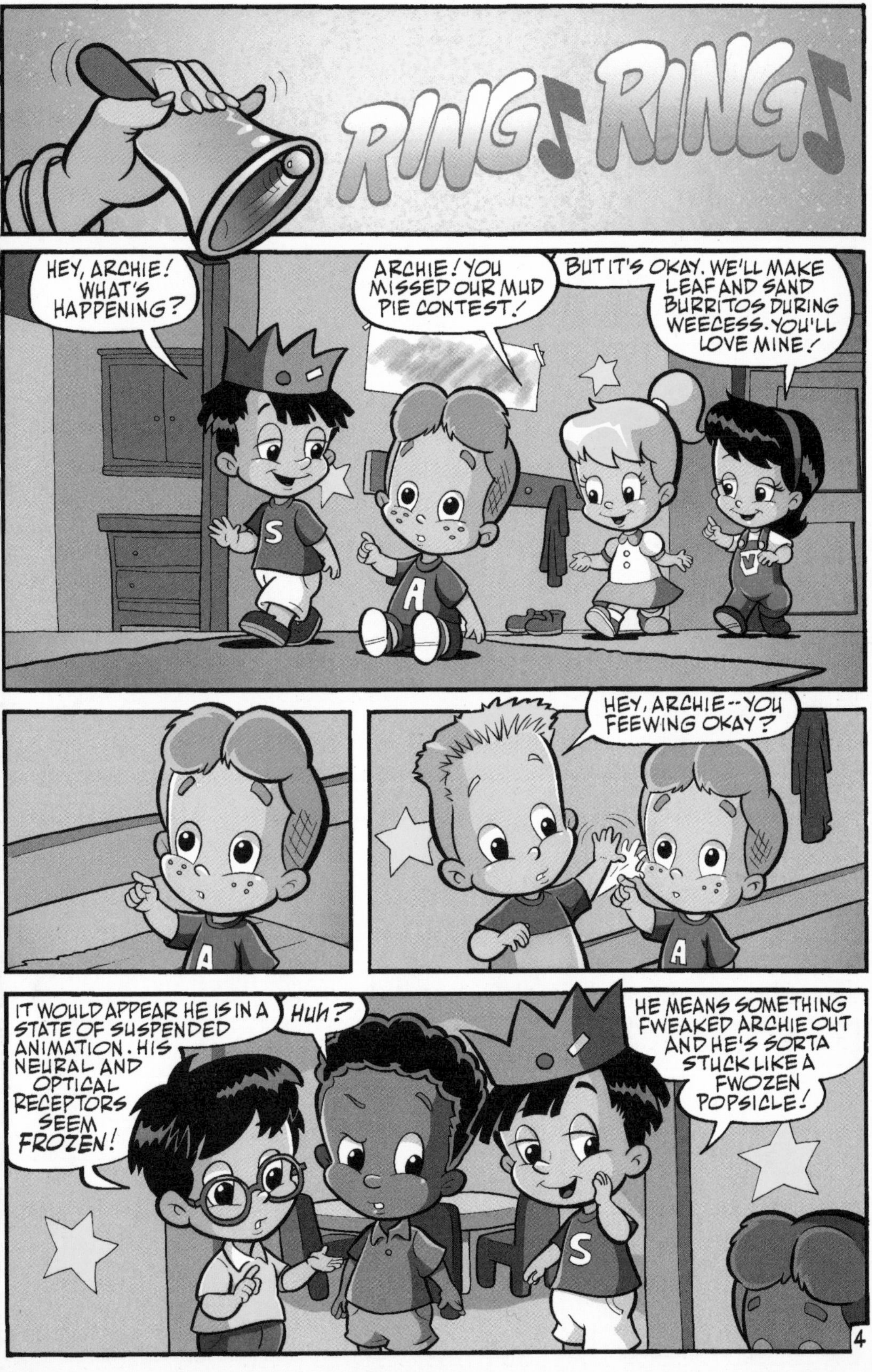
RING♪ RING♪
HEY, ARCHIE! WHAT'S HAPPENING?
ARCHIE! YOU MISSED OUR MUD PIE CONTEST!
BUT IT'S OKAY. WE'LL MAKE LEAF AND SAND BURRITOS DURING WEECESS. YOU'LL LOVE MINE!
HEY, ARCHIE--YOU FEEWING OKAY?
IT WOULD APPEAR HE IS IN A STATE OF SUSPENDED ANIMATION. HIS NEURAL AND OPTICAL RECEPTORS SEEM FROZEN!
HUH?
HE MEANS SOMETHING FWEAKED ARCHIE OUT AND HE'S SORTA STUCK LIKE A FWOZEN POPSICLE!

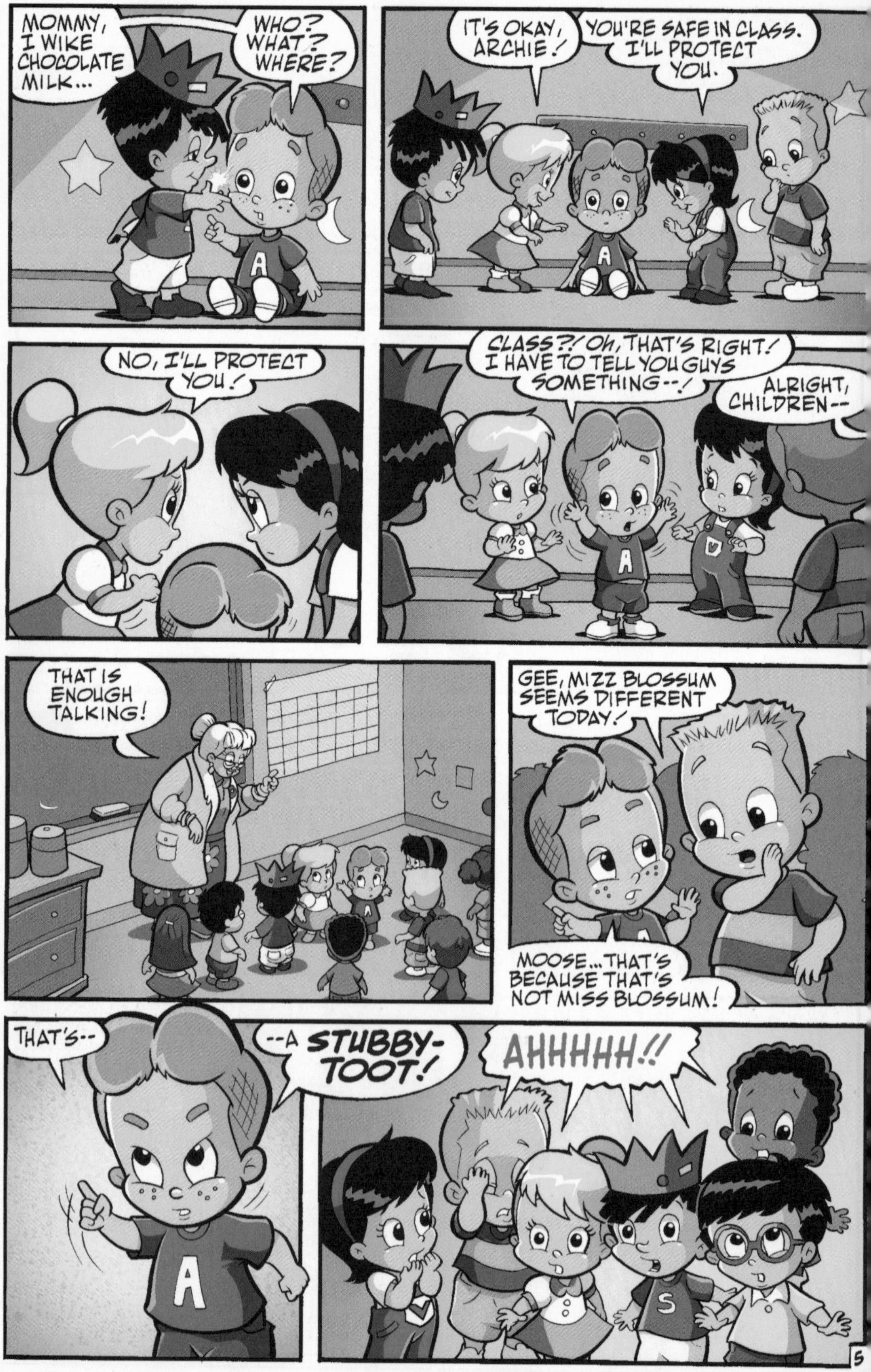
MOMMY, I WIKE CHOCOLATE MILK...
WHO? WHAT? WHERE?
IT'S OKAY, ARCHIE!
YOU'RE SAFE IN CLASS. I'LL PROTECT YOU.
NO, I'LL PROTECT YOU!
CLASS?! OH, THAT'S RIGHT! I HAVE TO TELL YOU GUYS SOMETHING--!
ALRIGHT, CHILDREN--
THAT IS ENOUGH TALKING!
GEE, MIZZ BLOSSUM SEEMS DIFFERENT TODAY!
MOOSE... THAT'S BECAUSE THAT'S NOT MISS BLOSSUM!
THAT'S--
--A STUBBY-TOOT!
AHHHHH!!

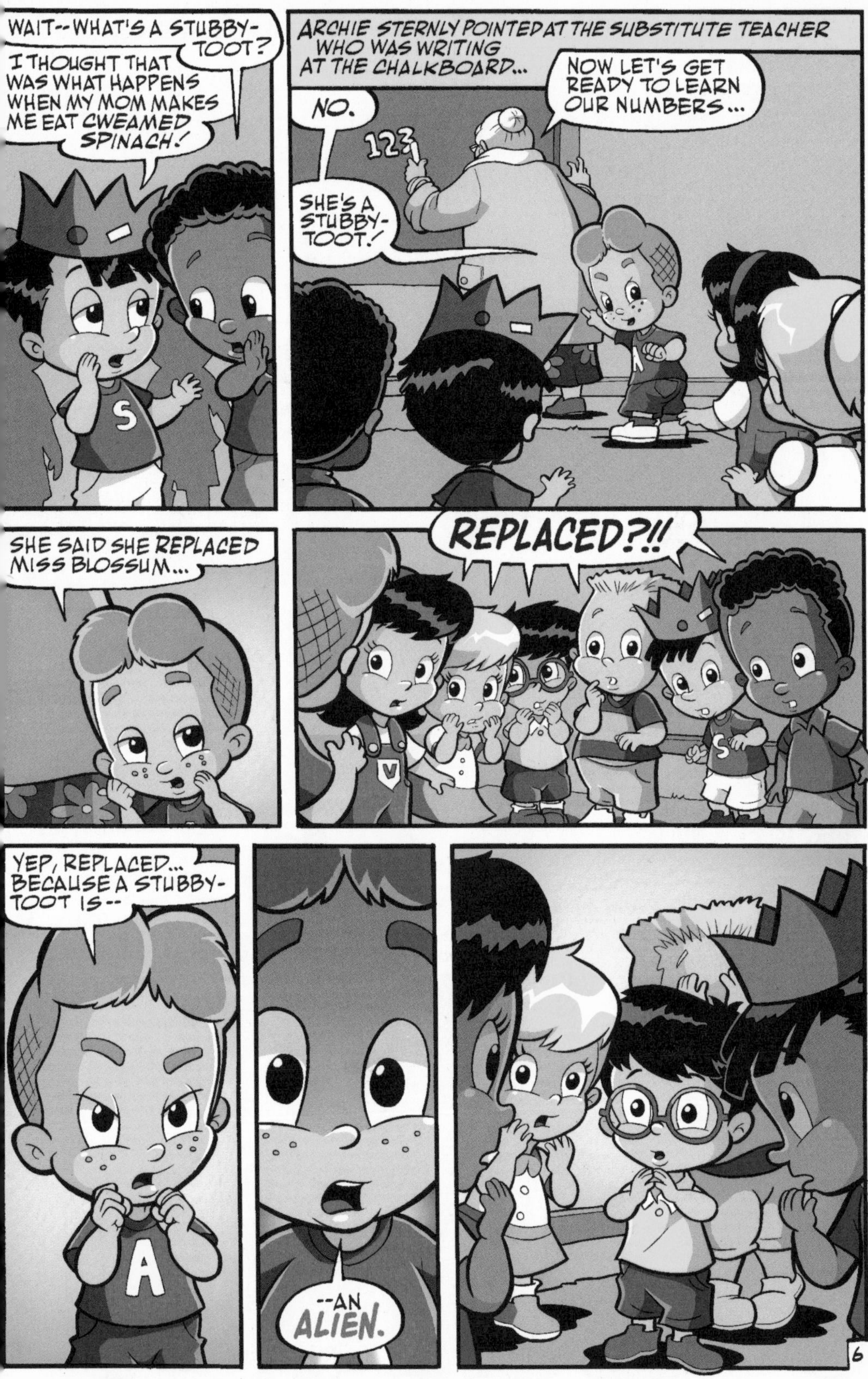
WAIT--WHAT'S A STUBBY-TOOT?
I THOUGHT THAT WAS WHAT HAPPENS WHEN MY MOM MAKES ME EAT CWEAMED SPINACH!
ARCHIE STERNLY POINTED AT THE SUBSTITUTE TEACHER WHO WAS WRITING AT THE CHALKBOARD...
NOW LET'S GET READY TO LEARN OUR NUMBERS...
NO.
123
SHE'S A STUBBY-TOOT!
SHE SAID SHE REPLACED MISS BLOSSUM...
REPLACED?!!
YEP, REPLACED... BECAUSE A STUBBY-TOOT IS--
--AN ALIEN.
6

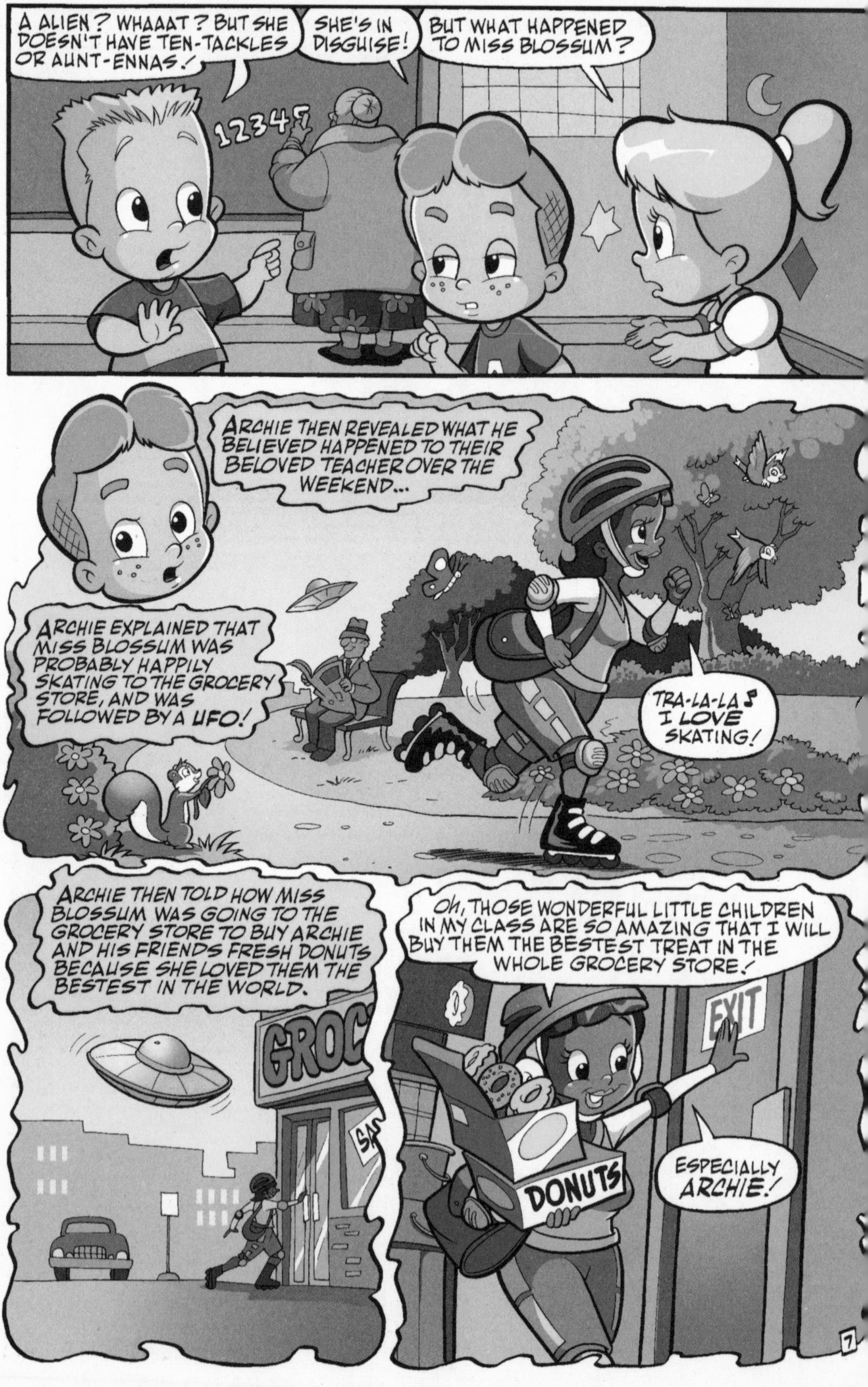
A ALIEN? WHAAAT? BUT SHE DOESN'T HAVE TEN-TACKLES OR AUNT-ENNAS!
SHE'S IN DISGUISE!
BUT WHAT HAPPENED TO MISS BLOSSUM?
12345
ARCHIE THEN REVEALED WHAT HE BELIEVED HAPPENED TO THEIR BELOVED TEACHER OVER THE WEEKEND...
ARCHIE EXPLAINED THAT MISS BLOSSUM WAS PROBABLY HAPPILY SKATING TO THE GROCERY STORE, AND WAS FOLLOWED BY A UFO!
TRA-LA-LA I LOVE SKATING!
ARCHIE THEN TOLD HOW MISS BLOSSUM WAS GOING TO THE GROCERY STORE TO BUY ARCHIE AND HIS FRIENDS FRESH DONUTS BECAUSE SHE LOVED THEM THE BESTEST IN THE WORLD.
Oh, THOSE WONDERFUL LITTLE CHILDREN IN MY CLASS ARE SO AMAZING THAT I WILL BUY THEM THE BESTEST TREAT IN THE WHOLE GROCERY STORE!
GROC
EXIT
DONUTS
ESPECIALLY ARCHIE!

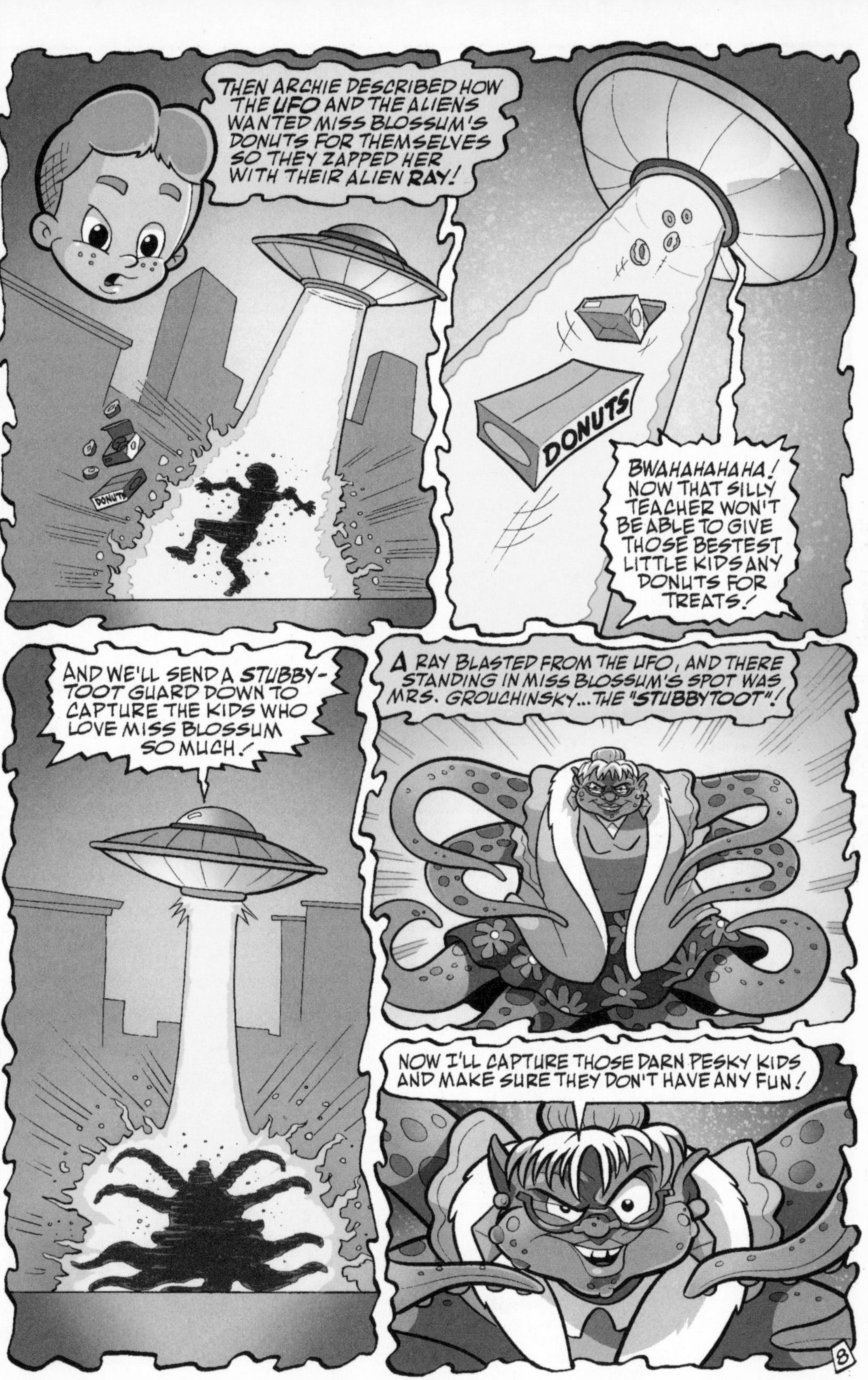
THEN ARCHIE DESCRIBED HOW THE UFO AND THE ALIENS WANTED MISS BLOSSUM'S DONUTS FOR THEMSELVES SO THEY ZAPPED HER WITH THEIR ALIEN RAY!
DONUTS
DONUTS
BWAHAHAHAHA! NOW THAT SILLY TEACHER WON'T BE ABLE TO GIVE THOSE BESTEST LITTLE KIDS ANY DONUTS FOR TREATS!
AND WE'LL SEND A STUBBY-TOOT GUARD DOWN TO CAPTURE THE KIDS WHO LOVE MISS BLOSSUM SO MUCH!
A RAY BLASTED FROM THE UFO, AND THERE STANDING IN MISS BLOSSUM'S SPOT WAS MRS. GROUCHINSKY... THE "STUBBYTOOT"!
NOW I'LL CAPTURE THOSE DARN PESKY KIDS AND MAKE SURE THEY DON'T HAVE ANY FUN!

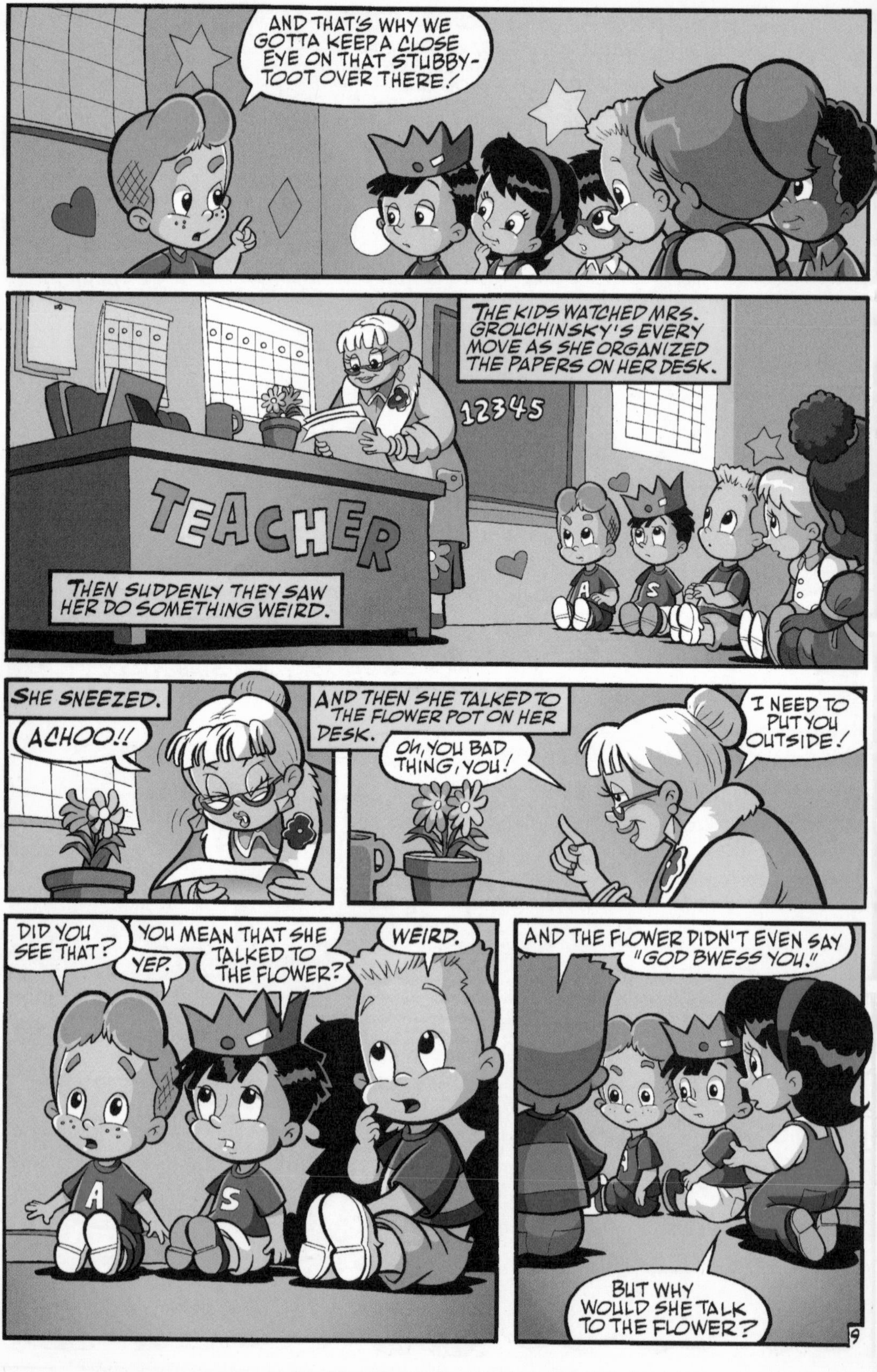
AND THAT'S WHY WE GOTTA KEEP A CLOSE EYE ON THAT STUBBY-TOOT OVER THERE!
THE KIDS WATCHED MRS. GROUCHINSKY'S EVERY MOVE AS SHE ORGANIZED THE PAPERS ON HER DESK.
12345
TEACHER
THEN SUDDENLY THEY SAW HER DO SOMETHING WEIRD.
SHE SNEEZED.
ACHOO!!
AND THEN SHE TALKED TO THE FLOWER POT ON HER DESK.
OH, YOU BAD THING, YOU!
I NEED TO PUT YOU OUTSIDE!
DID YOU SEE THAT?
YEP.
YOU MEAN THAT SHE TALKED TO THE FLOWER?
WEIRD.
AND THE FLOWER DIDN'T EVEN SAY "GOD BWESS YOU."
BUT WHY WOULD SHE TALK TO THE FLOWER?

 *oh, NO!*

 **IT'S MISS BLOSSUM!**

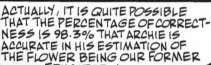
ACTUALLY, IT IS QUITE POSSIBLE THAT THE PERCENTAGE OF CORRECTNESS IS 98.3% THAT ARCHIE IS ACCURATE IN HIS ESTIMATION OF THE FLOWER BEING OUR FORMER EDUCATOR!

EXACTLY!

HUH?

DON'T YOU SEE? THE ALIENS PROBABLY TURNED MISS BLOSSUM INTO A EARTH PLANT SO THE STUBBYTOOT COULD BRING HER TO SCHOOL AND ASK HER HOW TO RUN THE CLASS.

ohhhh...

IF THE FLOWER IS MISS BLOSSUM...

...WHY IS THE STUBBY-TOOT PUTTING HER *OUTSIDE*?!!

SHE'S PROBABLY ALLERGIC TO HER AS A FLOWER AND WANTS TO GET HER FAR AWAY!

WE HAVE TO SAVE HER!

10

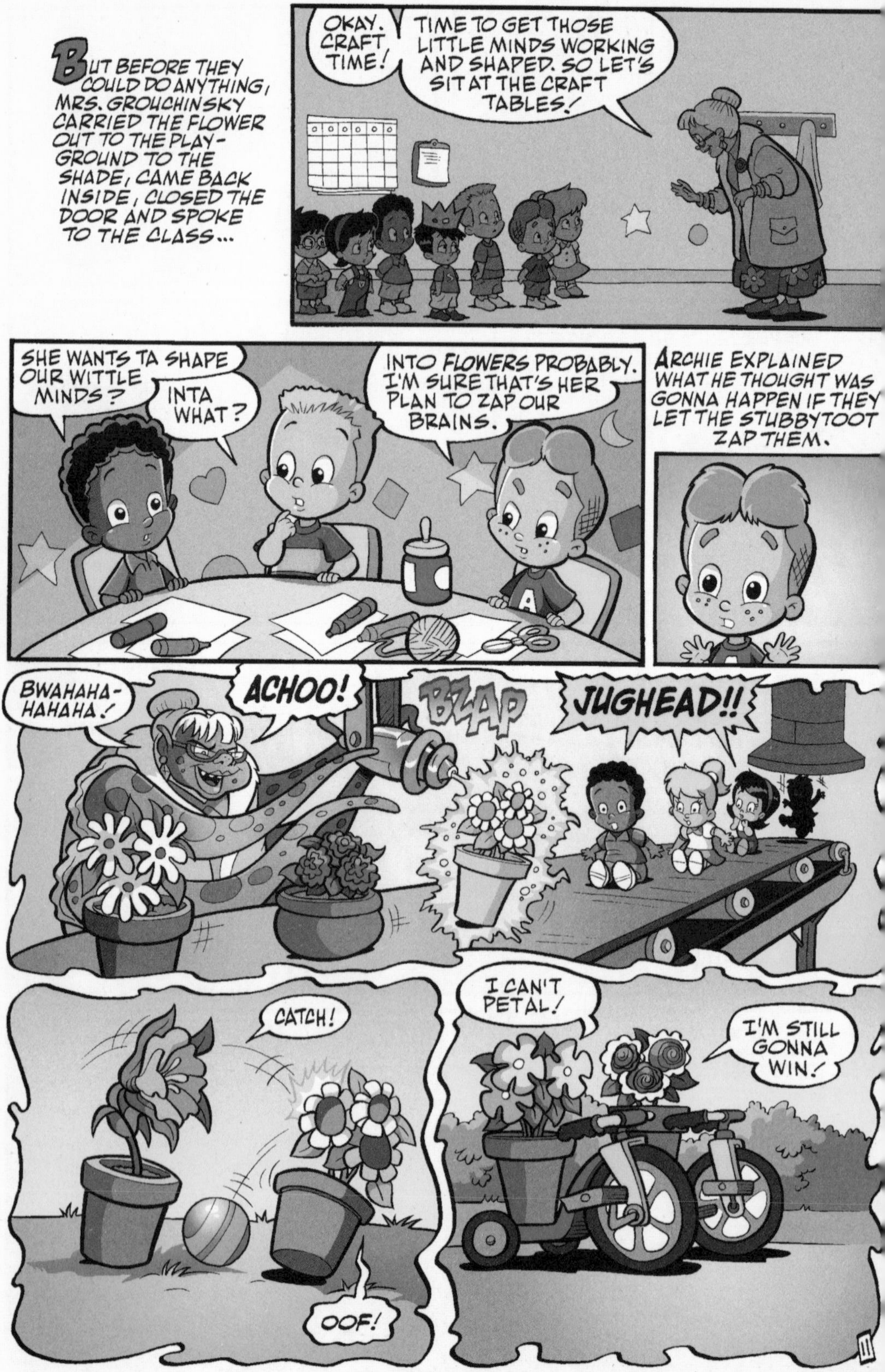

BUT BEFORE THEY COULD DO ANYTHING, MRS. GROUCHINSKY CARRIED THE FLOWER OUT TO THE PLAY-GROUND TO THE SHADE, CAME BACK INSIDE, CLOSED THE DOOR AND SPOKE TO THE CLASS...
OKAY. CRAFT TIME!
TIME TO GET THOSE LITTLE MINDS WORKING AND SHAPED. SO LET'S SIT AT THE CRAFT TABLES!
SHE WANTS TA SHAPE OUR WITTLE MINDS?
INTA WHAT?
INTO FLOWERS PROBABLY. I'M SURE THAT'S HER PLAN TO ZAP OUR BRAINS.
ARCHIE EXPLAINED WHAT HE THOUGHT WAS GONNA HAPPEN IF THEY LET THE STUBBYTOOT ZAP THEM.
BWAHAHA-HAHAHA!
ACHOO!
BZAP
JUGHEAD!!
CATCH!
OOF!
I CAN'T PETAL!
I'M STILL GONNA WIN!

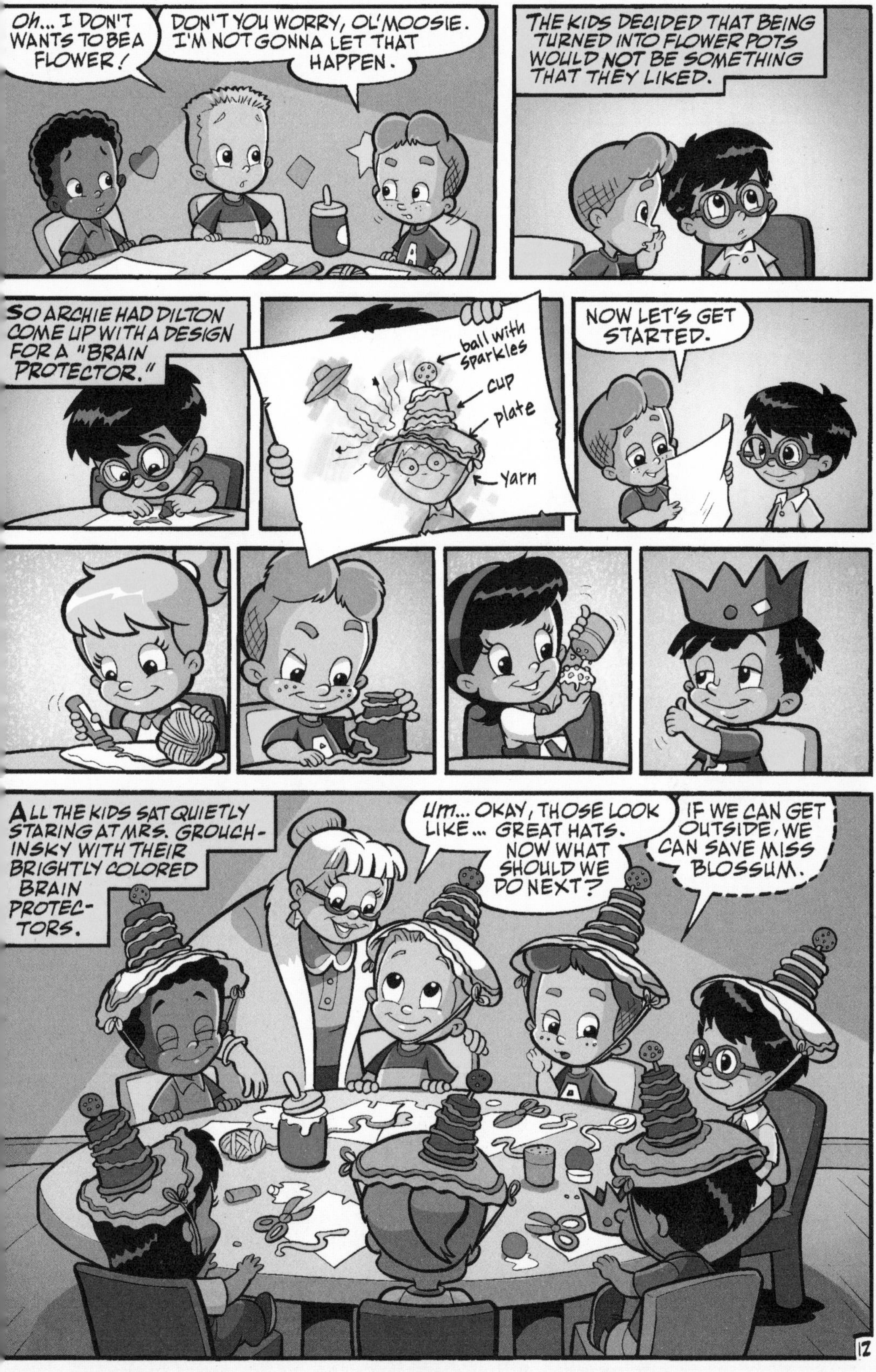

Oh... I DON'T WANTS TO BE A FLOWER!
DON'T YOU WORRY, OL' MOOSIE. I'M NOT GONNA LET THAT HAPPEN.
THE KIDS DECIDED THAT BEING TURNED INTO FLOWER POTS WOULD NOT BE SOMETHING THAT THEY LIKED.
SO ARCHIE HAD DILTON COME UP WITH A DESIGN FOR A "BRAIN PROTECTOR."
ball with sparkles
cup
plate
yarn
NOW LET'S GET STARTED.
ALL THE KIDS SAT QUIETLY STARING AT MRS. GROUCHINSKY WITH THEIR BRIGHTLY COLORED BRAIN PROTECTORS.
UM... OKAY, THOSE LOOK LIKE... GREAT HATS. NOW WHAT SHOULD WE DO NEXT?
IF WE CAN GET OUTSIDE, WE CAN SAVE MISS BLOSSUM.

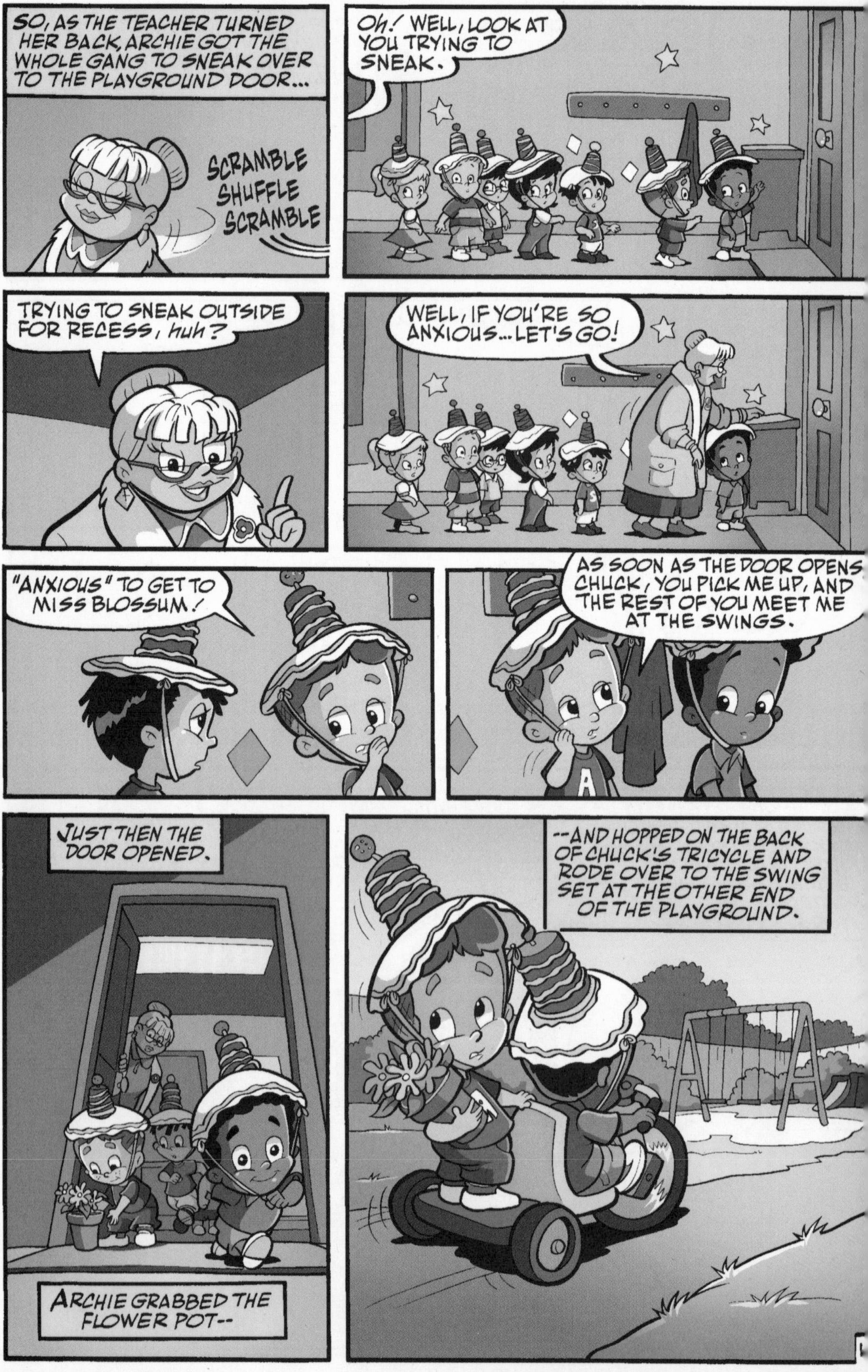
SO, AS THE TEACHER TURNED HER BACK, ARCHIE GOT THE WHOLE GANG TO SNEAK OVER TO THE PLAYGROUND DOOR...
SCRAMBLE SHUFFLE SCRAMBLE
Oh! WELL, LOOK AT YOU TRYING TO SNEAK.
TRYING TO SNEAK OUTSIDE FOR RECESS, huh?
WELL, IF YOU'RE SO ANXIOUS... LET'S GO!
"ANXIOUS" TO GET TO MISS BLOSSUM!
AS SOON AS THE DOOR OPENS CHUCK, YOU PICK ME UP, AND THE REST OF YOU MEET ME AT THE SWINGS.
JUST THEN THE DOOR OPENED.
ARCHIE GRABBED THE FLOWER POT--
--AND HOPPED ON THE BACK OF CHUCK'S TRICYCLE AND RODE OVER TO THE SWING SET AT THE OTHER END OF THE PLAYGROUND.
A
S

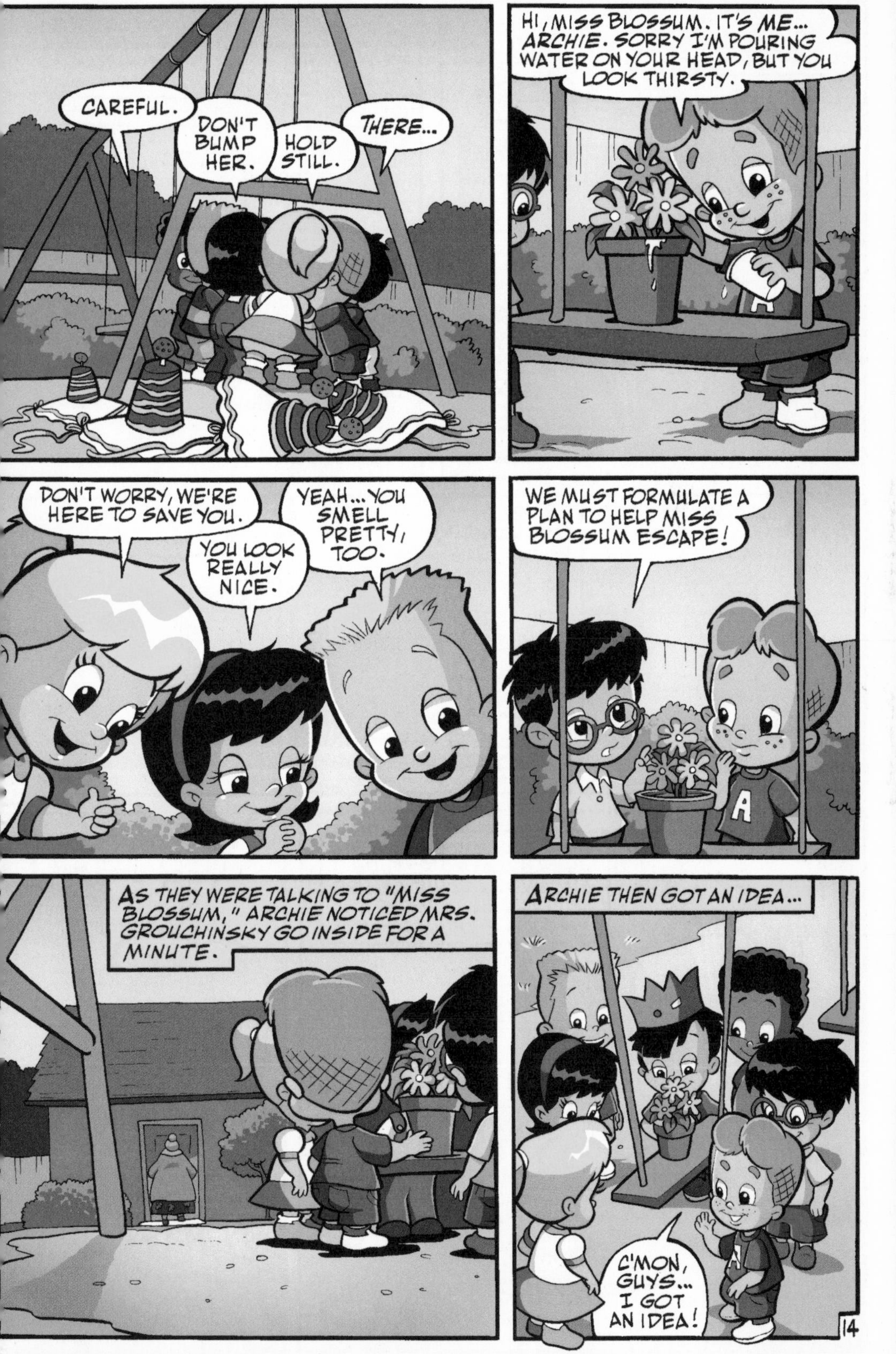
CAREFUL.
DON'T BUMP HER.
HOLD STILL.
THERE...
HI, MISS BLOSSUM. IT'S ME... ARCHIE. SORRY I'M POURING WATER ON YOUR HEAD, BUT YOU LOOK THIRSTY.
DON'T WORRY, WE'RE HERE TO SAVE YOU.
YOU LOOK REALLY NICE.
YEAH... YOU SMELL PRETTY, TOO.
WE MUST FORMULATE A PLAN TO HELP MISS BLOSSUM ESCAPE!
AS THEY WERE TALKING TO "MISS BLOSSUM," ARCHIE NOTICED MRS. GROUCHINSKY GO INSIDE FOR A MINUTE.
ARCHIE THEN GOT AN IDEA...
C'MON, GUYS... I GOT AN IDEA!
14

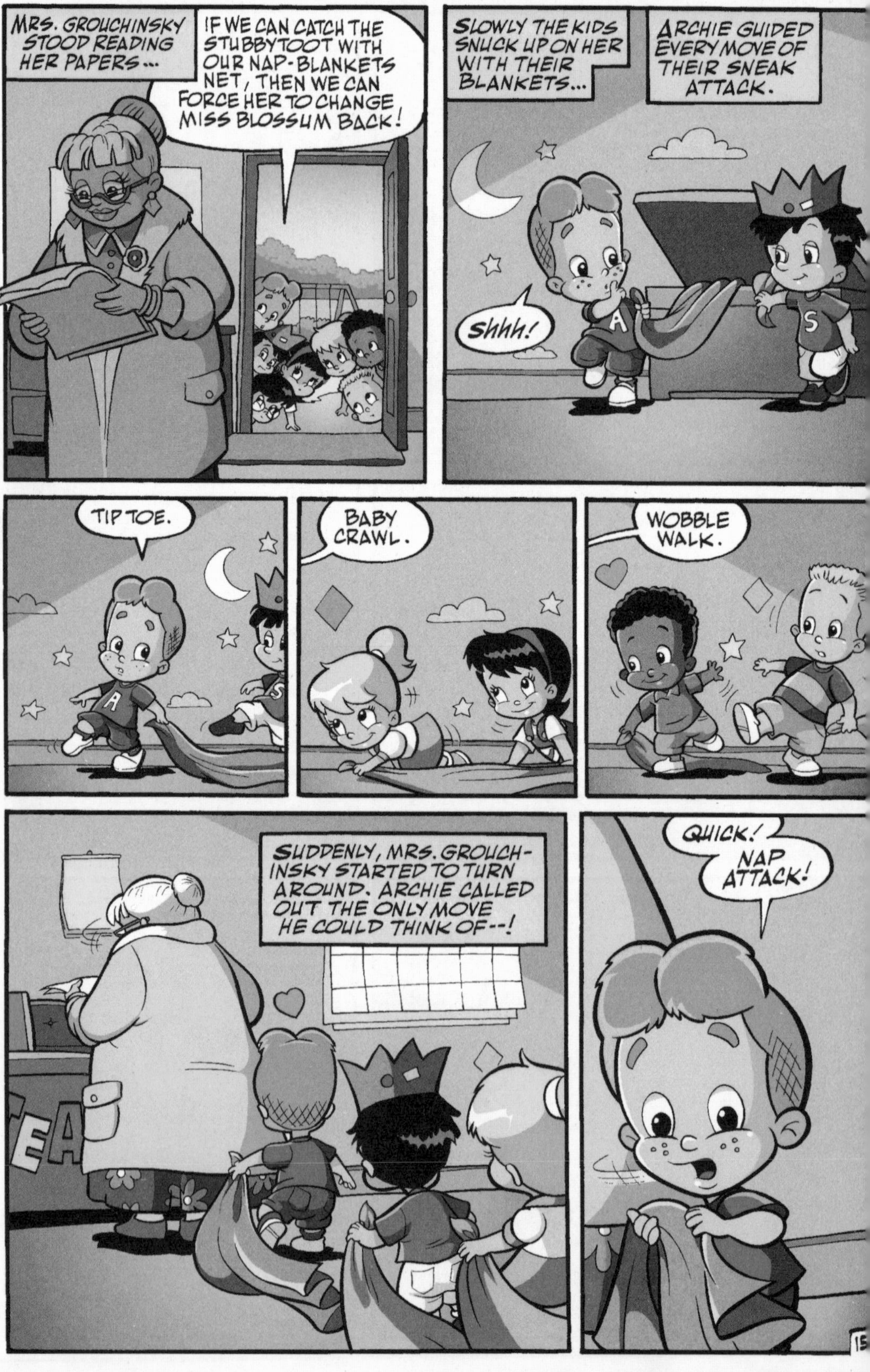
MRS. GROUCHINSKY STOOD READING HER PAPERS...
IF WE CAN CATCH THE STUBBYTOOT WITH OUR NAP-BLANKETS NET, THEN WE CAN FORCE HER TO CHANGE MISS BLOSSUM BACK!
SLOWLY THE KIDS SNUCK UP ON HER WITH THEIR BLANKETS...
ARCHIE GUIDED EVERY MOVE OF THEIR SNEAK ATTACK.
Shhh!
TIPTOE.
BABY CRAWL.
WOBBLE WALK.
SUDDENLY, MRS. GROUCHINSKY STARTED TO TURN AROUND. ARCHIE CALLED OUT THE ONLY MOVE HE COULD THINK OF--!
QUICK! NAP ATTACK!

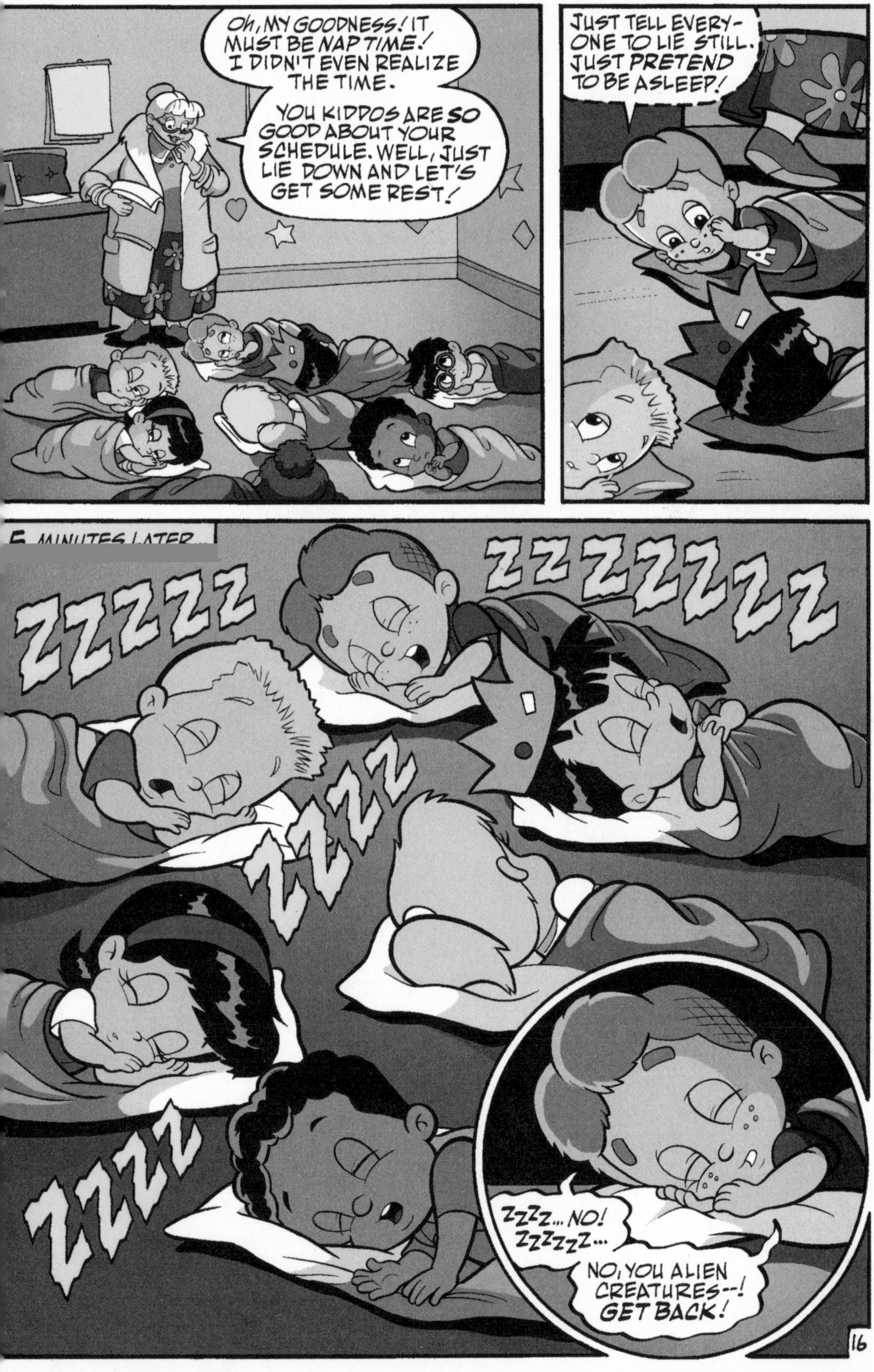

OH, MY GOODNESS! IT MUST BE NAP TIME! I DIDN'T EVEN REALIZE THE TIME.
YOU KIDDOS ARE SO GOOD ABOUT YOUR SCHEDULE. WELL, JUST LIE DOWN AND LET'S GET SOME REST!
JUST TELL EVERY-ONE TO LIE STILL. JUST PRETEND TO BE ASLEEP!
5 MINUTES LATER...
ZZZZZ
ZZZZZZZZZ
ZZZZZ
ZZZZ
ZZZZ... NO! ZZZZZZ...
NO, YOU ALIEN CREATURES--! GET BACK!

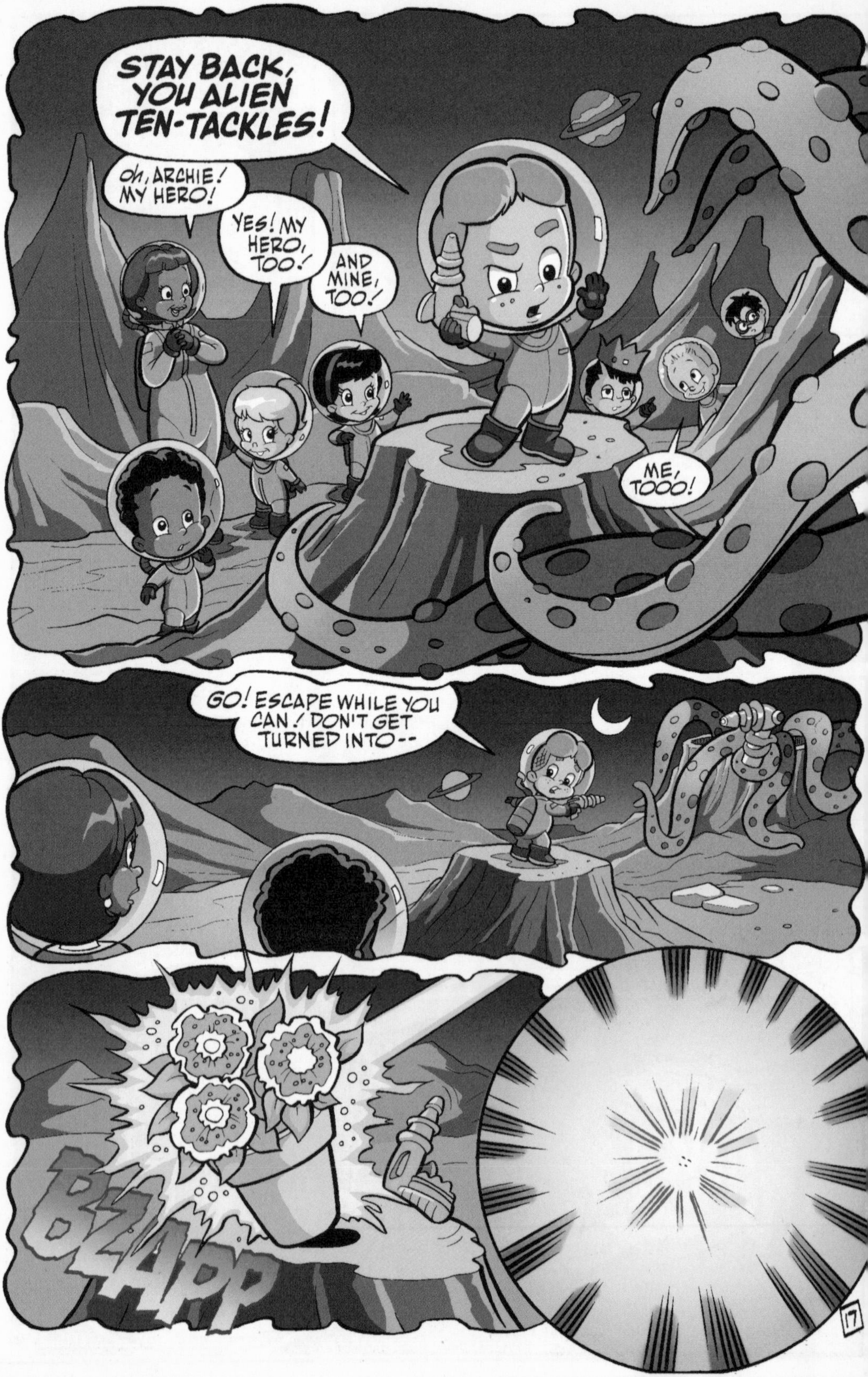
STAY BACK, YOU ALIEN TEN-TACKLES!
Oh, ARCHIE! MY HERO!
YES! MY HERO, TOO!
AND MINE, TOO!
ME, TOOO!
GO! ESCAPE WHILE YOU CAN! DON'T GET TURNED INTO--
BZAPP

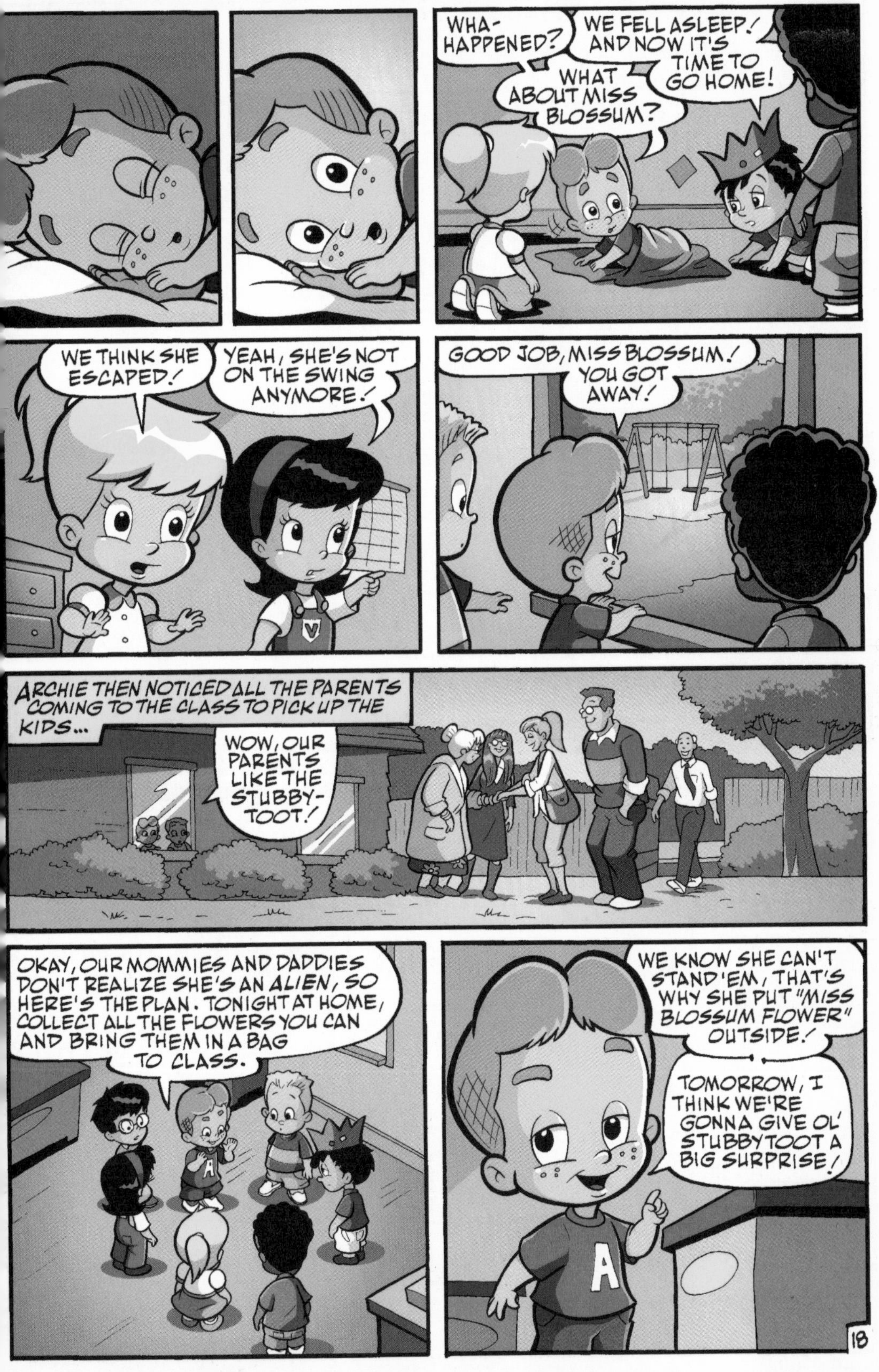
WHA-HAPPENED?
WE FELL ASLEEP! AND NOW IT'S TIME TO GO HOME!
WHAT ABOUT MISS BLOSSUM?
WE THINK SHE ESCAPED!
YEAH, SHE'S NOT ON THE SWING ANYMORE!
GOOD JOB, MISS BLOSSUM! YOU GOT AWAY!
ARCHIE THEN NOTICED ALL THE PARENTS COMING TO THE CLASS TO PICK UP THE KIDS...
WOW, OUR PARENTS LIKE THE STUBBY-TOOT!
OKAY, OUR MOMMIES AND DADDIES DON'T REALIZE SHE'S AN ALIEN, SO HERE'S THE PLAN. TONIGHT AT HOME, COLLECT ALL THE FLOWERS YOU CAN AND BRING THEM IN A BAG TO CLASS.
WE KNOW SHE CAN'T STAND 'EM, THAT'S WHY SHE PUT "MISS BLOSSUM FLOWER" OUTSIDE!
TOMORROW, I THINK WE'RE GONNA GIVE OL' STUBBYTOOT A BIG SURPRISE!

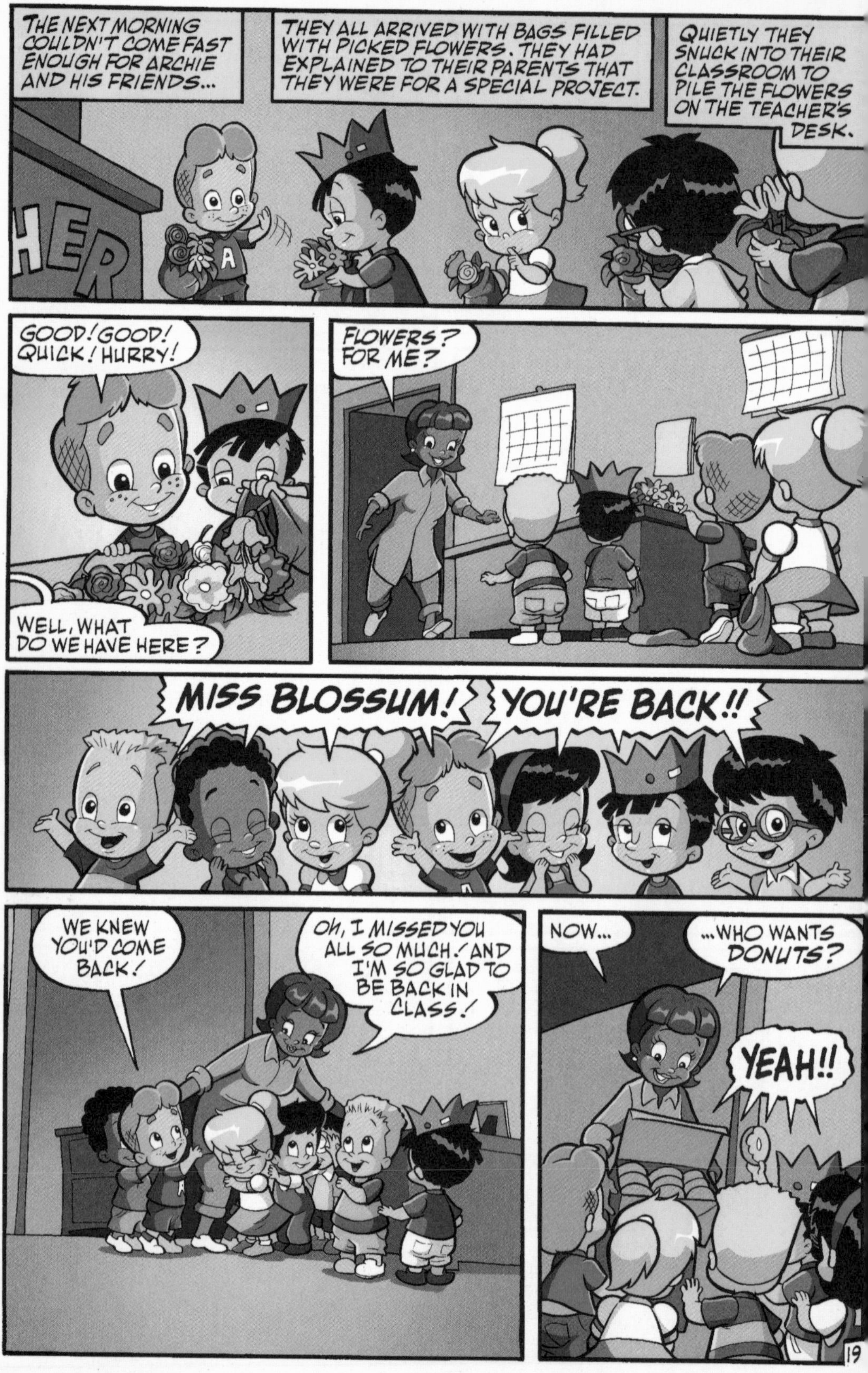
THE NEXT MORNING COULDN'T COME FAST ENOUGH FOR ARCHIE AND HIS FRIENDS...
THEY ALL ARRIVED WITH BAGS FILLED WITH PICKED FLOWERS. THEY HAD EXPLAINED TO THEIR PARENTS THAT THEY WERE FOR A SPECIAL PROJECT.
QUIETLY THEY SNUCK INTO THEIR CLASSROOM TO PILE THE FLOWERS ON THE TEACHER'S DESK.
HER
GOOD! GOOD! QUICK! HURRY!
WELL, WHAT DO WE HAVE HERE?
FLOWERS? FOR ME?
MISS BLOSSUM!
YOU'RE BACK!!
WE KNEW YOU'D COME BACK!
Oh, I MISSED YOU ALL SO MUCH! AND I'M SO GLAD TO BE BACK IN CLASS!
NOW...
...WHO WANTS DONUTS?
YEAH!!

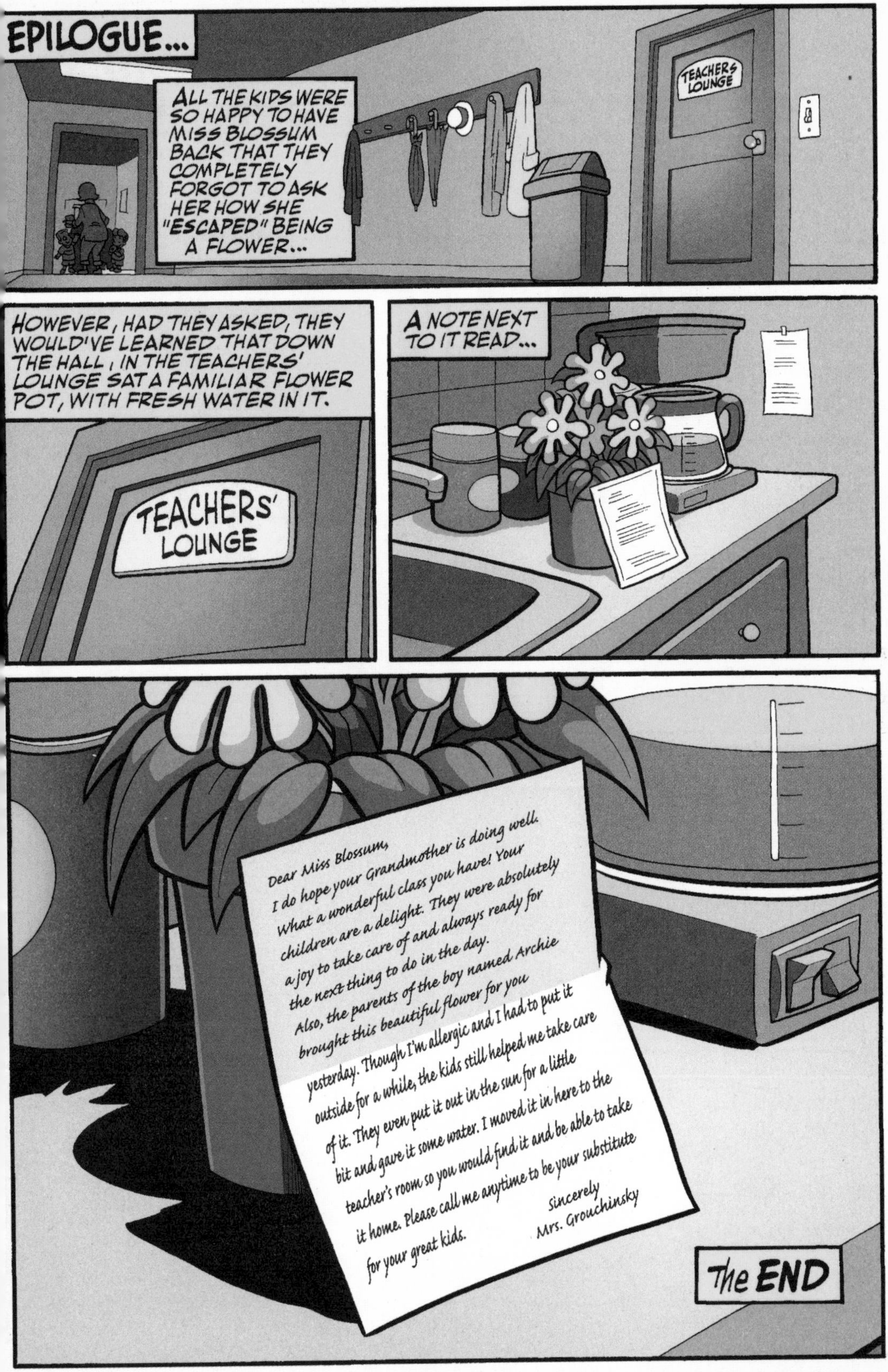
EPILOGUE...
ALL THE KIDS WERE SO HAPPY TO HAVE MISS BLOSSUM BACK THAT THEY COMPLETELY FORGOT TO ASK HER HOW SHE "ESCAPED" BEING A FLOWER...
TEACHERS LOUNGE
HOWEVER, HAD THEY ASKED, THEY WOULD'VE LEARNED THAT DOWN THE HALL, IN THE TEACHERS' LOUNGE SAT A FAMILIAR FLOWER POT, WITH FRESH WATER IN IT.
TEACHERS' LOUNGE
A NOTE NEXT TO IT READ...
Dear Miss Blossum,
I do hope your Grandmother is doing well.
What a wonderful class you have! Your
children are a delight. They were absolutely
a joy to take care of and always ready for
the next thing to do in the day.
Also, the parents of the boy named Archie
brought this beautiful flower for you
yesterday. Though I'm allergic and I had to put it
outside for a while, the kids still helped me take care
of it. They even put it out in the sun for a little
bit and gave it some water. I moved it in here to the
teacher's room so you would find it and be able to take
it home. Please call me anytime to be your substitute
for your great kids.
Sincerely
Mrs. Grouchinsky
The END

RECESS TIME

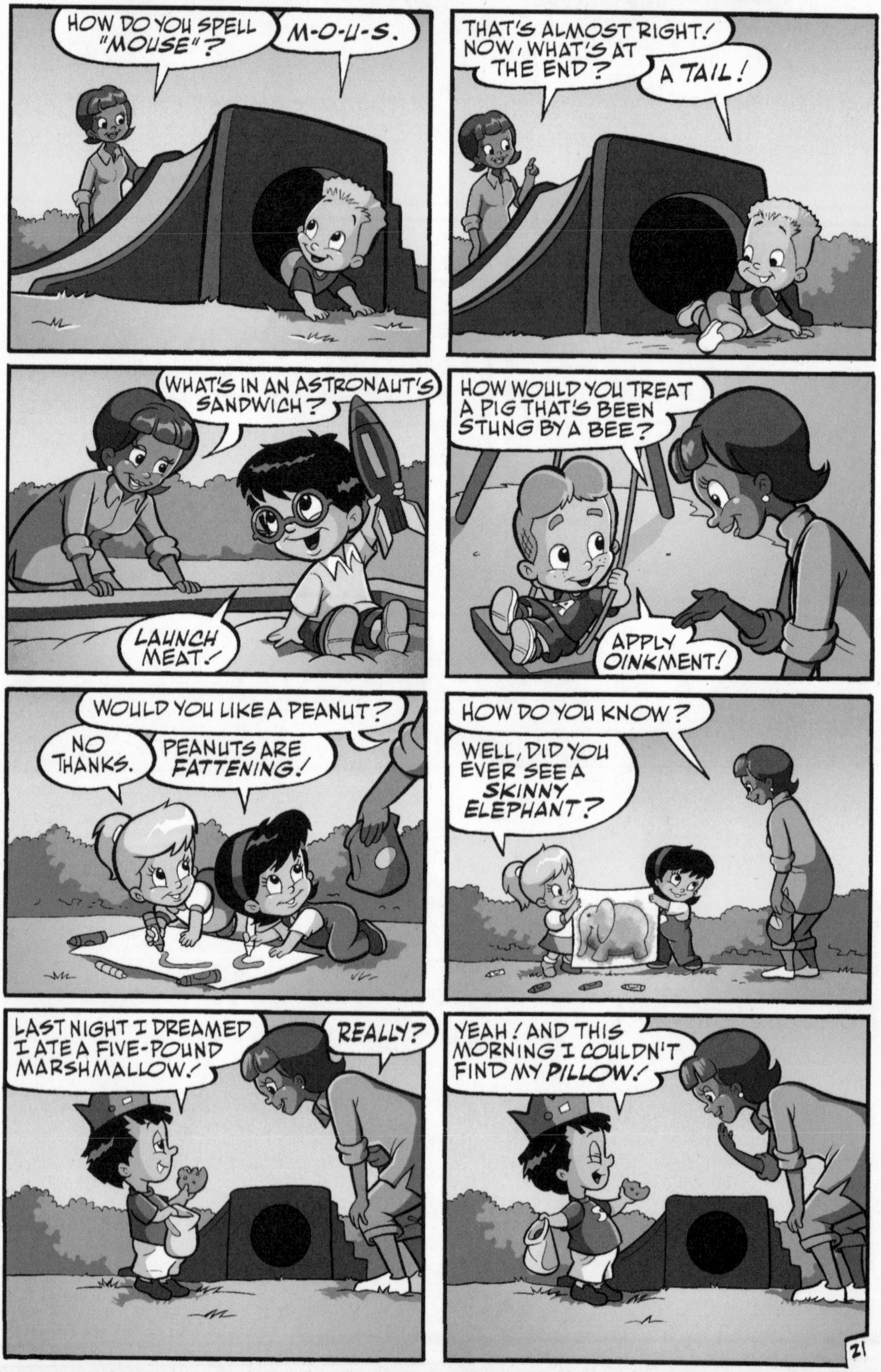

HOW DO YOU SPELL "MOUSE"?
M-O-U-S.
THAT'S ALMOST RIGHT! NOW, WHAT'S AT THE END?
A TAIL!
WHAT'S IN AN ASTRONAUT'S SANDWICH?
LAUNCH MEAT!
HOW WOULD YOU TREAT A PIG THAT'S BEEN STUNG BY A BEE?
APPLY OINKMENT!
WOULD YOU LIKE A PEANUT?
NO THANKS.
PEANUTS ARE FATTENING!
HOW DO YOU KNOW?
WELL, DID YOU EVER SEE A SKINNY ELEPHANT?
LAST NIGHT I DREAMED I ATE A FIVE-POUND MARSHMALLOW!
REALLY?
YEAH! AND THIS MORNING I COULDN'T FIND MY PILLOW!

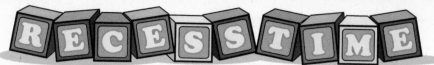

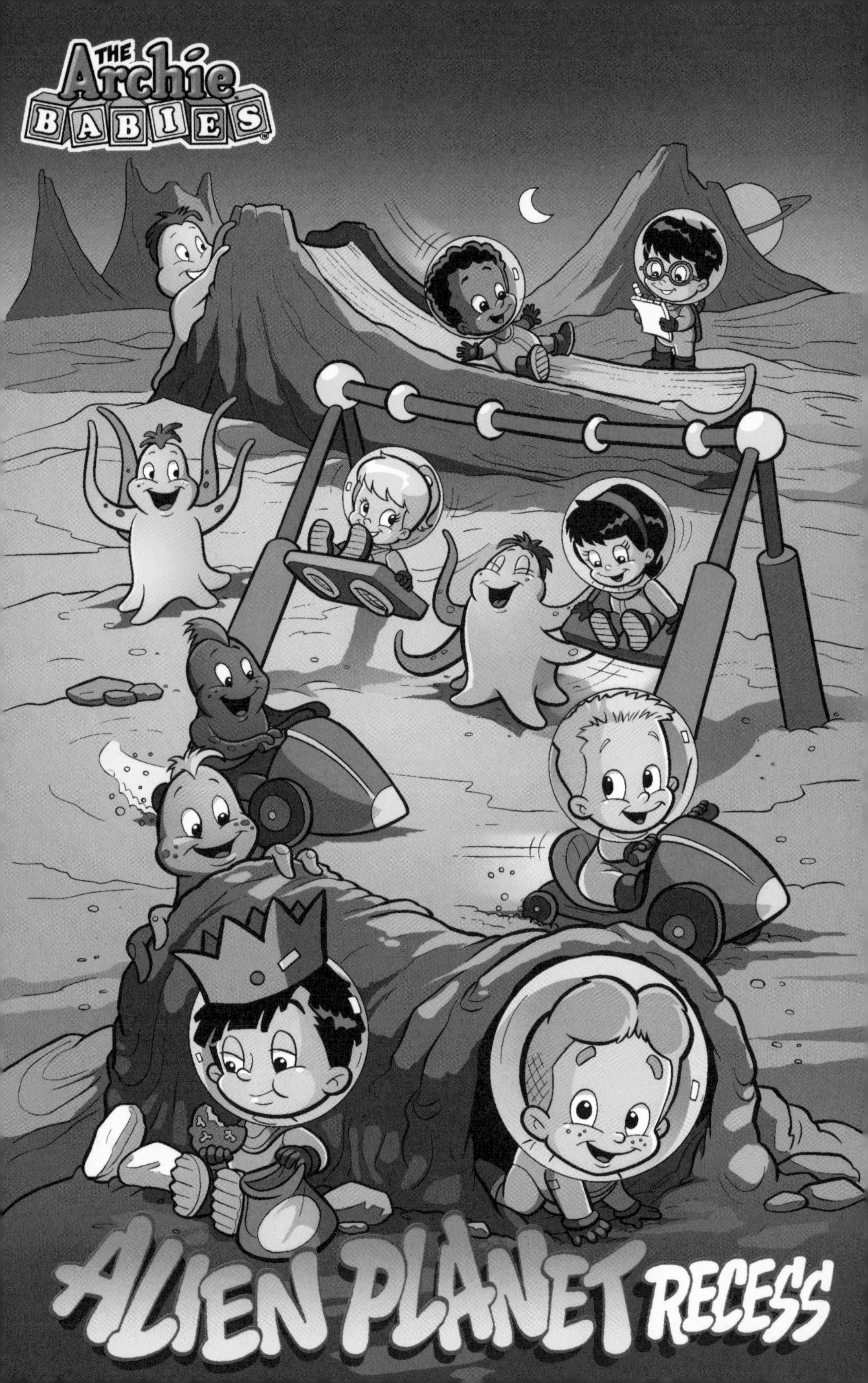
THE Archie BABIES
ALIEN PLANET RECESS

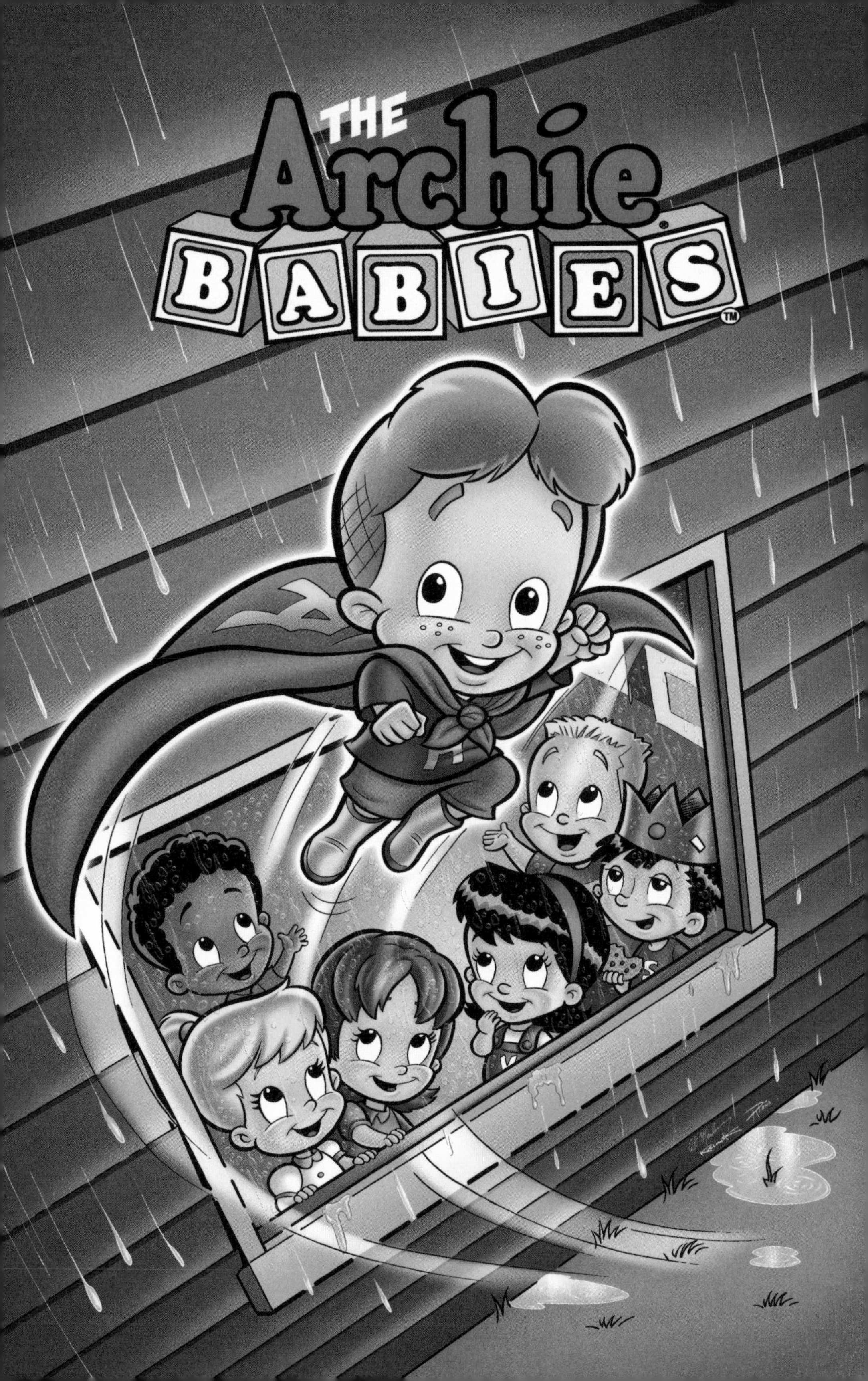
THE
Archie®
BABIES™

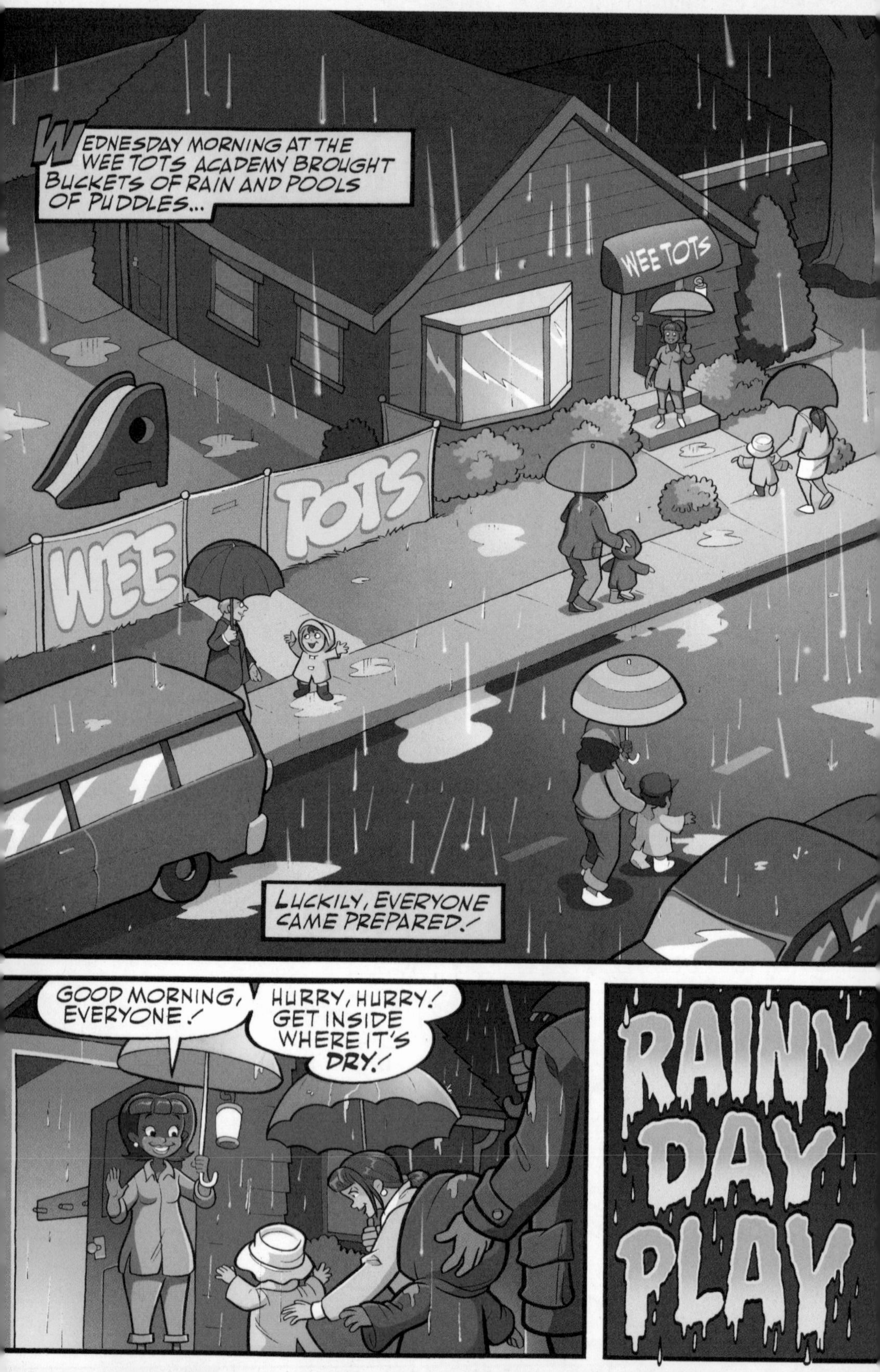
WEDNESDAY MORNING AT THE WEE TOTS ACADEMY BROUGHT BUCKETS OF RAIN AND POOLS OF PUDDLES...
WEE TOTS
WEE TOTS
LUCKILY, EVERYONE CAME PREPARED!
GOOD MORNING, EVERYONE!
HURRY, HURRY! GET INSIDE WHERE IT'S *DRY!*
RAINY DAY PLAY

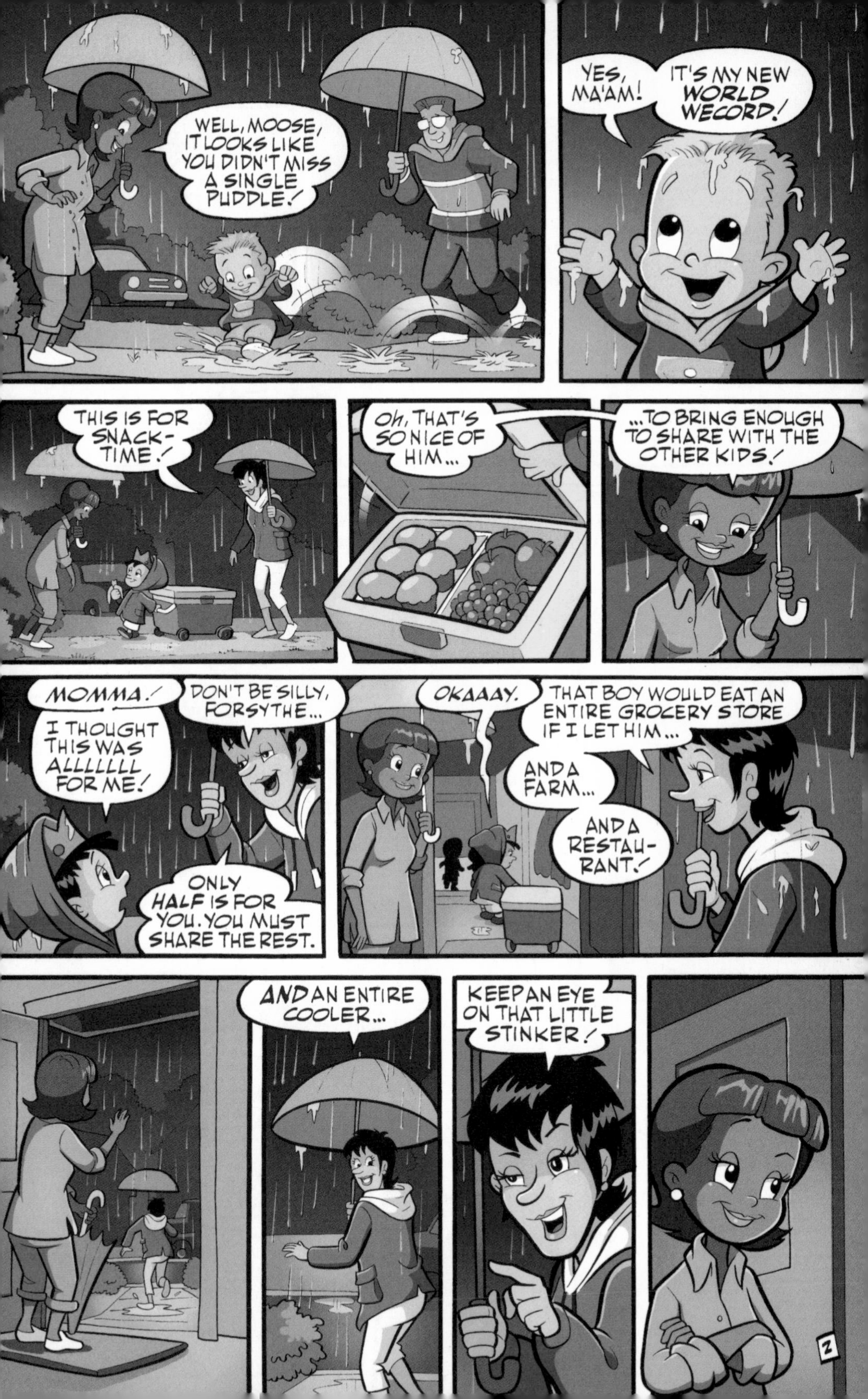
WELL, MOOSE, IT LOOKS LIKE YOU DIDN'T MISS A SINGLE PUDDLE!
YES, MA'AM!
IT'S MY NEW WORLD WECORD!
THIS IS FOR SNACK-TIME!
Oh, THAT'S SO NICE OF HIM...
...TO BRING ENOUGH TO SHARE WITH THE OTHER KIDS!
MOMMA!
I THOUGHT THIS WAS ALLLLLLL FOR ME!
DON'T BE SILLY, FORSYTHE...
ONLY HALF IS FOR YOU. YOU MUST SHARE THE REST.
OKAAAY.
THAT BOY WOULD EAT AN ENTIRE GROCERY STORE IF I LET HIM...
AND A FARM...
AND A RESTAU-RANT!
AND AN ENTIRE COOLER...
KEEP AN EYE ON THAT LITTLE STINKER!

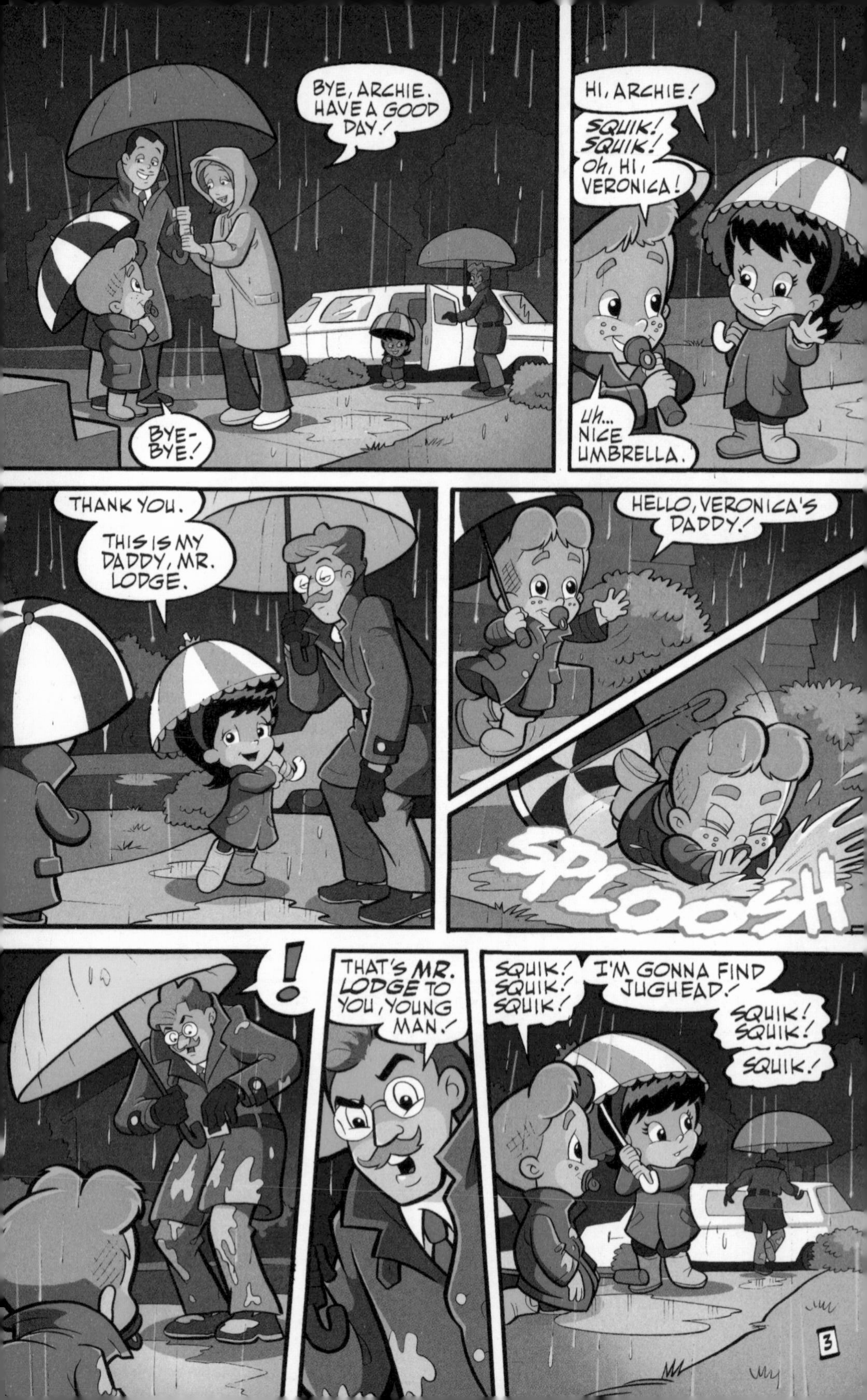
BYE, ARCHIE. HAVE A GOOD DAY!
BYE-BYE!
HI, ARCHIE!
SQUIK! SQUIK! Oh, HI, VERONICA!
uh... NICE UMBRELLA.
THANK YOU.
THIS IS MY DADDY, MR. LODGE.
HELLO, VERONICA'S DADDY!
SPLOOSH
!
THAT'S MR. LODGE TO YOU, YOUNG MAN!
SQUIK! SQUIK! SQUIK!
I'M GONNA FIND JUGHEAD!
SQUIK! SQUIK!
SQUIK!
3

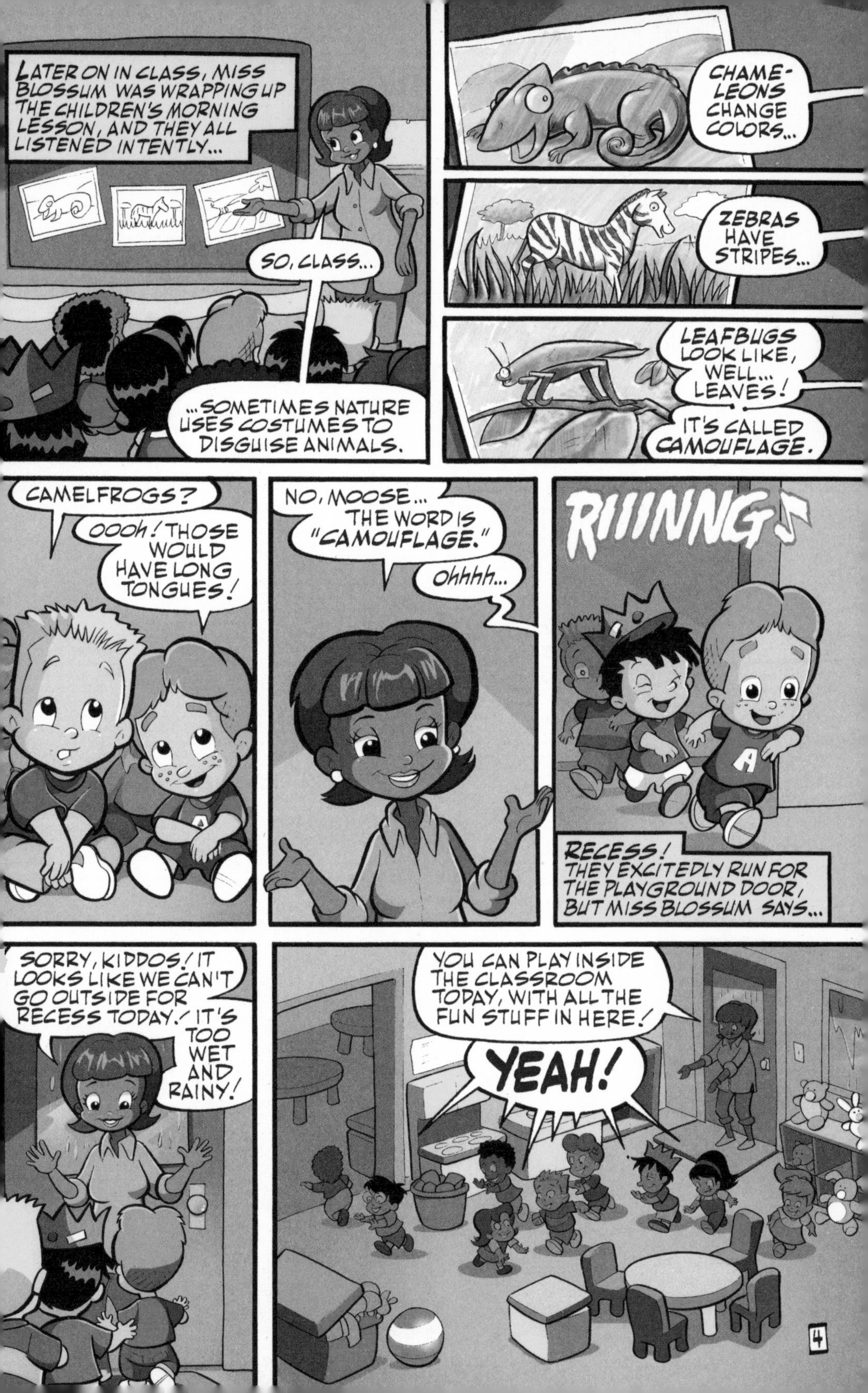
LATER ON IN CLASS, MISS BLOSSUM WAS WRAPPING UP THE CHILDREN'S MORNING LESSON, AND THEY ALL LISTENED INTENTLY...
SO, CLASS...
...SOMETIMES NATURE USES COSTUMES TO DISGUISE ANIMALS.
CHAMELEONS CHANGE COLORS...
ZEBRAS HAVE STRIPES...
LEAFBUGS LOOK LIKE, WELL... LEAVES!
IT'S CALLED CAMOUFLAGE.
CAMELFROGS?
OOOH! THOSE WOULD HAVE LONG TONGUES!
NO, MOOSE... THE WORD IS "CAMOUFLAGE."
OHHHH...
RIIINNG
RECESS! THEY EXCITEDLY RUN FOR THE PLAYGROUND DOOR, BUT MISS BLOSSUM SAYS...
SORRY, KIDDOS! IT LOOKS LIKE WE CAN'T GO OUTSIDE FOR RECESS TODAY! IT'S TOO WET AND RAINY!
YOU CAN PLAY INSIDE THE CLASSROOM TODAY, WITH ALL THE FUN STUFF IN HERE!
YEAH!
4

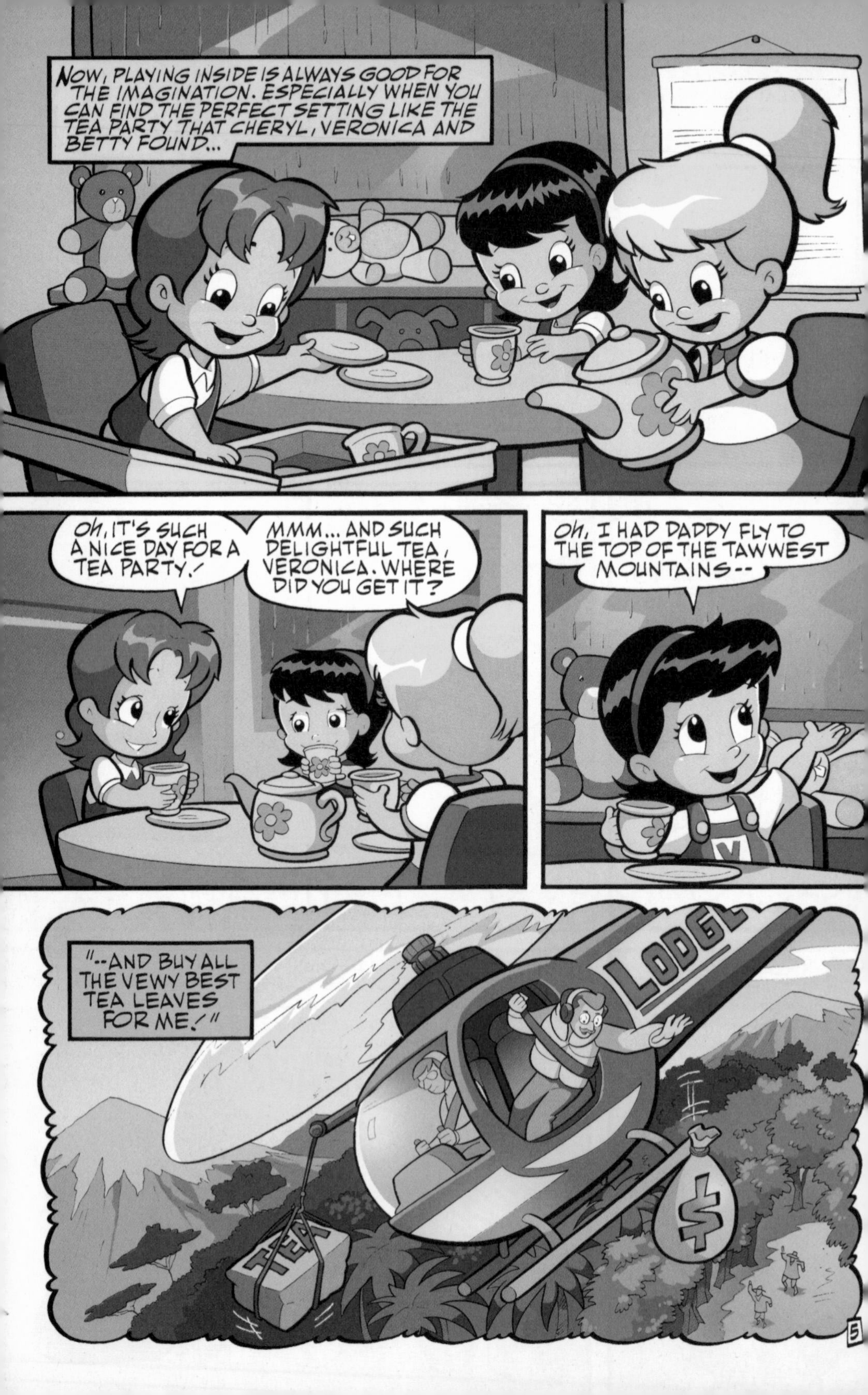

NOW, PLAYING INSIDE IS ALWAYS GOOD FOR THE IMAGINATION. ESPECIALLY WHEN YOU CAN FIND THE PERFECT SETTING LIKE THE TEA PARTY THAT CHERYL, VERONICA AND BETTY FOUND...
Oh, IT'S SUCH A NICE DAY FOR A TEA PARTY!
MMM... AND SUCH DELIGHTFUL TEA, VERONICA. WHERE DID YOU GET IT?
Oh, I HAD DADDY FLY TO THE TOP OF THE TAWWEST MOUNTAINS--
"--AND BUY ALL THE VEWY BEST TEA LEAVES FOR ME!"
LODGE
TEA
$

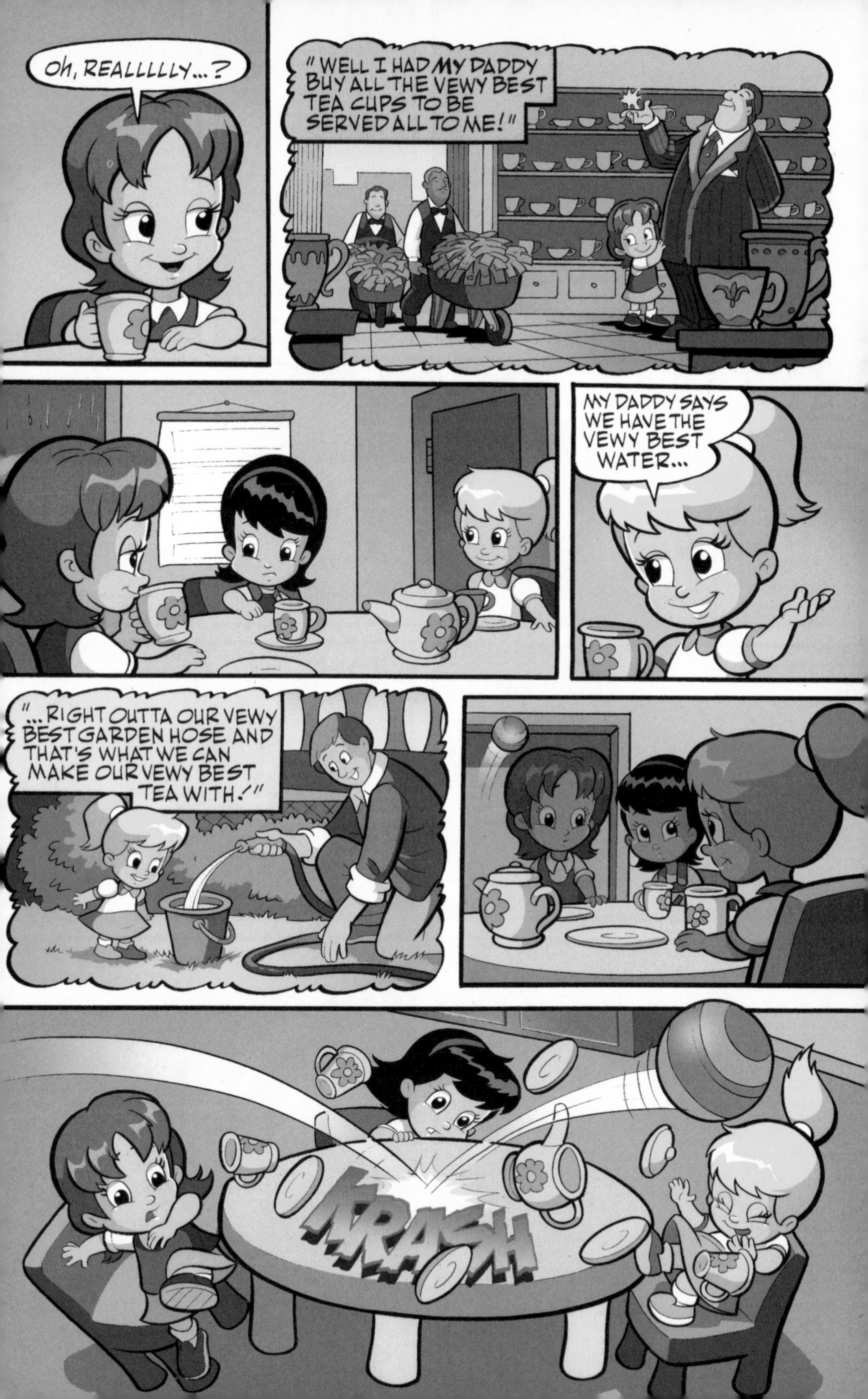
Oh, REALLLLLY...?
"WELL I HAD MY DADDY BUY ALL THE VEWY BEST TEA CUPS TO BE SERVED ALL TO ME!"
MY DADDY SAYS WE HAVE THE VEWY BEST WATER...
"...RIGHT OUTTA OUR VEWY BEST GARDEN HOSE AND THAT'S WHAT WE CAN MAKE OUR VEWY BEST TEA WITH!"
KRASH

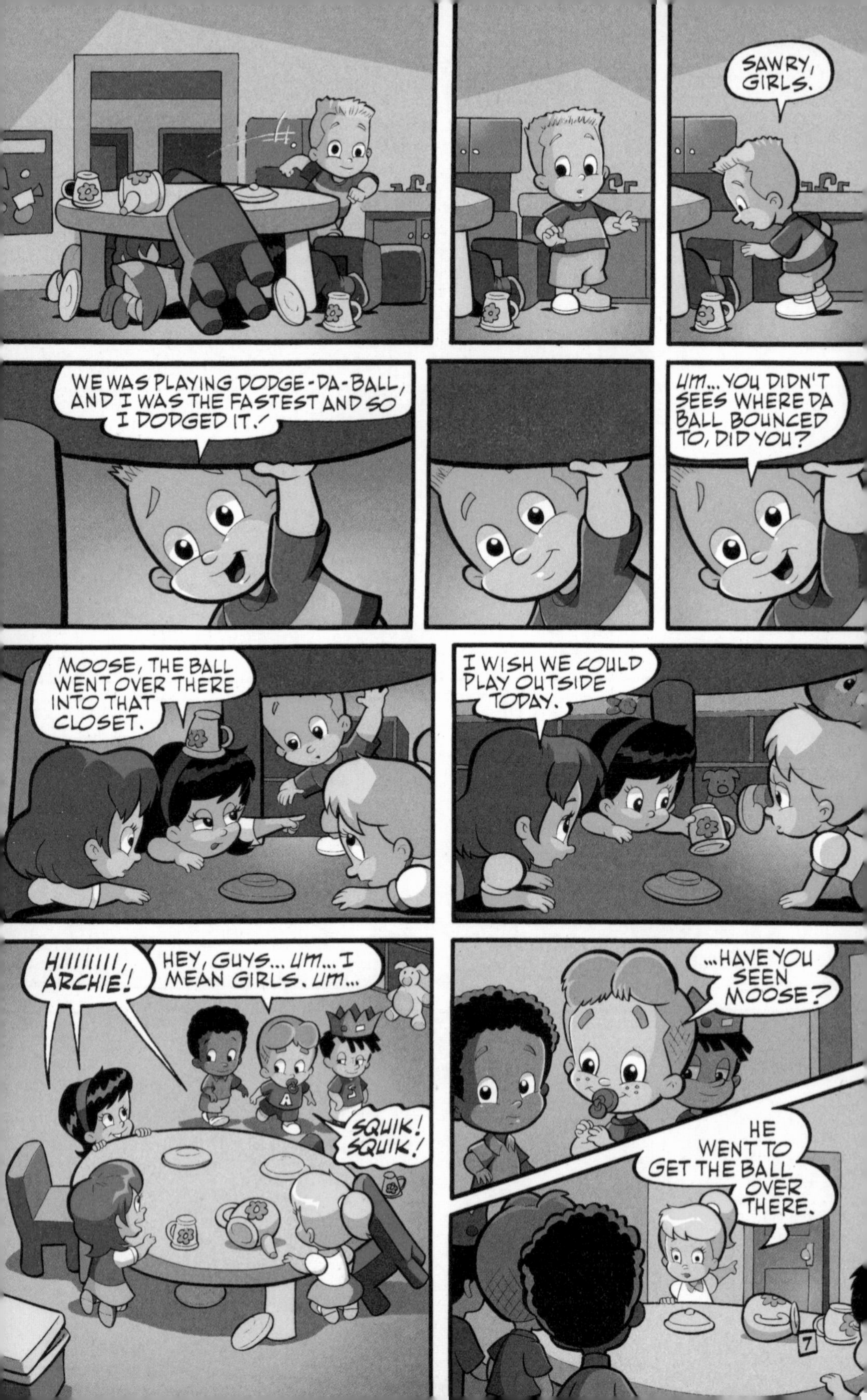
SAWRY, GIRLS.
WE WAS PLAYING DODGE-DA-BALL, AND I WAS THE FASTEST AND SO I DODGED IT!
UM... YOU DIDN'T SEES WHERE DA BALL BOUNCED TO, DID YOU?
MOOSE, THE BALL WENT OVER THERE INTO THAT CLOSET.
I WISH WE COULD PLAY OUTSIDE TODAY.
HIIIIIIII, ARCHIE!
HEY, GUYS... UM... I MEAN GIRLS. UM...
SQUIK! SQUIK!
...HAVE YOU SEEN MOOSE?
HE WENT TO GET THE BALL OVER THERE.
7

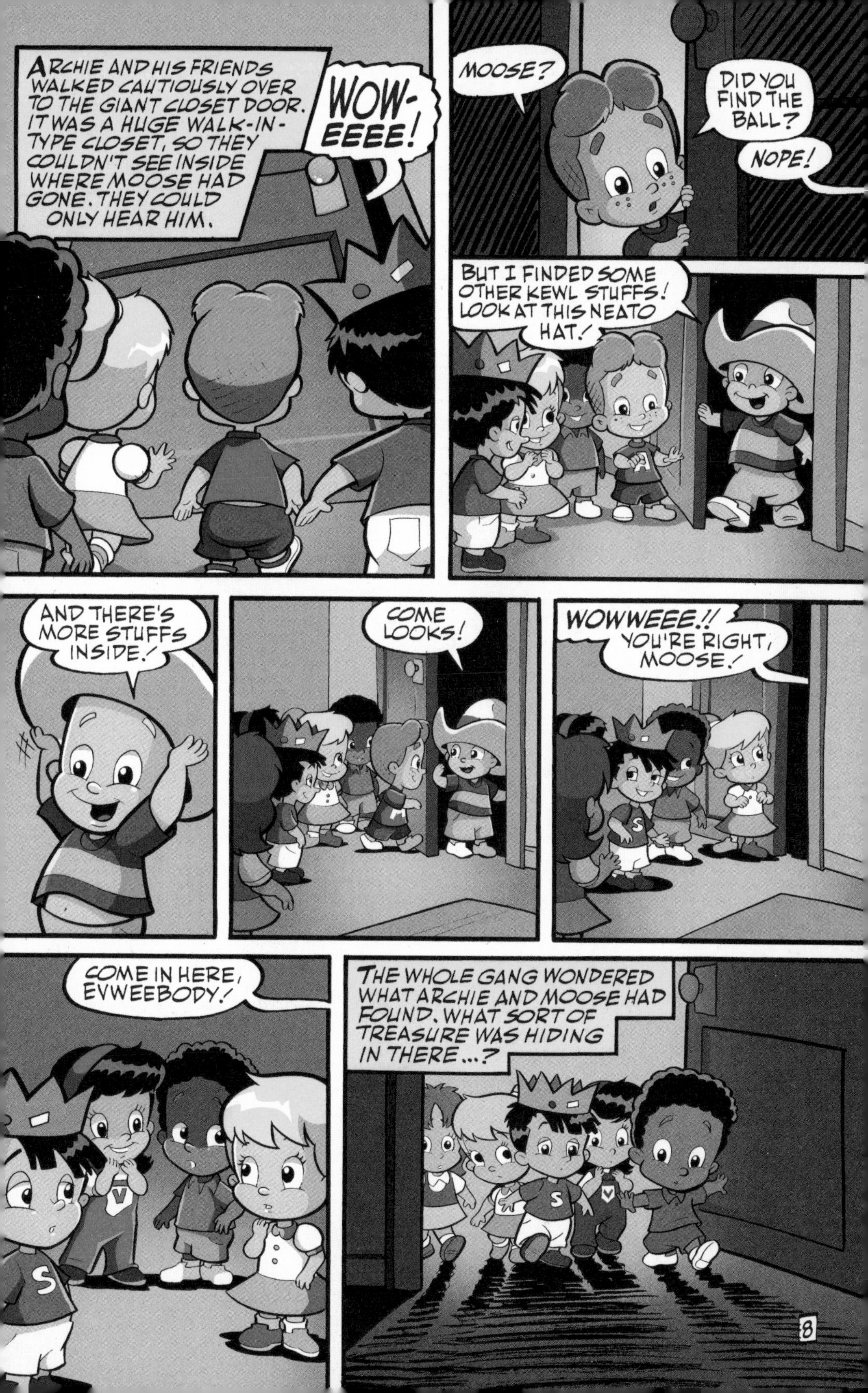
ARCHIE AND HIS FRIENDS WALKED CAUTIOUSLY OVER TO THE GIANT CLOSET DOOR. IT WAS A HUGE WALK-IN-TYPE CLOSET, SO THEY COULDN'T SEE INSIDE WHERE MOOSE HAD GONE. THEY COULD ONLY HEAR HIM.
WOW-EEEE!
MOOSE?
DID YOU FIND THE BALL?
NOPE!
BUT I FINDED SOME OTHER KEWL STUFFS! LOOK AT THIS NEATO HAT!
AND THERE'S MORE STUFFS INSIDE!
COME LOOKS!
WOWWEEE!! YOU'RE RIGHT, MOOSE!
COME IN HERE, EVWEEBODY!
THE WHOLE GANG WONDERED WHAT ARCHIE AND MOOSE HAD FOUND. WHAT SORT OF TREASURE WAS HIDING IN THERE...?
8

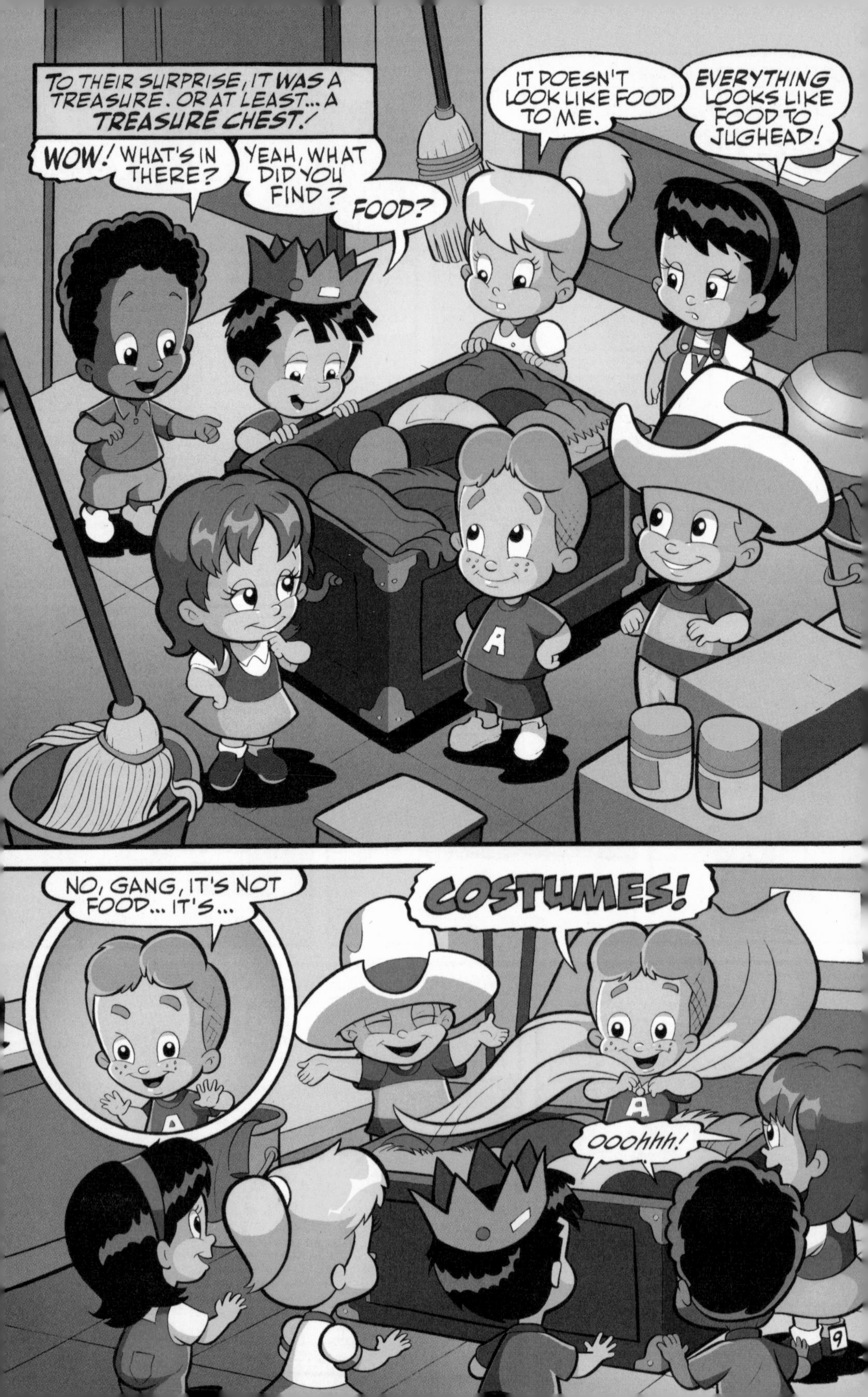
TO THEIR SURPRISE, IT WAS A TREASURE. OR AT LEAST... A TREASURE CHEST!
WOW! WHAT'S IN THERE?
YEAH, WHAT DID YOU FIND?
FOOD?
IT DOESN'T LOOK LIKE FOOD TO ME.
EVERYTHING LOOKS LIKE FOOD TO JUGHEAD!
NO, GANG, IT'S NOT FOOD... IT'S...
COSTUMES!
OOOHHH!
9

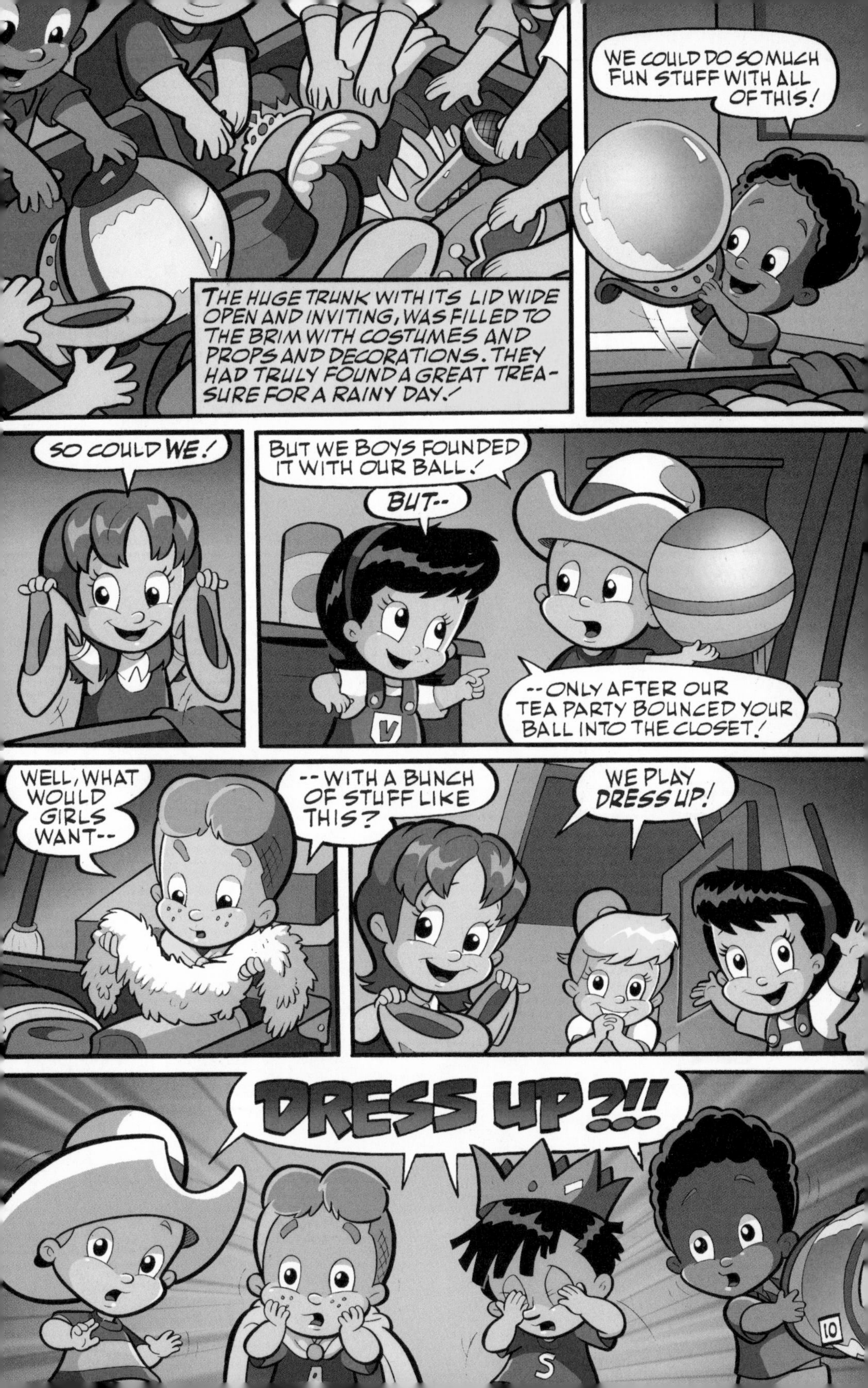
THE HUGE TRUNK WITH ITS LID WIDE OPEN AND INVITING, WAS FILLED TO THE BRIM WITH COSTUMES AND PROPS AND DECORATIONS. THEY HAD TRULY FOUND A GREAT TREA-SURE FOR A RAINY DAY!
WE COULD DO SO MUCH FUN STUFF WITH ALL OF THIS!
SO COULD WE!
BUT WE BOYS FOUNDED IT WITH OUR BALL!
BUT--
--ONLY AFTER OUR TEA PARTY BOUNCED YOUR BALL INTO THE CLOSET!
WELL, WHAT WOULD GIRLS WANT--
--WITH A BUNCH OF STUFF LIKE THIS?
WE PLAY DRESS UP!
DRESS UP?!!
10

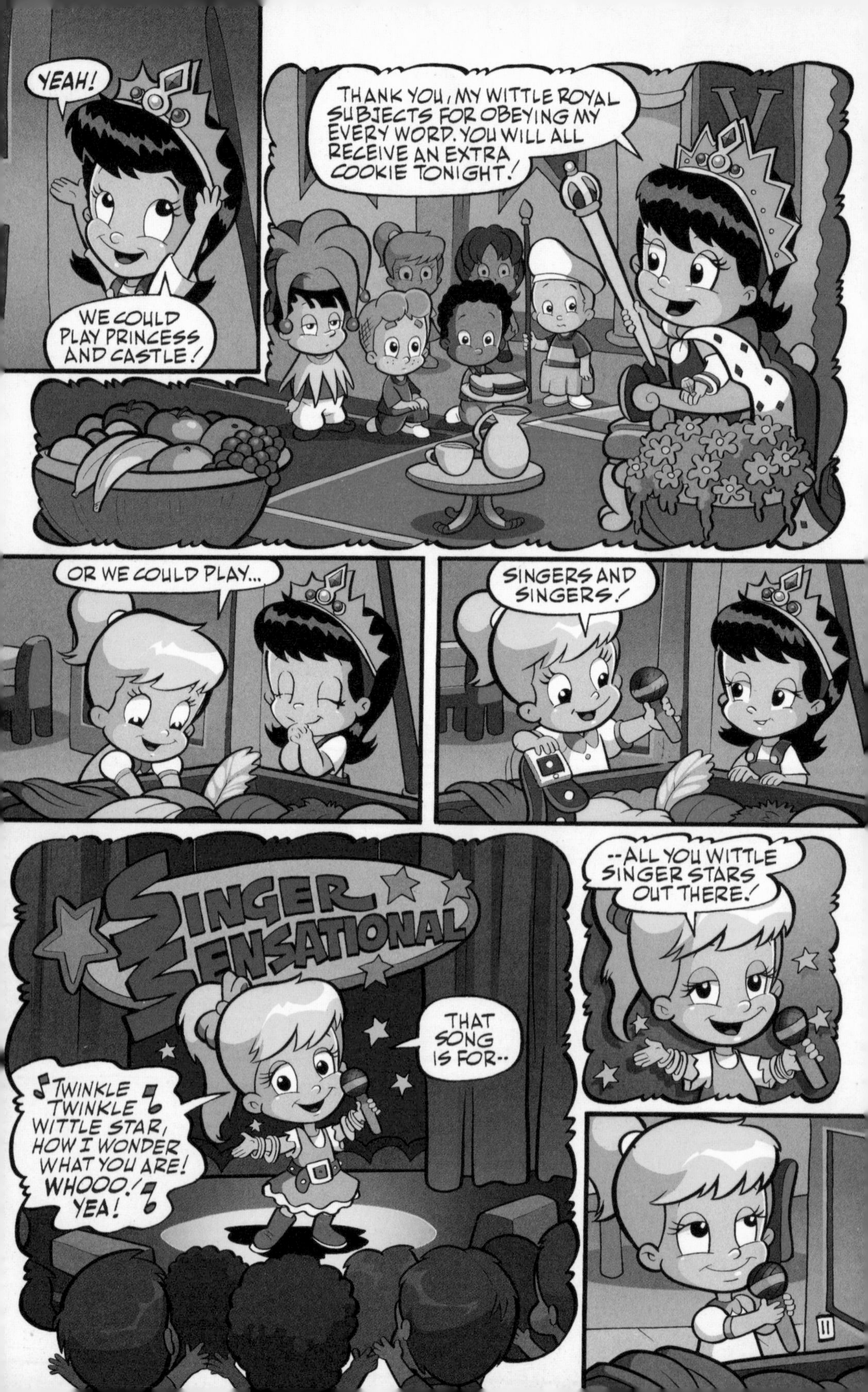
YEAH!
WE COULD PLAY PRINCESS AND CASTLE!
THANK YOU, MY WITTLE ROYAL SUBJECTS FOR OBEYING MY EVERY WORD. YOU WILL ALL RECEIVE AN EXTRA COOKIE TONIGHT!
OR WE COULD PLAY...
SINGERS AND SINGERS!
SINGER SENSATIONAL
TWINKLE TWINKLE WITTLE STAR, HOW I WONDER WHAT YOU ARE! WHOOO! YEA!
THAT SONG IS FOR--
--ALL YOU WITTLE SINGER STARS OUT THERE!

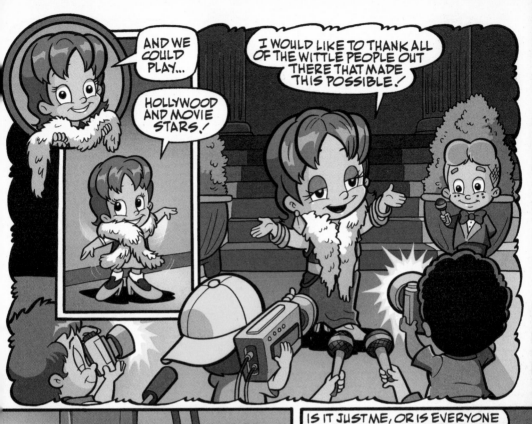

AND WE COULD PLAY...

HOLLYWOOD AND MOVIE STARS!

I WOULD LIKE TO THANK ALL OF THE WITTLE PEOPLE OUT THERE THAT MADE THIS POSSIBLE!

IS IT JUST ME, OR IS EVERYONE "WITTLE" IN THEIR DREAMS?

IT'S COSTUMES, LIKE MISS BLOSSOM SAID "CAMELFROGS" WEAR TO DISGUISE THEM-SELVES!

CAMELFROGS WEAR DRESSES?!

NO WAY, MOOSE!

IZ

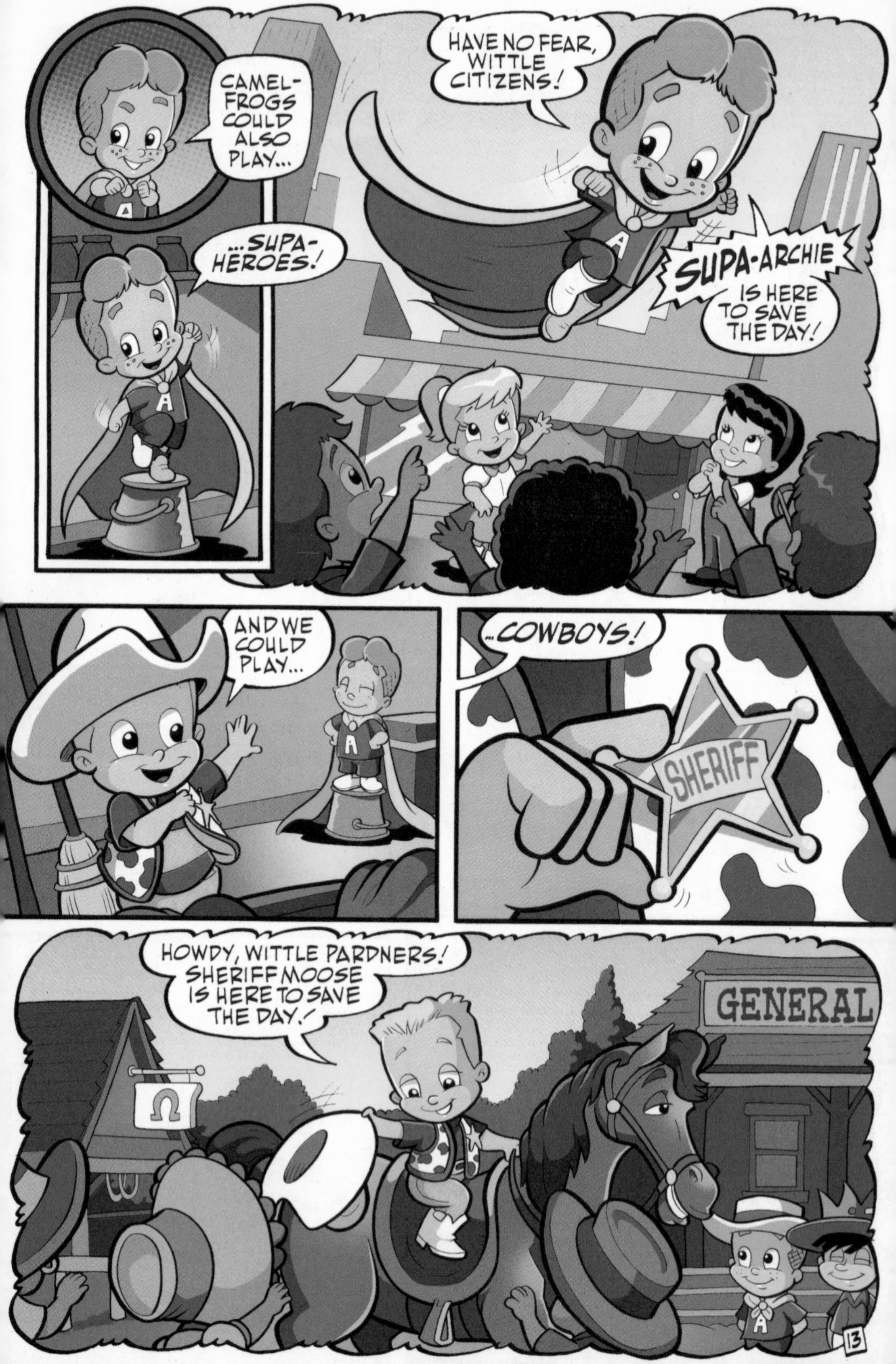

CAMEL-FROGS COULD ALSO PLAY...
...SUPA-HEROES!
HAVE NO FEAR, WITTLE CITIZENS!
SUPA-ARCHIE IS HERE TO SAVE THE DAY!
AND WE COULD PLAY...
...COWBOYS!
SHERIFF
HOWDY, WITTLE PARDNERS! SHERIFF MOOSE IS HERE TO SAVE THE DAY!
GENERAL

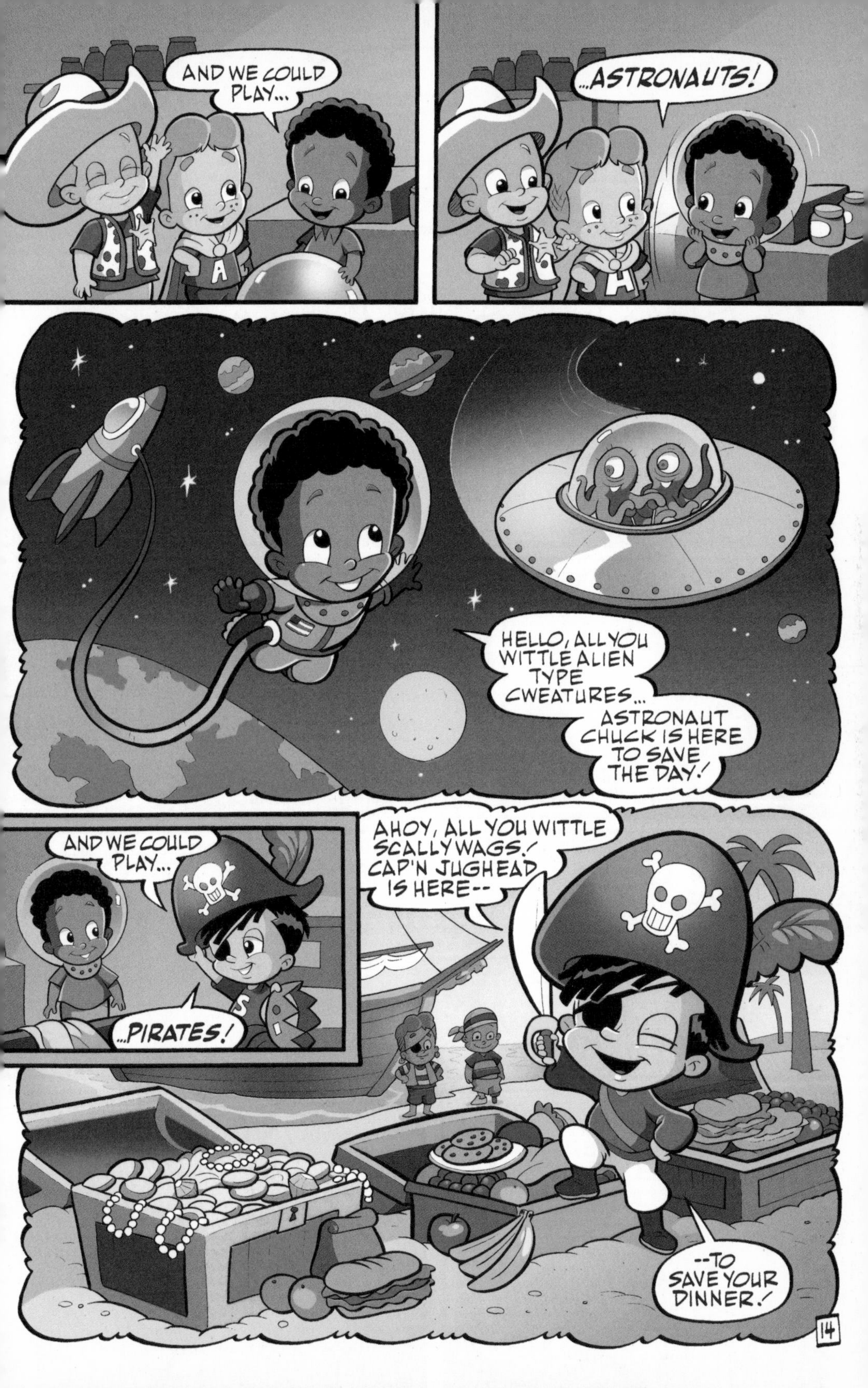
AND WE COULD PLAY...
...ASTRONAUTS!
HELLO, ALL YOU WITTLE ALIEN TYPE CWEATURES...
ASTRONAUT CHUCK IS HERE TO SAVE THE DAY!
AND WE COULD PLAY...
...PIRATES!
AHOY, ALL YOU WITTLE SCALLYWAGS! CAP'N JUGHEAD IS HERE--
--TO SAVE YOUR DINNER!
14

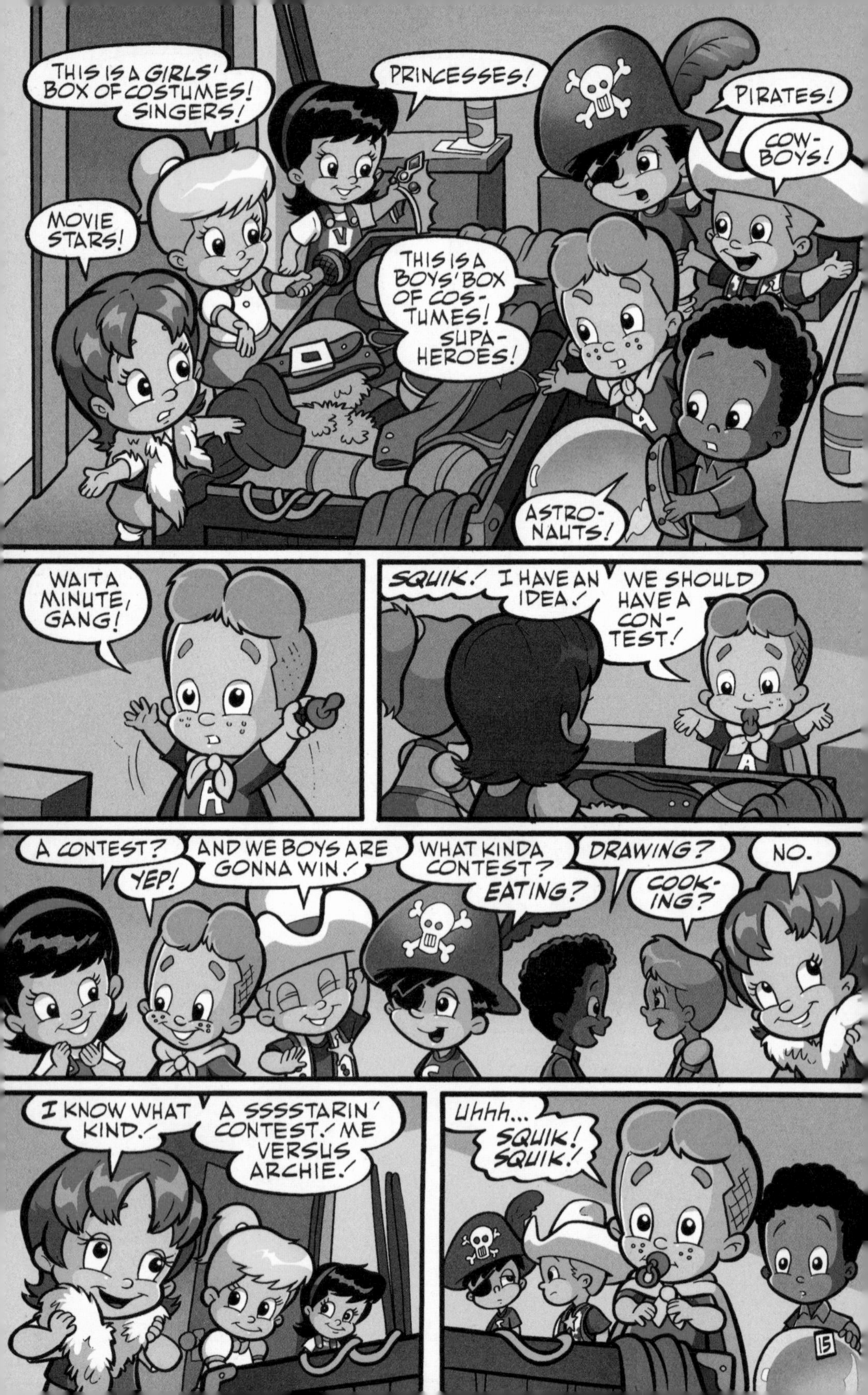
THIS IS A GIRLS' BOX OF COSTUMES! SINGERS!
PRINCESSES!
PIRATES!
COW-BOYS!
MOVIE STARS!
THIS IS A BOYS' BOX OF COS-TUMES! SUPA-HEROES!
ASTRO-NAUTS!
WAIT A MINUTE, GANG!
SQUIK! I HAVE AN IDEA!
WE SHOULD HAVE A CON-TEST!
A CONTEST?
YEP!
AND WE BOYS ARE GONNA WIN!
WHAT KINDA CONTEST?
EATING?
DRAWING?
COOK-ING?
NO.
I KNOW WHAT KIND!
A SSSSTARIN' CONTEST! ME VERSUS ARCHIE!
Uhhh...
SQUIK! SQUIK!
15

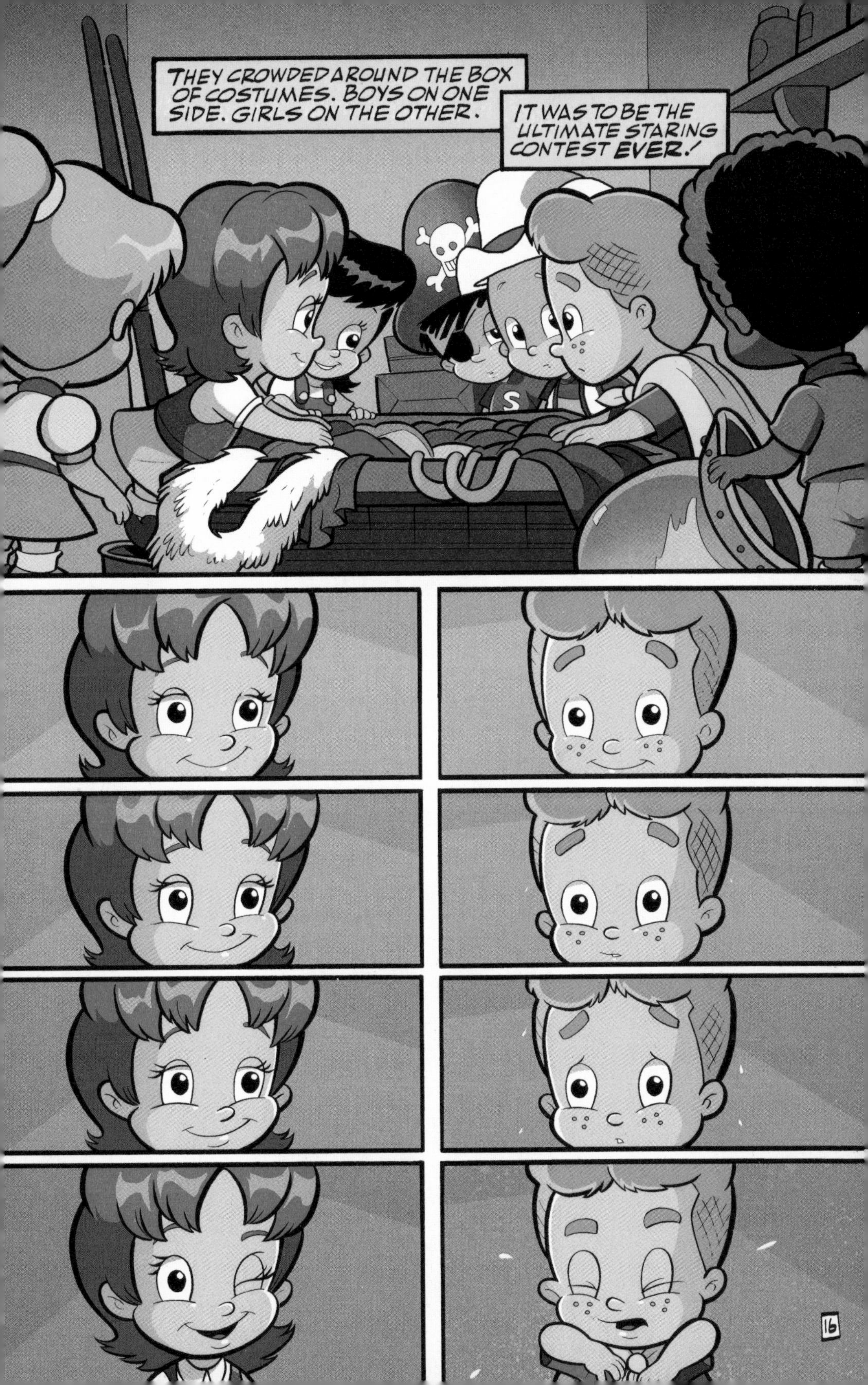
THEY CROWDED AROUND THE BOX OF COSTUMES. BOYS ON ONE SIDE. GIRLS ON THE OTHER.
IT WAS TO BE THE ULTIMATE STARING CONTEST EVER!
S

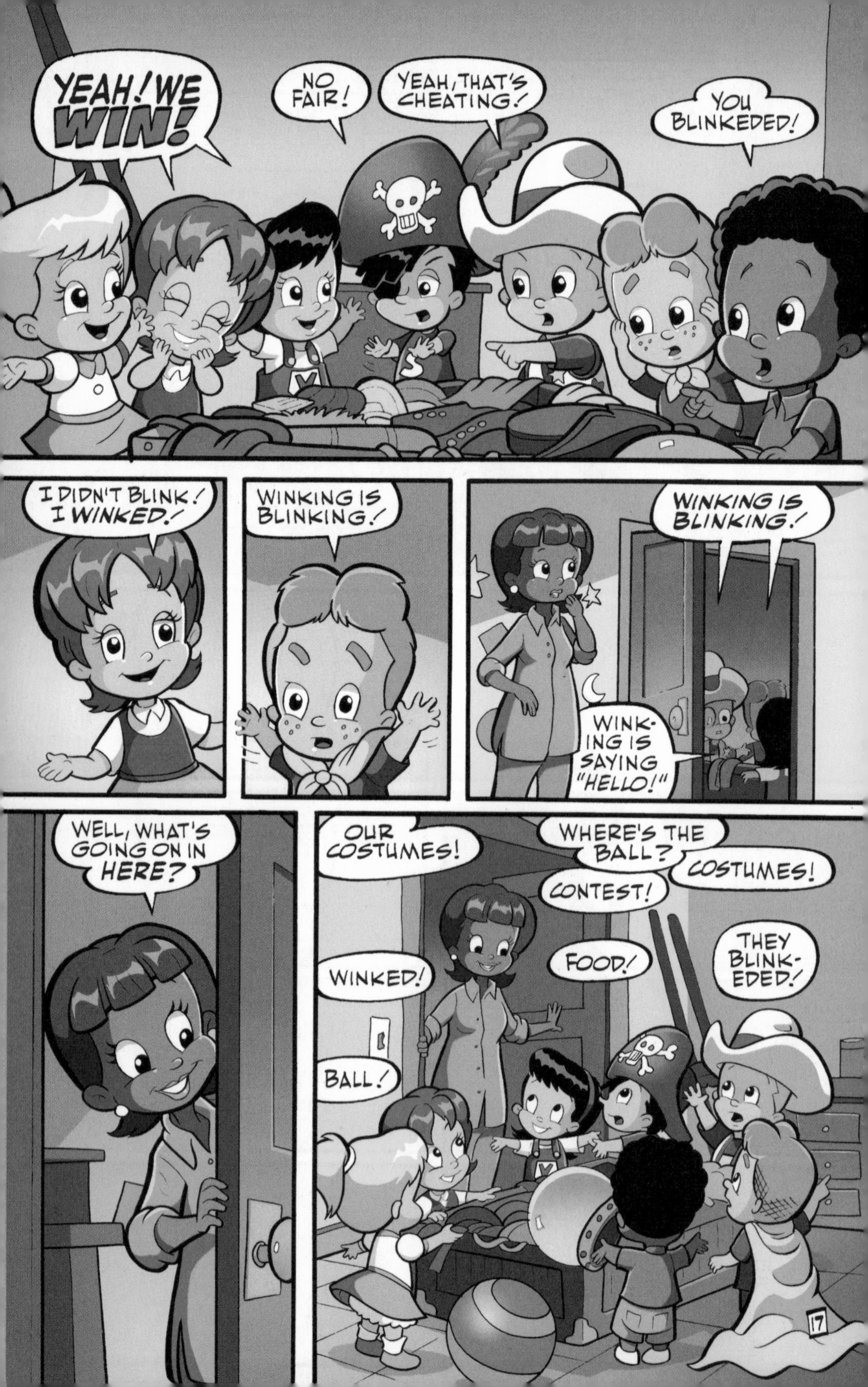
YEAH! WE WIN!
NO FAIR!
YEAH, THAT'S CHEATING!
YOU BLINKEDED!
I DIDN'T BLINK! I WINKED!
WINKING IS BLINKING!
WINKING IS BLINKING!
WINK-ING IS SAYING "HELLO!"
WELL, WHAT'S GOING ON IN HERE?
OUR COSTUMES!
WHERE'S THE BALL?
COSTUMES!
CONTEST!
THEY BLINK-EDED!
FOOD!
WINKED!
BALL!

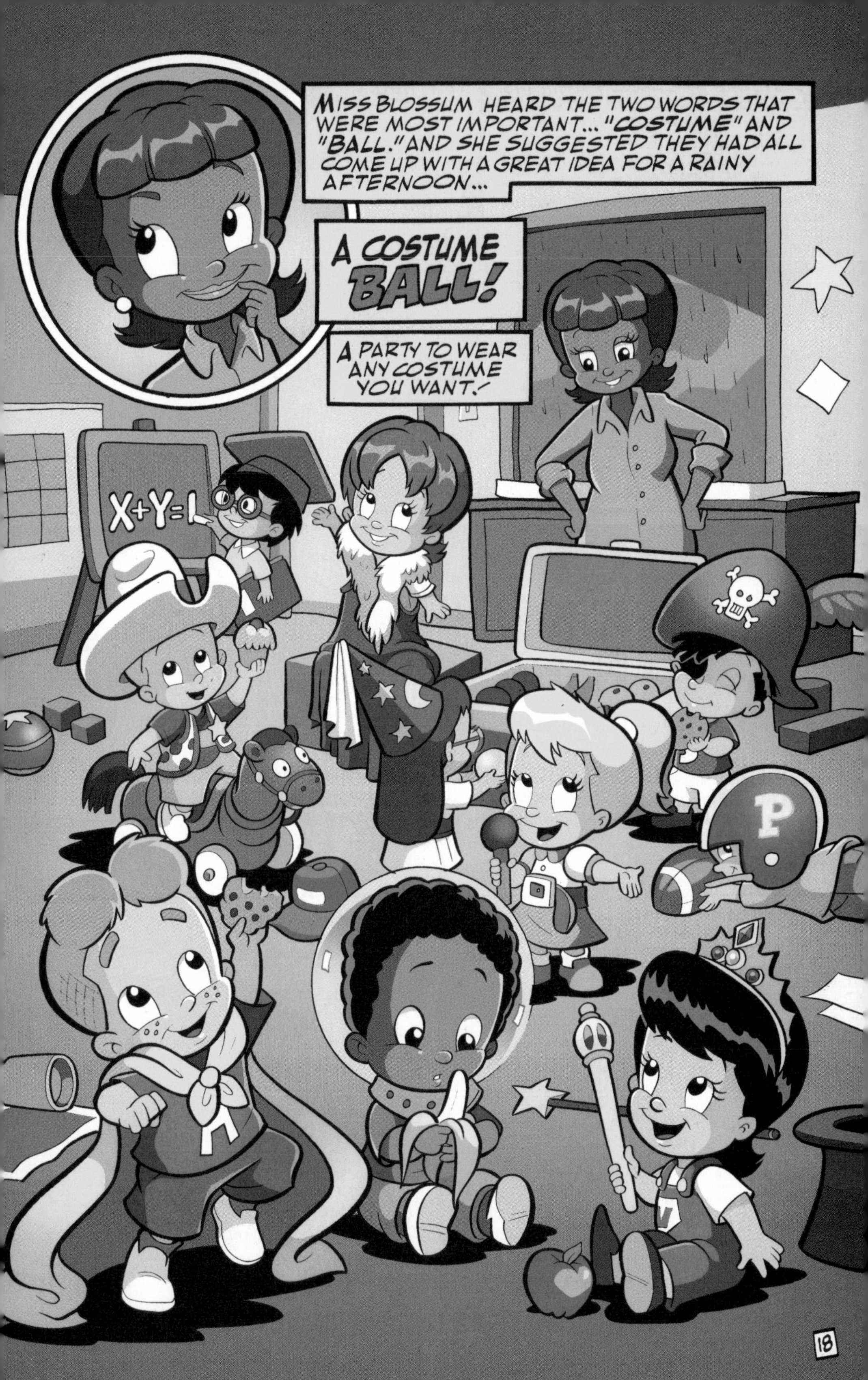
MISS BLOSSUM HEARD THE TWO WORDS THAT WERE MOST IMPORTANT... "COSTUME" AND "BALL." AND SHE SUGGESTED THEY HAD ALL COME UP WITH A GREAT IDEA FOR A RAINY AFTERNOON...
A COSTUME BALL!
A PARTY TO WEAR ANY COSTUME YOU WANT!
X+Y=1
P

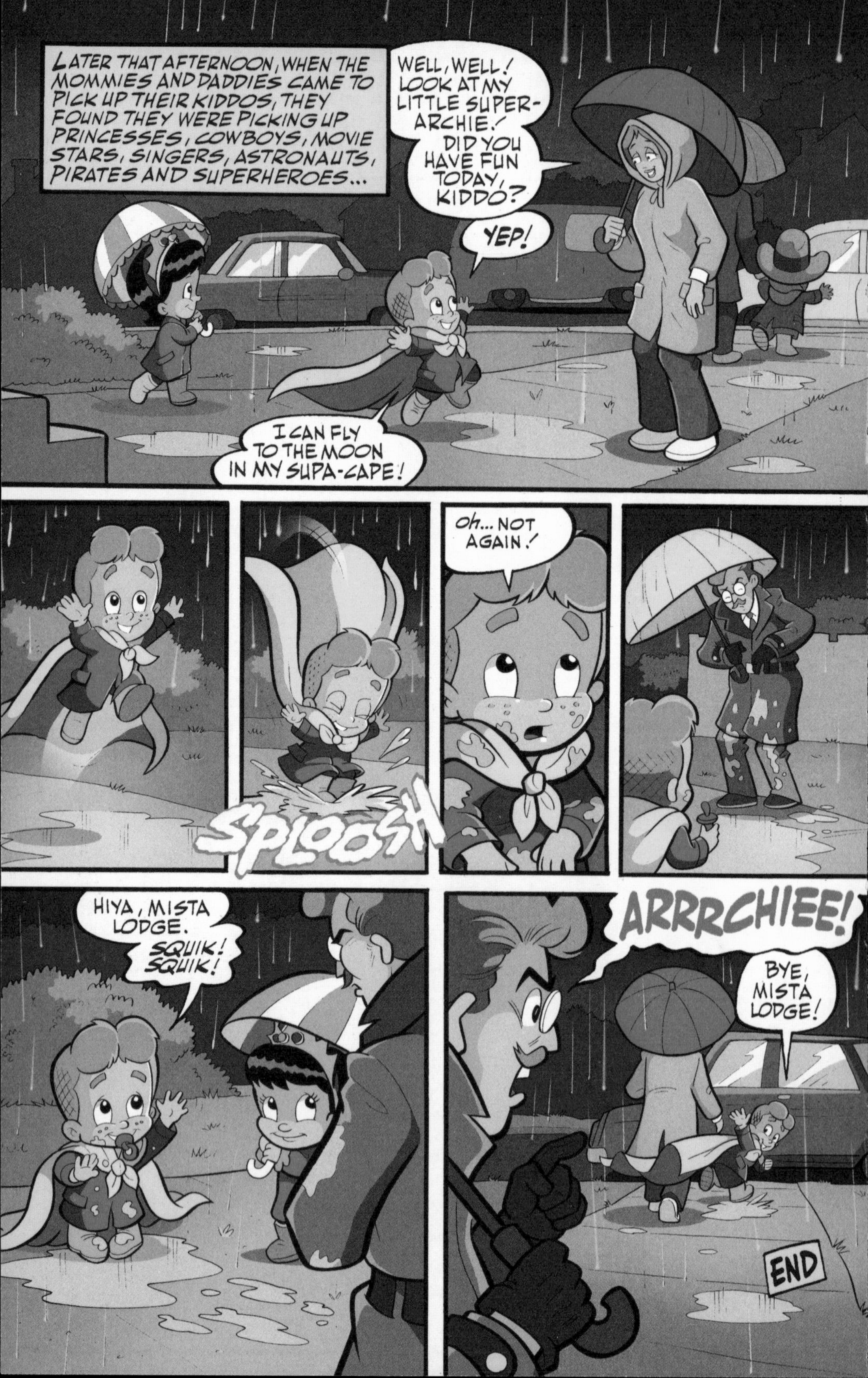
LATER THAT AFTERNOON, WHEN THE MOMMIES AND DADDIES CAME TO PICK UP THEIR KIDDOS, THEY FOUND THEY WERE PICKING UP PRINCESSES, COWBOYS, MOVIE STARS, SINGERS, ASTRONAUTS, PIRATES AND SUPERHEROES...
WELL, WELL! LOOK AT MY LITTLE SUPER-ARCHIE! DID YOU HAVE FUN TODAY, KIDDO?
YEP!
I CAN FLY TO THE MOON IN MY SUPA-CAPE!
SPLOOSH
Oh... NOT AGAIN!
HIYA, MISTA LODGE. SQUIK! SQUIK!
ARRRCHIEE!
BYE, MISTA LODGE!
END

RECESS TIME

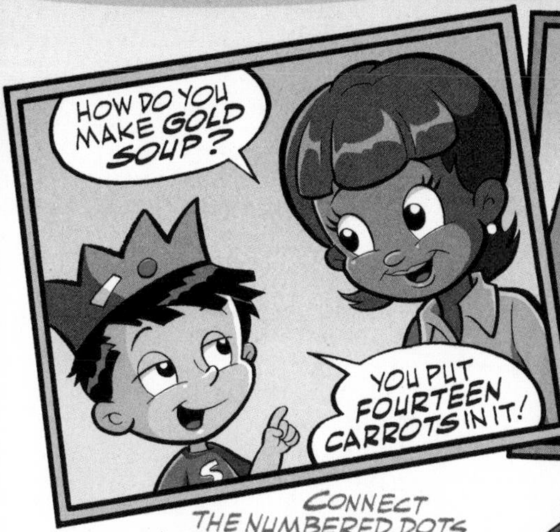
HOW DO YOU MAKE GOLD SOUP?
YOU PUT FOURTEEN CARROTS IN IT!

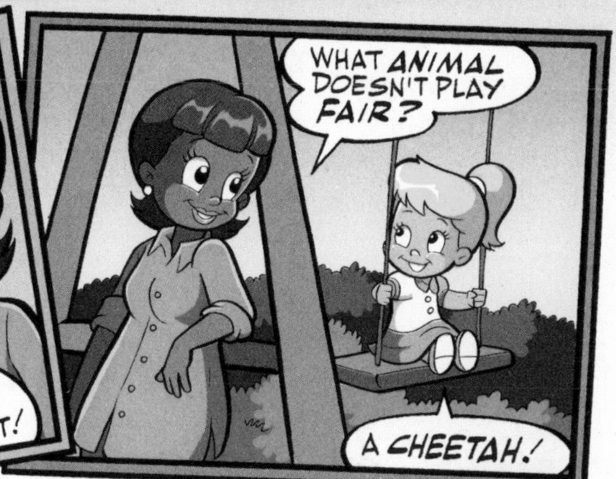
WHAT ANIMAL DOESN'T PLAY FAIR?
A CHEETAH!

CONNECT THE NUMBERED DOTS IN ORDER, AND YOU'LL FIND A SPECIAL FRIEND!

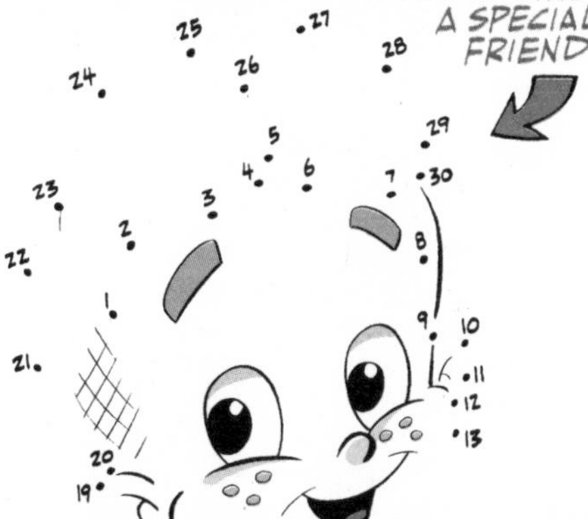

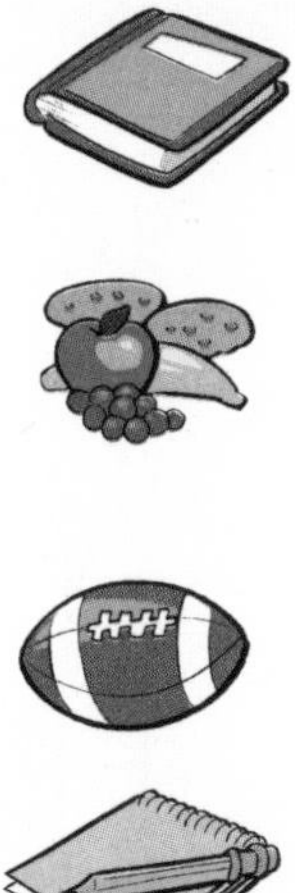

CAN YOU HELP MISS BLOSSUM TO CONNECT EACH OBJECT--

--WITH HER WEE TOTS STUDENT WHO MIGHT ENJOY IT THE MOST?

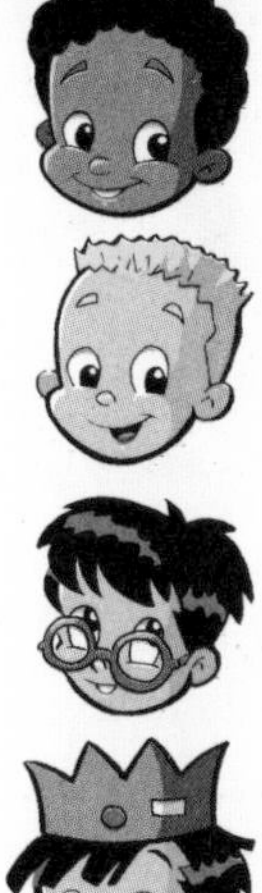

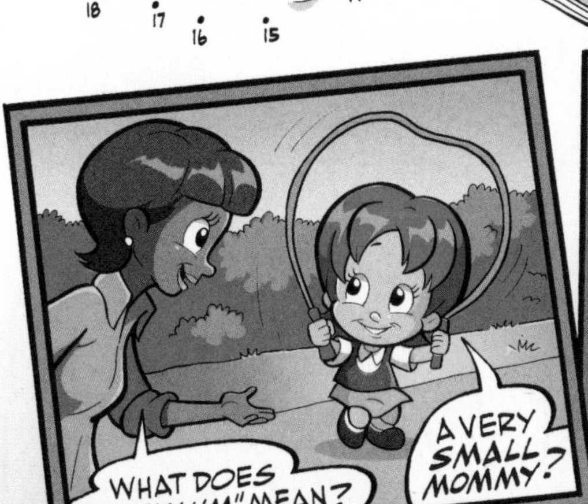
WHAT DOES "MINIMUM" MEAN?
A VERY SMALL MOMMY?

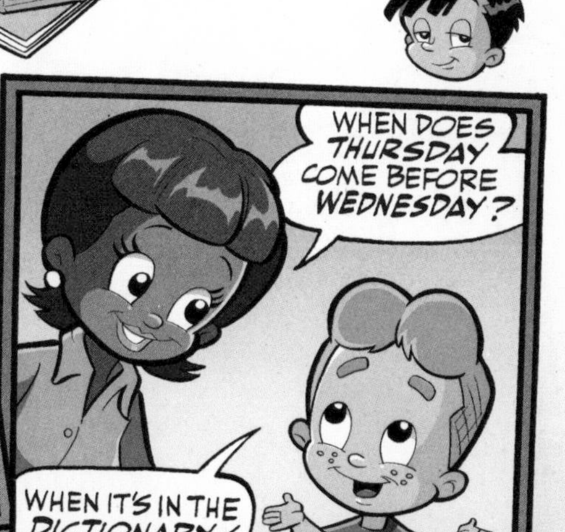
WHEN DOES THURSDAY COME BEFORE WEDNESDAY?
WHEN IT'S IN THE DICTIONARY!

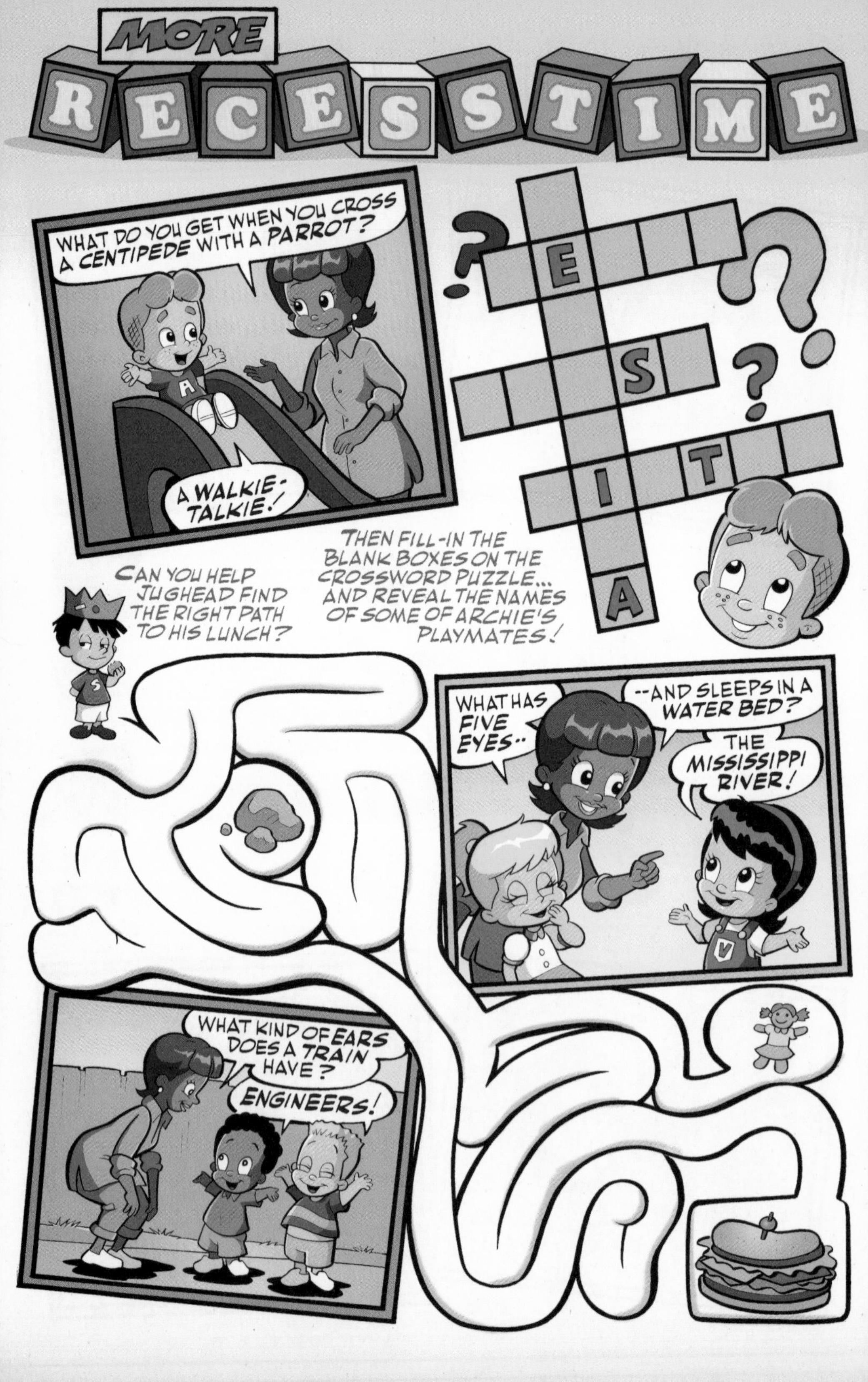
MORE
RECESS TIME
WHAT DO YOU GET WHEN YOU CROSS A CENTIPEDE WITH A PARROT?
A WALKIE-TALKIE!
E
S
I
T
A
CAN YOU HELP JUGHEAD FIND THE RIGHT PATH TO HIS LUNCH?
THEN FILL-IN THE BLANK BOXES ON THE CROSSWORD PUZZLE... AND REVEAL THE NAMES OF SOME OF ARCHIE'S PLAYMATES!
WHAT HAS FIVE EYES..
--AND SLEEPS IN A WATER BED?
THE MISSISSIPPI RIVER!
WHAT KIND OF EARS DOES A TRAIN HAVE?
ENGINEERS!

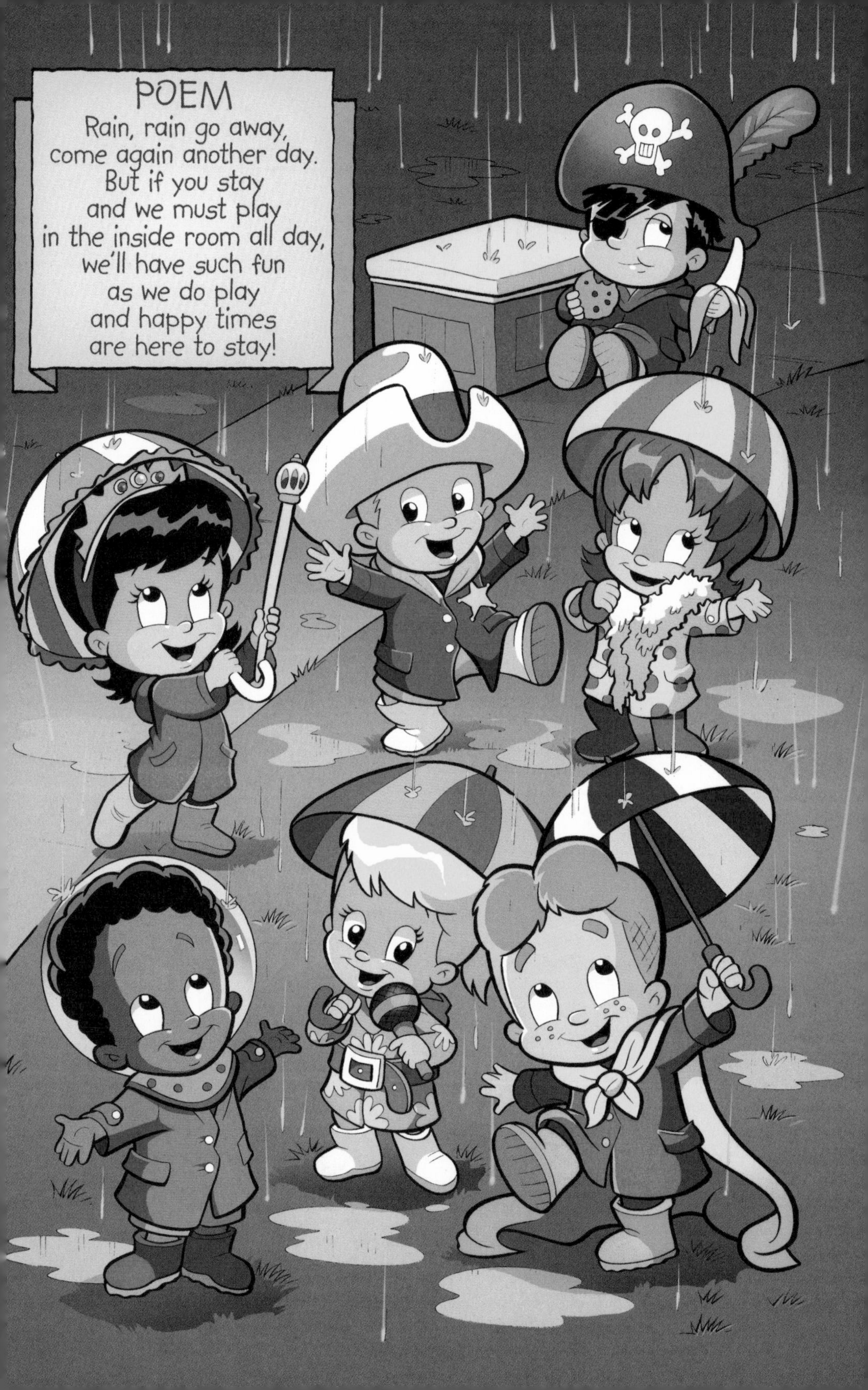
POEM
Rain, rain go away,
come again another day.
But if you stay
and we must play
in the inside room all day,
we'll have such fun
as we do play
and happy times
are here to stay!

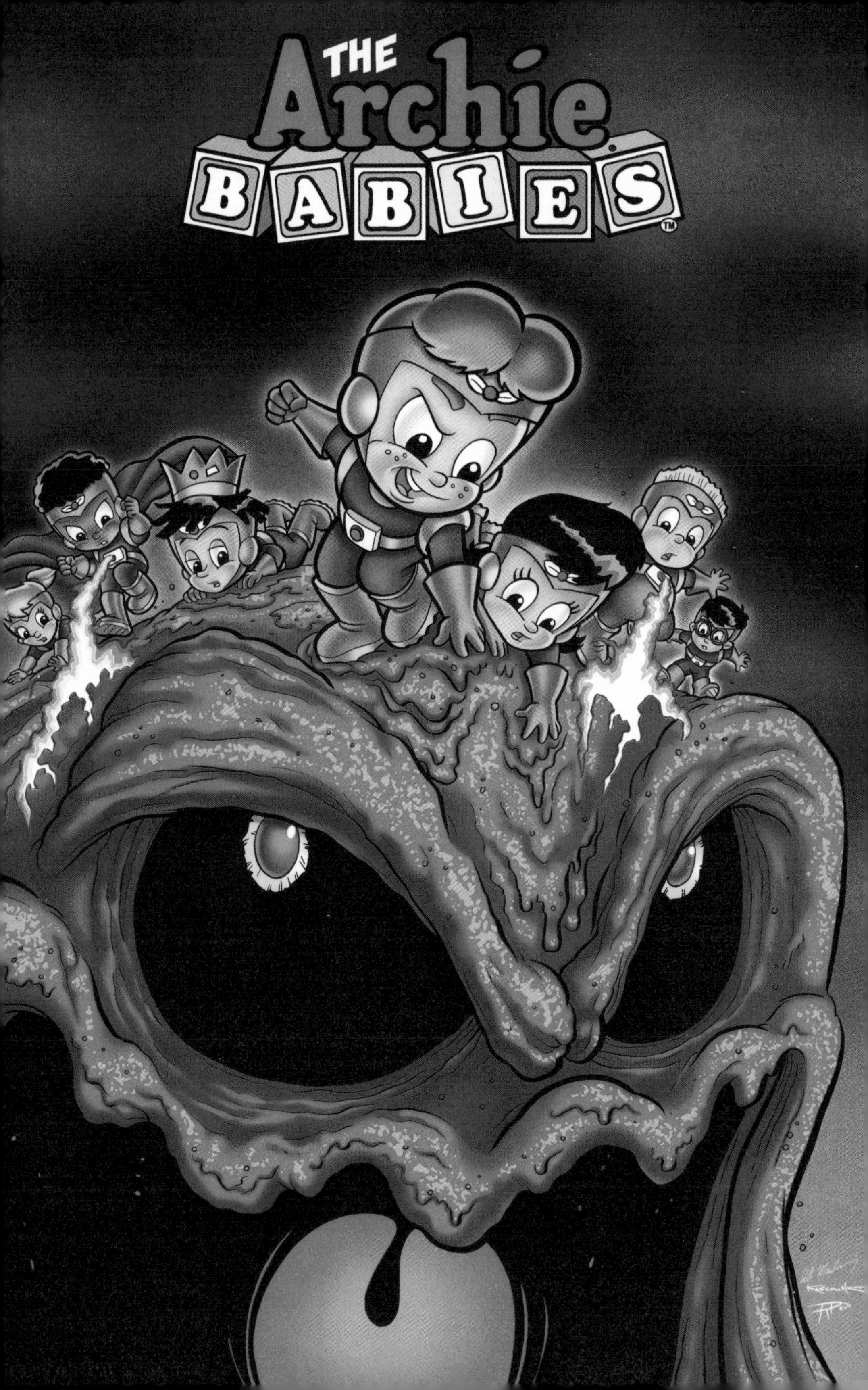
THE Archie
BABIES™

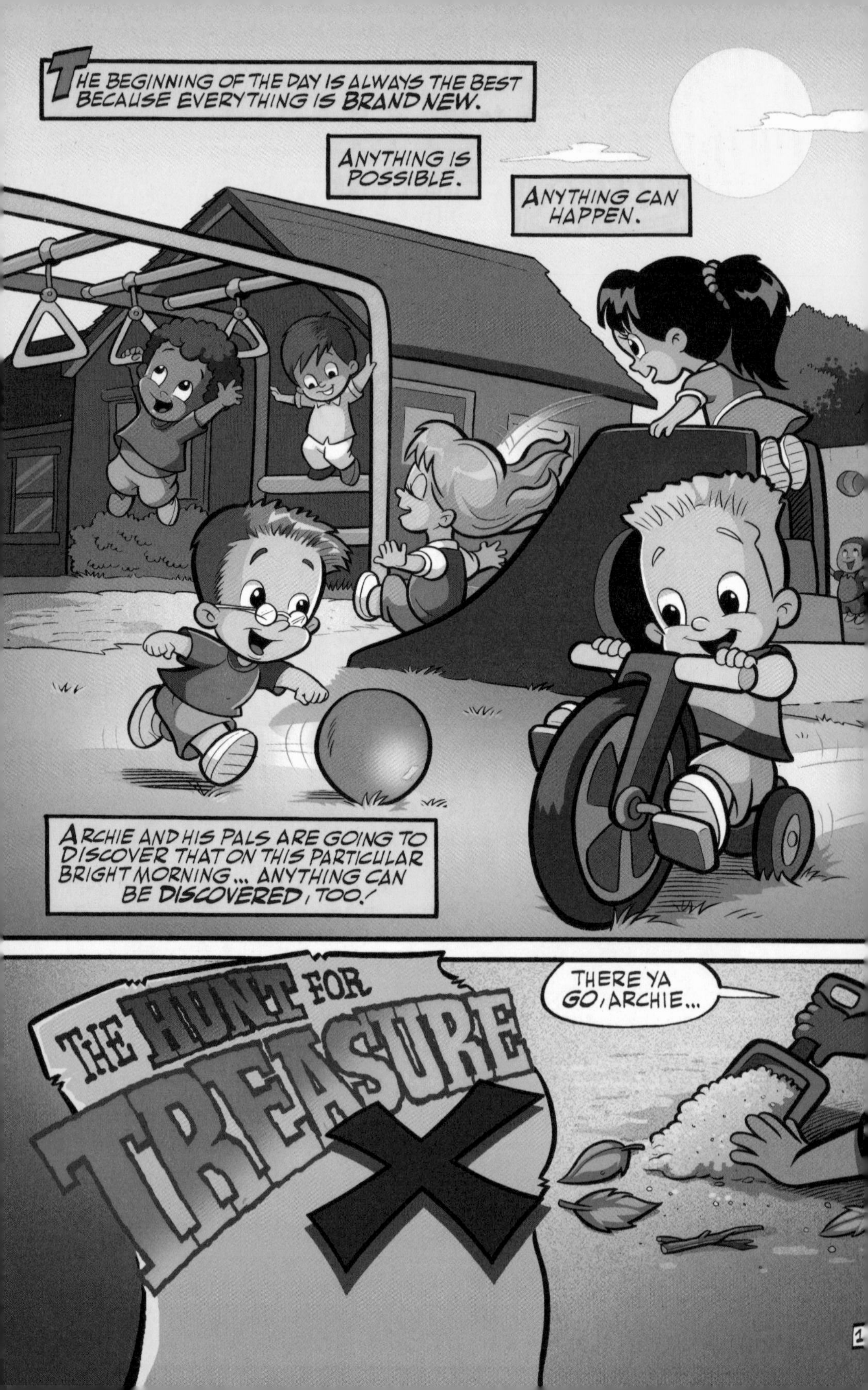
THE BEGINNING OF THE DAY IS ALWAYS THE BEST BECAUSE EVERYTHING IS BRAND NEW.
ANYTHING IS POSSIBLE.
ANYTHING CAN HAPPEN.
ARCHIE AND HIS PALS ARE GOING TO DISCOVER THAT ON THIS PARTICULAR BRIGHT MORNING... ANYTHING CAN BE DISCOVERED, TOO!
THE HUNT FOR TREASURE
THERE YA GO, ARCHIE...

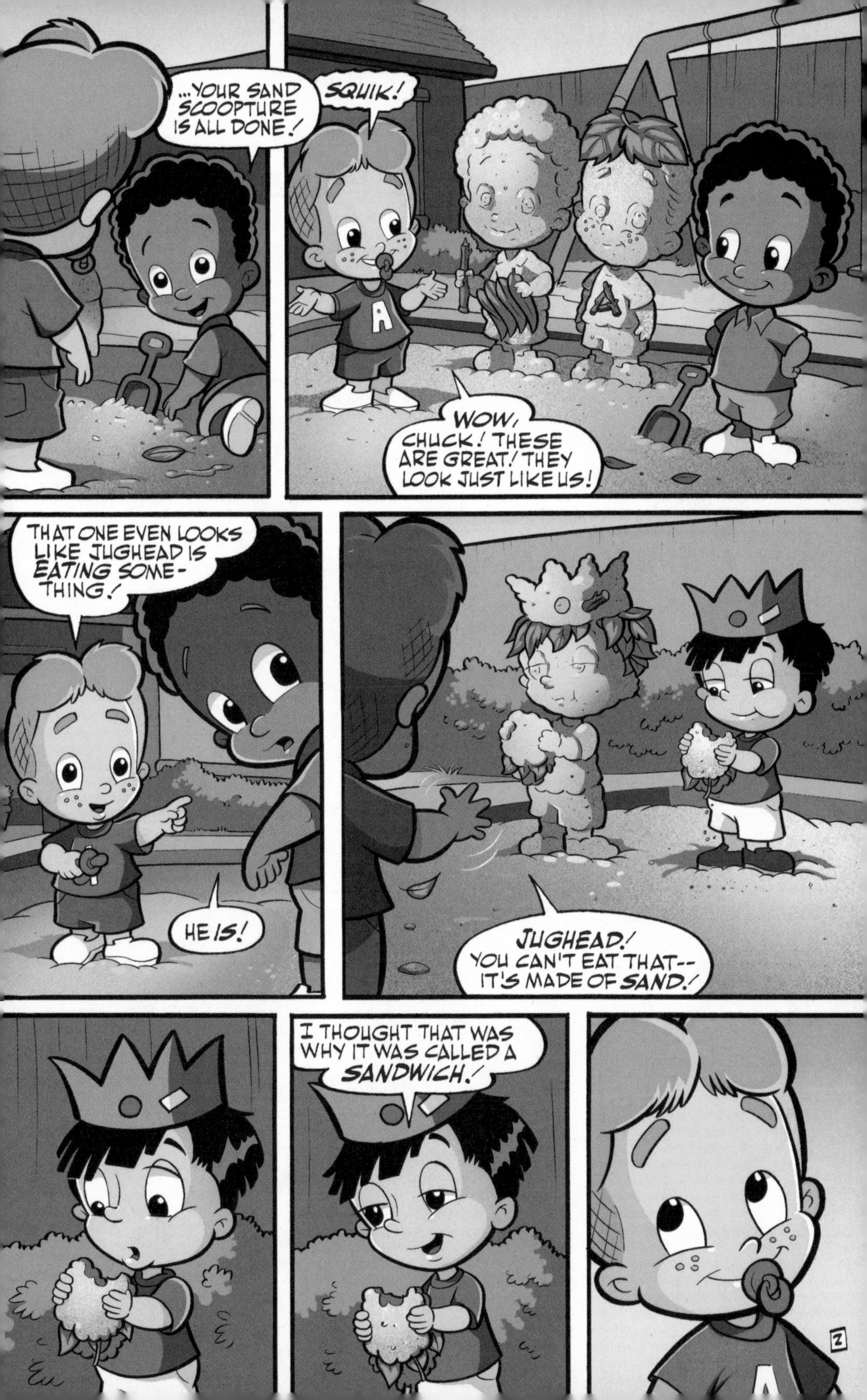
...YOUR SAND SCOOPTURE IS ALL DONE!
SQUIK!
WOW, CHUCK! THESE ARE GREAT! THEY LOOK JUST LIKE US!
THAT ONE EVEN LOOKS LIKE JUGHEAD IS EATING SOMETHING!
HE IS!
JUGHEAD! YOU CAN'T EAT THAT-- IT'S MADE OF SAND!
I THOUGHT THAT WAS WHY IT WAS CALLED A SANDWICH!

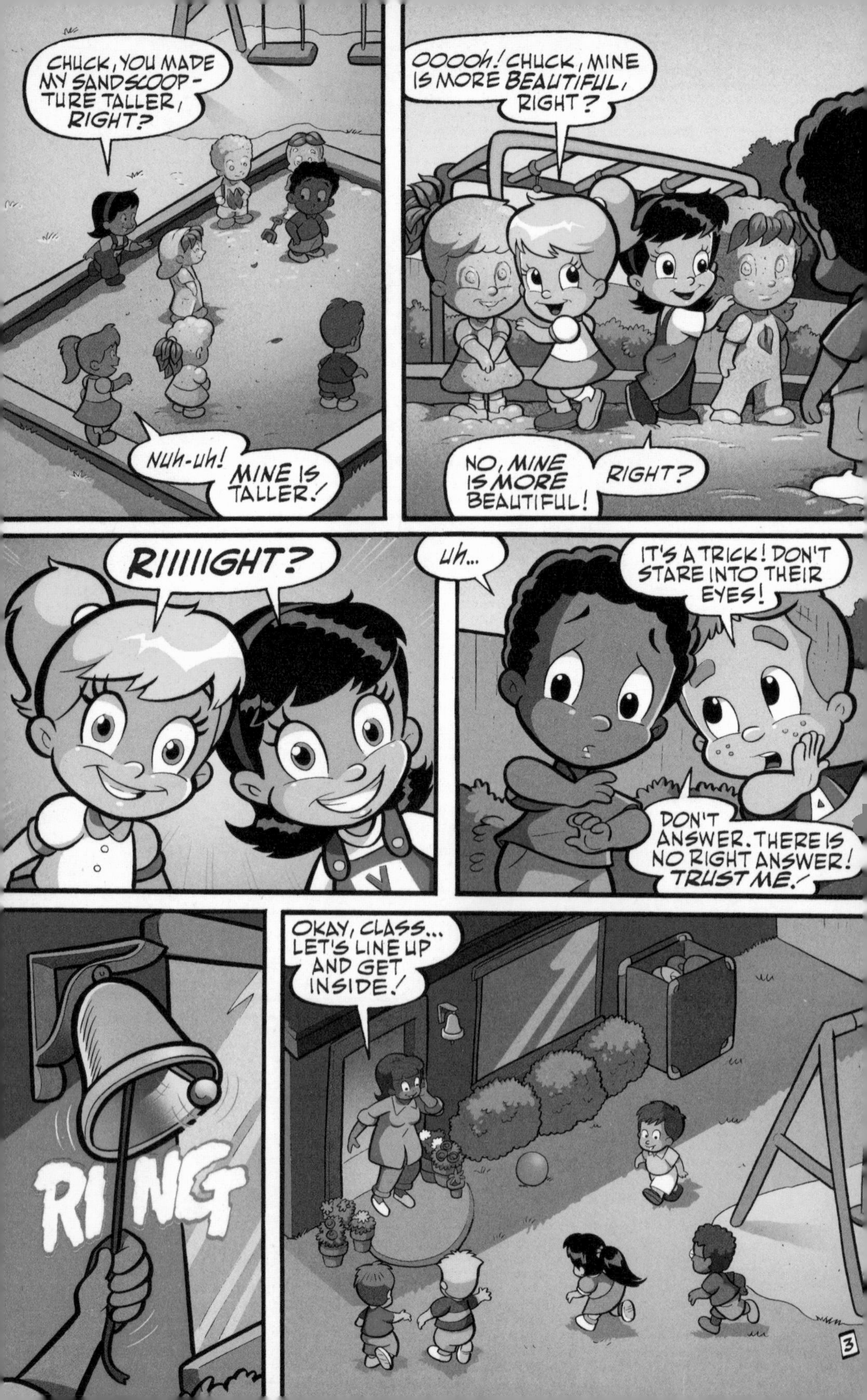
CHUCK, YOU MADE MY SANDSCOOP-TURE TALLER, RIGHT?
Nuh-uh! MINE IS TALLER!
OOOOh! CHUCK, MINE IS MORE BEAUTIFUL, RIGHT?
NO, MINE IS MORE BEAUTIFUL!
RIGHT?
RIIIIGHT?
uh...
IT'S A TRICK! DON'T STARE INTO THEIR EYES!
DON'T ANSWER. THERE IS NO RIGHT ANSWER! TRUST ME.!
RING
OKAY, CLASS... LET'S LINE UP AND GET INSIDE!
3

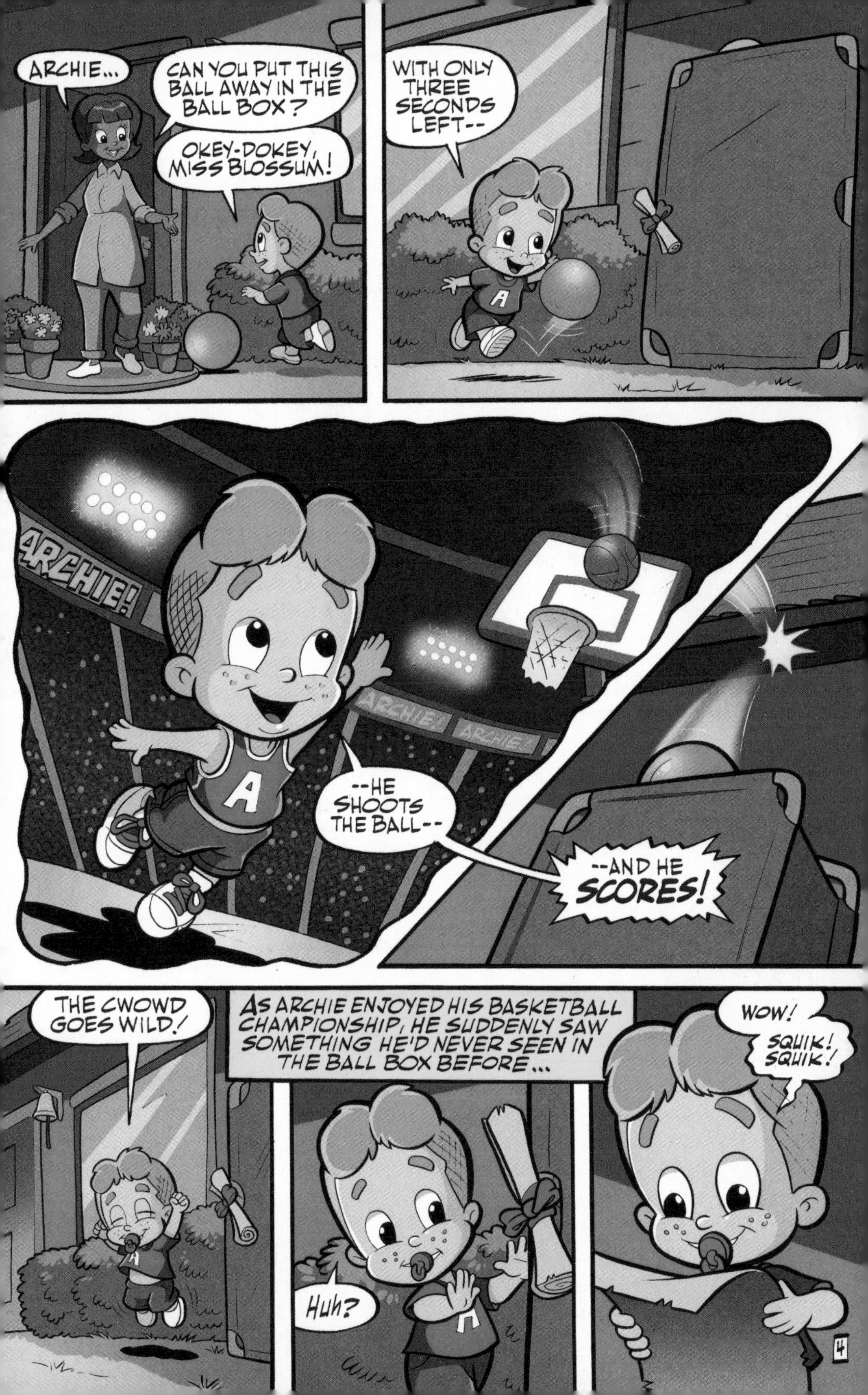
ARCHIE...
CAN YOU PUT THIS BALL AWAY IN THE BALL BOX?
OKEY-DOKEY, MISS BLOSSUM!
WITH ONLY THREE SECONDS LEFT--
ARCHIE!
ARCHIE!
ARCHIE!
--HE SHOOTS THE BALL--
--AND HE SCORES!
THE CWOWD GOES WILD!
AS ARCHIE ENJOYED HIS BASKETBALL CHAMPIONSHIP, HE SUDDENLY SAW SOMETHING HE'D NEVER SEEN IN THE BALL BOX BEFORE...
Huh?
WOW!
SQUIK! SQUIK!
4

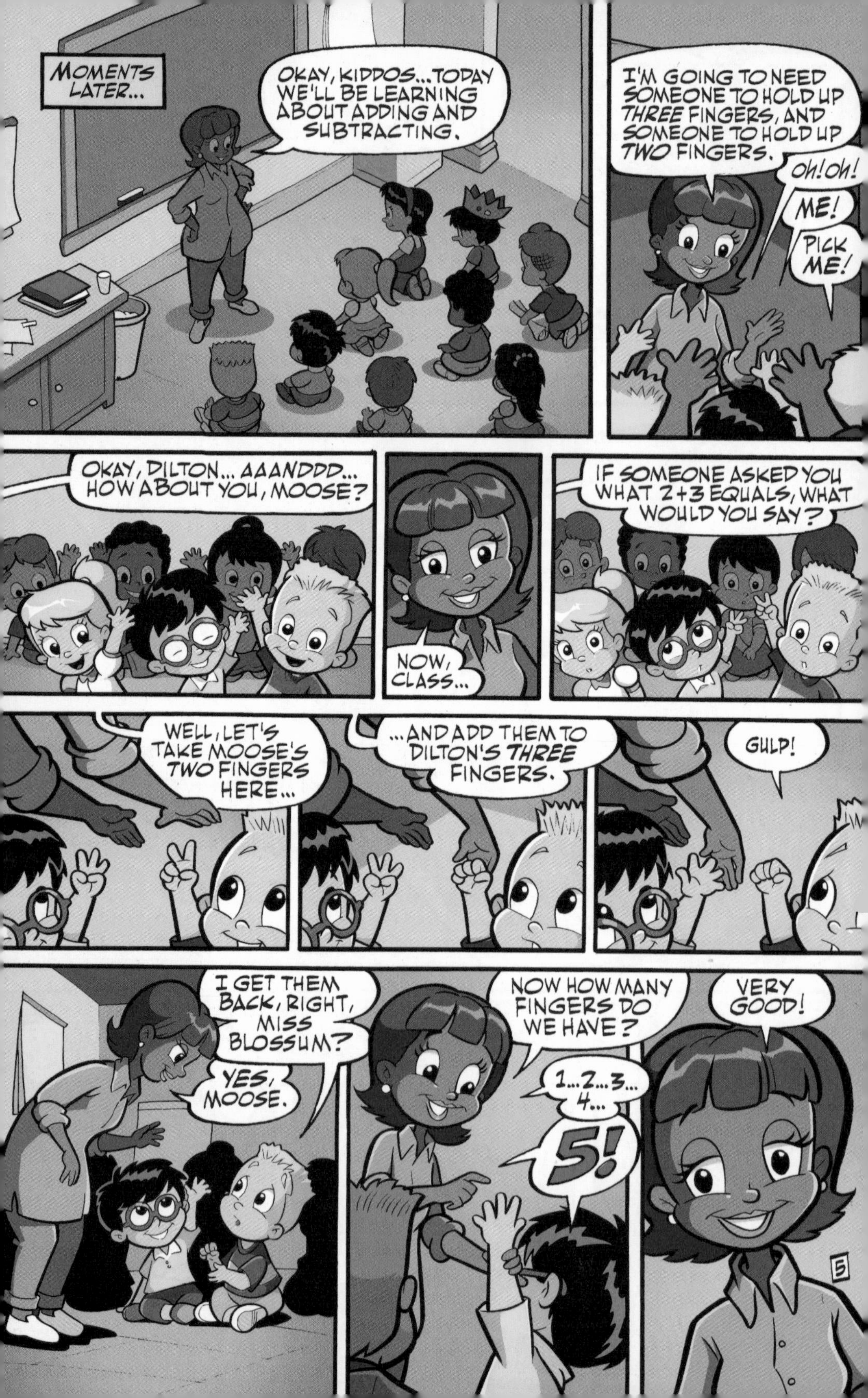
MOMENTS LATER...
OKAY, KIDDOS...TODAY WE'LL BE LEARNING ABOUT ADDING AND SUBTRACTING.
I'M GOING TO NEED SOMEONE TO HOLD UP THREE FINGERS, AND SOMEONE TO HOLD UP TWO FINGERS.
oh! oh!
ME!
PICK ME!
OKAY, DILTON... AAANDDD... HOW ABOUT YOU, MOOSE?
NOW, CLASS...
IF SOMEONE ASKED YOU WHAT 2+3 EQUALS, WHAT WOULD YOU SAY?
WELL, LET'S TAKE MOOSE'S TWO FINGERS HERE...
...AND ADD THEM TO DILTON'S THREE FINGERS.
GULP!
I GET THEM BACK, RIGHT, MISS BLOSSUM?
YES, MOOSE.
NOW HOW MANY FINGERS DO WE HAVE?
1...2...3... 4...
5!
VERY GOOD!
5

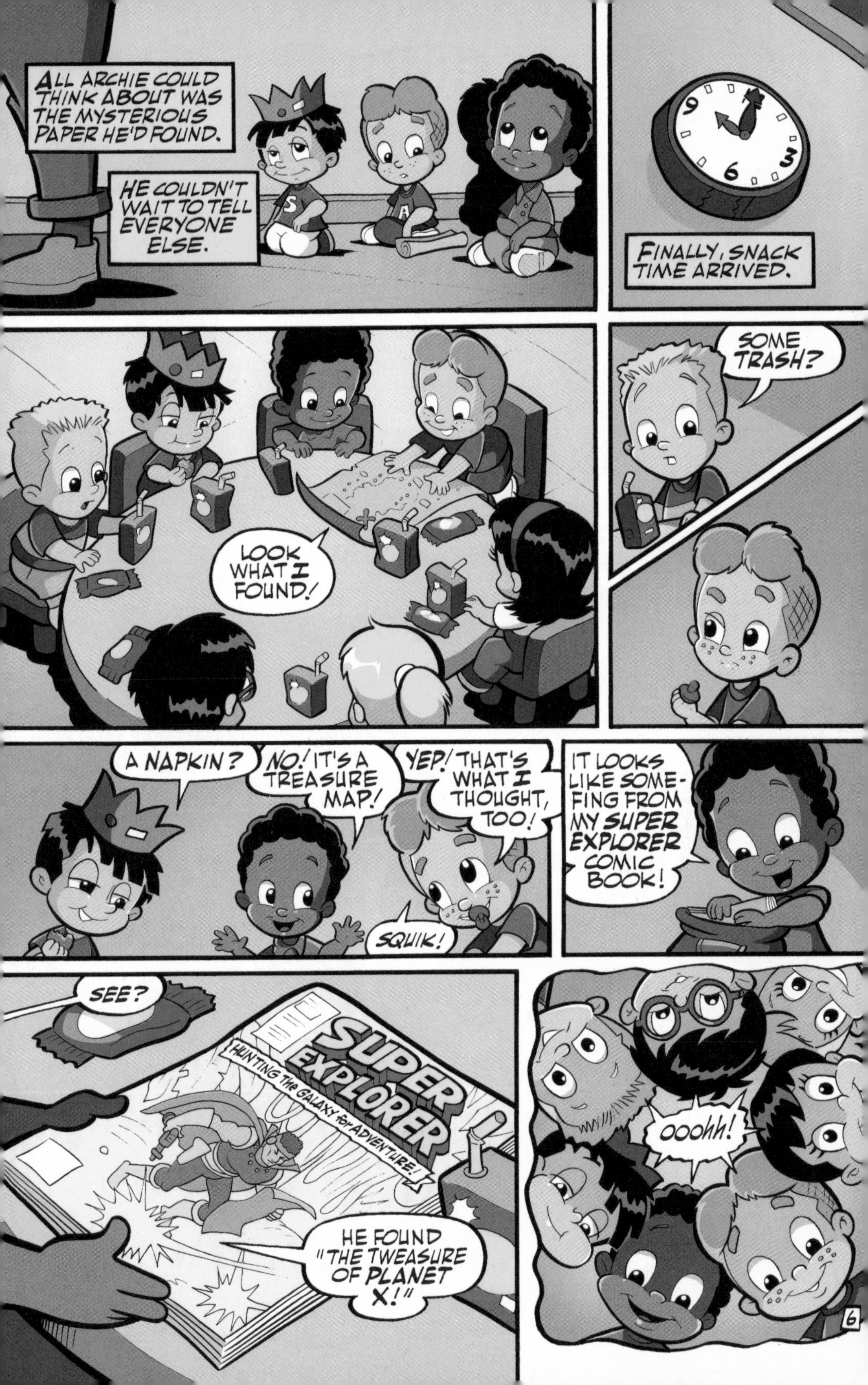
ALL ARCHIE COULD THINK ABOUT WAS THE MYSTERIOUS PAPER HE'D FOUND.
HE COULDN'T WAIT TO TELL EVERYONE ELSE.
FINALLY, SNACK TIME ARRIVED.
LOOK WHAT I FOUND!
SOME TRASH?
A NAPKIN?
NO! IT'S A TREASURE MAP!
YEP! THAT'S WHAT I THOUGHT, TOO!
SQUIK!
IT LOOKS LIKE SOME-FING FROM MY SUPER EXPLORER COMIC BOOK!
SEE?
SUPER EXPLORER
HUNTING THE GALAXY FOR ADVENTURE!
HE FOUND "THE TWEASURE OF PLANET X!"
oooh!
6

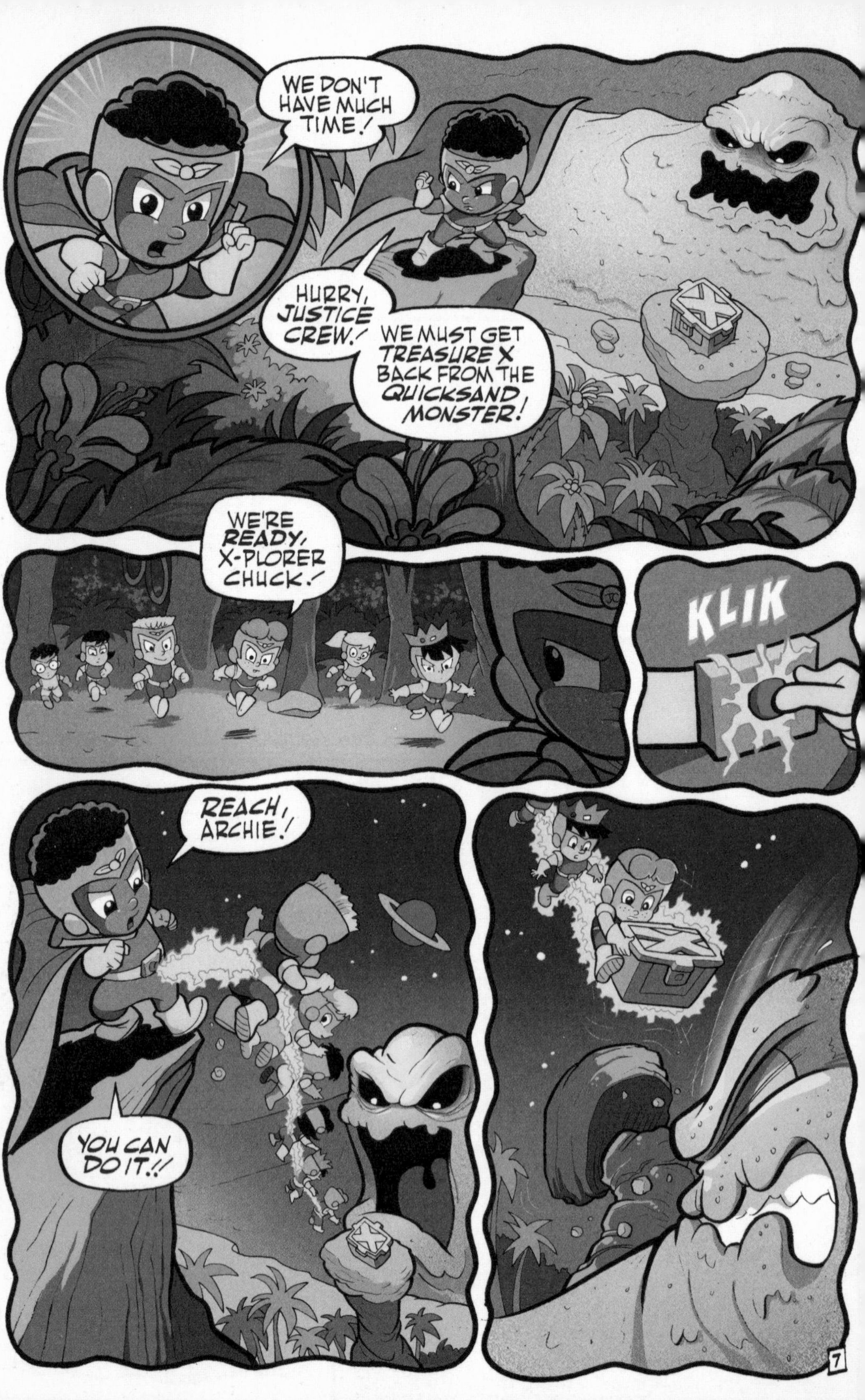
WE DON'T HAVE MUCH TIME!
HURRY, JUSTICE CREW!
WE MUST GET TREASURE X BACK FROM THE QUICKSAND MONSTER!
WE'RE READY, X-PLORER CHUCK!
KLIK
REACH, ARCHIE!
YOU CAN DO IT!!

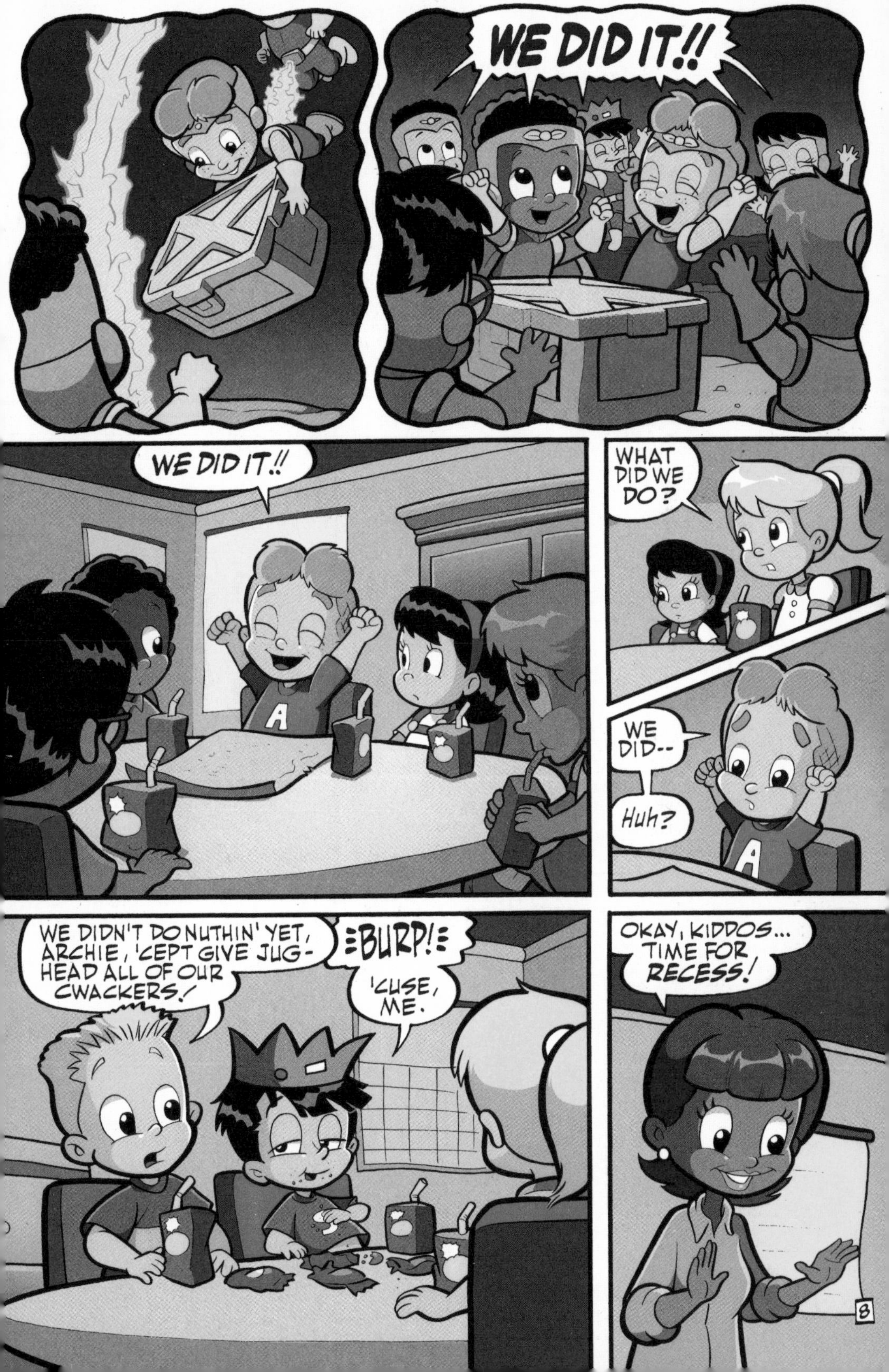
WE DID IT!!
WE DID IT!!
WHAT DID WE DO?
WE DID--
Huh?
WE DIDN'T DO NUTHIN' YET, ARCHIE, 'CEPT GIVE JUG-HEAD ALL OF OUR CWACKERS!
BURP!
'CUSE, ME.
OKAY, KIDDOS... TIME FOR RECESS!
8

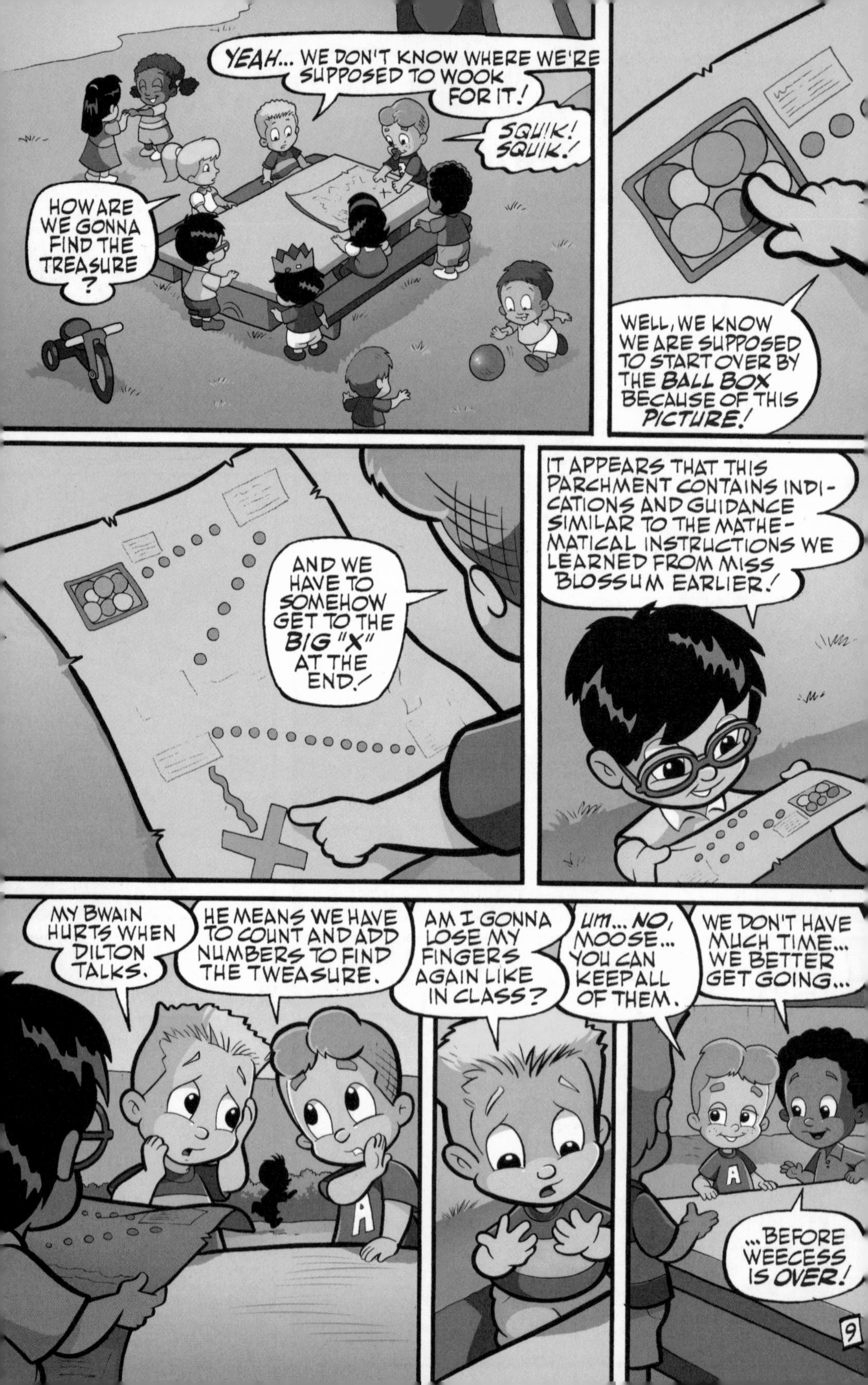
YEAH... WE DON'T KNOW WHERE WE'RE SUPPOSED TO WOOK FOR IT!
SQUIK! SQUIK!
HOW ARE WE GONNA FIND THE TREASURE?
WELL, WE KNOW WE ARE SUPPOSED TO START OVER BY THE BALL BOX BECAUSE OF THIS PICTURE!
AND WE HAVE TO SOMEHOW GET TO THE BIG "X" AT THE END!
IT APPEARS THAT THIS PARCHMENT CONTAINS INDI-CATIONS AND GUIDANCE SIMILAR TO THE MATHE-MATICAL INSTRUCTIONS WE LEARNED FROM MISS BLOSSUM EARLIER!
MY BWAIN HURTS WHEN DILTON TALKS.
HE MEANS WE HAVE TO COUNT AND ADD NUMBERS TO FIND THE TWEASURE.
AM I GONNA LOSE MY FINGERS AGAIN LIKE IN CLASS?
UM... NO, MOOSE... YOU CAN KEEP ALL OF THEM.
WE DON'T HAVE MUCH TIME... WE BETTER GET GOING...
...BEFORE WEECESS IS OVER!

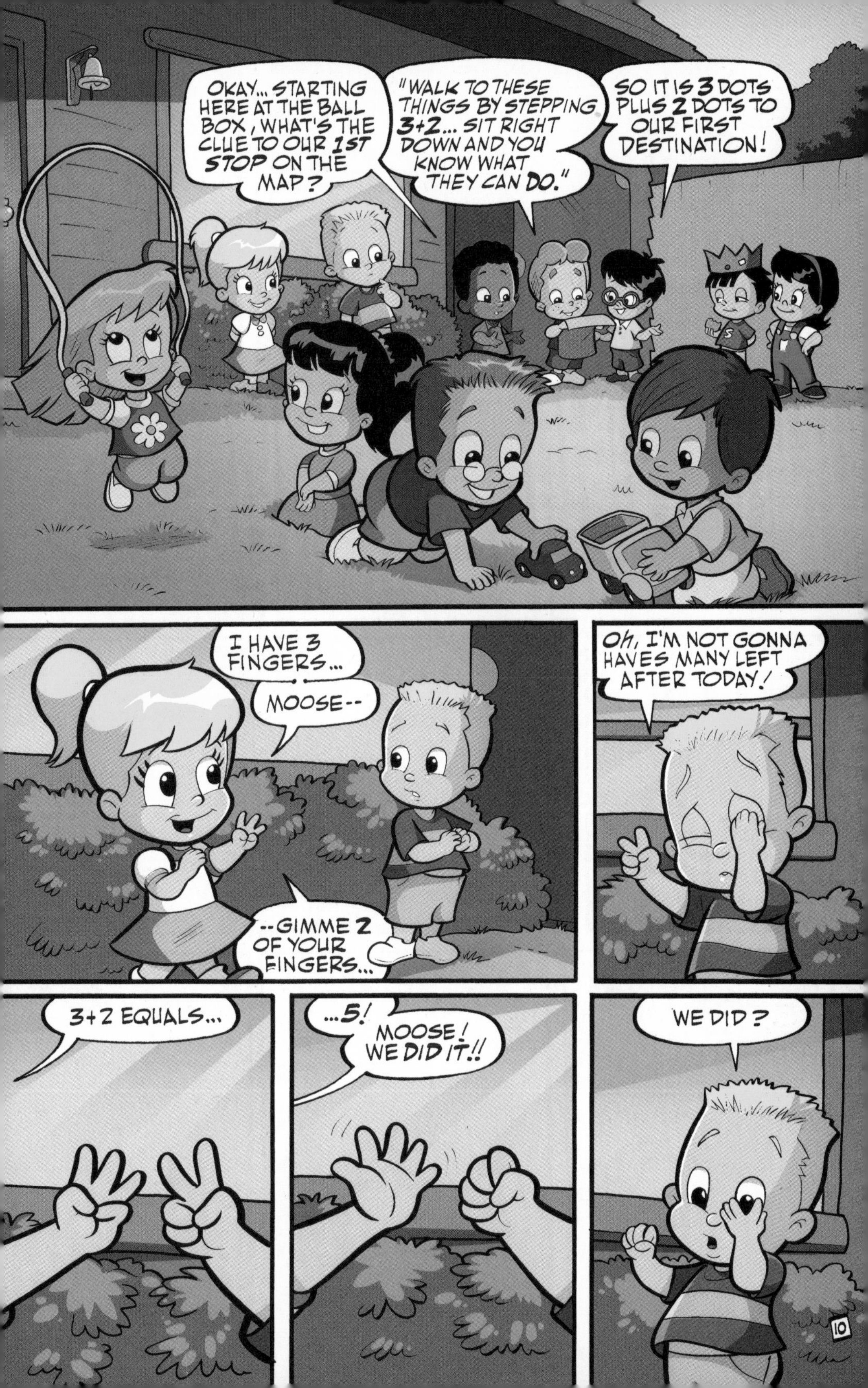

OKAY... STARTING HERE AT THE BALL BOX, WHAT'S THE CLUE TO OUR 1ST STOP ON THE MAP?
"WALK TO THESE THINGS BY STEPPING 3+2... SIT RIGHT DOWN AND YOU KNOW WHAT THEY CAN DO."
SO IT IS 3 DOTS PLUS 2 DOTS TO OUR FIRST DESTINATION!
I HAVE 3 FINGERS...
MOOSE--
--GIMME 2 OF YOUR FINGERS...
Oh, I'M NOT GONNA HAVES MANY LEFT AFTER TODAY!
3+2 EQUALS...
...5!
MOOSE! WE DID IT!!
WE DID?

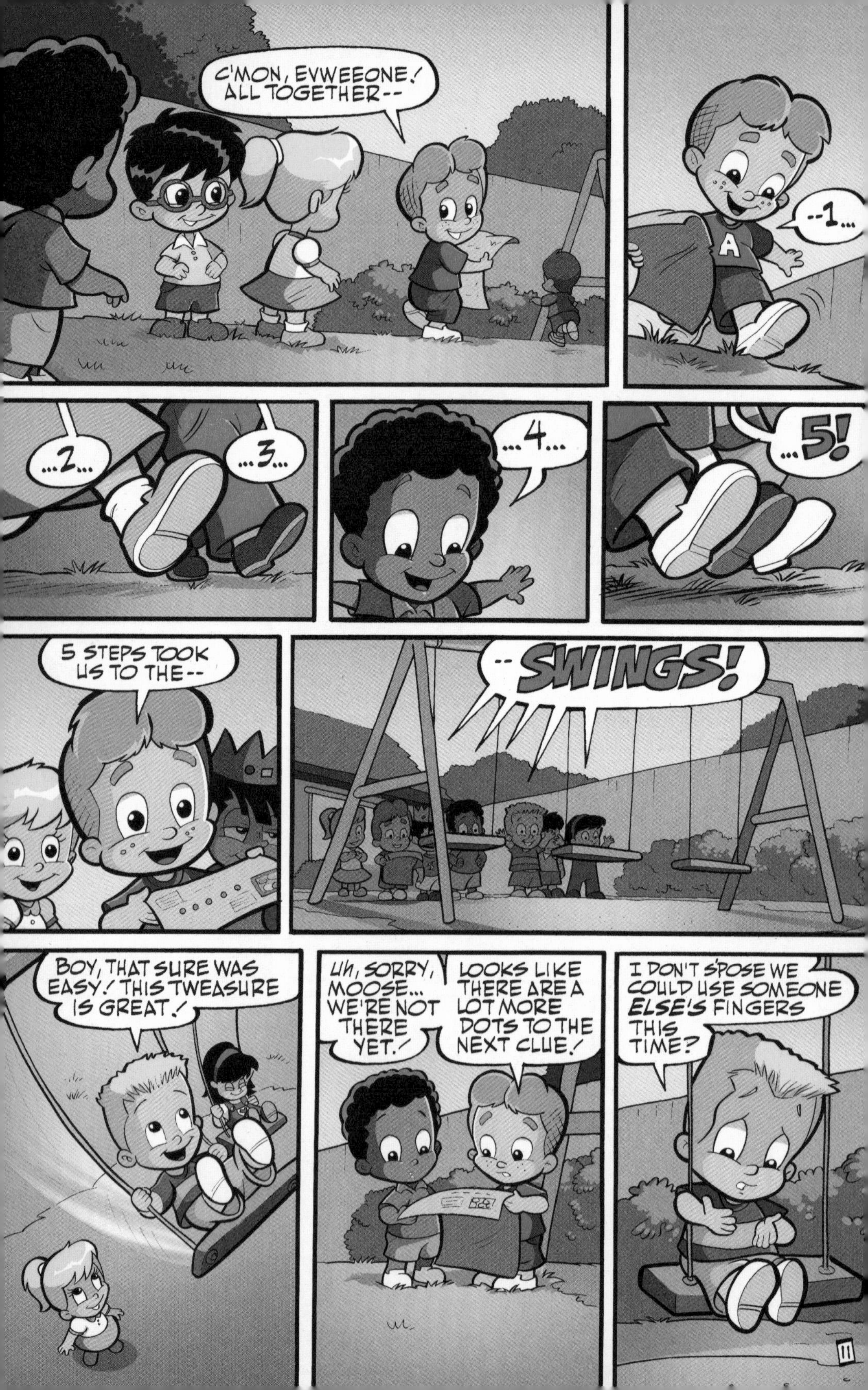
C'MON, EVWEEONE! ALL TOGETHER--
--1...
...2...
...3...
...4...
...5!
5 STEPS TOOK US TO THE--
--SWINGS!
BOY, THAT SURE WAS EASY! THIS TWEASURE IS GREAT!
UH, SORRY, MOOSE... WE'RE NOT THERE YET.
LOOKS LIKE THERE ARE A LOT MORE DOTS TO THE NEXT CLUE!
I DON'T S'POSE WE COULD USE SOMEONE *ELSE'S* FINGERS THIS TIME?

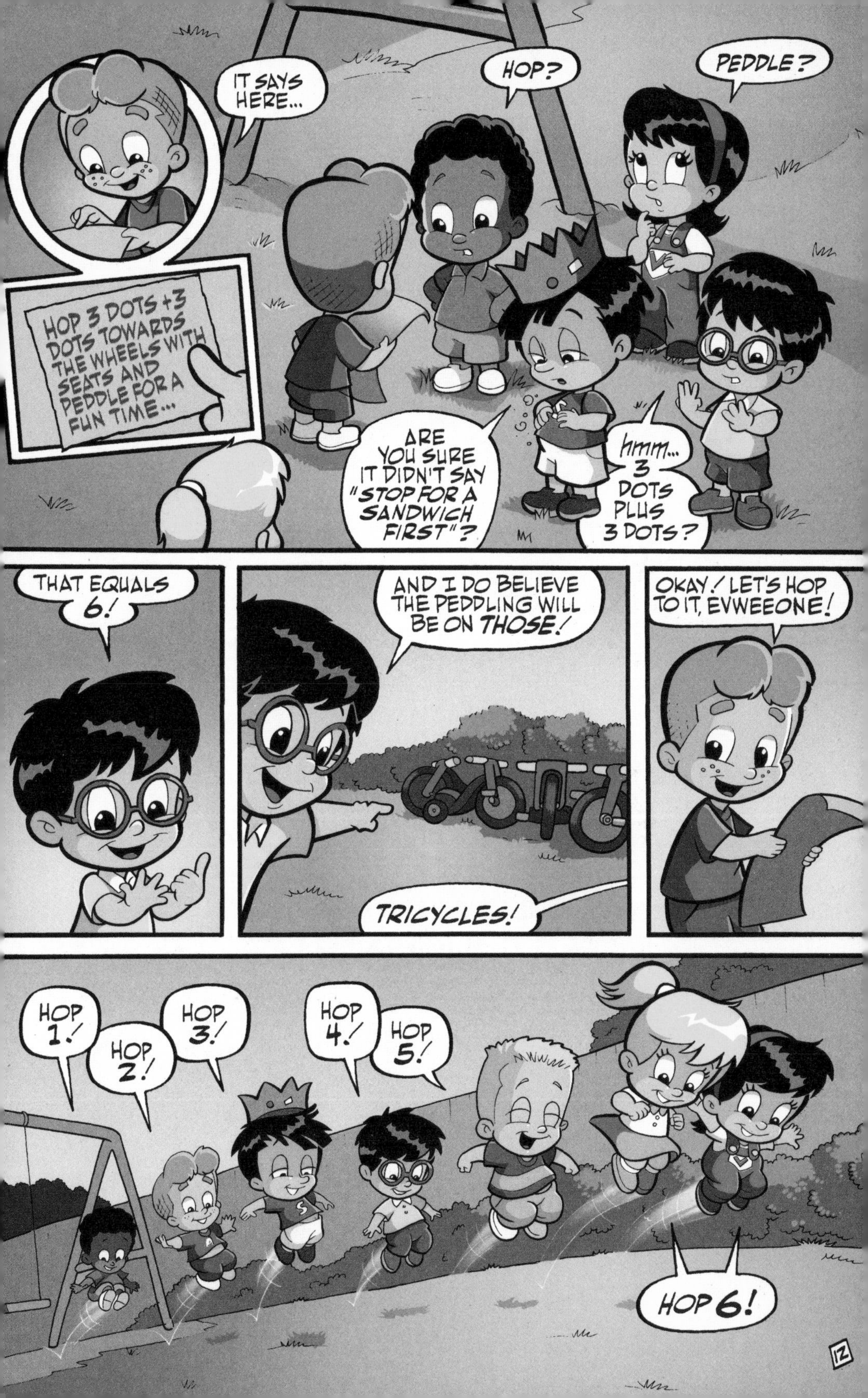
IT SAYS HERE...
HOP?
PEDDLE?
HOP 3 DOTS +3 DOTS TOWARDS THE WHEELS WITH SEATS AND PEDDLE FOR A FUN TIME...
ARE YOU SURE IT DIDN'T SAY "STOP FOR A SANDWICH FIRST"?
hmm... 3 DOTS PLUS 3 DOTS?
THAT EQUALS 6!
AND I DO BELIEVE THE PEDDLING WILL BE ON THOSE!
TRICYCLES!
OKAY! LET'S HOP TO IT, EVWEEONE!
HOP 1!
HOP 2!
HOP 3!
HOP 4!
HOP 5!
HOP 6!
12

OKAY, WE MADE IT... BUT WHERE DO WE RIDE TO?

THE MAP SAYS:

"NOW PEDDLE YOUR WAY TO A LADDER UP AND A RAMP DOWN AND EVERYONE RIDES FROM THE TOP TO THE GROUND!"

HUH?

WHERE COULD THAT BE?

HEY, ARCHIE... CAN I SEE THE MAP PAPER REAL QUICK?

SURE!

A LADDER AND A RAMP? HMMM...

I GOT IT!!

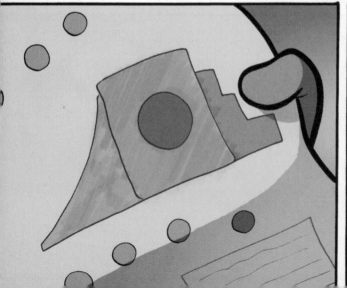

THE SLIDE!

13

TO THE SLIDE!

IT SAYS TO GO FROM TOP TO BOTTOM ONLY 1+1 TIMES.

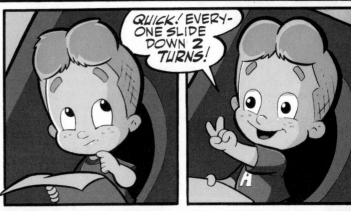

QUICK! EVERY-ONE SLIDE DOWN 2 TURNS!

WHEW! THAT WAS FUN!

YOU THINK THAT WAS FUN? LISTEN TO THIS!

14

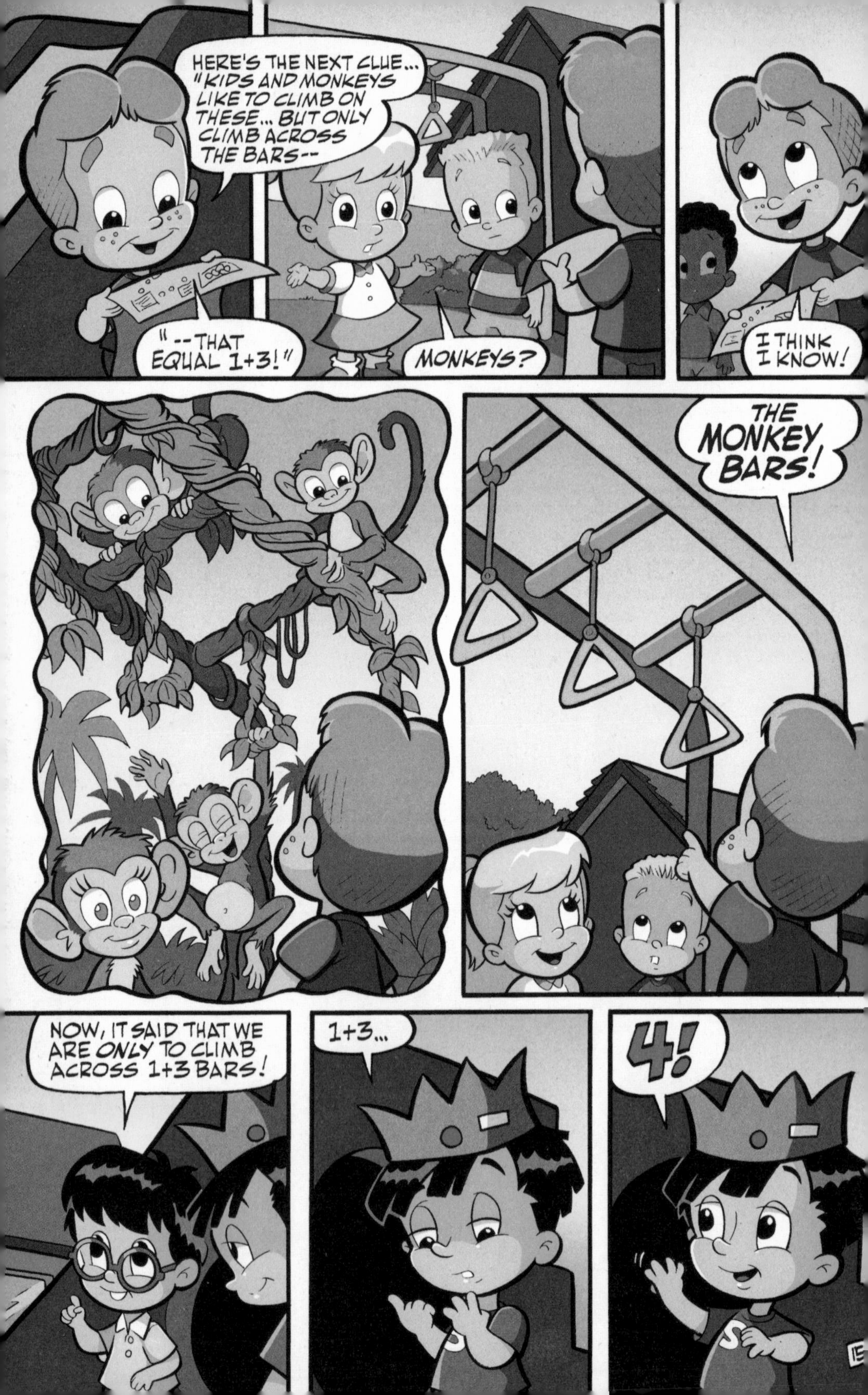
HERE'S THE NEXT CLUE... "KIDS AND MONKEYS LIKE TO CLIMB ON THESE... BUT ONLY CLIMB ACROSS THE BARS--
"--THAT EQUAL 1+3!"
MONKEYS?
I THINK I KNOW!
THE MONKEY BARS!
NOW, IT SAID THAT WE ARE ONLY TO CLIMB ACROSS 1+3 BARS!
1+3...
4!

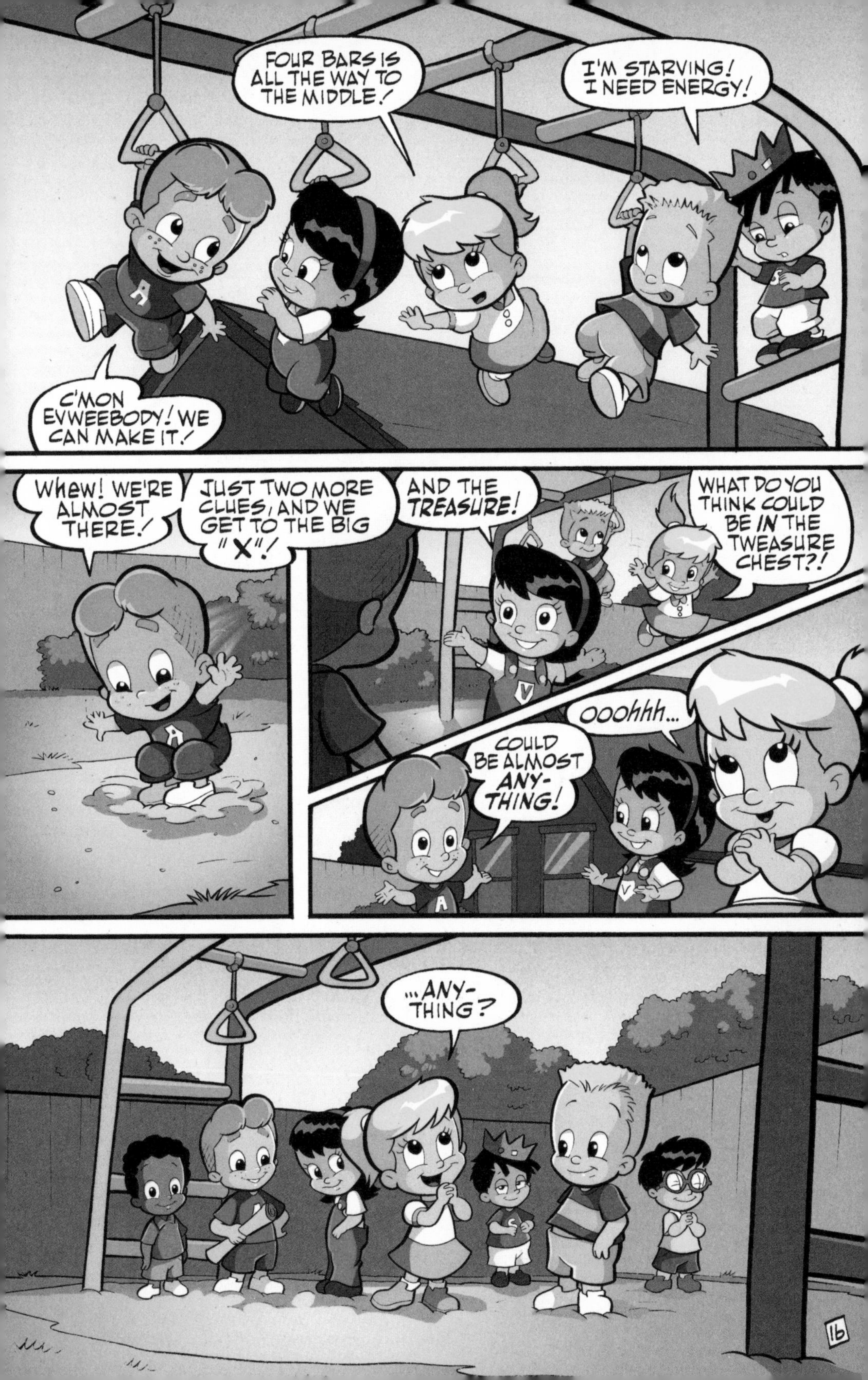
FOUR BARS IS ALL THE WAY TO THE MIDDLE!
I'M STARVING! I NEED ENERGY!
C'MON EVWEEBODY! WE CAN MAKE IT!
Whew! WE'RE ALMOST THERE!
JUST TWO MORE CLUES, AND WE GET TO THE BIG "X"!
AND THE TREASURE!
WHAT DO YOU THINK COULD BE IN THE TWEASURE CHEST?!
ooohhh...
COULD BE ALMOST ANY-THING!
...ANY-THING?
16

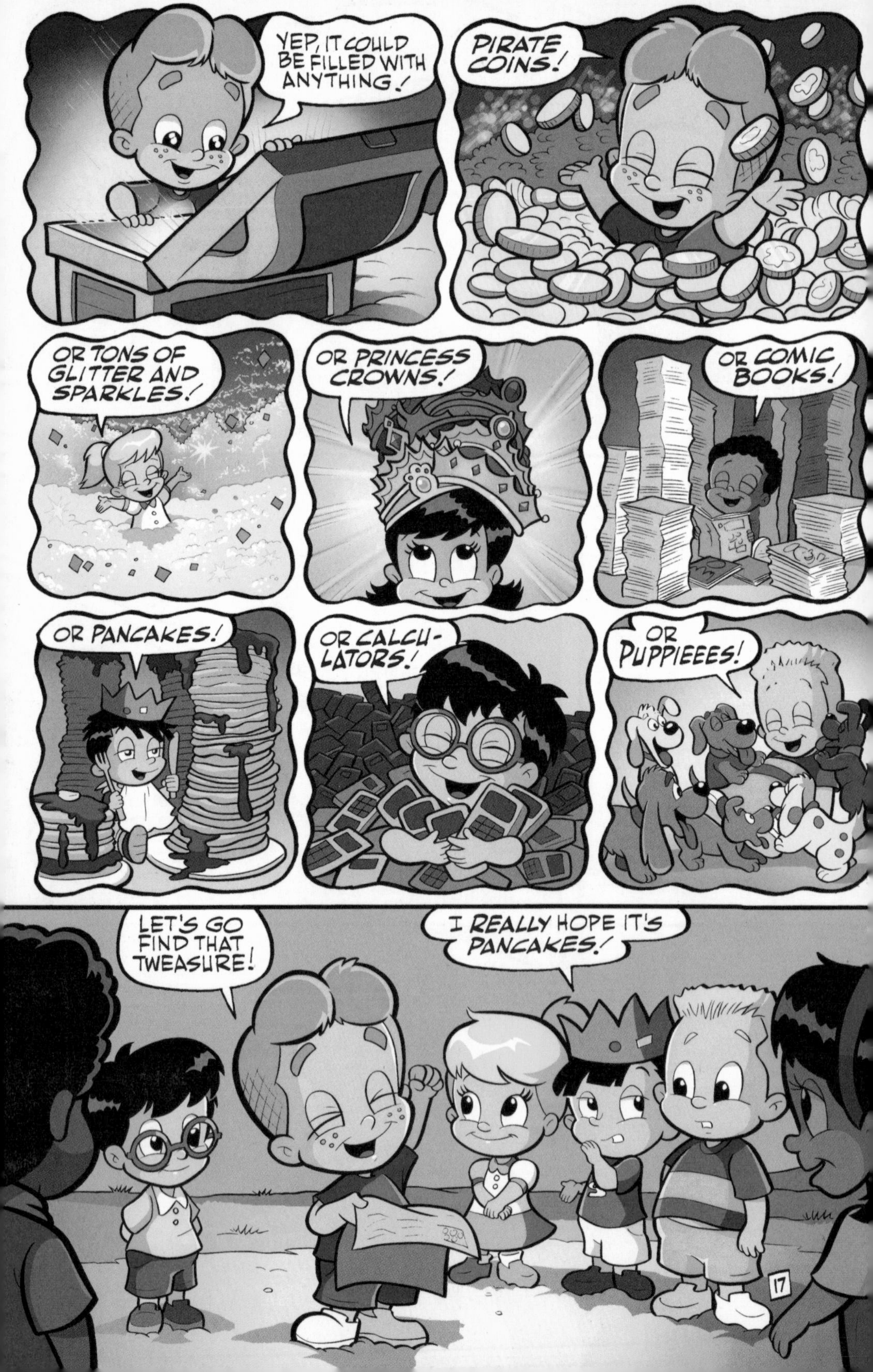

YEP, IT COULD BE FILLED WITH ANYTHING!
PIRATE COINS!
OR TONS OF GLITTER AND SPARKLES!
OR PRINCESS CROWNS!
OR COMIC BOOKS!
OR PANCAKES!
OR CALCU-LATORS!
OR PUPPIEEES!
LET'S GO FIND THAT TWEASURE!
I REALLY HOPE IT'S PANCAKES!

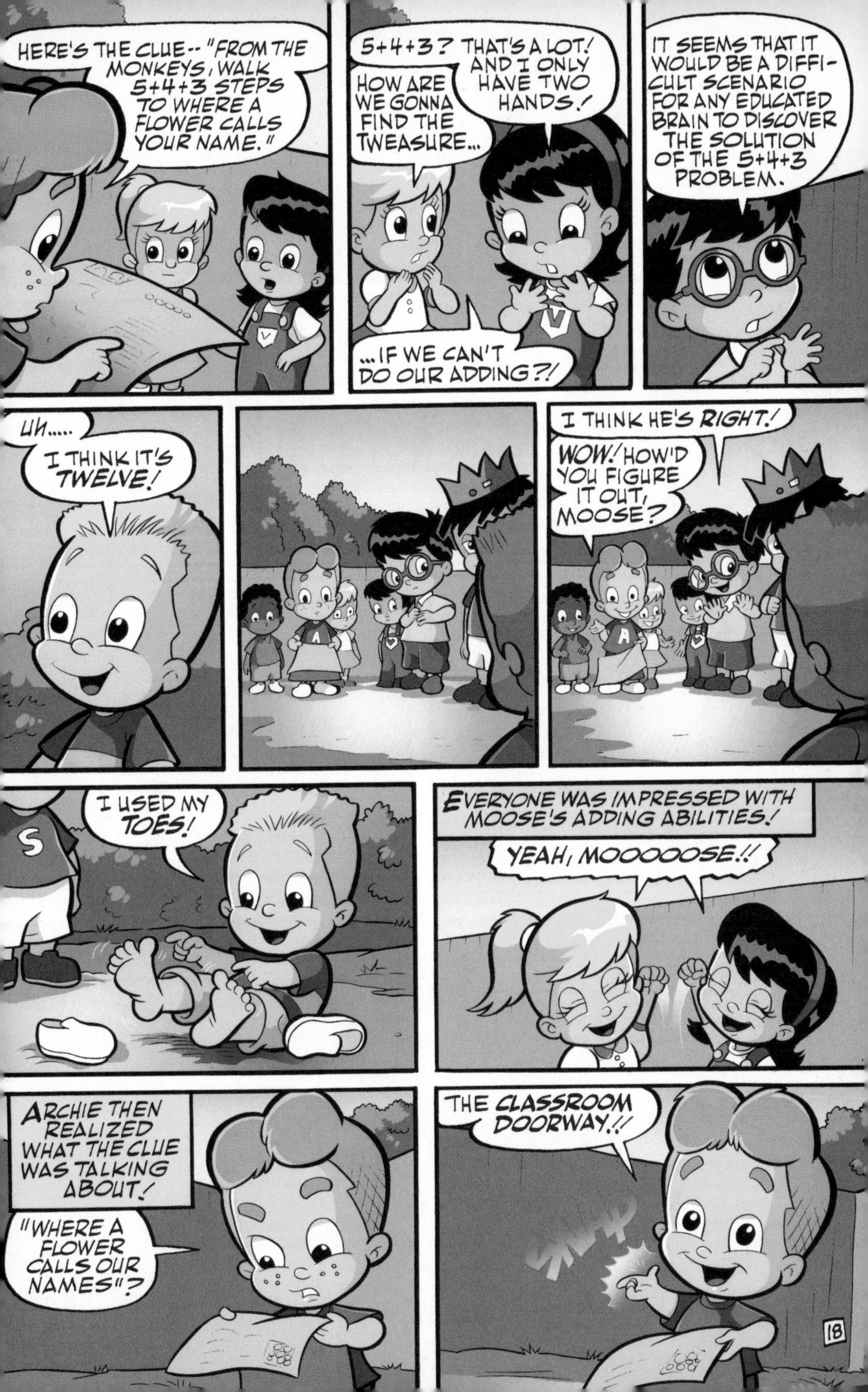
HERE'S THE CLUE-- "FROM THE MONKEYS, WALK 5+4+3 STEPS TO WHERE A FLOWER CALLS YOUR NAME."
5+4+3? THAT'S A LOT! AND I ONLY HAVE TWO HANDS!
HOW ARE WE GONNA FIND THE TWEASURE...
...IF WE CAN'T DO OUR ADDING?!
IT SEEMS THAT IT WOULD BE A DIFFI-CULT SCENARIO FOR ANY EDUCATED BRAIN TO DISCOVER THE SOLUTION OF THE 5+4+3 PROBLEM.
UH.....
I THINK IT'S TWELVE!
I THINK HE'S RIGHT!
WOW! HOW'D YOU FIGURE IT OUT, MOOSE?
I USED MY TOES!
EVERYONE WAS IMPRESSED WITH MOOSE'S ADDING ABILITIES!
YEAH, MOOOOOSE!!
ARCHIE THEN REALIZED WHAT THE CLUE WAS TALKING ABOUT!
"WHERE A FLOWER CALLS OUR NAMES"?
THE CLASSROOM DOORWAY!!
SNAP
18

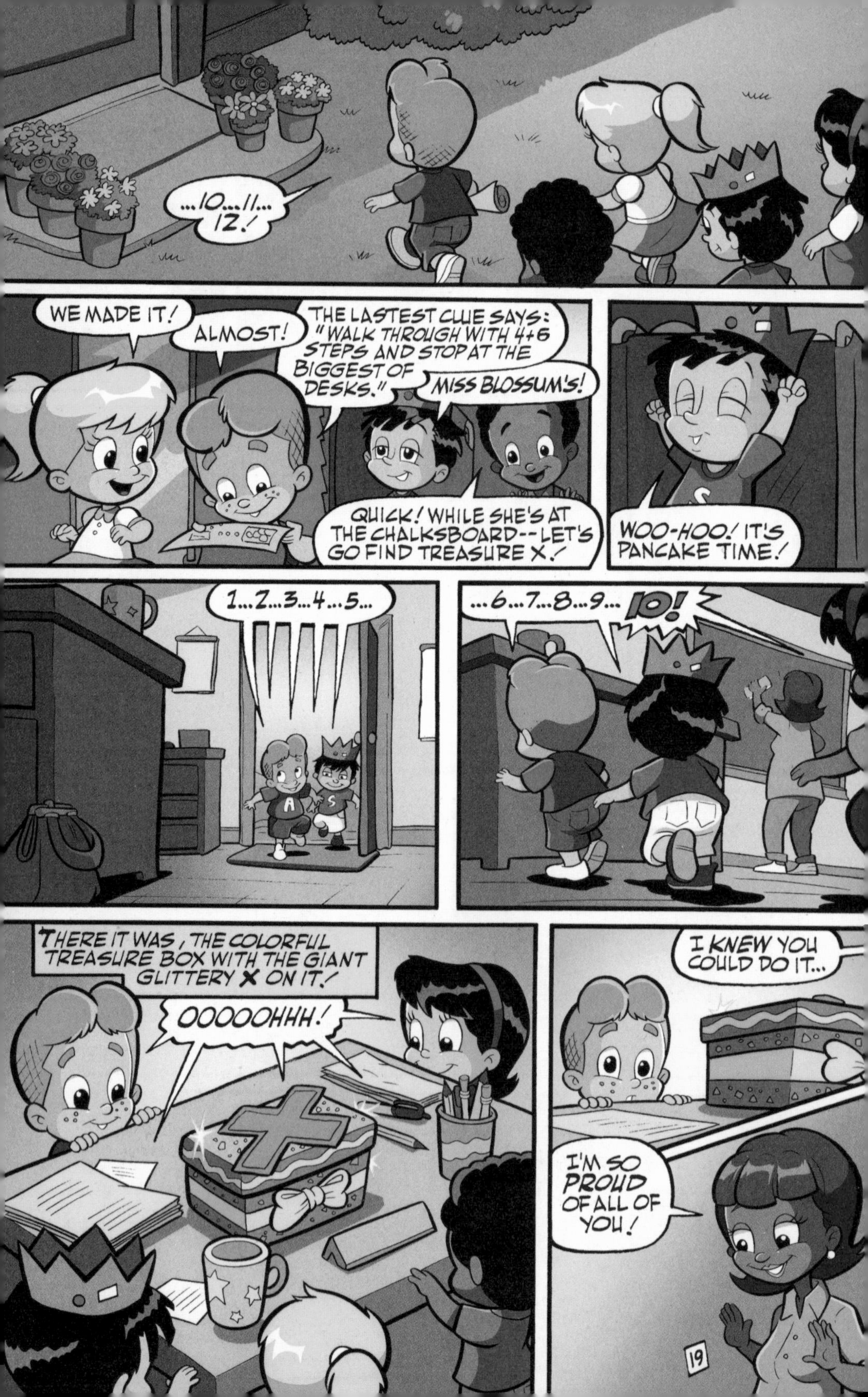
...10...11...12!
WE MADE IT!
ALMOST!
THE LASTEST CLUE SAYS: "WALK THROUGH WITH 4+6 STEPS AND STOP AT THE BIGGEST OF DESKS."
MISS BLOSSUM'S!
QUICK! WHILE SHE'S AT THE CHALKSBOARD--LET'S GO FIND TREASURE X!
WOO-HOO! IT'S PANCAKE TIME!
1...2...3...4...5...
...6...7...8...9... 10!
THERE IT WAS, THE COLORFUL TREASURE BOX WITH THE GIANT GLITTERY X ON IT!
OOOOOHHH!
I KNEW YOU COULD DO IT...
I'M SO PROUD OF ALL OF YOU!
19

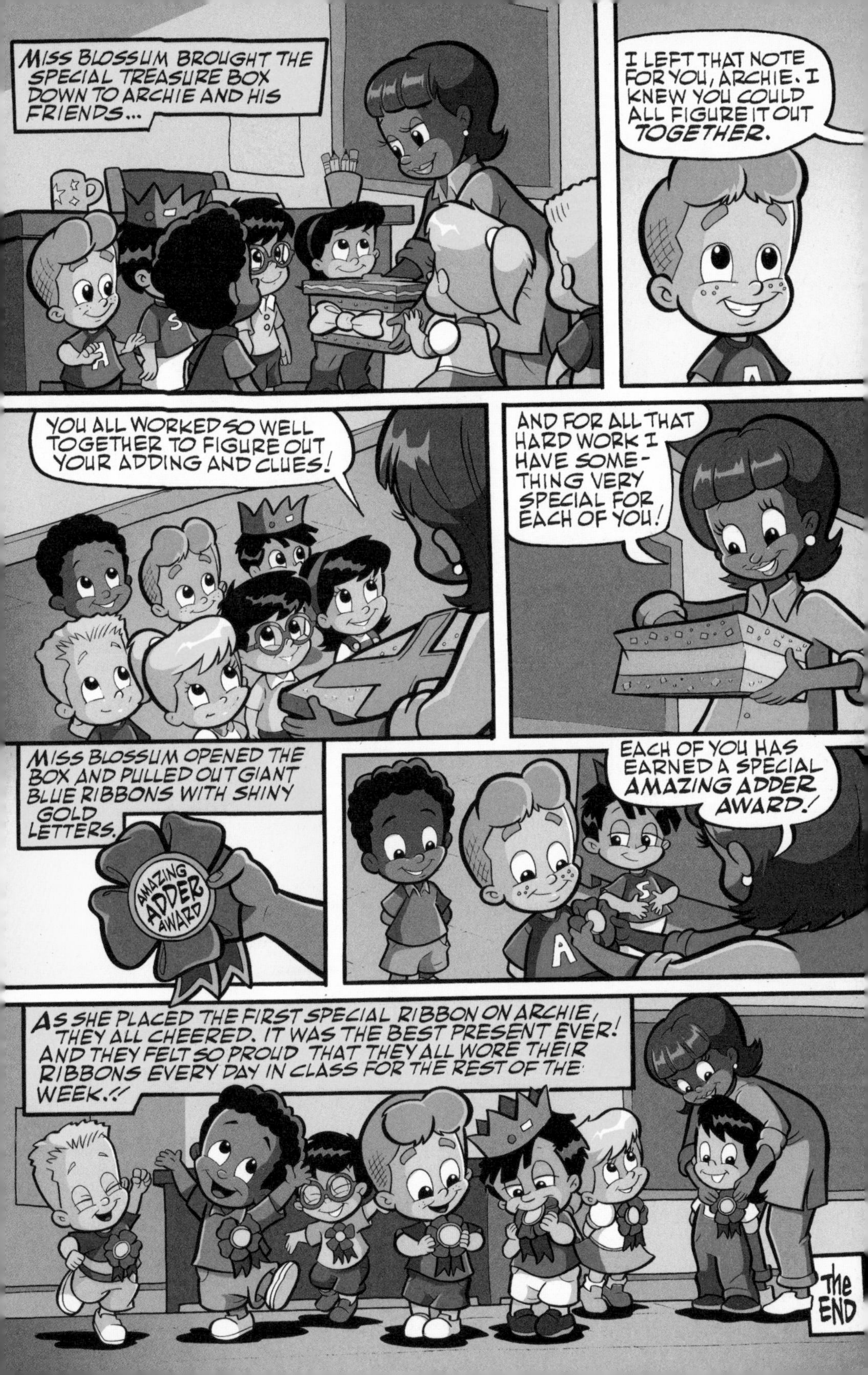
MISS BLOSSUM BROUGHT THE SPECIAL TREASURE BOX DOWN TO ARCHIE AND HIS FRIENDS...
I LEFT THAT NOTE FOR YOU, ARCHIE. I KNEW YOU COULD ALL FIGURE IT OUT TOGETHER.
YOU ALL WORKED SO WELL TOGETHER TO FIGURE OUT YOUR ADDING AND CLUES!
AND FOR ALL THAT HARD WORK I HAVE SOME-THING VERY SPECIAL FOR EACH OF YOU!
MISS BLOSSUM OPENED THE BOX AND PULLED OUT GIANT BLUE RIBBONS WITH SHINY GOLD LETTERS.
AMAZING ADDER AWARD
EACH OF YOU HAS EARNED A SPECIAL AMAZING ADDER AWARD!
AS SHE PLACED THE FIRST SPECIAL RIBBON ON ARCHIE, THEY ALL CHEERED. IT WAS THE BEST PRESENT EVER! AND THEY FELT SO PROUD THAT THEY ALL WORE THEIR RIBBONS EVERY DAY IN CLASS FOR THE REST OF THE WEEK.!!
The END

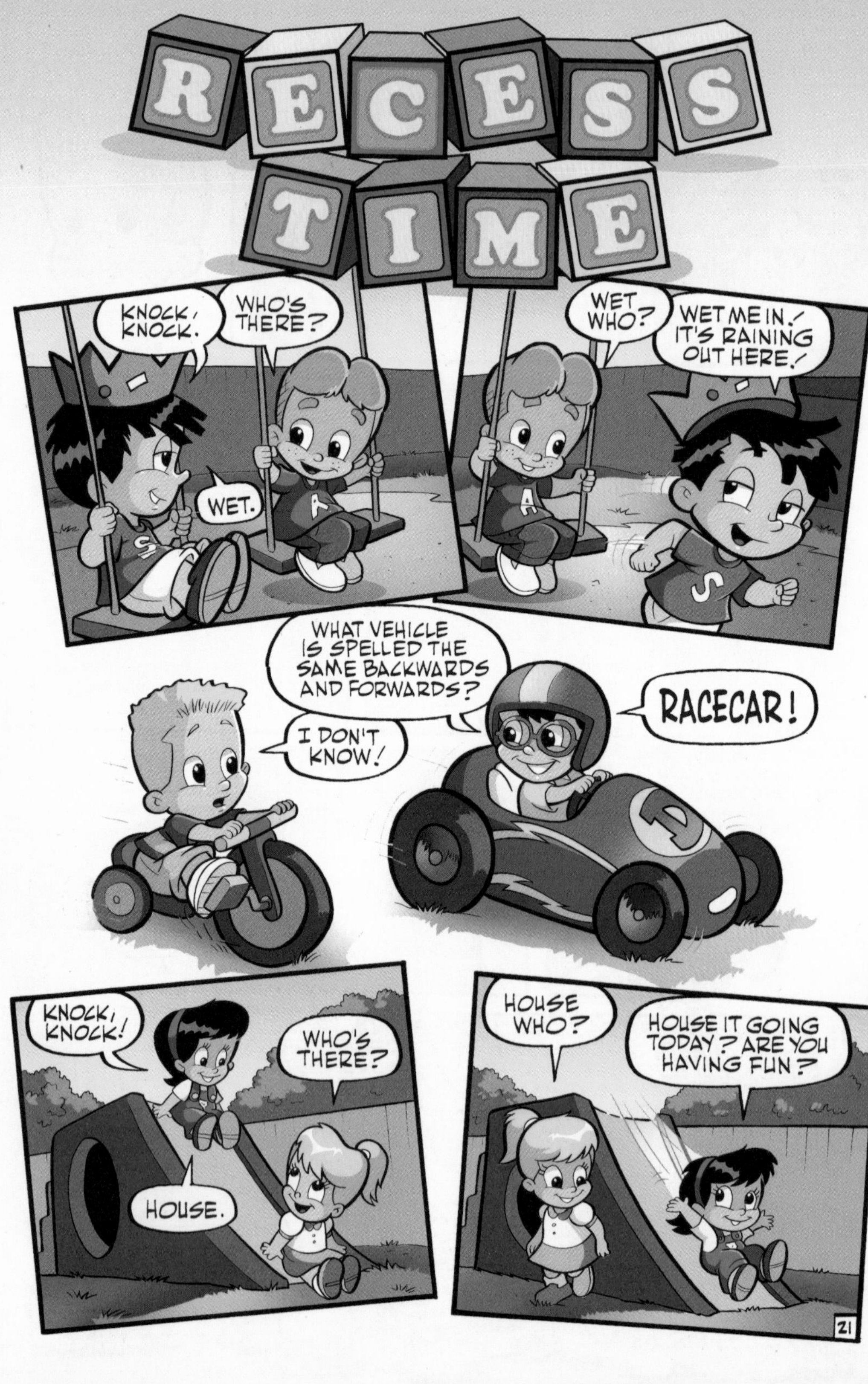
RECESS TIME
KNOCK, KNOCK.
WHO'S THERE?
WET.
WET WHO?
WET ME IN! IT'S RAINING OUT HERE!
WHAT VEHICLE IS SPELLED THE SAME BACKWARDS AND FORWARDS?
I DON'T KNOW!
RACECAR!
KNOCK, KNOCK!
WHO'S THERE?
HOUSE.
HOUSE WHO?
HOUSE IT GOING TODAY? ARE YOU HAVING FUN?

MAKE YOUR OWN TREASURE HUNT

LIST of SUPPLIES

- 1 PENCIL
- 1 GIANT PIECE OF PAPER
- 1 BIG "X" CUT OUT OF CARD-BOARD (MAKE SURE YOUR PARENTS HELP YOU WITH THE CUTTING!)
- 2 LONG PIECES OF RED RIBBON
- 1 PLASTIC ZIP-LOCK BAG
- 10 PENNIES

INSTRUCTIONS

- PUT THE PENNIES IN THE ZIPLOCK BAG AND TIE THE RIBBON AROUND IT...
- HIDE THE BAG IN YOUR BACK YARD BY A PLANT OR A TREE...
- PLACE THE CARDBOARD "X" OVER THE PENNIES...
- DRAW A TREE ON YOUR PAPER...
- DRAW AN "X" NEXT TO THE TREE. THIS IS WHERE YOUR TREASURE IS...
- COUNT HOW MANY STEPS IT TAKES TO WALK FROM THE TREE TO YOUR REFRIGERATOR...
- DRAW A RECTANGLE TO BE YOUR REFRIGERATOR IN THE MIDDLE OF THE PAPER... DRAW A LINE FROM THE "X" TO THE RECTANGLE, AND WRITE THE NUMBER OF STEPS ALONGSIDE IT...
- DRAW A BOX AT THE BOTTOM OF THE PAPER AND WRITE "TV" IN IT... COUNT THE STEPS FROM YOUR REFRIGERATOR TO YOUR TV...
- DRAW A LINE FROM THE "REFRIGERATOR" TO THE "TV" AND WRITE THE NUMBER OF STEPS NEXT TO THE LINE...

FINALLY!

ROLL UP THE PAPER AND TIE A RIBBON AROUND IT AND GIVE IT TO YOUR PARENTS, SIBLINGS OR FRIENDS AND SEE IF THEY CAN *FIND THE TREASURE!*

The GREAT LION HUNT!

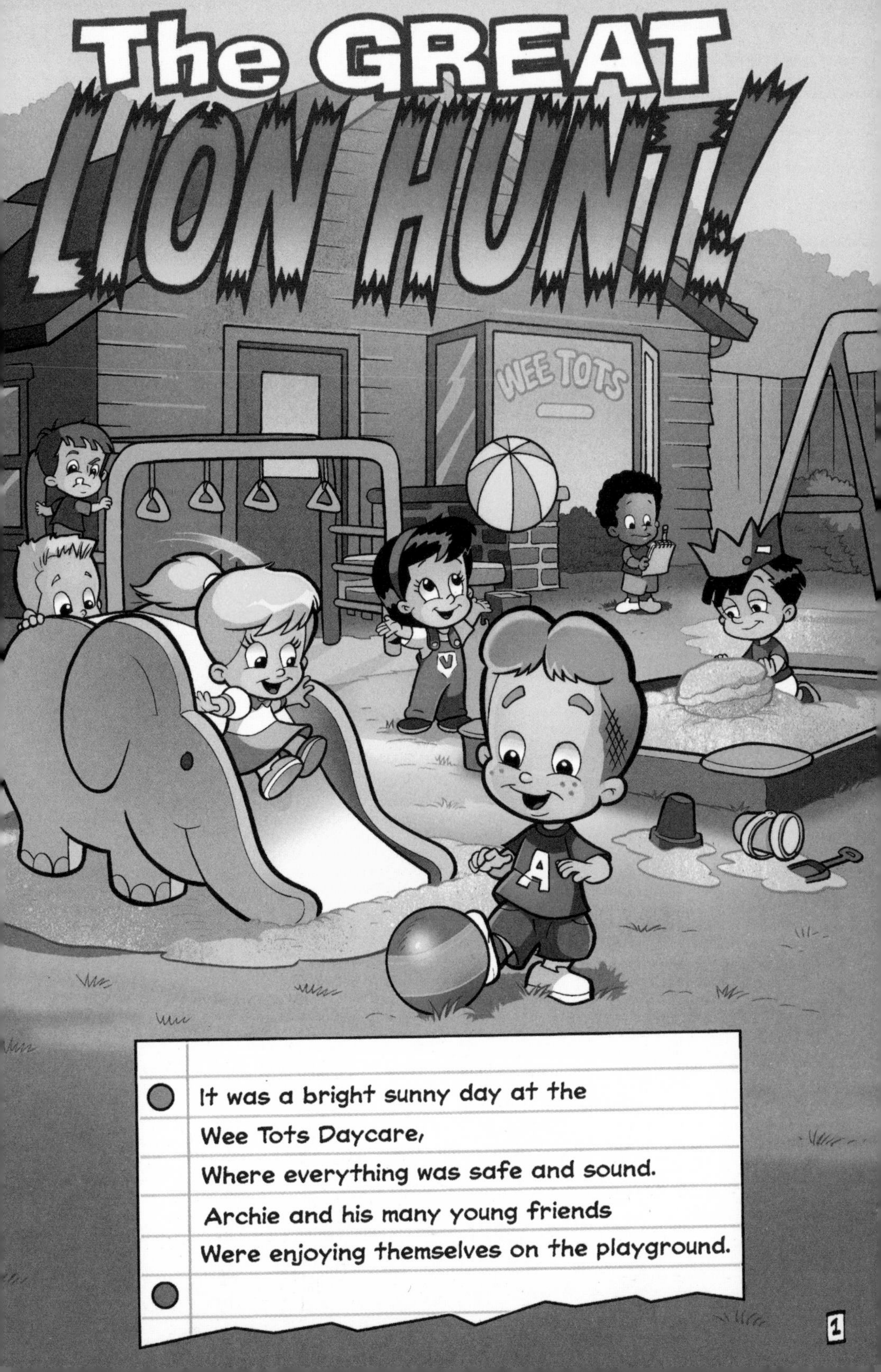
WEE TOTS

It was a bright sunny day at the
Wee Tots Daycare,
Where everything was safe and sound.
Archie and his many young friends
Were enjoying themselves on the playground.

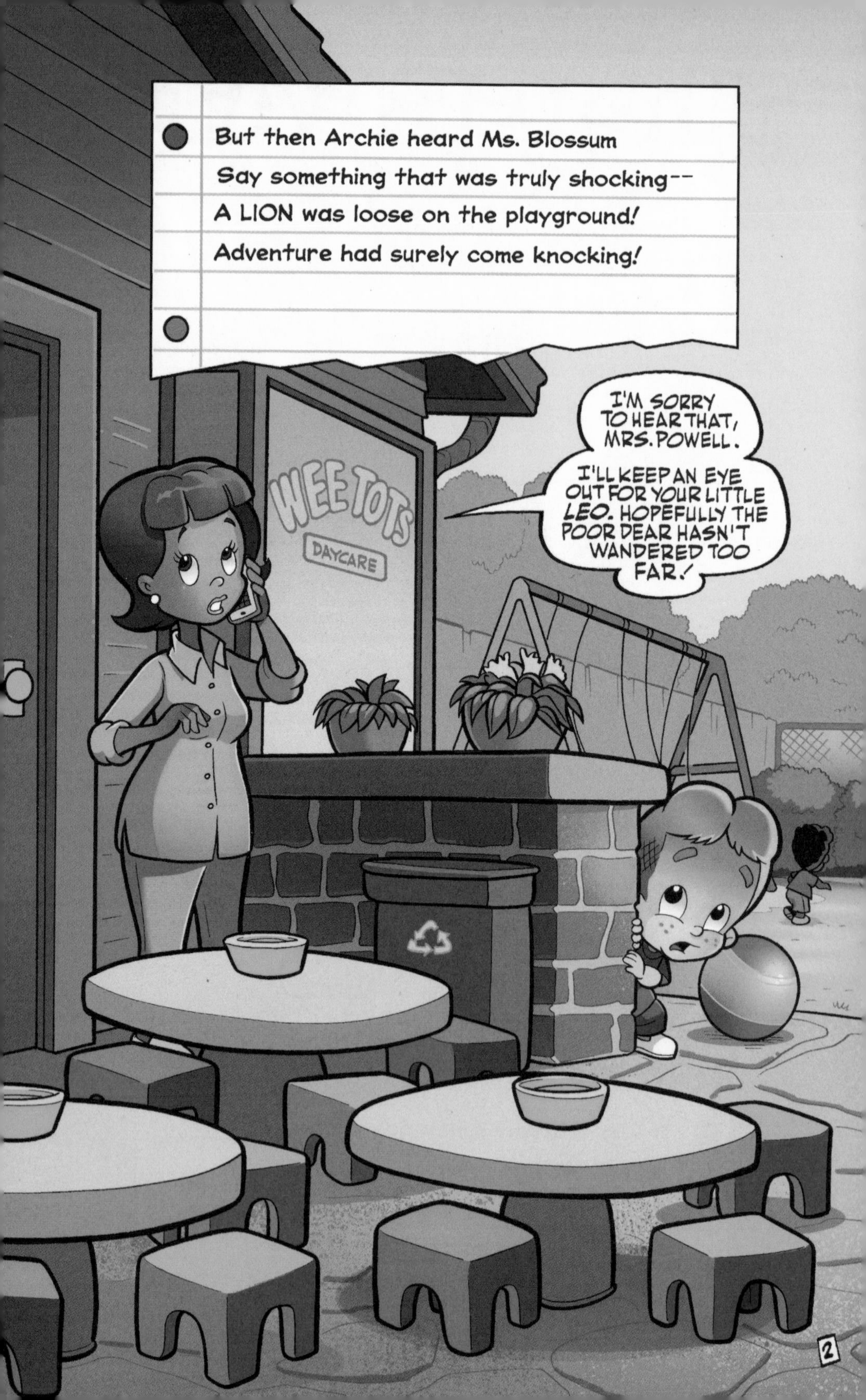
But then Archie heard Ms. Blossum
Say something that was truly shocking--
A LION was loose on the playground!
Adventure had surely come knocking!
WEE TOTS
DAYCARE
I'M SORRY TO HEAR THAT, MRS. POWELL.
I'LL KEEP AN EYE OUT FOR YOUR LITTLE LEO. HOPEFULLY THE POOR DEAR HASN'T WANDERED TOO FAR!
2

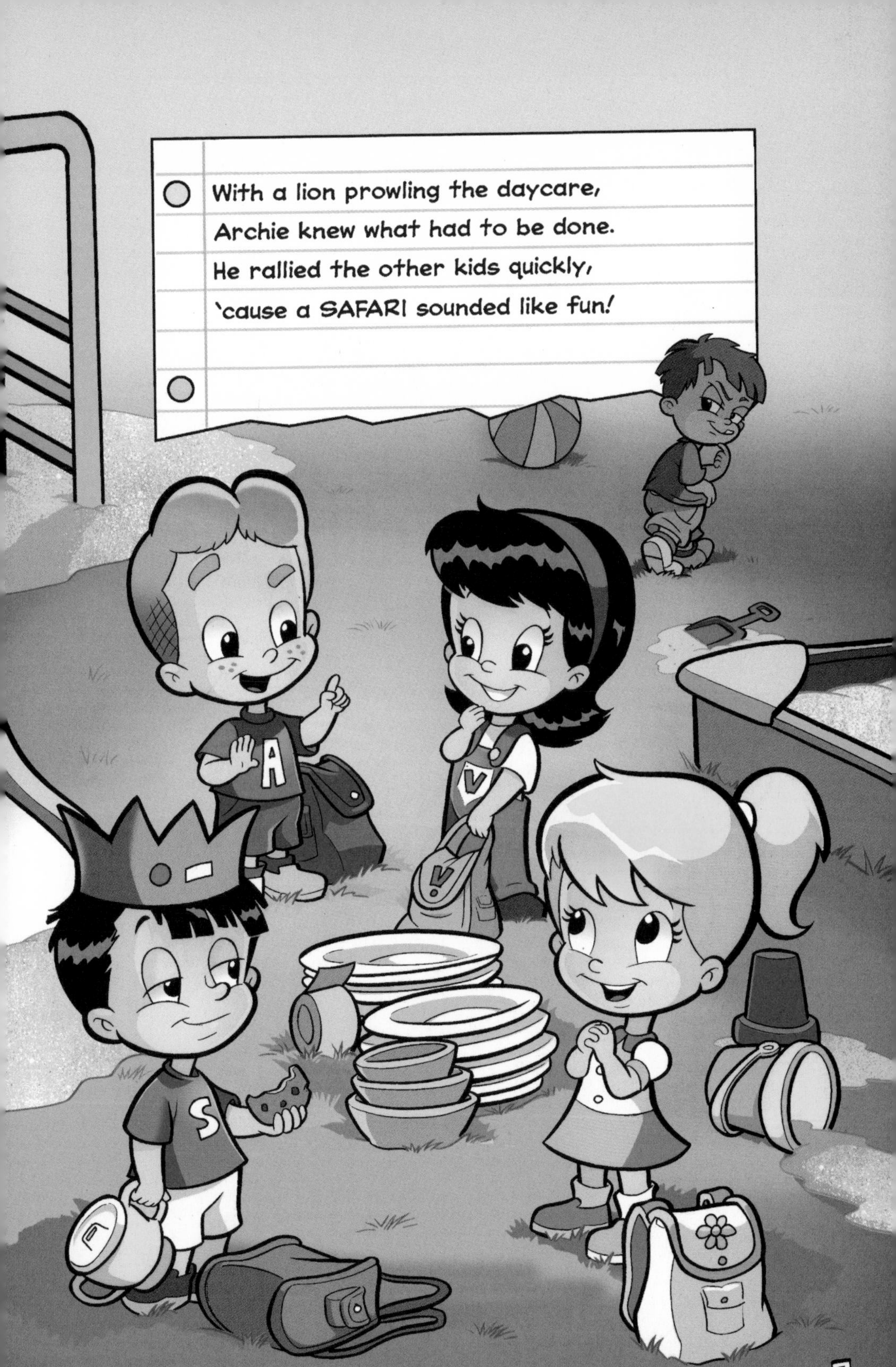
With a lion prowling the daycare,
Archie knew what had to be done.
He rallied the other kids quickly,
'cause a SAFARI sounded like fun!

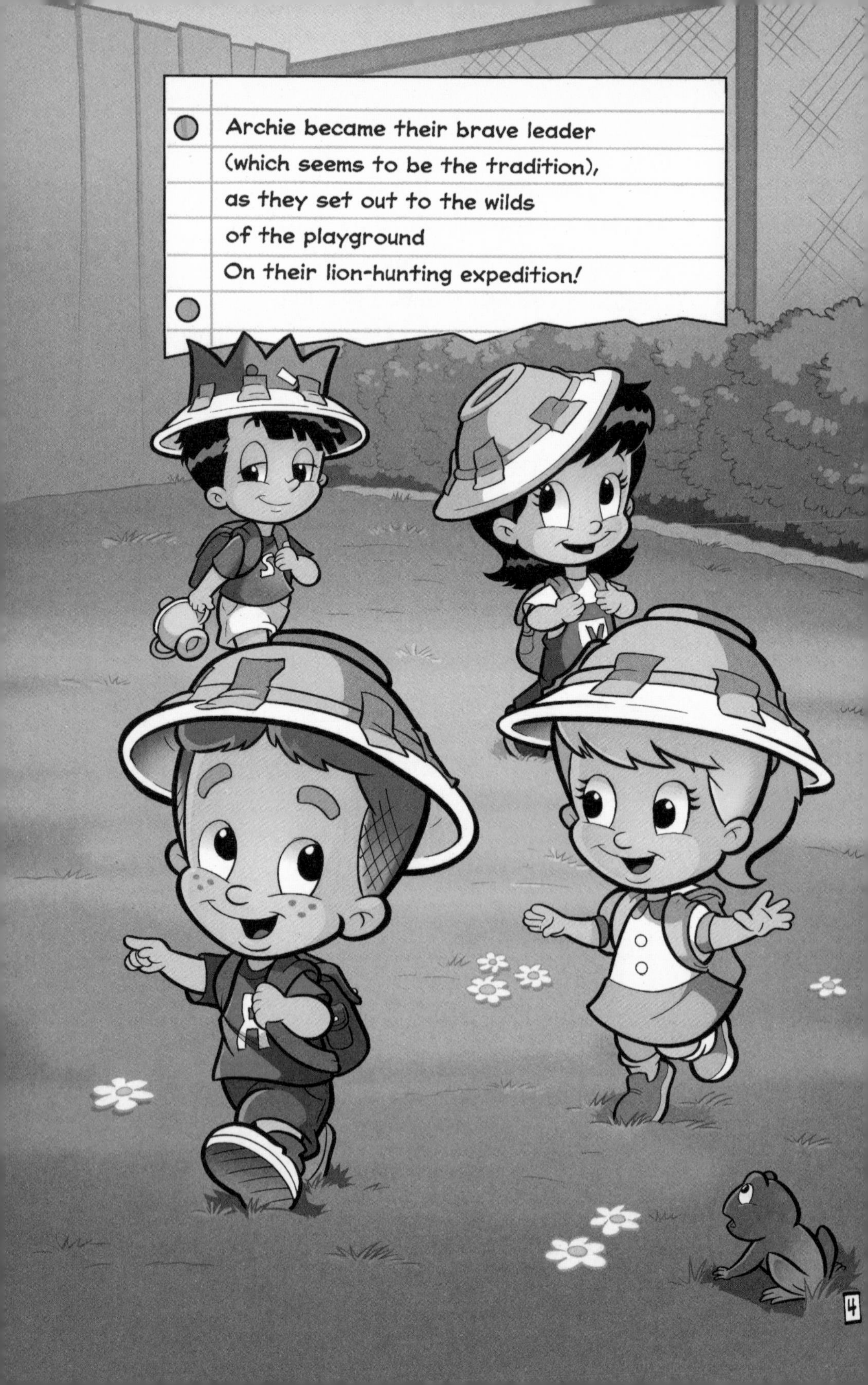
Archie became their brave leader
(which seems to be the tradition),
as they set out to the wilds
of the playground
On their lion-hunting expedition!

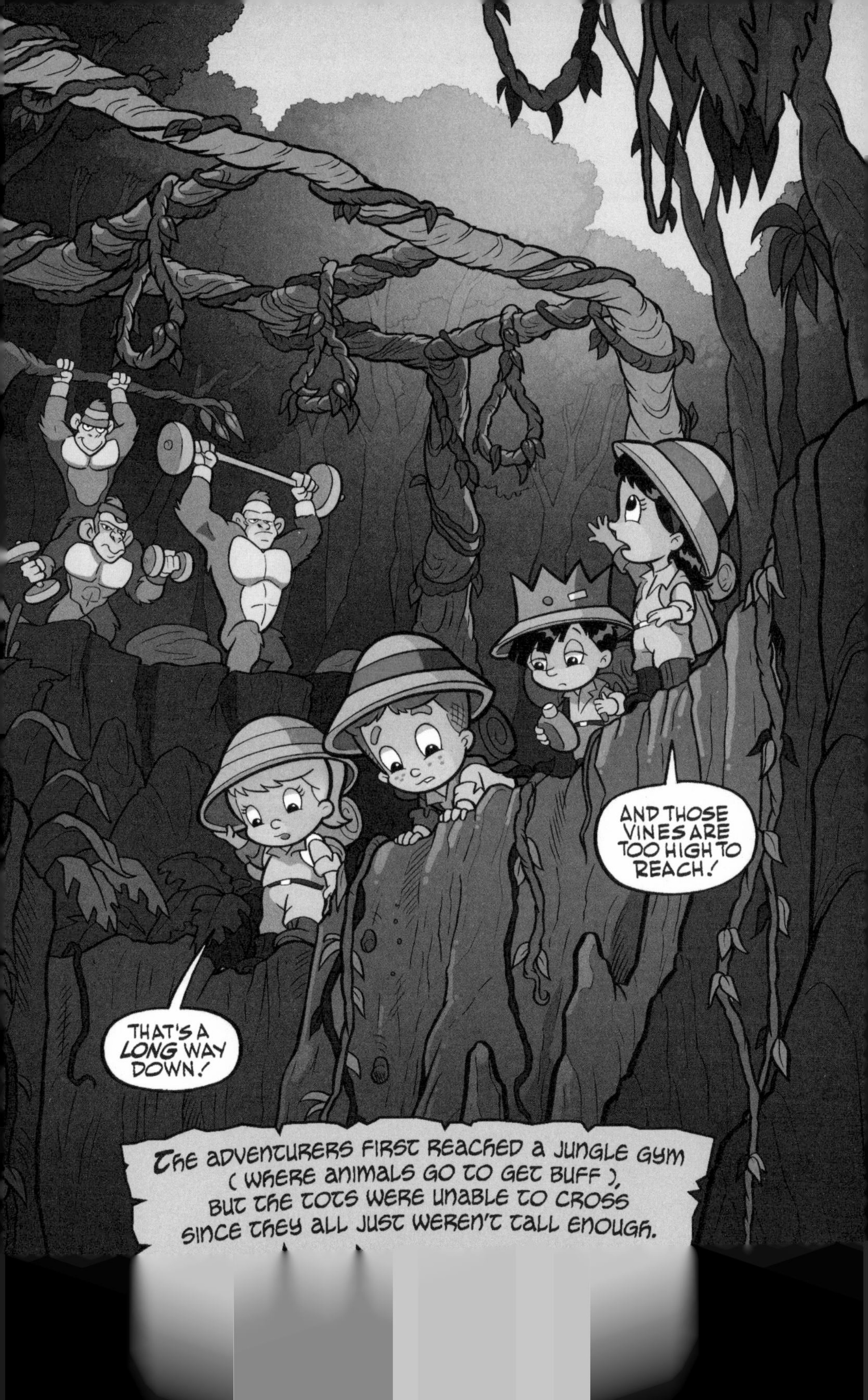
AND THOSE VINES ARE TOO HIGH TO REACH!
THAT'S A LONG WAY DOWN!
THE ADVENTURERS FIRST REACHED A JUNGLE GYM (WHERE ANIMALS GO TO GET BUFF), BUT THE TOTS WERE UNABLE TO CROSS SINCE THEY ALL JUST WEREN'T TALL ENOUGH.

But the kids knew they could help each other, and together they crossed over with ease. With the first jungle peril behind them, this lion hunt would be a BREEZE!

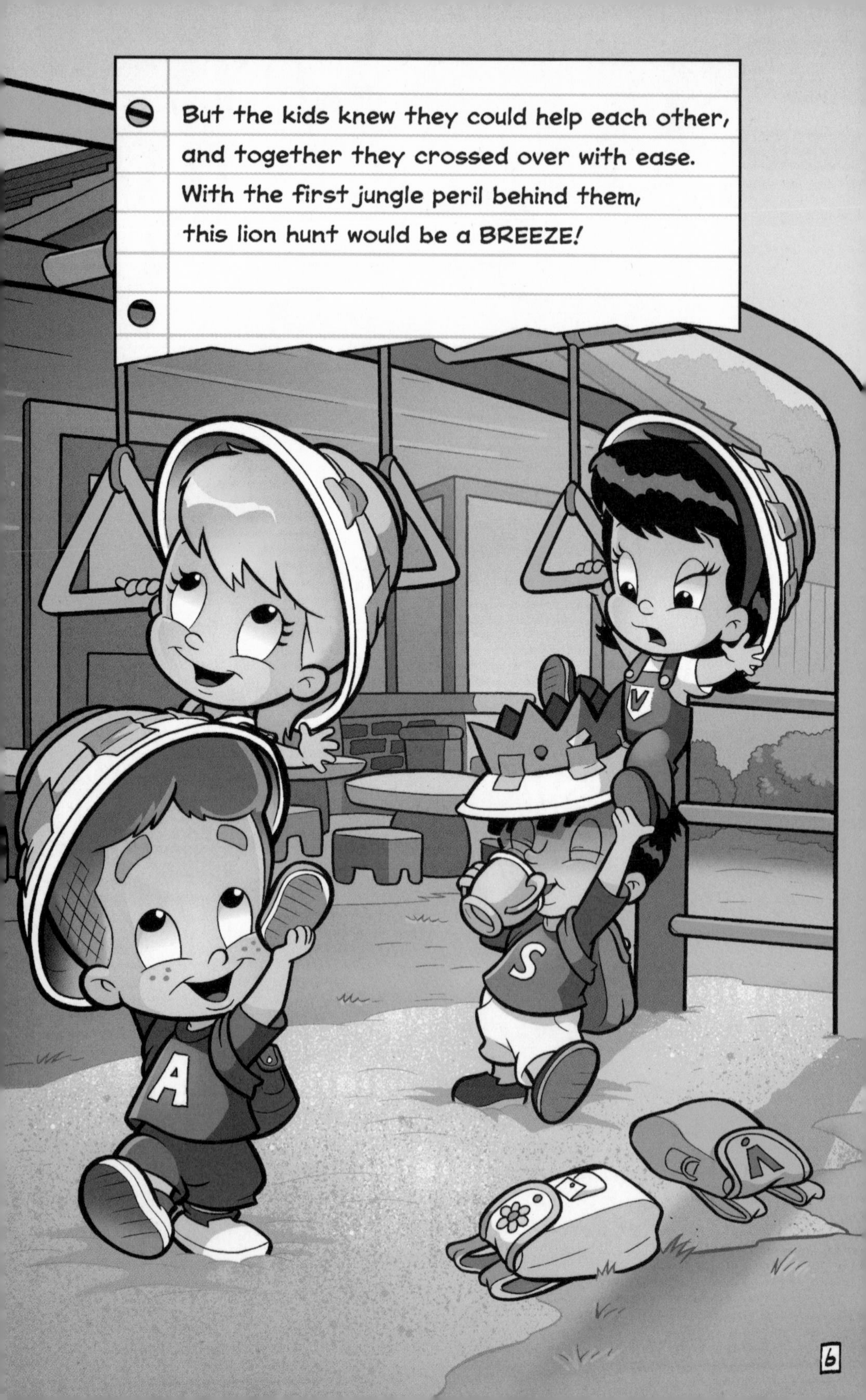

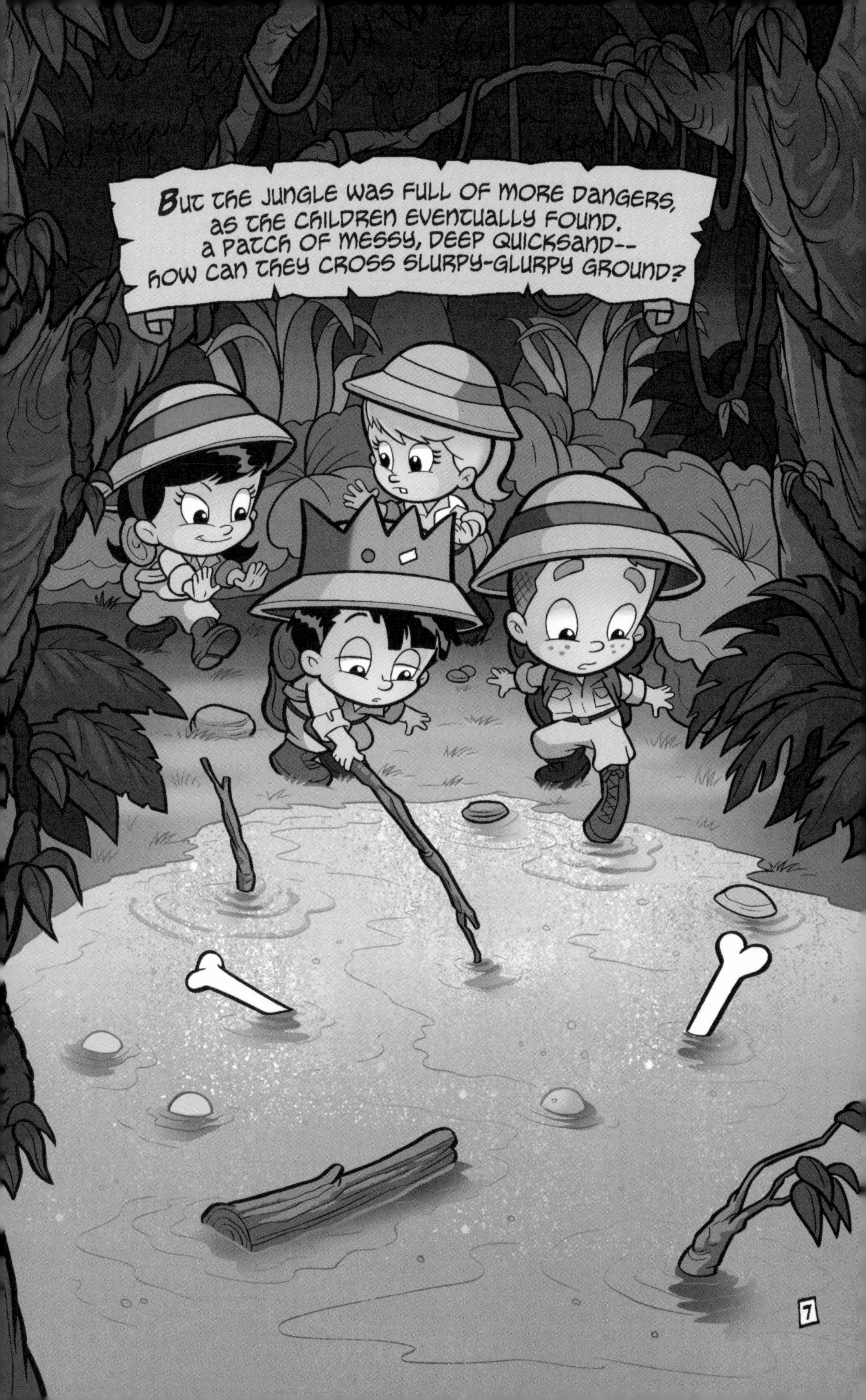
BUT THE JUNGLE WAS FULL OF MORE DANGERS,
AS THE CHILDREN EVENTUALLY FOUND.
A PATCH OF MESSY, DEEP QUICKSAND--
HOW CAN THEY CROSS SLURPY-GLURPY GROUND?

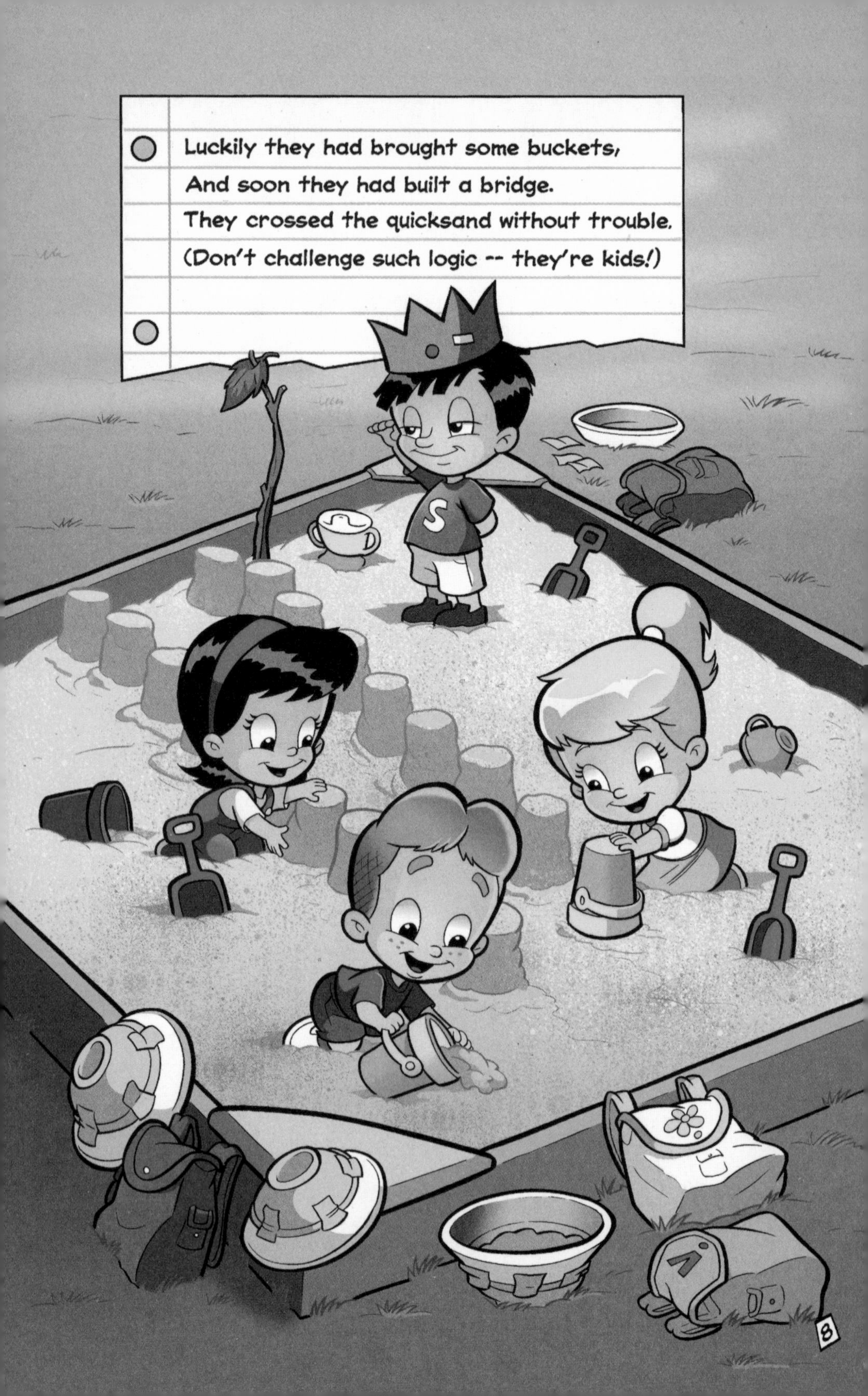
Luckily they had brought some buckets,
And soon they had built a bridge.
They crossed the quicksand without trouble.
(Don't challenge such logic -- they're kids!)

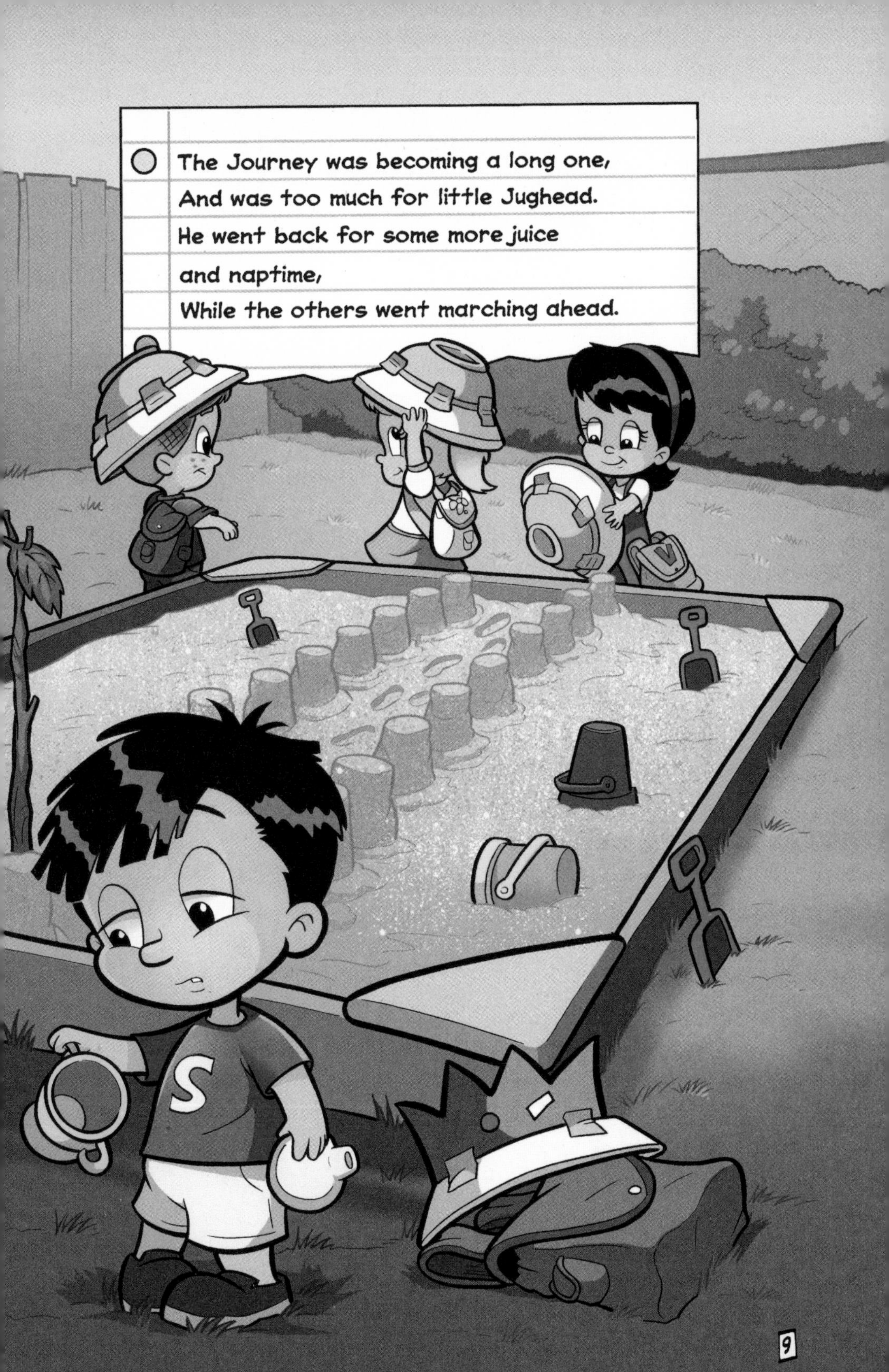
The Journey was becoming a long one,
And was too much for little Jughead.
He went back for some more juice
and naptime,
While the others went marching ahead.

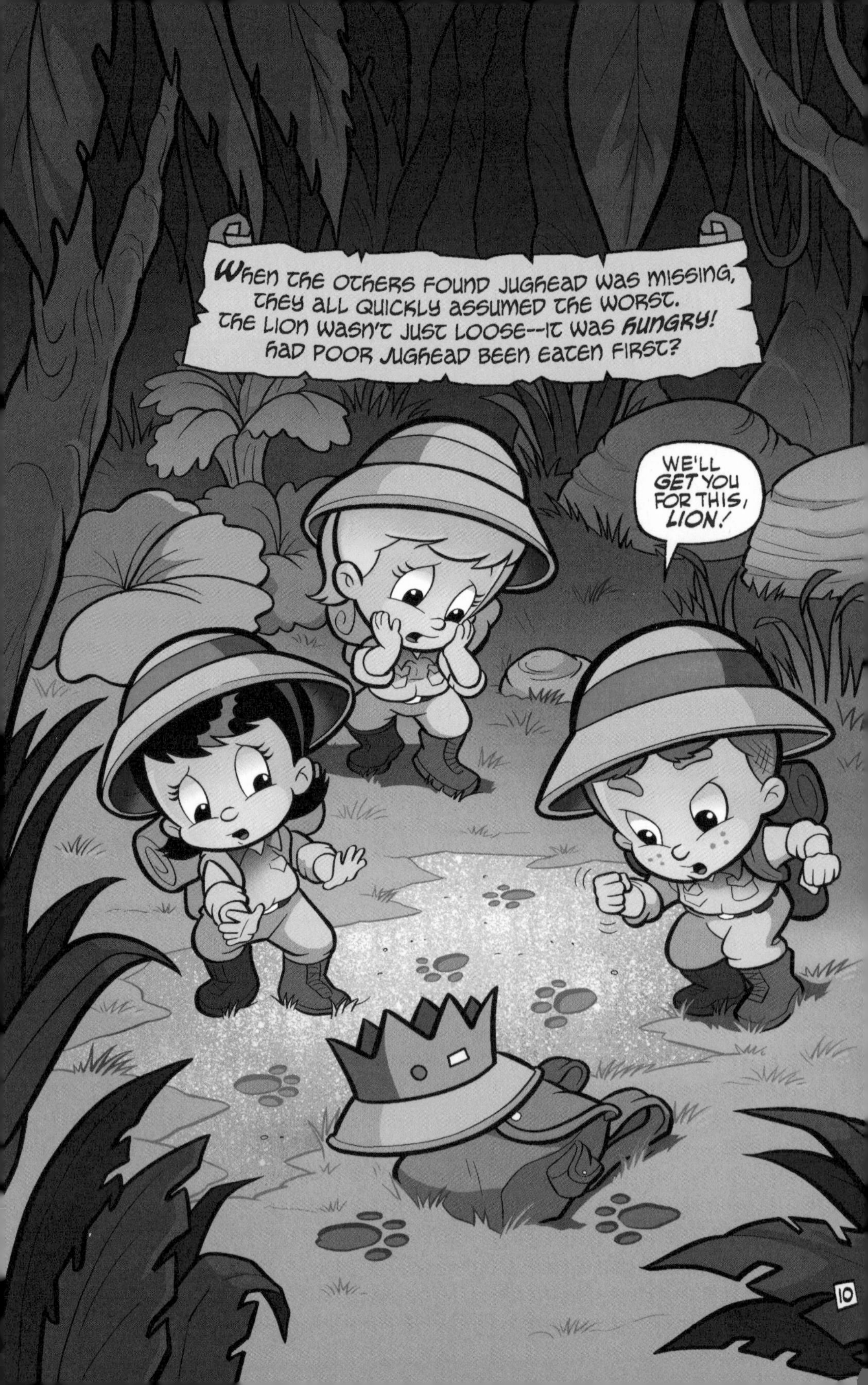
WHEN THE OTHERS FOUND JUGHEAD WAS MISSING, THEY ALL QUICKLY ASSUMED THE WORST. THE LION WASN'T JUST LOOSE--IT WAS HUNGRY! HAD POOR JUGHEAD BEEN EATEN FIRST?
WE'LL GET YOU FOR THIS, LION!
10

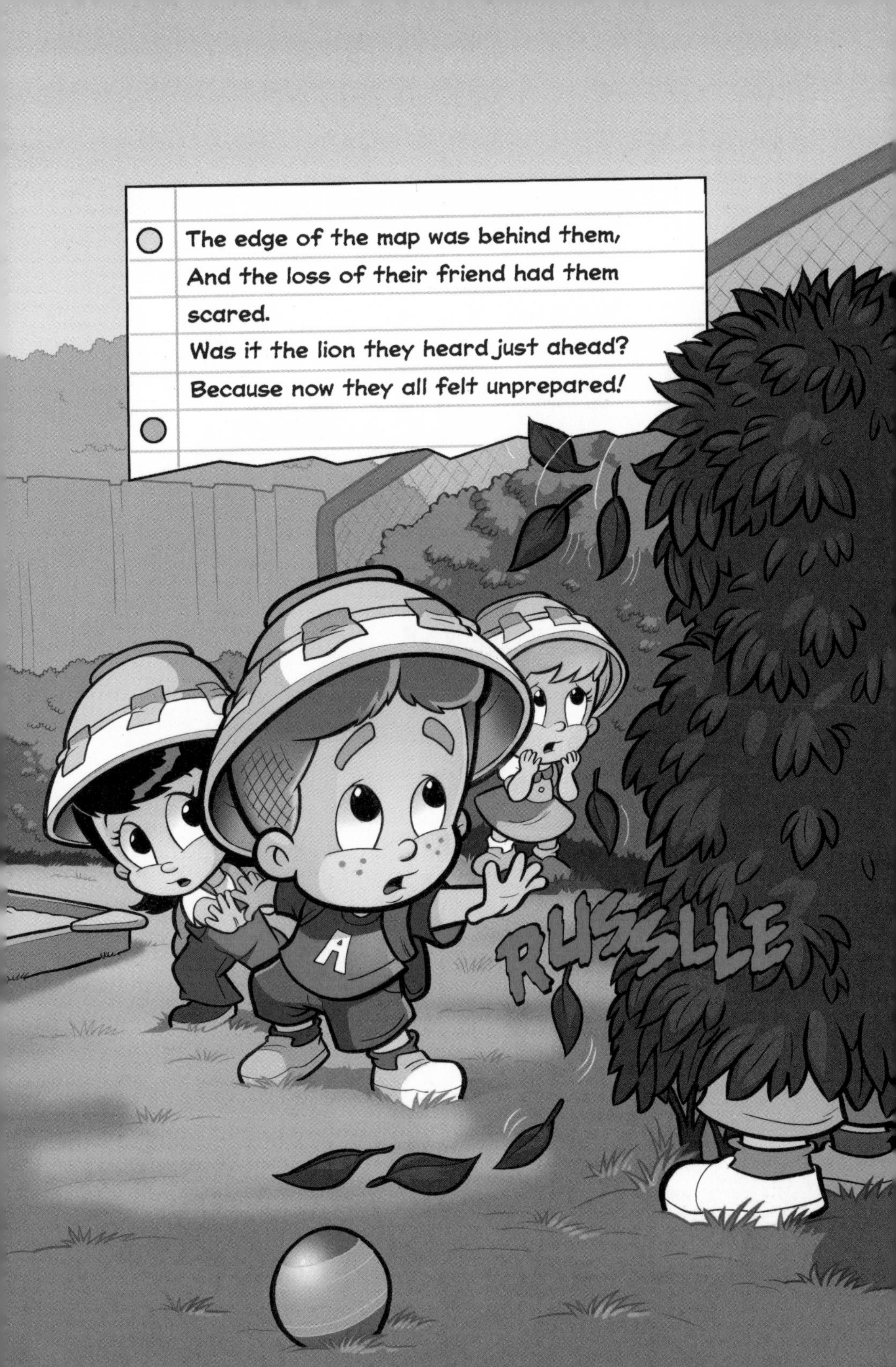
The edge of the map was behind them,
And the loss of their friend had them scared.
Was it the lion they heard just ahead?
Because now they all felt unprepared!
RUSSLLE

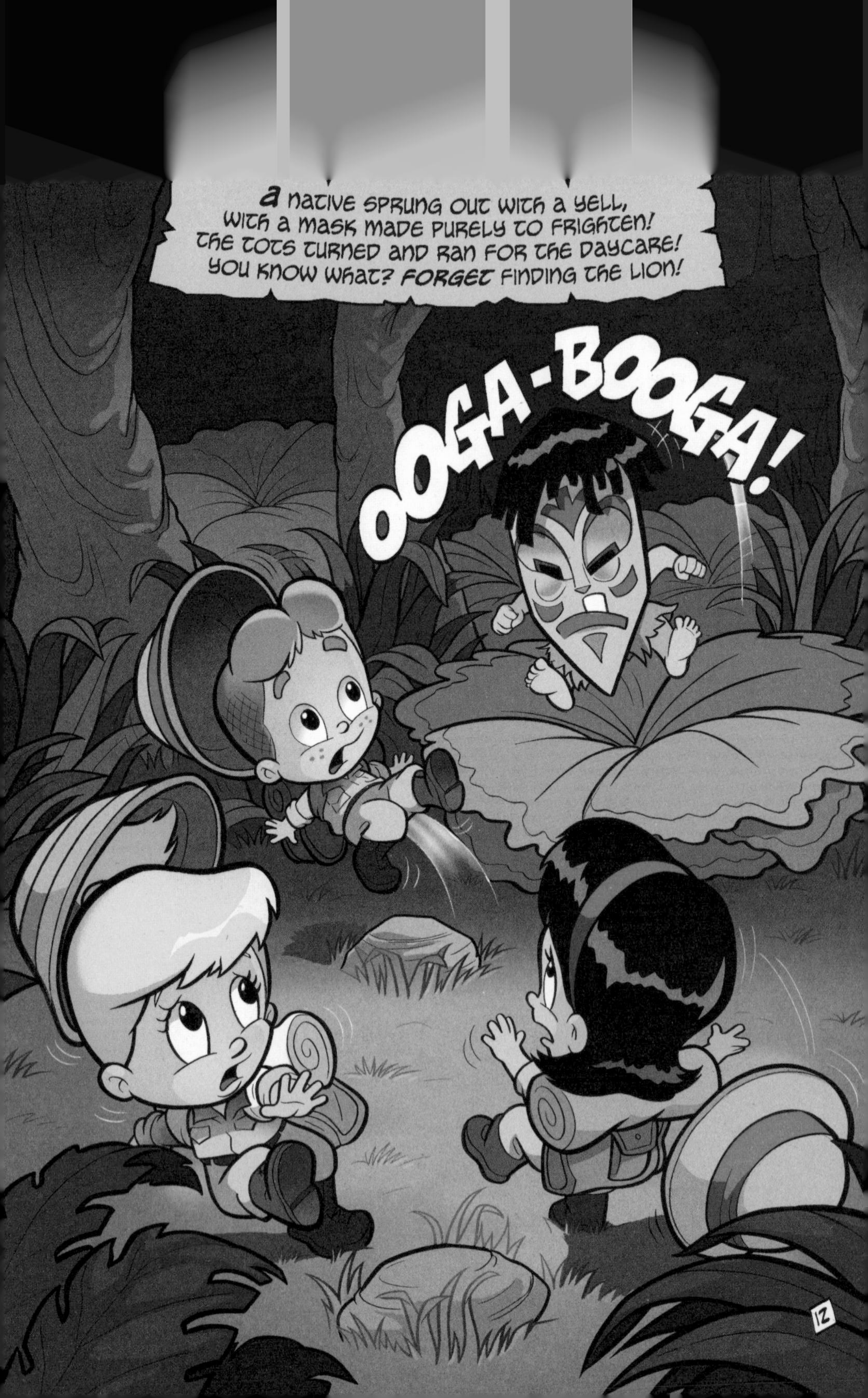
A NATIVE SPRUNG OUT WITH A YELL,
WITH A MASK MADE PURELY TO FRIGHTEN!
THE TOTS TURNED AND RAN FOR THE DAYCARE!
YOU KNOW WHAT? FORGET FINDING THE LION!
OOGA-BOOGA!

AND WHAT OF OUR BRAVE LEADER, ARCHIE?
WHY, HE RAN AHEAD AS A DECOY...
SO THE GIRLS COULD ESCAPE TO SAFETY.
(HOW BRAVE FOR SUCH A YOUNG BOY!)
BOOGA BOOGA BOOGA BOOGA!!

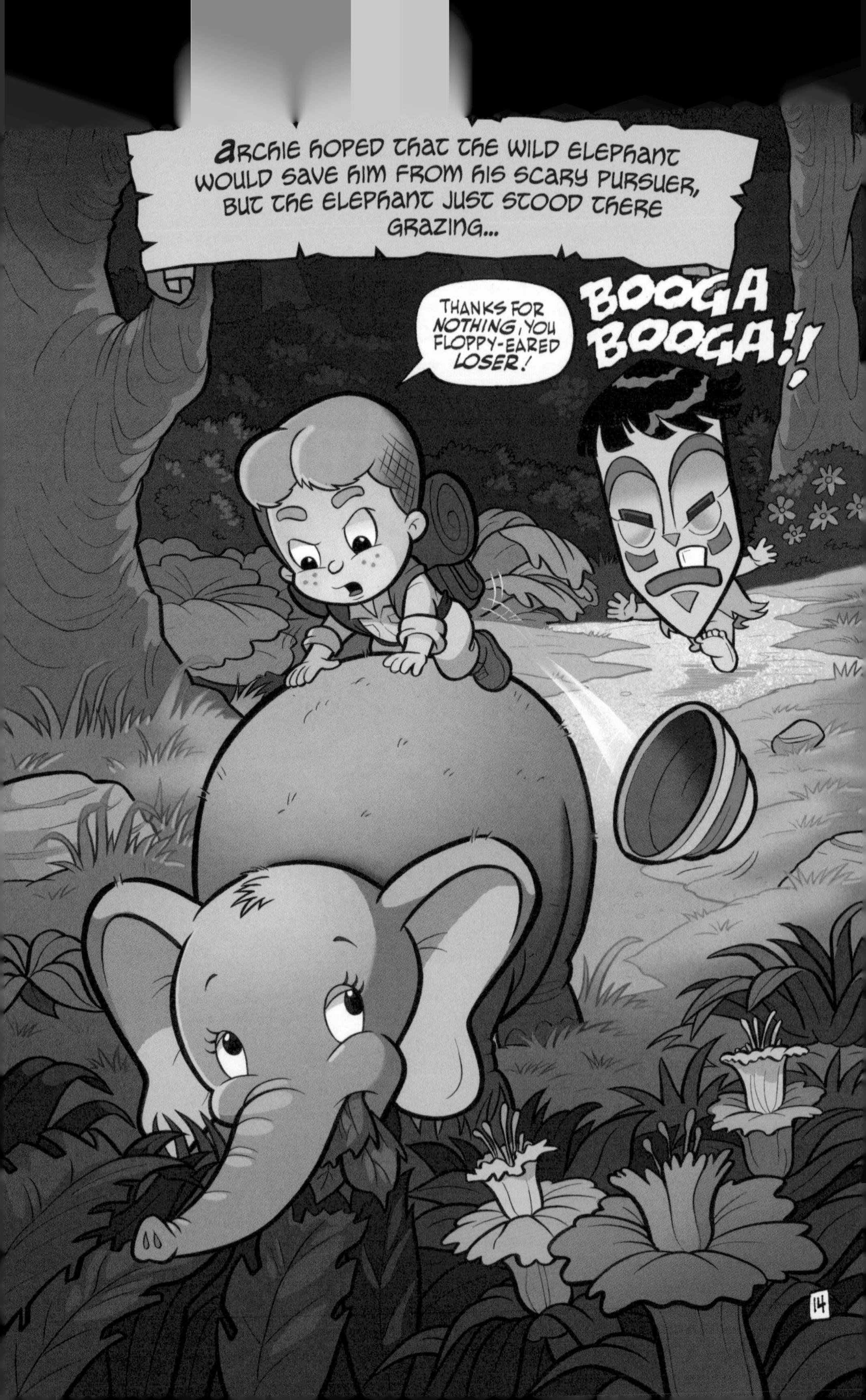
ARCHIE HOPED THAT THE WILD ELEPHANT WOULD SAVE HIM FROM HIS SCARY PURSUER, BUT THE ELEPHANT JUST STOOD THERE GRAZING...
THANKS FOR NOTHING, YOU FLOPPY-EARED LOSER!
BOOGA BOOGA!!
14

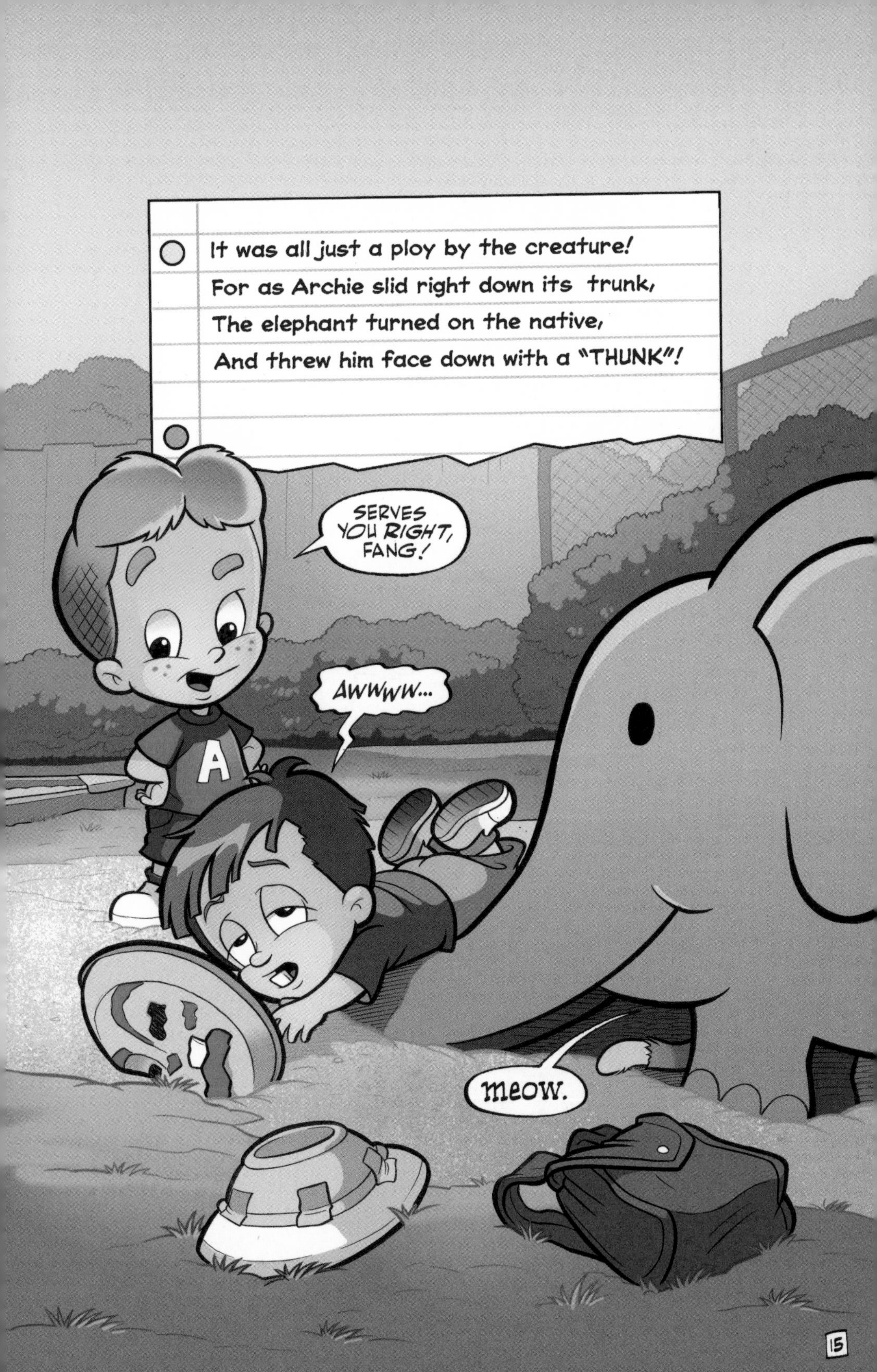
It was all just a ploy by the creature!
For as Archie slid right down its trunk,
The elephant turned on the native,
And threw him face down with a "THUNK"!
SERVES YOU RIGHT, FANG!
AWWWW...
meow.

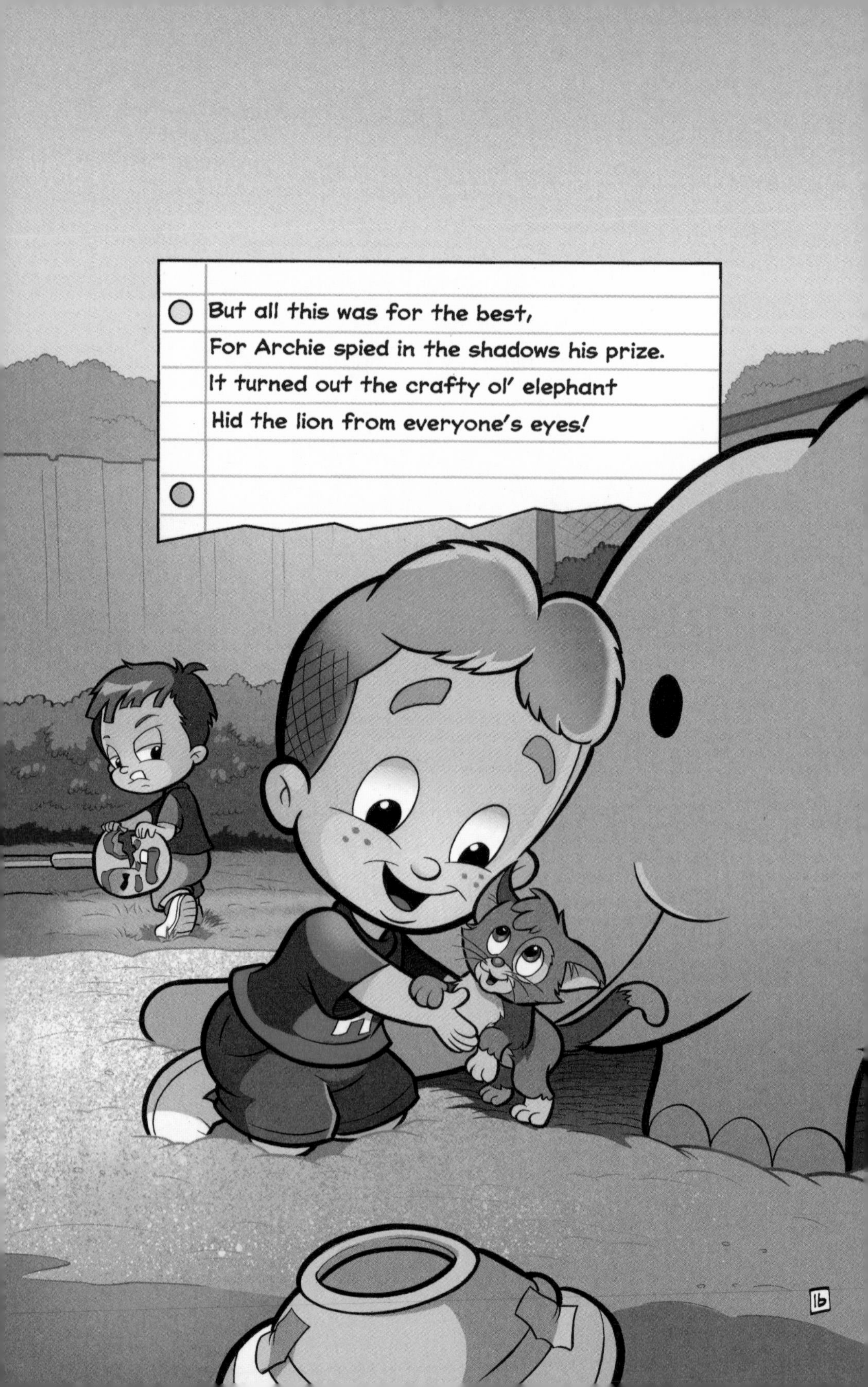
But all this was for the best,
For Archie spied in the shadows his prize.
It turned out the crafty ol' elephant
Hid the lion from everyone's eyes!

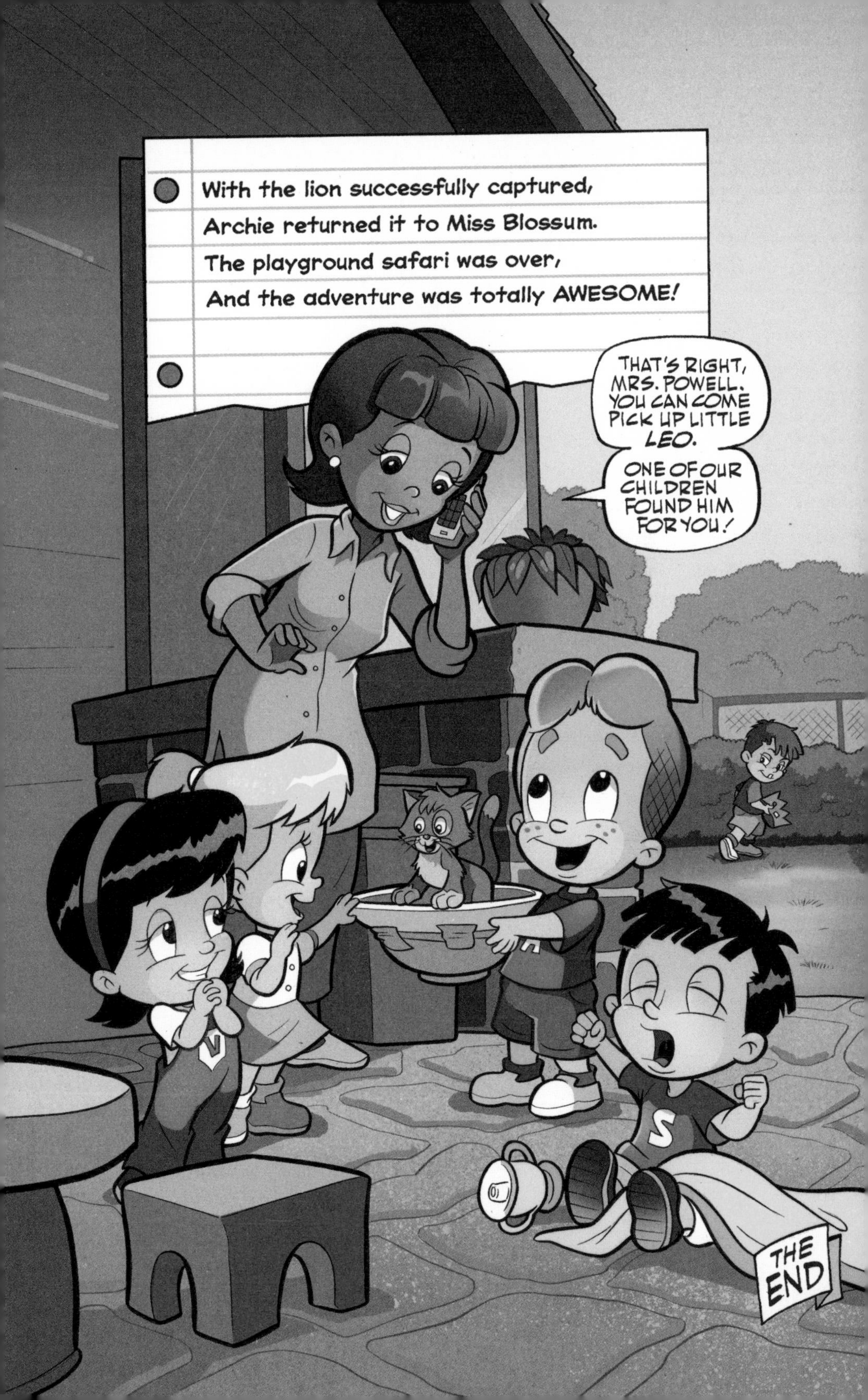

With the lion successfully captured,
Archie returned it to Miss Blossum.
The playground safari was over,
And the adventure was totally AWESOME!
THAT'S RIGHT, MRS. POWELL. YOU CAN COME PICK UP LITTLE LEO.
ONE OF OUR CHILDREN FOUND HIM FOR YOU!
THE END

THE END

(NAP TIME)

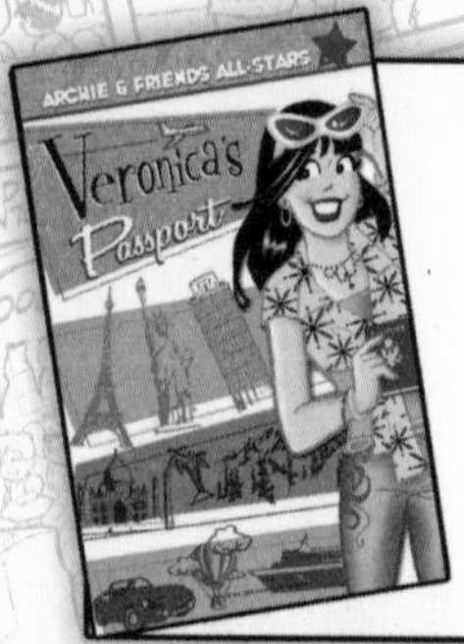
ARCHIE & FRIENDS ALL-STARS
Veronica's Passport

Veronica's Passport

Go on a globetrotting adventure with the sophisticated Veronica Lodge!

ISBN: 978-1-879794-43-6

The Best of Betty's Diary

People think they know Betty, but even the girl next door has secrets!

ISBN: 978-1-879794-46-7

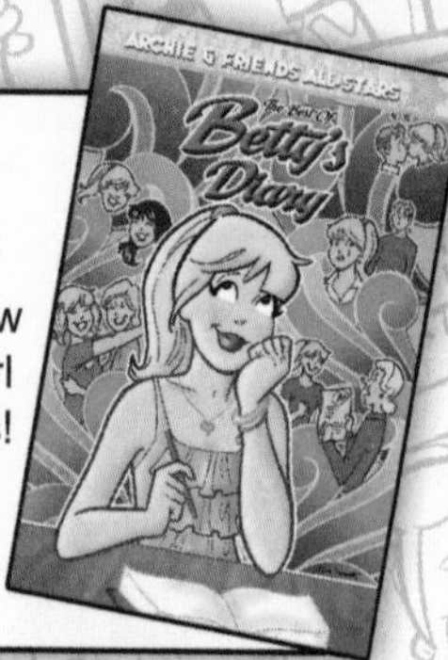
ARCHIE & FRIENDS ALL-STARS
The Best of Betty's Diary

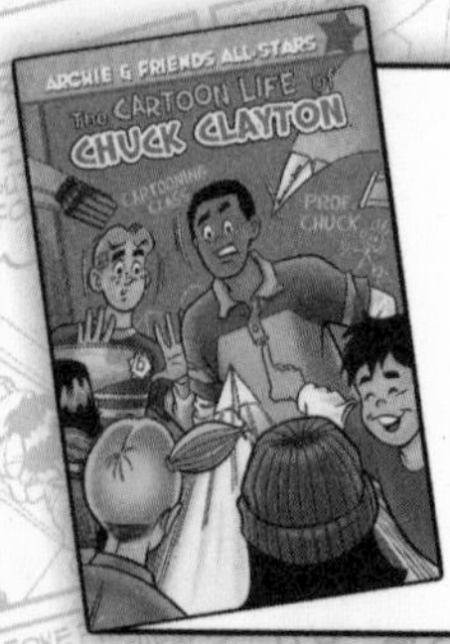
ARCHIE & FRIENDS ALL-STARS
The Cartoon Life of Chuck Clayton

The Cartoon Life of Chuck Clayton

Go on a wild ride where life imitates art with Chuck Clayton!

ISBN: 978-1-879794-48-1

Betty & Veronica: Beach Party

Grab your surfboard and put on your swimsuit because the gang is ready to party!

ISBN: 978-1-879794-50-4

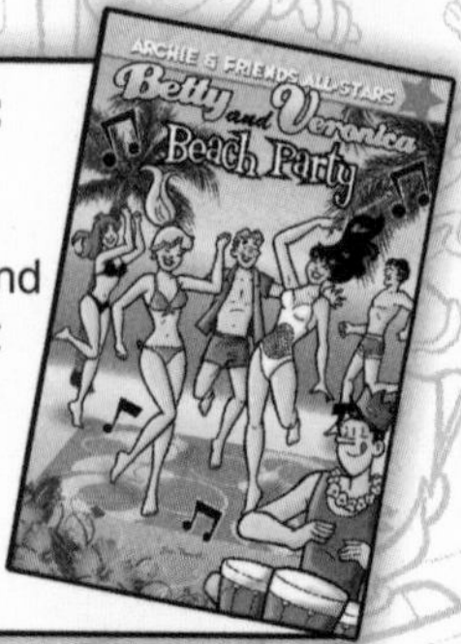
ARCHIE & FRIENDS ALL-STARS
Betty and Veronica
Beach Party

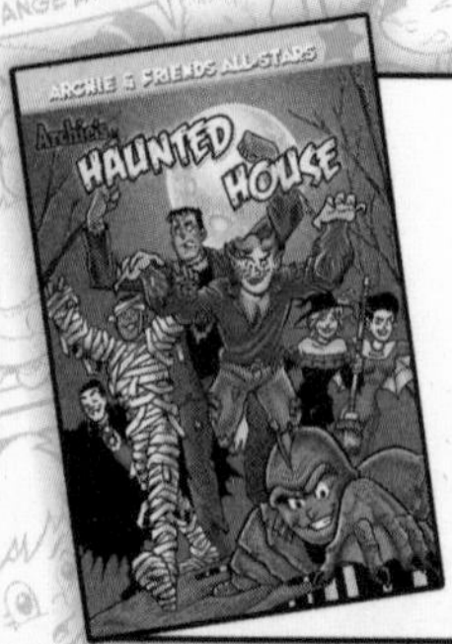
ARCHIE & FRIENDS ALL-STARS
Archie's
HAUNTED HOUSE

Archie's Haunted House

Get ready to have a howling good time!

ISBN: 978-1-879794-52-8

Christmas Stocking

It's a Riverdale Wonderland in this cool Christmas collection!

ISBN: 978-1-879794-57-3

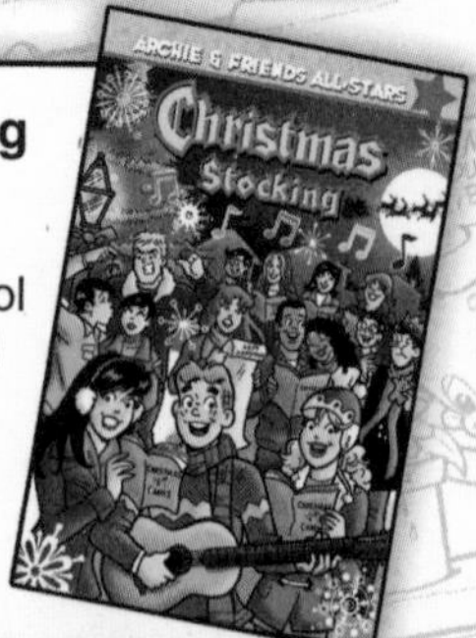
ARCHIE & FRIENDS ALL-STARS
Christmas
Stocking

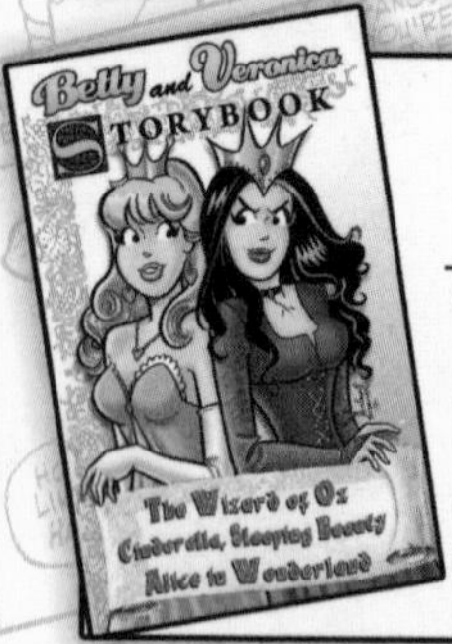
Betty and Veronica
STORYBOOK
The Wizard of Oz
Cinderella, Sleeping Beauty
Alice in Wonderland

Betty & Veronica: Storybook

The ladies of Riverdale live happily ever after when they take center stage in four classic fairy tales!

ISBN: 978-1-879794-60-3

The Archies & Josie and the Pussycats

Two of the hottest bands get together to make some sweet music!

ISBN: 978-1-879794-61-0

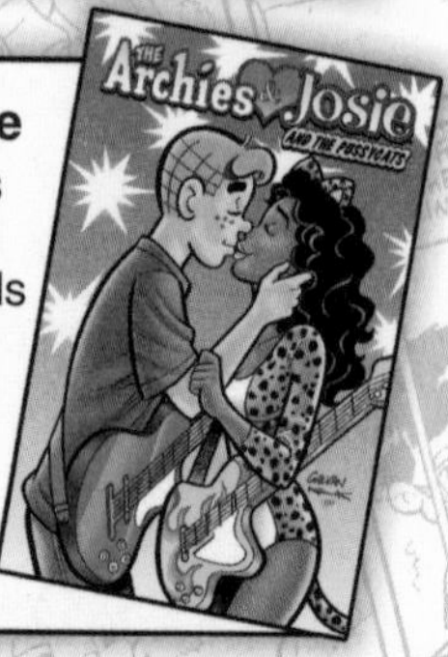
THE Archies
Josie
AND THE PUSSYCATS

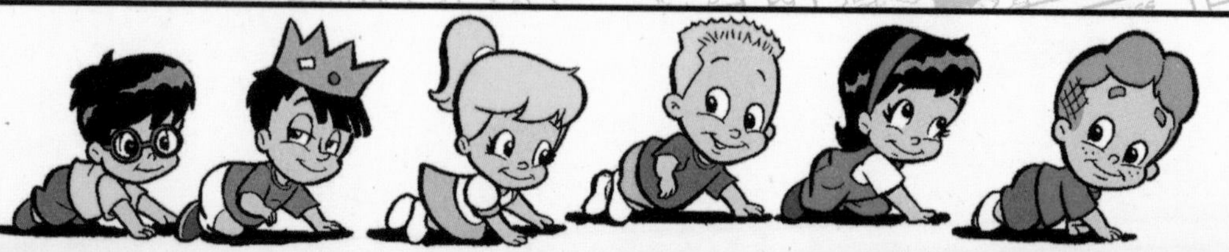

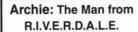

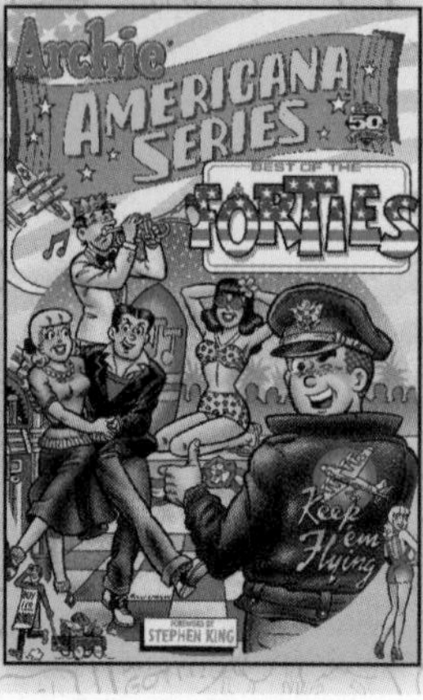
Archie
AMERICANA SERIES
BEST OF THE FORTIES
Keep 'em Flying
STEPHEN KING
ISBN: 9781879794009

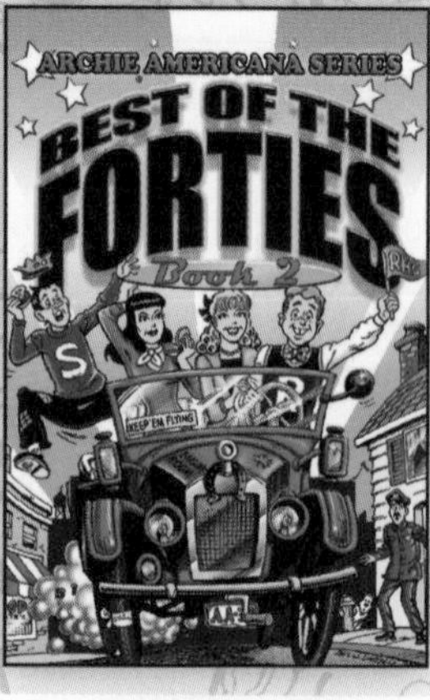
ARCHIE AMERICANA SERIES
BEST OF THE FORTIES
Book 2
ISBN: 9781879794092

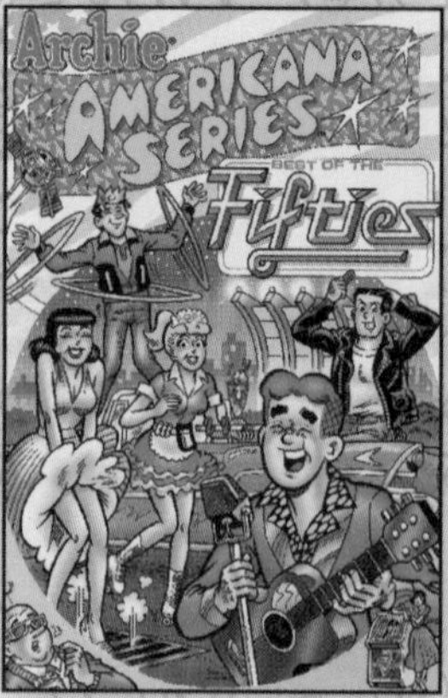
Archie
AMERICANA SERIES
BEST OF THE
Fifties
ISBN: 9781879794016

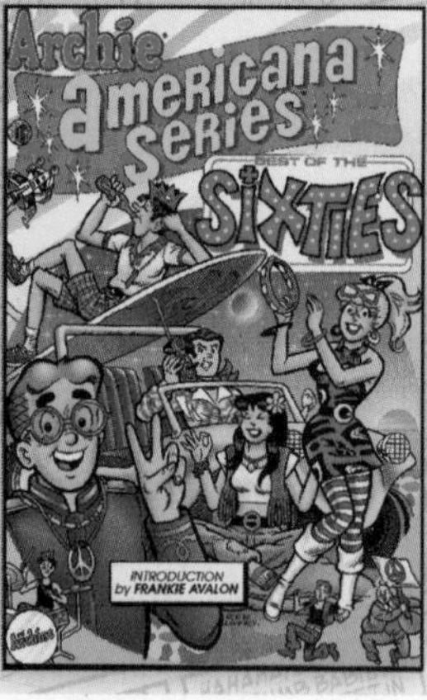
Archie
americana Series
BEST OF THE
SIXTIES
INTRODUCTION by FRANKIE AVALON
ISBN: 9781879794023

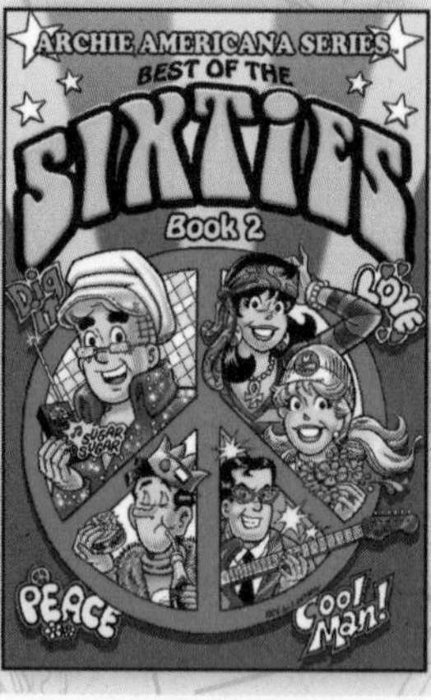
ARCHIE AMERICANA SERIES
BEST OF THE
SIXTIES
Book 2
Dig It
Love
PEACE
Cool Man!
ISBN: 9781879794313

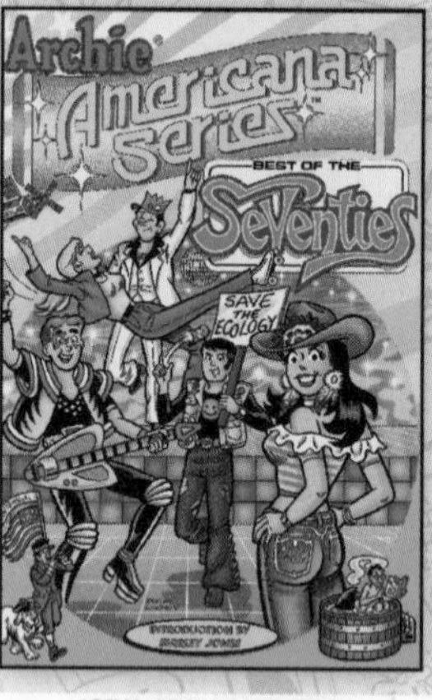
Archie
Americana Series
BEST OF THE
Seventies
SAVE THE ECOLOGY
ISBN: 9781879794054

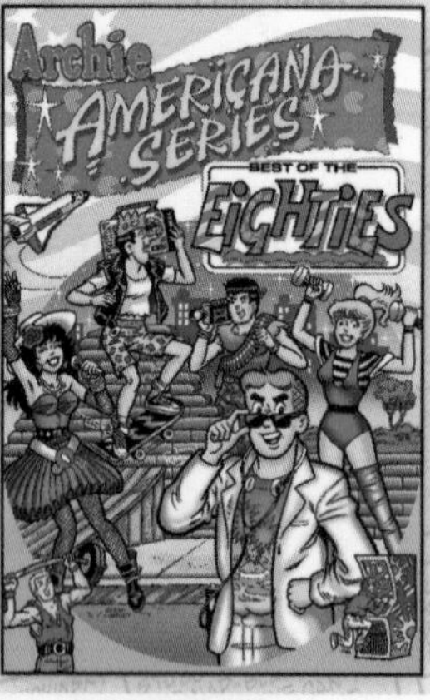
Archie
AMERICANA SERIES
BEST OF THE
EIGHTIES
ISBN: 9781879794061

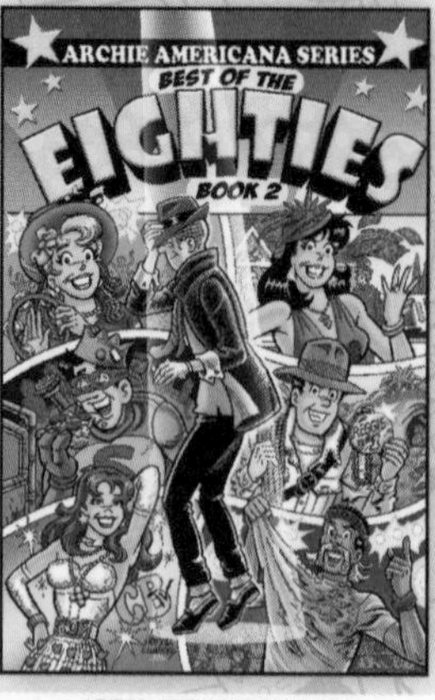
ARCHIE AMERICANA SERIES
BEST OF THE
EIGHTIES
BOOK 2
ISBN: 9781879794580

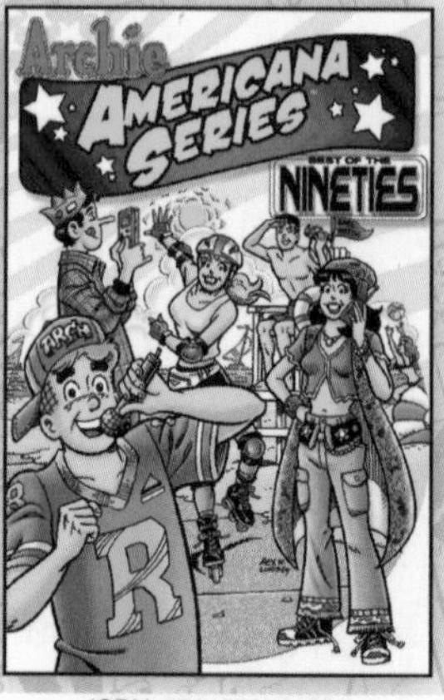
Archie
AMERICANA SERIES
BEST OF THE
NINETIES
ISBN: 9781879794351

Archie® COMICS

COLLECT ALL 12 VOLUMES OF THE
ARCHIE AMERICANA SERIES!

LOOK FOR THESE AND OTHER GRAPHIC NOVELS AT COMIC SHOPS AND BOOKSTORES EVERYWHERE!

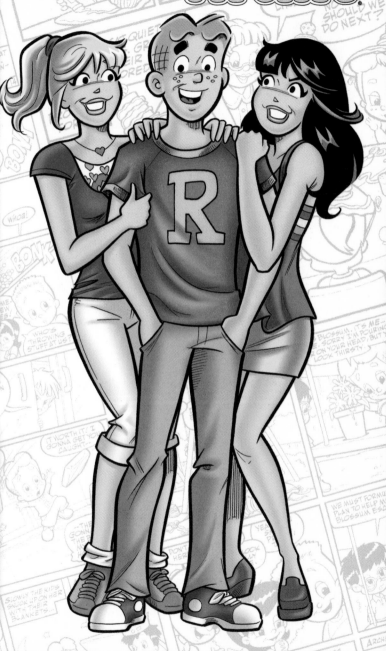

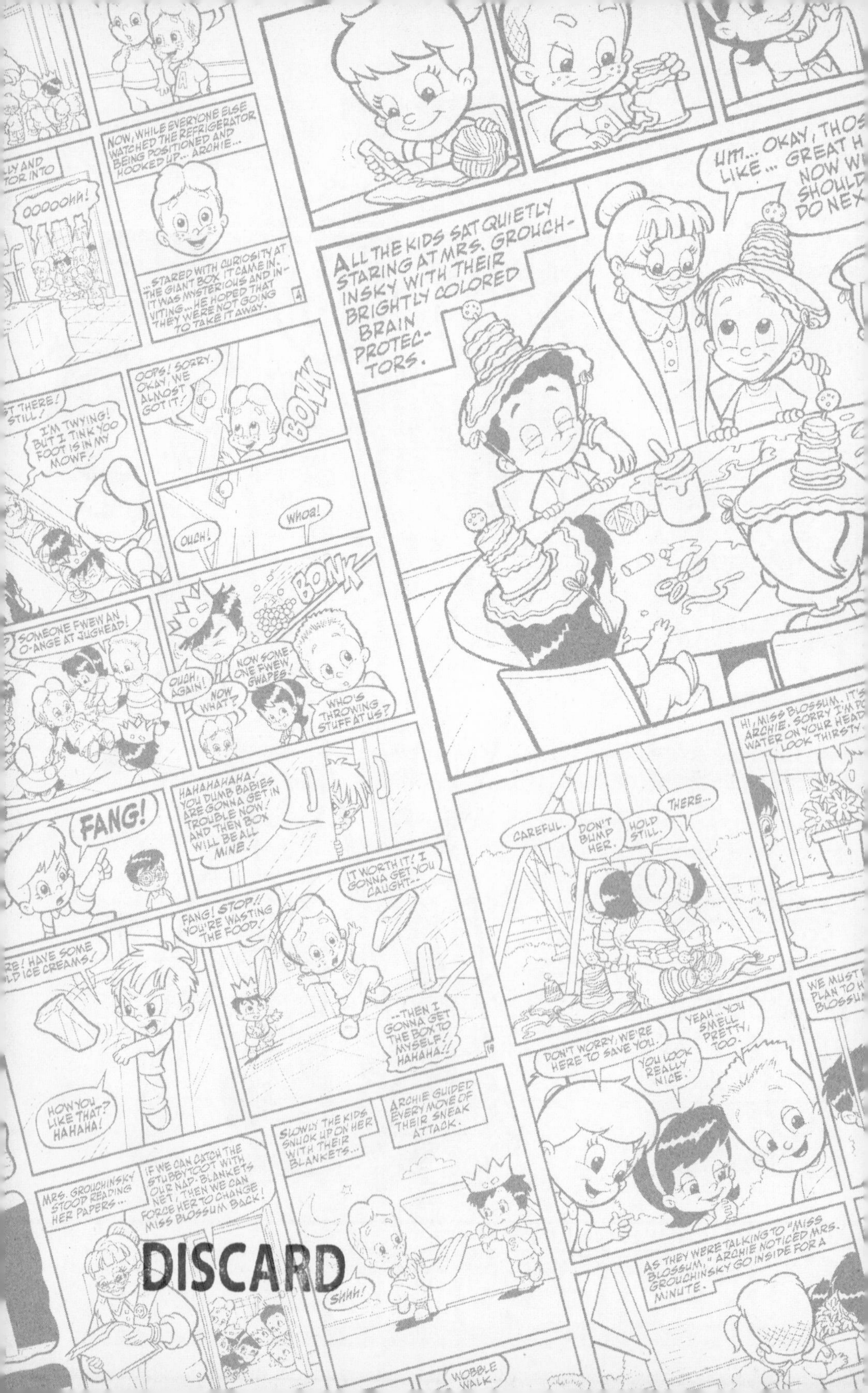

NOW, WHILE EVERYONE ELSE WATCHED THE REFRIGERATOR BEING POSITIONED AND HOOKED UP... ARCHIE...
OOOOOhh!
...STARED WITH CURIOSITY AT THE GIANT BOX IT CAME IN. IT WAS MYSTERIOUS AND INVITING... HE HOPED THAT THEY WERE NOT GOING TO TAKE IT AWAY.
ALL THE KIDS SAT QUIETLY STARING AT MRS. GROUCHINSKY WITH THEIR BRIGHTLY COLORED BRAIN PROTECTORS.
OOPS! SORRY. OKAY, WE ALMOST GOT IT!
BONK
I'M TWYING! BUT I TINK YOO FOOT IS IN MY MOWF.
OUCH!
Whoa!
BONK
SOMEONE FWEW AN O-ANGE AT JUGHEAD!
OUCH! AGAIN!
NOW WHAT?
NOW SOMEONE FWEW GWAPES!
WHO'S THROWING STUFF AT US?
FANG!
HAHAHAHAHA! YOU DUMB BABIES ARE GONNA GET IN TROUBLE NOW! AND THEN BOX WILL BE ALL MINE!
IT WORTH IT! I GONNA GET YOU CAUGHT--
FANG! STOP!! YOU'RE WASTING THE FOOD!
--THEN I GONNA GET THE BOX TO MYSELF! HAHAHA!!
HOW YOU LIKE THAT? HAHAHA!
CAREFUL.
DON'T BUMP HER.
HOLD STILL.
THERE...
DON'T WORRY, WE'RE HERE TO SAVE YOU.
YOU LOOK REALLY NICE.
YEAH... YOU SMELL PRETTY, TOO.
ARCHIE GUIDED EVERY MOVE OF THEIR SNEAK ATTACK.
SLOWLY THE KIDS SNUCK UP ON HER WITH THEIR BLANKETS...
IF WE CAN CATCH THE STUBBYTOOT WITH OUR NAP-BLANKETS NET, THEN WE CAN FORCE HER TO CHANGE MISS BLOSSUM BACK!
MRS. GROUCHINSKY STOOD READING HER PAPERS...
Shhh!
AS THEY WERE TALKING TO "MISS BLOSSUM," ARCHIE NOTICED MRS. GROUCHINSKY GO INSIDE FOR A MINUTE.
WOBBLE WALK.